JOANNE TRACEY

ESCAPE TO Curlew COTTAGE

First published in Australia in 2021

by Joanne Tracey

https://joannetracey.com

Copyright © Joanne Tracey 2021

Print ISBN 978-0-6450735-0-8

Kindle ISBN 978-0-6484533-9-0

Epub ISBN 978-0-6450735-1-5

Cover design by Louise West of Book Coverology

A catalogue record for this book is available from the National Library of Australia

For Grant and Sarah...

Always

CHAPTER ONE

On a rainy Tuesday in the last week of October Claire Mansfield, host of the popular reality TV series, *Time for Tea*, frowned as the waitress plonked her salad on the table with such force some leaves flew off the plate.

'Excuse me,' Claire called after the waitress who'd already flounced away with a flick of her purple hair.

Sitting across the table from her, Harris Bartholomew, known to friends and clients alike as Barty – and Claire was both friend and client – grinned. 'Somehow, I don't think they hired her for her sparkling personality and excellent customer service skills.'

Claire giggled. 'I'm not sure they hired the chef for his ability in the kitchen either. Just how pretentious was that starter? And please tell me that dark green dusty stuff on the outside of the plate wasn't kale dust? And that's something I bet you never thought you'd hear me say.'

'I'm afraid it might've been.'

'Oh dear.' Claire tried to keep her face expressionless

and gave up the pretence. 'It's all rather appalling, isn't it?'

Barty nodded slowly. 'Yes, very grim indeed.'

Claire wrinkled her nose as she took in the sparse decor of *Bella Donna*, the latest offering by London-based restaurant supremo Bruno Belucci.

'And what's with the name? Isn't belladonna some sort of poisonous plant? It seems a strange name to give to a restaurant.'

'It also means beautiful lady in Italian,' said Barty. 'And I think Bruno was going for that direction, rather than a toxic reference.'

Claire pushed the limp lettuce around her plate with her fork. 'Are you sure this poor excuse for a salad vegetable isn't the poisonous plant?'

'Okay,' said Barty, 'I know you don't like Bruno, but can you please contain your glee at this travesty of a restaurant and concentrate on business for just a few minutes? Then you can bitch to your heart's content about everything you don't like about this place.'

'But it's so much more fun to talk about a potential Belucci failure.'

As Barty raised his eyebrows at her continued attempts to avoid work, Claire finally nodded her agreement. 'I suppose if you're to write-off the ridiculous expense of eating here as a tax deduction, we do need to discuss a little business. But please don't talk to me about that Christmas show again.' Her shoulders slumped dramatically.

'Claire, sweetie, I'm your manager, it's my job to talk to you about the Christmas special. And don't try your diva out on me, we both know it's not something that comes naturally to you.'

She groaned and tipped her head back, closing her eyes briefly. When she opened them again, Barty was watching her, a faint smile on his face.

'I don't understand why you're so hesitant,' he said. 'You host the most popular TV show in the country at the moment.'

'Perhaps, but I can't remember the last time I did any baking myself. What makes you think I'd want to show all of Britain that while I can spend my days judging scones, I probably no longer have any idea how to cook one?'

'*Celebrity Christmas Cook-off* is for charity so no one will care whether or not you can cook a scone – in fact, it's more entertaining if you can't. I'd like to bet none of the other guests have time to cook for themselves either.'

'Just because it's for charity doesn't make it any more forgiving. If I messed up a baking challenge, it would be mortifying!' Relenting slightly, she added, 'I suppose if I practised, I could probably do you some puddings and gingerbreads and maybe even a biscuit or two, and I'm sure I could still roast a chicken, but I've never roasted a turkey and wouldn't know where to start with the stuffing. Actually, where do you stuff a turkey?'

'I hate to think, but I'm sure there'd be a YouTube video for it.' His voice took on a soothing note. 'The production team said you get plenty of time to practice the first round at home, and because you're all celebrities and therefore hopeless, they'll make the technical challenge doable. It's bound to be baking something Christmassy, and you've always liked Christmas. You can't tell me honestly you don't have a copy of Delia Smith's "Christmas" somewhere in that pile of cookbooks you and Giles share your flat with?'

Claire's sheepish look was admission enough.

'I know you already come across as the girl next door, but this is a good chance to reinforce that and let the public see you can get just as flustered in the kitchen as they do.' His smile was reassuring as he pushed home his advantage. 'Seriously, sweetie, this will be no more difficult than following a recipe – anyone can do that. You can do that. You did it for a living when you wrote that column of yours. I remember how we had to sit through endless variations of the same recipe until you decided which version was the best.'

Claire grimaced and twisted her thick chestnut hair into a makeshift ponytail. There was something that didn't feel right, something she couldn't put her finger on. Perhaps it was the idea of cooking on television? Maybe it was just that it had been too long since she last prepared anything in the kitchen that didn't involve a tea bag and a toaster. She couldn't remember the last time she'd eaten at home, let alone had the time to cook a meal for her and Giles, and now she was expected to do it in front of cameras. She took a deep breath, 'I don't know, Barty, I'm out of practice, and I don't have the time to do anything about that. Plus, they usually have actresses and singers or athletes, and I'm just a food writer who used to bake a bit and who got lucky with a drunken proposal for a reality TV program and somehow ended up here.'

'Isn't that the way it usually happens? Nigella wasn't a chef and look at what she's done.'

'I don't think Nigella would've drunk too much cheap champagne at a party and slurred a half-thought-through idea into the ear of a BBC producer – not that I knew Ed was a producer. None of her ideas would be half-thought-through, and she certainly wouldn't be slurring them. Besides, look at me Barty, I'm no Nigella.'

Barty placed his elbow on the table, his cheek resting against the back of his fist. If he was feeling impatient, it didn't show on his face. 'No, sweetie, you're nothing like Nigella and thank goodness for that; we only have room for one Nigella. *Time for Tea* wouldn't work if Nigella were hosting it; it works because you're you.'

'No, *Time for Tea* works because I don't try to be anything more than a presenter and because everybody we have on the show is lovely,' she said.

'They're contestants, darling. Don't ever forget that.'

'They might compete for a weekly prize, but it's not exactly life-changing, and everyone's really sweet. I don't think I could stand in front of a camera and cook for judges.'

'I understand where you're coming from, but don't forget this isn't live television and you get plenty of lead time to plan and practice everything other than the technical dish.'   He raised his eyebrows and smiled until she smiled back. 'I think you should do it – it's for charity and who knows, it could turn out to be really fun. Trust me, darling, nothing could possibly go wrong. Now, where's the rest of our lunch?'

After that, Barty made a concerted effort to bring the conversation onto safer grounds, and Claire relaxed back into her chair and enjoyed his banter and pushed the next disappointing course of food around her plate.

When the meal was finally and blessedly over, Barty stood and announced he was off to check out the bathroom. 'I hear the décor's fabulous,' he said.

Claire looked around with disdain, the beige walls and bland décor paired perfectly with the soulless meal they'd endured. 'You also heard the food was fabulous, so I wouldn't be trusting that source in the future.'

As Barty disappeared down the corridor, thoughts of how it had all began flooded back.

She and Barty had become friends in university; they both answered an advertisement for a share house. When she got the job to host *Time for Tea*, he'd become her manager by default and had managed her career ever since, guiding her towards opportunities that had made her one of the most loved and respected presenters on British television. If it hadn't been for Barty, none of it would've happened; she owed everything to him. As much as Claire baulked at the idea of doing *Celebrity Christmas Cook-off*, Barty's reasoning was sound – as were his instincts.

Yet, while she'd never admitted it out loud, sometimes she lay awake at 3 am, her heart pounding at the thought that one day, maybe not too far in the future, it would all be over. On those nights she'd look across at Giles snoring softly beside her and reach out a hand to be reassured he was there. That he at least was solid. Sometimes it seemed he and Nigel, her cocker spaniel, and their little apartment in Pimlico were the only things in her world that were.

Time for Tea was her dream job, but TV audiences were fickle, and her longevity was at the pleasure of the studio and the ratings – which was why Barty was encouraging her to branch out a little with guest appearances on podcasts and other shows.

'Sorry, darling.' Barty slid back into his chair.

'How are the bathrooms?'

'Fabulous. Amazing pink mosaics and enormous mirrors with lights all around them and shiny gold tap fittings. All very glitzy and over the top.' He leaned across the table and lowered his voice. 'I suspect Bruno used a different designer in there to what he did out here.'

Claire chuckled. 'You're probably right.' She paused briefly and then said, 'Okay, Barty, I'll do it. The Christmas cooking thing. I'll do it.'

'There was never any doubt.'

'You've already told them I would, haven't you?'

'As I said, sweetie, there was never any doubt.'

CHAPTER TWO

Tallis Harlow sat seventy-seven miles away, not in an expensive London restaurant, but eating defrosted soup in her house just outside Fenwyck in The Cotswolds.

As she ripped off the end of the baguette she'd bought in the high street that morning and dunked it into her soup, she took in the large open-plan kitchen of the refurbished Georgian house. It was way too large for the three of them, but Derek had been so proud when they'd bought it five years ago. She had been too, even though she hadn't wanted to leave Bristol and all their friends.

She didn't see any of them anymore; Derek's success had seen the others drop away, one by one. Tallis had tried to stay in touch, but soon the mutual discomfort made her give up. To be honest, she didn't see much of Derek now either. He found it easier to stay in Bristol during the week rather than commute the sixty-something miles back home to Fenwyck each day. She couldn't blame him for that.

As for their son, Adam, a few mornings a week,

before school, he had a paper run, and most days after school he'd go to Anna's house. Not only was Anna his girlfriend, but she was also the daughter of Tallis' closest friend, Gail Longmuir. Next year he'd be finished school and moving away for university, and then Tallis really would be alone, rattling around in this big house all day with nothing to do, just her and the dogs.

The problem was, this life and this big house were what Derek had always said he wanted for her, not what she'd wanted. Tallis hadn't minded working in an office – she had always enjoyed the company of her colleagues and the knowledge she was doing something worthwhile.

When they'd first moved here, Derek hired a cleaner and a gardener and had all his work clothes laundered and ironed in Bristol. The notion she no longer had any real purpose was confronting. When she'd said as much to him, he'd sighed heavily in that way men do and then said, 'Make new friends and go for lunch like other wives do. Get your nails done, do some shopping.' Then he'd thrown his hands up in the air. 'I don't know, I've worked hard to give you the life of leisure you've always wanted, and now you're complaining about being bored? Well, that's certainly not the gratitude I'd expected.'

The truth was Tallis struggled to fit in with the other Fenwyck wives – who all seemed to fall into one of three categories:

1. The old money-horsey set who spent their days on estates doing horsey things and looked down their well-bred noses at the likes of Tallis and Derek, who'd made a lot of new money; or

2. Working women who spent their days juggling jobs, bills, children and domestic life and thought Tallis, in her expensive clothes with her fresh blow-dry and large house, was looking down her nose at the likes of them; or

3. Wives whose husbands spent their weeks doing something unintelligible, but obviously important in the city and who amused themselves with tennis, health clubs, lunches and shopping trips to Oxford, Bath or London, and who spend very little time in Fenwyck.

So Tallis spent her days' shopping, having her hair and nails done, and coming home to cook meals for herself and Adam, who'd also, until he met Anna, found it hard to make friends here.

At least that was how Tallis spent her days before she met Gail – and through her, Caro Norton and Fee Perry.

Tallis was contemplating this when the doorbell rang.

'Gail, I was just thinking about you.'

'Good things, I hope?' Gail followed Tallis into

the kitchen and placed the cloth-covered basket she'd been carrying on the bench. 'I'm interrupting your lunch,' she said, indicating the soup bowl.

'It's fine. I was thinking about Adam and Anna and how we met.'

'When I decided that seeing as how our kids were spending so much time together it was time I got to know you too.'

The memory bought a smile to Tallis' face. 'You brought scones that day.'

'I'd seen you around town and was so worried you'd be too posh for me, and certainly too posh to eat carbs, but you weren't posh at all.' Gail switched on the kettle and helped herself to a teacup. 'You finish your soup. Do you want tea?'

'Thanks,' said Tallis, sitting back down at the bench. 'What's in the basket?'

'A new scone I'm trying out. It's spiced pumpkin – for Christmas.'

'For the show?' asked Tallis.

'Yes. Have you heard yet?'

Both women looked at the laptop open on the bench. 'No,' said Tallis. 'The producers said the email would be through today though. Shouldn't you be at work?'

Gail worked for a solicitor in town. 'I should, but Liam was so tired of me checking my phone every two minutes that he told me to go home.' She grinned. 'On the strict proviso I call him as soon as we find out. I figured you'd be sitting here waiting, so I thought I'd wait with you and we could taste test these scones.' She took the cloth off the top of the basket and pulled out a plate of golden scones, which she waved under Tallis' nose.

'They smell good,' said Tallis, pushing aside her now-empty bowl. 'We should try them now before—'

The doorbell sounded again. Tallis raised her eyebrows at Gail and went to the front door, returning with two familiar faces.

'Caro and Fee!' Gail laughed. 'Let me guess, you were just passing?'

'Shouldn't you be at work?' Fee asked Gail.

'Probably, but I couldn't concentrate so Liam took pity on me. Besides, I brought Christmas scones,' said Gail.

'I brought ginger biscuits,' said Caro.

'I didn't bother bringing anything,' said Fee. 'Have you any news?'

'Not yet,' said Tallis.

'We can all wait together then,' said Caro, placing biscuits on a plate.

Brought together by a mutual love of baking, the four of them met each month to cook a shared meal at Tallis'. At one of these lunches, back in February, Tallis had suggested that as a group they should apply to appear on the TV show *Time for Tea*. Fee, predictably, had jumped at the opportunity, although Caro and Gail were at first hesitant about the idea.

'I think it would be fun,' Fee had said. 'The four of us putting on a giant afternoon tea for the whole of Fenwyck.'

'Well,' said Tallis, 'maybe not the whole of Fenwyck, but at least as many as can come along.'

'And it's for a good cause,' said Fee. 'We get to choose which charity the proceeds go towards.'

'I'm not sure,' said Caro. 'Don't they usually hold the tea in a grand hall or marquee somewhere? Would we need to arrange that too or do we just turn up and bake?'

'I've looked into it,' said Tallis, who had done little else but research the idea all the previous week. 'We'd need to come up with a potential venue and the theme of our tea, but the production team will make all the other arrangements and even dress the room for us. We'd also need to decide on our charity and publicise the event in town.' She'd looked around at the other faces; Fee, who was always ready and willing to try something new, Caro, who'd done nothing like this before, and Gail, who was wavering. She took a deep breath before continuing.

'Before I met you ladies, I would never have proposed anything like this, but this group has shown me I'm more than Derek's wife and Adam's mother. I enjoy planning our lunches and, this might sound selfish, but I'd like to do this not just because it's for charity, but because I need a project.' She paused and met the eyes of each of her friends. 'It would be fun, don't you think?'

Gail nodded slowly. 'It would be fun, but do you think we're good enough?'

'We certainly are,' said Fee. 'This little club has also given me something to look forward to. When I booted out husband number two, I thought I couldn't be alone, that I needed a number three, but thanks to you ladies I've finally decided that it's okay to be single.' She grinned. 'It's just a pity it took me until the age of fifty-nine to work that out. I think Tallis would make a fabulous organiser and I could think of nothing better than to spend a day baking for the good people of Fenwyck with you three.'

'I've never put myself out there like that before.' Caro's face still wore a worried look.

'There's always a first time,' said Fee. 'Besides, we might not even get chosen.'

'I'd like to meet Claire Mansfield,' said Gail. 'She seems really warm and lovely. You know she comes from The Cotswolds?'

'I think I read that somewhere,' said Tallis. 'Brookford, wasn't it? She still has a little of the accent from around here.'

'I like that,' said Gail. 'It makes her more approachable.'

'What if she's not like she is on the telly?' Caro was still hesitant.

Tallis picked up the magazine she'd been reading before the others had arrived. Claire was on the cover. Although casually dressed in jeans, long brown boots and a blue jumper, she still looked slim and elegant. Her chestnut hair hung loosely around her shoulders, and her smile was warm. She could've been any of a thousand attractive women until you noticed her eyes that were the most startling blue Tallis had ever seen. Those eyes lifted Claire's face from ordinary to extraordinary. 'I think she'll be exactly like she is on the telly,' she said.

'What if we mess up?' asked Caro.

Fee shook her head. 'With Tallis managing us? That's not going to happen. Gail, what about you? Are you in?'

A smile had spread slowly across Gail's face. 'You know what? Why not?'

Tallis had been watching *Time for Tea* since the first show and knew what the producers would want to see. After getting the go-ahead from the others, she'd re-watched episodes with a notepad beside her, creating a checklist covering everything from potential venues and local charities to accommodation options for the production team.

Time for Tea was part travelogue, so Tallis had included in her application, information about local sights, pieces of history, and growers and providores Claire could be filmed visiting. Her submission, the others agreed, had covered all possible bases.

Then they waited. In May, Tallis received an email saying their application was being considered. Then in September, Ed Wilson, the executive producer, came down for the day with two junior producers and met with them.

And they waited some more. Last week Tallis had received an email advising the final placement for the Christmas episode would be announced today – so here they were waiting again.

'We've got to be a good chance to be selected,' said Gail. 'Your proposal covered everything. You even convinced Lady Elliott to let us hold the tea at Fountains Hall.'

'Then there's the tea itself,' said Caro. 'I'd like to bet our application is the only one that included illustrations of how our Christmas-themed tea would look. Anna did a wonderful job with that.'

'I've heard our major competitors are in Burford,' said Fee, referring to a market town on the way to Oxford. 'But I think Fountains Hall will clinch it for us.'

'I think so too,' said Gail. 'Does anyone want another scone?'

it was quiet for a few minutes as everyone savoured Gail's spiced creation. The ping of an incoming email caused them all to pause and look at Tallis, who rose slowly and calmly walked around to where her laptop stood open.

Three pairs of eyes watched her intently as she read the message. Turning around, she said with a straight face, 'it's just as well those scones are as good as they are.' Unable to hold her grin back any longer, she put her hands in the air. 'We're on!'

CHAPTER THREE

The Spoonman, by Alex Spooner

Bella Donna, Knightsbridge

Meal for two, including drinks and service: way, way too much.

These are challenging times for London's Italian restaurants. There's still room for the classics — dishes the way Nonna made them. There are a few restaurants in Soho doing very well on that formula — and have done so since Nonna was a twinkle in her mamma's eye.

For new players, it's not easy. The modern diner wants something, well, modern — unless they don't. Then they want traditional, but only if it's vintage traditional. It's the same with fashion; there's a vast difference between vintage and old — and a large part of that difference is who's wearing it.

It gets even more complicated at the top end of town. Fine diners don't lend themselves to Italian cuisine. Of course, there're exceptions, Bruno Belucci's flagship, Belucci's, being one that's consistently on point – traditional Italian food in a space that's extravagantly over the top Roman grandeur without falling into kitsch. Belucci's consistently turns out Italian food that's better than you'd get in many establishments in Rome.

That's not to say Italian restaurants can't get away with charging a fortune for what they call cucina povera *or peasant's food; there are plenty doing just that. This is why I was excited when the press release for Bella Donna,* il tuo locale Italiano *landed on my desk. The term* il tuo locale Italiano *means "your Italian local". If anyone could pull that off, I thought it would be Bruno Belucci. Sadly, this wasn't the case.*

I suppose the word "local" could mean many things and, indeed, if you happen to live in Knightsbridge, Bella Donna would be local to you – in much the same way as the food hall at Harrods could be considered your corner store. As for the price point? Let's just say I could feel my credit card screaming – as was I on the inside.

First up, let's have a little chat about the service. Poor service, like mediocre food, doesn't usually have any place in a Belucci establishment. Someone didn't get the memo at Bella Donna. My companion and I were left waiting at reception for a good five minutes before anyone deigned to notice us. It was a further five before we were led to our table, and still longer before menus were given to us. Our drinks arrived marginally before the starters, but only marginally, and my companion's wine glass had a lipstick stain on it. Following this incident service improved slightly but could still be described as inconsistent at best.

We could, perhaps, have forgiven the service – or, rather, lack thereof – if the food had been great, but again, dear reader, I was disappointed. The menu was a series of ingredients rather than cohesive dishes, and in many cases, it was blatantly obvious those ingredients hadn't been introduced to each other.

Instead, we received overly complicated dishes with smears, sprays, foams, and freeze-dried kale that had been ground into fine dust and sprinkled liberally over every unsmeared, unfoamed and unsprayed surface. I'm positive there was even a fine sprinkling of kale dust on the limp lettuce that appeared to have come straight from the bottom of the plastic bag at the back of the vegetable crisper and tossed onto a plate. At least, I hope it was kale dust – and that's not a phrase I ever thought would come from my mouth.

As well as meaning beautiful woman, belladonna is also a poisonous plant – deadly nightshade. Perhaps that might've been a welcome alternative to what came next: the pudding. I know I should tell you more about the pudding, but to be perfectly honest, I've spent the time in between eating that and writing this trying to erase it from my memory.

Dear Reader, I ate it so you won't have to – it was a selfless act of sacrifice on my part.

On the upside, the bathroom is a work of art. Where the decor inside the restaurant can be described as benignly minimalist with a Scandinavian twist, the bathroom is over-the-top glamour with pink mosaic tiles and gold fixtures. We weren't, however, there to admire a bathroom. In fact, and I'm going out on a limb here, but I wouldn't be at all surprised to hear you could spend the same amount of money we did on our meal on a budget flight to Rome, eat real Italian home-cooked food and still have change. Further, despite the queues and budget economy class and the inevitable delays, you'd probably have a more enjoyable experience.

You would, however, miss out on seeing the bathroom. It's an exceptional bathroom.

CHAPTER FOUR

Claire closed the newspaper and stood to take her teacup and breakfast plate across to the sink. The early December sun might have been thinking about greeting Monday but was as yet undecided. She wrinkled her nose at the thought of the cold outside and turned back to where Giles sat reading his newspaper, sniggering to himself.

'What's so funny?' she asked.

'The Spoonman's column. Have you read it today?'

'I glanced at it, but …' Claire shrugged as she leaned back against the bench and crossed her arms. 'I used to think The Spoonman was funny in a bitchy kind of way, but don't you think his reviews are all becoming a little same-same?'

'Do you think? It's hilarious today. He's only gone to town on Belucci's new place – Bella Donna, the one you went to a month back. How many restaurants does one man need?'

At the kitchen sink, Claire contemplated whether she had time for another cup of tea. 'Who knows? He's got his flagship, *Belucci's*, other than that they come and go. Mind you, I think this one is one too many. What was the verdict?'

'That the service was lazy, the food was overly complicated and, at best, average, and the prices inflated.' Giles paused as he read back through the article.

'That sounds like our experience,' said Claire. 'The food was dismal, the décor bland and the service was off. Barty didn't seem to dislike it as much as I did, although come to think on it he hardly ate anything – not that there's anything unusual about that, it's no wonder he's always so thin. A fabulous mosaic feature wall in the bathroom, though.'

'It's a concern if the best thing you can say about a place was that the toilet wall was fabulous.'

'I suppose. And the salad dressing was good, even though the leaves were a little, um, flaccid.' Claire chuckled as Giles raised his eyebrows at her description. 'I know, probably not the best choice of words, but the lettuce was limp. Why doesn't anyone do iceberg anymore? At least it keeps its crunch.'

'Why go then?'

'Barty wanted to try it. You know what he's like – give him a celebrity chef and a waiting list, and he's a happy man.'

Giles smirked. 'That's pretty much what Spooner says. He's even made fun of the name – *Bella Donna*. Listen to this, Claire: "Belladonna is a poisonous plant

– deadly nightshade. Perhaps that might've been a welcome alternative to what came next: the pudding." Ouch!' He looked up and grinned. 'A review like that couldn't happen to a better person. It's about time Belucci was taken down a peg or two. Spooner's done it here.' He tapped at the newspaper. 'And Belucci's name has come up in my investigation too; the wage-breaching story I was telling you about.'

Giles was an investigative journalist and had been chasing a story about wage breaching and bullying of apprentices in the restaurant industry for the past couple of months.

'I have to say,' he said in a conspiratorial tone, 'I was quite happy when it did. I still haven't forgotten how he behaved toward you back when you were starting on *Time for Tea*, and then he snubbed you at that awards dinner back in the summer.'

Claire nodded slowly at the memory. 'He told me I had no right to be there, that allowing reality show home cooks to attend an industry awards event was cheapening the tone of the night. He also ignored you and was quite unpleasant to Barty too. Besides, I don't think he's ever forgotten I turned him down; I don't think many people say no to Bruno Belucci.'

'How long is the man going to hold that against you? He made a pass, you said no, end of story. You'd think in today's climate he'd be more careful about things like that.' He paused and gazed at the ceiling, the newspaper still in one hand, idly pulling at his ear with the other.

It was Giles' classic "there could be a story in this if I think about it" pose.

'I wonder if he's tried that move on others. Maybe that's another angle I could take with the story. Sexual harassment in the workplace and all that.'

Giles' mind was razor sharp and was continually looking to put links, random information, and people together.

'Have you heard any whispers along those lines?'

Claire rinsed her teacup and set it on the drying rack. 'No, but I hardly move in those circles. I only know the chefs we've used as guest judges on the show and those I've come across at events. That sort of thing wouldn't get spoken about at that level. Plus, everyone who knows me knows I'm with you and what you do. They'd hardly be likely to confide in me.'

'Hmm, I suppose. Unless they wanted to use you to drop me information.'

'Well, I haven't heard anything.' Claire wiped her hands on a tea towel, her back still to Giles. 'I can't help feeling sorry for Bruno though; it can't be nice opening the paper to reviews like that over your morning coffee.'

'There's no point feeling sorry for the guy if what The Spoonman has said was right.'

'I suppose.' She walked back to the kitchen counter where Giles sat and put her arms around his neck, resting her chin against the top of his head. 'My car will be here soon, so I'd better think about being ready. Do you have much on this week?' she asked him. Giles was always juggling multiple stories and deadlines.

'I have some sources to follow up and other than that my regular column with the *Guardian* and I need to finish that piece I'm doing for the weekend magazine. Where are you this week?' he asked, reaching up to hold her hand against his heart.

'Fenwyck – in The Cotswolds. It's our last show for the year, and I haven't been there for years, so it should be nice.'

He tilted his head back so her lips could meet his. 'It's always nice. You're the nicest person on British television with the nicest show.' He smiled tenderly. 'It can't help but be nice. How far is Fenwyck from Brookford? Are you going to be able to duck home? I know you saw your sister last month when she was in town, but it's been a while since you've been back.'

'It's not too far,' she said, 'but Gracie and Milo are down in Somerset visiting Bill's mother. I'll see them before Christmas, though. I know that Gracie was hoping Mum and Dad might come home for Christmas too, but they'll stay in Sydney with Stephen and Hayley and the kids. Maybe next year.' She kissed him again. 'I love you.'

'And I love you,' he said as she straightened. 'When will you be back?'

'Friday night. We have that booking at Lily James, remember? At eight?'

'How could I forget? No one can get a booking there until February, and we have one in the middle of the Christmas party rush – and on a Friday night. Sometimes it's worth having a TV star as a girlfriend.'

She laughed at that. 'I'm hardly a star, darling. It's just a little cooking show, and I eat a lot of scones.'

'You are to me, and it's more than that.'

If anyone else had said it, the words would've sounded false, but from Giles, they were just right.

'As for Friday night, I'm looking forward to it. There's something particular I want to talk to you about.'

'Sounds intriguing. You can't give me a hint now?'

'Okay, a tiny hint – only because I know you'll pester me otherwise. It's something I always said I didn't want to do, but I've changed my mind now. In any case, it can wait until Friday.'

Claire searched his face for a clue.

'You can wait until Friday for any more than that,' he teased. 'Now, say goodbye to Nigel and get out of here.' He playfully slapped at her bottom.

She bent down to kiss him again. 'Miss you already.'

'Me too,' he murmured, pulling her to his side so he could rest his head against her belly.

The ding of an incoming text interrupted the moment. 'That'll be my car,' she said, wrenching away from him. 'Nigel!' Claire's voice roused the cocker spaniel snoring loudly on the sofa. He raised his head and reluctantly, yet luxuriantly, stretched before jumping off the sofa and into her arms for a doggy cuddle. 'I'll see you on Friday,' she told him. Nigel squirmed out of her arms and wagged his tail as if he understood what she was saying.

Claire picked up the bag and coat she had waiting at the door. In the kitchen, Giles already had his head buried back in the newspaper. 'See you on Friday, darling,' she called.

'Love you,' he called back, but he didn't raise his head.

A few hours later Claire and her producer Ed introduced themselves to this week's bakers. A group of women Ed had taken to referring to as the Fenwyck Four – even though Claire had pointed out such a moniker would usually describe bank robbers or drug mules rather than bakers. The women had poured the tea and warmed the scones and were chatting away, allowing Claire to get to know them a little better.

First to introduce herself, and the other women was Gail. She was, Claire struggled for the right description, sunny – the type of woman who could immediately brighten the mood of a room just by being there. Gail was, she explained, a single mother to a seventeen-year-old daughter named Anna, who was dating Tallis' son Adam, who was also seventeen.

'I understand we have you to thank for being here in Fenwyck.' Claire said to Tallis.

After reading Tallis' application, Claire had assumed that Tallis would be a confident, well presented, professional woman, and her first impression of Tallis was precisely that. She seemed very different from the others and was, Claire cringed even as she thought it, obviously of very different financial means and class. Yet when Tallis smiled, it was a shy smile, and when she spoke, it was with a broad West Country accent.

'It was very much a team effort,' said Tallis, the diamonds on her well-manicured fingers glinting as she crossed her arms.

'Don't listen to her,' said Fiona 'It was all down to Tallis. And please,' she added, 'call me Fee – everyone does. I don't think I've been called Fiona in years.'

'Probably not since the last time you got married,' said Caroline. 'And while we're at it, please call me Caro.'

Caro and Fee had, they told Claire, been best friends since school. Physically, they couldn't have been more opposite. Fee was of medium height and slim with short blonde hair, liberally yet naturally streaked with grey, and other than an animal print scarf around her neck dressed all in black. Caro was shorter and more comfortable in appearance and wore her auburn hair in a loose bun; her outfit simple, black pants and a rust-coloured jumper.

'We were each other's bridesmaids,' said Caro.

'But in my case, the husband has moved on,' said Fee.

'Don't you mean both husbands?' Caro corrected her.

'Okay, both husbands, and no, I can't see a number three in my future,' Fee stated emphatically.

Claire smiled at Fee's determination.

'We're also godmothers to each other's babies,' continued Caro.

'Although our babies have grown up now and have their own babies.'

'And because my son married one of Fee's daughters, we're also grandmothers to our baby's babies.'

Claire and Ed exchanged grins as Caro and Fee finished each other's sentences.

'How long have you been baking for?' Claire asked.

'Forever,' said Caro.

'As long as I can remember,' said Fee. 'Caro's mother was a member of the WI, the Women's Institute,' she clarified. 'And she used to help at Fountains Hall if they had big parties. I used to love going to Caro's house after school because there'd always be something sweet and yummy just out of the oven. Caro's mother had the lightest touch for pastry.'

'And her Victoria Sponge!' Caro's eyes softened at the memory. 'Try as I might, I can never get mine to taste the way hers did.'

'I remember the mother of my best friend at school baked an amazing sponge,' said Claire. 'She passed away when I was just eighteen. I'm taken right back to that kitchen and Mrs Gallagher every time I eat a good one.'

'I'm the same,' said Caro. 'My mother died soon after I got married and I still can't eat a sponge cake without thinking of her.'

'Did you bake very much for your children?' Claire asked.

'Sadly, no. Neither Fee nor I baked as much as we would've liked when the kids were little, but now that we're grandmothers we've gotten back into it again.'

'Especially since Caro's husband retired and she needed an excuse to get out of the house,' Fee said, smiling conspiratorially at her friend.

'It's a funny thing how suddenly I was incapable of doing anything on my own – even the groceries.'

Claire suppressed a chuckle – it was a story she heard a lot.

'Do you have any baking specialties?' asked Claire.

'Caro is our pastry queen, and I make an excellent chocolate biscuit – if I do say so myself.' Fee answered for them both, something she'd probably been doing for most of their friendship.

'Fee's also our sandwich maker. Her ribbon sandwiches are so neat and pretty,' said Caro with a smile at her friend.

Claire turned to Gail. 'What about you Gail?

What's your baking background?'

'I didn't have one. My mother was never much of a cook – she's still suspicious of anything that doesn't come out of a can or can't be cooked in the microwave – so I never really learnt. My childhood was either ready meals or grey food.

'I remember one time when I was growing up, I took the labels off all the tins in the cupboard. Mum was so angry with me – especially when she didn't know what cans held baked beans and which ones were the tinned peaches. Dinner was quite the surprise.' She paused as everyone laughed at the image. 'My husband left when Anna was still a baby, so I worked a couple of jobs to keep a roof over our heads and didn't have the time or the money to cook anything fresh. I used to dread those days when we'd have to take a cake for morning tea at school. All the other mothers would have these gorgeous homemade cakes, and I'd have something in plastic I'd grabbed from Tesco on the way there.'

'What got you started then?' asked Claire.

'Anna and I moved here about five years ago, and I got a job at a solicitor's firm in town. For the first time since Anna was born, I was earning enough to not only keep our heads above water but also to put a little away. It meant I didn't have to work extra jobs to make ends meet and had some spare time after work and on weekends. Fee came into work one day—'

'It was when I was divorcing husband number

two.' Fee rolled her eyes.

'And because Liam – he's my boss – was running late we got talking, and Fee said she was hoping Liam wouldn't be too much longer because she and her friend Caro had a date to do some baking for their grandson's birthday party.'

'Gail mentioned she had always wanted to learn how to bake but had no idea where to start,' said Fee.

Gail smiled at her friend. 'Fee invited me to her house the next weekend for afternoon tea. I met Caro there, and the next thing I knew I had an apron on and they were showing me how to make scones with lemonade, cream and flour.'

'The easiest scones in the world,' said Caro. 'They're not as great as a perfect traditionally made scone, but you get an excellent result for not a lot of work. It's the best way to lift a new cook's confidence, I think.'

Fee nodded her agreement.

'After that, I got the bug. The perfectionist in me wouldn't rest until I'd baked a proper scone. Since then I've experimented with cheese and herbs, pumpkin, and even Christmas flavours.'

'Gail is the scone maker in the group,' Caro said.

'I'm keen to try your Christmas flavours,' Claire said. 'Scones were always my favourite thing to bake as well.' Even as she said it, she felt like a hypocrite given how long it had been since she'd baked any. Keen to change the subject, Claire switched her focus to Tallis, who up to now had said little. 'What about you, Tallis?'

'Unlike Gail, I've always had a lot of time on my hands – some might say too much time. Derek has a business in Bristol and has always worked long hours and travelled quite a bit for work – you know, conferences and the like.' She lowered her eyes briefly to the table before raising them and smiling at Gail.

'I was *that* mother that Gail hated – the one who spent hours making sure my cake was better and prettier than all the others at morning tea. I was also the woman who always had a plate of something home-baked on the table for when Adam got home from school and a hot meal in the oven for Derek – not that he's home too often during the week these days.' She paused, deciding whether to say anymore. 'We weren't always well-off, you see. When Derek's business took off, he wanted to show the world how far we'd come, so about five years ago he bought the house here – at about the same time Gail and Anna arrived.' She sent a smile to her friend.

'When we first came here, it was quite strange. I didn't belong in my old life, and I didn't belong in my new life either – swanning around in a big Georgian pile like Lady Muck while my old friends were still working their fingers to the bone. I was in this in-between place. Then my Adam and Gail's Anna became friends – although they're more than friends now – and Gail turned up on my doorstep with a plate of scones and introduced herself.'

Gail grinned. 'It was something I knew I had to do but had been dreading doing it. I'd seen Tallis around town, and she always looked so perfect and put together. I thought she was outside my league and might look down her nose at Anna and me. That day over the scones, Tallis and I started talking, and I realised she wasn't snobby, she was just shy and, like me, didn't know where she belonged. Anyway, she asked me how I got my scones so light and fluffy, and I told her how Fee and Caro had taught me.'

'Gail took me along the next time she met with Fee and Caro, and we began baking together,' said Tallis.

'And one thing led to another, and we formed a book club – although it wasn't your normal sort of book club, it was a cookery book club. We meet once a month – usually at Tallis' house – and we all cook a meal together using recipes from whatever book was our book of the month. I can't even remember whose idea it was in the first place – although I think it was probably yours, Tallis,' said Fee.

'I'd never been a member of any sort of club before,' said Gail.

'None of us had been,' said Caro.

'I've never belonged to anything like that either and think it's the sort of book club I'd very much like to be part of,' Claire said.

'You can be an honorary member,' Gail impulsively offered. 'What do you think, girls?'

'Absolutely,' said Caro and Fee together.

'If you can't be here in spirit, maybe you could email us what you would've cooked if you were here,' suggested Tallis, looking away from Claire as she spoke, expecting to be turned down.

'Perhaps I could,' Claire said, wondering whether she meant it and feeling surprised when she did.

'The thing is,' said Gail, 'we'd all been drifting a bit, trying to find our purpose and this gave us something.'

'You'd be surprised at how often I hear that,' said Claire, 'that baking with other women can give a purpose and community that so many of us need.'

After they'd chatted some more, Ed walked everyone through what would happen over the next few days.

'Claire will be visiting some tea shops and specialist food stores in town and getting some background footage we can use to show Fenwyck at its best. We've got the list of growers you sent through to us, so we've organised for Claire to call in on them. We'll also be visiting each of you at home and will film you cooking something to serve family and friends.'

'We're due to have our monthly book club meeting next Saturday,' said Gail. 'Maybe we should move it forward a week, and you could come along.' She looked at the others for approval, and they all nodded. 'Sorry,' she said, 'I have a habit of speaking before I think things through. We wouldn't expect you to make something; you can just come along.' She looked down and away before speaking again. 'It's just that I can't imagine it would be great footage watching me serving up a meal to my daughter.' She grinned. 'Although you could film me yelling at her to take her earphones out and get to the table.'

'That's a lovely idea,' said Claire, 'but we'll come only on the condition I get to muck in and prepare something too. Besides, our crew is always hungry, so we'll need plenty of food. Are you sure you'll be fine to bring it forward to tomorrow night?'

'Absolutely,' said Caro.

'Caro and I have already decided what we're doing,' said Fee.

'We're cooking from "Nigella Express" this month,' said Tallis, 'so the whole point is for quick and easy food you can either make ahead or at the end of a hard day. There's bound to be something in there you can rustle up and put together at the house. I'll drop a copy of the book off to you later this afternoon. Where are you staying?'

Claire named the hotel where she and Ed were staying. 'We'll bring the wine as well.'

'Well, if you're bringing wine …' Gail laughed.

'This will be so exciting,' said Fee.

'We're so happy to be involved with the show this week as it is, but this will be the icing on the cake!' Caro chortled. 'Did you hear what I did then? Icing on the cake!'

Everyone groaned.

'As much as I'm enjoying this,' said Ed, 'Claire and I are due at Fountains Hall, and we still need to talk about Thursday and the actual afternoon tea.'

Once everyone was listening again, he continued with his usual spiel. 'I know you've already sent through a menu, but for the afternoon tea itself, you need to serve up a three-tiered tea plate to each table – one stand for every two people. You need, for each person, one plain scone and one savoury or flavoured scone, plus homemade jam and cream – it doesn't have to be clotted, but if you're serving clotted cream, it has to be homemade. You should also have a layered cake, a slice or filled biscuit, and two kinds of finger sandwiches using locally sourced fillings. Everything is to be baked or prepared on the day except for the jam and, if you're using it, the clotted cream – you can do that in advance.'

He looked around the table, and all the women nodded their acknowledgement.

'Please provide us with any changes to the menu or the shopping list you sent through to us by tomorrow morning. We'll ensure the kitchen at Fountains Hall is fully stocked and ready for you. We'll also arrange copies of your menu for each of the tables.

'Thanks, Tallis, for clearing the way for us with Lady Elliott. After talking to her, she's convinced the whole thing is her idea.'

Tallis laughed at the expression on Ed's face. 'That doesn't surprise me at all.'

'We've organised the marquee, and you have full access to the kitchen in the estate's tearoom for your preparations. The production team is there now checking on arrangements, and will be setting up on Wednesday and Thursday. If you need anything at all, these are the guys who can make it happen for you. Jody is in charge, and her details are here.' Ed placed some business cards in the middle of the table.

'You'll have access to the kitchen from 7 am with your tea plates ready to be served by 2 pm. Claire, a representative from your chosen charity, which is the local donkey and farm animal sanctuary, and a special guest "judge" will taste your food. This week's guest grew up here in The Cotswolds. He's been head chef in a couple of Michelin starred restaurants in London and Yorkshire and is passionate about cooking classical British dishes with seasonal and local produce.' Ed looked at each of the women to see if they had any idea as to the guest's identity. 'He's also now come full circle and is the head chef and owner of *The Lamb* at Brookford – which is Claire's hometown. In fact, Claire, you might know him – it's Owen Gallagher.'

Claire choked on the tea she'd just sipped. Owen Gallagher. After all these years. Her tummy plummeted into a void. Had Ed made a mistake? Was there another chef named Owen Gallagher who'd grown up in

Brookford? It absolutely couldn't be her Owen. That Owen had never cooked anything other than toast.

Most importantly, that Owen left to see the world in the summer they both turned eighteen. Even as Claire reasoned why it couldn't be the Owen Gallagher who'd broken her young heart into so many little pieces that for a time she feared it could never be glued back together again, she knew with absolute certainty it was her Owen. On Thursday she'd be seeing him again for the first time since that horrible summer.

Claire sat motionless, willing her expression to remain neutral as the guilt that had haunted her over their parting all those years ago flooded through her. Her past, it would appear, was about to catch up with her.

CHAPTER FIVE

Tallis arrived home to find Adam standing in front of the open fridge. She kissed his cheek, 'Good day?'

He grunted. 'I guess. What's for dinner?'

Tallis smiled at his predictability. 'I was thinking a chicken tray bake?'

'The one with the potatoes and the crispy skin and the chorizo?'

'Sure is.'

'Yeah, that would be good. Before I forget, Dad rang earlier. I think he wanted to know how the TV thing went.'

Adam sounded deliberately casual, which meant he wanted to know too.

'It went really well. Claire Mansfield seems lovely and warm. Exactly as she is on the show.' She paused for a second, 'which is fortunate because they're all coming here for dinner tomorrow night.'

'What?'

'Gail suggested we move our monthly cook-off forward so they can film it.'

'Wow, that's big. The entire film crew in here?'

'Yes. We have the room, and the crew were going to be here filming at some point anyway.'

'I suppose. Do I have to be here?'

'It's up to you.'

He nodded. 'I might go to Anna's. Does Dad know?'

'Not yet.' Tallis grimaced at the thought of the conversation. Derek hadn't liked the idea of them applying for the show, but had reasoned they wouldn't be chosen. He'd been in a sulk ever since he heard the news that Tallis and her friends would feature on the show.

'You know he wasn't pleased about you doing this, but I reckon he'll like the idea of showing off the house.' Adam's grin was conspiratorial. 'It's probably lucky he won't have time to come home and place some business cards or merchandise around for advertising – just in case someone on the crew wants to put up a conservatory.'

'You might be right,' said Tallis with a short laugh. 'I need to duck back into town to drop a cookbook around to Claire, so is there's anything you need while I'm there?'

'"I need to drop a cookbook around to Claire." Is it like that? Are you and Claire new best friends?'

'Absolutely.' Tallis laughed. 'Claire and I are like this.' She crossed her fingers on both hands and held them up. 'New BFFs.'

He screwed his face up in mock exasperation. 'Seriously, Mum, does anyone say that anymore?'

Tallis was about to make an appropriate response when her phone rang. 'It's your father,' she mouthed to Adam.

'Have you met with the television people?' Derek asked.

Tallis raised her eyebrows at his lack of greeting. 'Yes, I'm not long home. They seem nice.'

'People like that are trained to be nice to your face; it's all part of the business.'

'I don't think it was an act,' said Tallis.

Derek harrumphed. 'You're definitely going ahead with it then?'

'Of course,' said Tallis. 'I can't let the others down.'

'I'm only saying it because I don't want to see you embarrass yourself on national TV,' he said.

What he meant was that he didn't want her embarrassing *him* on national TV.

'I don't know why you need to be involved with those women anyway. Couldn't you join the tennis club or maybe you should take up golf? You don't want to get fat from all that baking. Whose idea did you say this was?'

Tallis bit lightly on her tongue. 'I didn't.'

'It would be Gail's, I bet,' said Derek.

'You never did like Gail,' Tallis muttered under her

breath. 'Will you be home tomorrow night?'

'No, of course not, why?'

'We're doing our club meeting tomorrow night and—'

'Now I'm thrilled I've got a client dinner,' he said and then laughed.

'And,' Tallis continued, 'the crew will be coming here to film it. Claire Mansfield's even going to cook and eat with us.'

Tallis imagined him sitting at his desk debating the potential business upside to coming home, the wheels ticking over in his mind.

'Do you want me to move the dinner so I can be there for you?'

'No, Derek, it's fine. Caro's Malcolm won't be there either, so it would be strange if you were. Besides, the house looks great, and I've put the Christmas tree up. It would be a shame to put your clients off for something that will probably be over with very quickly.'

'If you're sure …'

'Absolutely. The camera will be more focused on Claire than it will be on any of us.'

'Okay. You can tell me all about it on Saturday.'

'You're not home on Friday night?'

'Didn't I say? Jerry wants to take me out to say thanks for sending some business his way. I'll be home on Saturday instead.'

Rather than pointing out what they both knew,

which was that he hadn't mentioned Friday night, Tallis sighed inwardly and said goodbye.

It was only after she'd hung up the phone, picked up the cookbook, her handbag and keys and prepared to leave the house that she wondered who Derek was really going out with on Friday night.

Tallis had seen the looks her friends had tried to hide from her, and knew they suspected his absences weren't strictly business. None of them had ever said as much to Tallis, although Gail had almost gone there more than once. It was almost as if they understood that once they'd voiced the suspicion, Tallis would need to choose a course of action – even if the decision she made was to continue to tolerate what she suspected were Derek's extra-curricular activities. For now, though, shutting the front door behind her, she would continue to build a life here in Fenwyck that included the occasional visit by Derek; and that seemed to be working out for Tallis just fine.

Claire pushed thoughts of Owen Gallagher to the back of her mind and concentrated instead on work.

'This could be gold, Claire. Firstly, it's a different kind of book club, a cookbook club; secondly, rather than the usual stock images of family meals, we can do the bulk of the filming at the cookbook club meeting – although we need to come up with a snappier title than that. The best bit of all, though, is your involvement.

That's priceless.'

'It is, but I'm a bit concerned about holding my own with them – I'm out of practice in the kitchen.'

Ed shook his head, his eyes still focused on the road. 'You'll be fine. Select a couple of dishes you can throw together from ingredients we can source in town. Instead of the usual meet and greets with shop owners, we can show you buying the produce and talking to them about what you'll be using it for and what else they have on offer. Then we get the footage of you all mucking in together – that whole wine and conversation thing that makes everybody feel good. It's such a brilliant idea; I don't know why I hadn't thought of it before now.'

'Yes,' Claire agreed absently, 'it'll be fun.' She turned away and pretended to be absorbed in the landscape. The hedgerows were sparse, and the fields mostly bare and ploughed ready for planting. Here and there pheasants were scratching away at the surface, their brightly plumed tails golden as the setting sun hit them.

'Hey,' said Ed, sounding unusually hesitant, 'this Owen Gallagher that we have coming along on Thursday ... Was it my imagination, or won't you be overjoyed to see him? You do know him, right? Is he the son of the Mrs Gallagher you mentioned who made the sponge cakes? The one who died when you were eighteen?'

Claire's smile was wry. 'You don't miss much do you? Yes, I know him, we went to school together.' She forced a laugh into her voice. 'You know what it's like when you meet up with people from your school years – everyone is either married or divorced or both, and hardly anyone is doing what they said they would. It can just be a bit embarrassing. I haven't spoken to him since we left school.' Claire reasoned that at least her last statement wasn't a lie.

'Is that all it is? You referred to him as your best friend when you were talking about his mother.' He paused and snuck a quick look her way. 'I don't want to place you in an uncomfortable position, Claire.'

Claire cursed Ed's sharp mind. 'We were friends, and then we weren't. That's all there is. When I knew Owen, my ambition was to be a serious journalist and look what happened to that? The closest I got to becoming a journalist was writing a little column about the history of British cakes and biscuits and played around with some recipes.'

'I would've thought you'd done pretty well for yourself. You front one of the highest rating shows on TV at the moment, and most of the country knows who you are. You've nothing to be embarrassed about.'

'When you look at it that way I suppose, but the Owen I knew was quite serious. I doubt he even watches TV. And there he is, a real chef and owning the restaurant in the pub we used to get wasted in before we were old enough to do so.'

'Did he always want to be a chef?'

Claire shook her head. 'No. He was going to study – environmental science. He was one of those guys who aced maths and the sciences without even trying.'

'So not exactly kitchen apprentice material.'

'No. Isn't it awful how people assume that? That if you get marks like Owen got, you'd be wasted in a kitchen. It's just a different sort of smarts. I remember the headmaster at our school thought he was Oxford or Cambridge material.'

Claire didn't tell Ed that Owen had wanted to go to Bristol to study purely because he wanted to stay out of the whole Oxbridge scene. With Owen, it was almost a reverse snobbery. 'How much of a hypocrite would that make me Della?' he'd asked, using her childhood nickname. 'I can't do what I want to do from within that system. I want to study with people who are just like me and who want to change things for the better.'

Instead of going to university, he'd bought a one-way ticket to Vietnam, leaving without even saying goodbye.

'Well,' Ed was saying, 'whatever he might've wanted to have done with his life, he's certainly fallen on his feet now. He had a pretty big hiccup when he got sacked from *Belucci's*, and he seems to have come back from that.'

Claire turned back to Ed with a start. 'I didn't know he worked at *Belucci's*. When was that?'

'It would've been a few years ago now – maybe

just before we started with our first series. I'm surprised you didn't hear about it?'

'I wasn't exactly mixing in those circles back then. Although, I've eaten at *Belucci's* – a couple of times. The food was amazing.'

'Not everyone thought the same. The Spoonman wrote a review that totally slammed the restaurant and, if I remember correctly, Owen himself. Belucci responded by sacking Owen. He hasn't let it get him down – *The Lamb* is getting some great reviews. Have you been?'

'No, I haven't been back to Brookford in months. Next time I'm there, I'll be sure to try it. I'm surprised my sister didn't tell me he was there – news like that travels fast in a village. Back to tomorrow night though, I hope Tallis doesn't forget to drop me around a copy of that book. I'd like to settle on what I'm going to prepare so we can film it tomorrow.' As a change of subject, it was an effective one and brought Ed back onto the subject of what he was now calling the Cotswolds Cookbook Club. It had, he said, a better ring and less of a criminal connotation than the Fenwyck Four.

After dodging countless numbers of pheasants on the narrow road that led to the estate, Ed finally drove through the gates of Fountains Hall about thirty minutes later than they'd planned. As they arrived, another car on its way out stopped. The driver, a woman wearing a frown so deep it looked as though it never cleared, wound down the window and said, 'are you with the television people?'

'Yes, we are,' said Ed. 'Ed Wilson and Claire Mansfield.'

'Hmm. Lady Elliott was expecting you much earlier than this, and she doesn't like tardiness.' She shook her head, conveying a lifetime of being disappointed into that single movement. 'Just drive up to the estate office, and she'll come out and greet you. There's no need to be bothering her at the house.'

With that, she drove away, and Claire and Ed looked at each other and laughed. 'That's a good start,' he said. 'The lady of the manor isn't happy with us.'

'You'll just have to charm her back into happiness with your Scottish good humour,' said Claire.

No sooner had they parked the car than a middle-aged woman wearing muddy jeans, wellingtons and a forest-green wool jumper strode out to greet them. She thrust her hand into Claire's and shook it vigorously. 'You must be Claire Mansfield. I'm Jane Elliott, and I'm very pleased to have you all here.'

'Thank you for agreeing to open your lovely grounds to us,' said Claire.

'You're welcome. Plus, it's for a worthy cause. I went to school with Esther Paxton, you know – from the donkey sanctuary.' She turned to Ed and shook his hand too. 'It's nice to put a face to the name, Mr Wilson.'

'Please call me Ed, Lady Elliott.'

'And you must call me Jane – I don't hold stock with any of that Lady Elliott nonsense.'

'Oh, but—' Claire started.

'Aah. You must have met Joan on the way out. Pay no attention to her. Her parents worked here too, and I think she's horrified how George and I don't stand on as much ceremony as she thinks we ought. She still hasn't recovered from the indignity of opening the grounds to the paying public in the spring. But these old houses cost a fortune to maintain, and it seems a pity other people don't get to enjoy them as well as us.'

'Well, we're certainly grateful you're so generous.'

She waved Claire's thanks away. 'I'm looking forward to it. If Caro is as good a cook as her mother was, we'll be in for a treat. Anyway,' she said, a purposeful look on her face, 'walk me through the arrangements for the next few days.'

Claire stood back and let Ed take the lead.

Tallis was just walking out of the hotel when Ed and Claire pulled into the parking space. Ed greeted her and quickly excused himself. 'I'm sorry to run off,' he said to Tallis, 'but I need to make a call back to the office. I'll leave you in Claire's capable hands. I'll see you inside, Claire.'

Tallis smiled, 'That's okay.' To Claire, she said, 'I've left the book with reception.' Then she asked tentatively, 'Are you sure you want to do this, Claire?

We did spring it on you.'

'Absolutely. I can't remember the last time I cooked with anyone else, so it's a real treat and a privilege to be involved. I only hope I can keep up with you.' She smiled reassuringly at Tallis.

Tallis laughed, a look of relief on her face, 'I'm sure you will. Did you just want to prepare a starter? We'll serve everything on platters in the middle of the table so it would look like a feast for the cameras. What do we need to do for the film crew?'

'Don't worry about them – like the vultures most of them are when it comes to food, they'll descend on the remains the minute we've finished eating. Trust me, it doesn't matter how much we cook; there'll be no leftovers. I have to say though, Ed is worried about one thing.'

A slight frown crossed her face. 'Oh?'

'He says that you need to come up with a name for your cookbook club. He's suggested The Cotswolds Cookbook Club or The Cotswolds Ladies Culinary Society.' Claire shrugged a shoulder. 'What can I say? He's not great with titles.'

She smiled at that. 'I'll talk it over with the others, but maybe The Cotswolds Culinary Society? That has a certain ring to it.'

'You'll want to be careful – after everyone sees how much fun it is, you'll get requests from all over the country to join.'

'Oh, I hope not.' Tallis was suddenly serious. 'We want to keep it to invitation only. The club has filled gaps for each of us in different ways, and we all get on so well that we wouldn't want to risk messing with that.'

'In that case, I'm very honoured you considered me.'

Tallis' smile was hesitant before her cheeks coloured. 'I'd better be off home and leave you to it. Have you finished work for the day?'

'No, Ed wants to film me going through this cookbook over a pint in the bar, so I haven't quite knocked off just yet.' Claire lifted one shoulder in a no-rest-for-the-wicked you-know how-it-is gesture.

Tallis laughed. 'I think we've created a lot more work for you.'

'Perhaps, but we all think the episode will be so much better for the changes.'

'I hope so. Anyway, we'll see you tomorrow night. The others will be there by about six, but you'll be wanting to set up, so just let me know how you want to do that or if there's anything special you need.' She turned to go, 'Also we don't dress up for these things – Gail and I normally wear jeans and Fee and Caro dress down too.'

'That's good for me.' Claire lowered her voice, 'between you and me, I don't feel comfortable in anything else.'

'It sounds like you'll fit in perfectly,' said Tallis

before impulsively hugging Claire goodbye.

Claire stood outside for a few minutes more after she'd left. Although it was only just gone 5 pm, the sun had well and truly set, and the cold and dark had descended. Across the road, the Christmas lights on the market hall shone brightly and the Christmas trees at either side of the door added a festive touch that was echoed in most of the shopfronts along the high street. Claire hunched deeper into her jacket as she watched Tallis drive away.

Although Ed was thrilled at the way the day had gone and the filming they'd be doing tomorrow night at Tallis', and while Claire was looking forward to cooking with the other women, she couldn't shake her unease about doing it on camera. She loosened her scarf and rubbed absently at the prickle on the back of her neck.

Who was she kidding? It wasn't tomorrow night she was worried about – Ed would ensure any stuff-ups didn't make the final edit. No, what was creating this vague feeling of unease, the sudden flutter in her belly, was the thought of seeing Owen again. She'd told Ed that Owen probably wouldn't remember her, but she didn't believe it for a second – not after the way they'd parted. But then, maybe it hadn't meant as much to him as it had for her and that, perhaps, worried her more.

A drizzle had begun to fall, the drops hanging in the light, creating a kaleidoscope of colours. The lightshow distracted Claire for long enough to regain her composure before she shrugged lightly and walked into the bar where she knew Ed and the crew would be waiting for her. She could think about Owen as much as she wanted later; for now, there was still work to be done.

CHAPTER SIX

As Claire walked into the main bar, Ed slid his phone back in his pocket. 'There you are, I was beginning to think you'd run away,' he said.

'Why would I do that?' she asked with a forced laugh.

'Oh, I don't know,' he said, his eyes not leaving hers. 'Maybe so you don't need to meet a certain guest chef on Thursday?'

She shook her head, faking a smile. 'As I said earlier, he probably won't even remember me.'

'So you said. Something is worrying you though; it's not like you to leave the crew waiting.'

'No, not at all. I just got talking to Tallis, and then the lights on the market hall got me thinking. I wonder if there's anyone in town who could tell me about its heyday and when people used to come in for market day?'

'That's a great idea. Let me work on that. Now, I wanted to get some footage of you going through the cookbook and deciding on what to cook, so why don't you settle yourself into that chair; I'll get someone to get you a drink, and you spend the next thirty minutes not thinking about Owen Gallagher.' He raised his eyebrows and grinned, letting Claire know she hadn't fooled him with her attempted distraction. 'It's been a long day, so let's try and get this done so everyone can have some dinner and a few drinks.'

Warmth rose to her cheeks, and she nodded. 'It's okay, Ed, I'm focused. You get the guys to set up while I'm reading. One take – three at the most,' she promised. 'Then the first round of drinks is on me.'

Before packing the gear away for the night, they'd filmed Claire reading the book Tallis had left. With a pint of ale in front of her, she announced to the camera she'd decided to prepare two starters for the following evening: a mozzarella, herb and chilli gremolata, and a simple tuna and beans dish. 'With a couple of baguettes and some excellent olive oil, it'll make a promising beginning to our feast,' she'd said. 'And I think I might know exactly the place to get it.' Then she'd smiled into the camera and picked up her pint glass. 'But that's for tomorrow, and right now I'm thirsty. Cheers.'

The crew had stayed at the pub for dinner, and while everyone surrounded her, Claire could focus on work and the week ahead. Back in the quiet of her room, it was a different story, and despite her best efforts, her thoughts drifted back to Owen. Rather than thinking about why she was thinking about him, and why she seemed unable to stop thinking about him, she called Giles.

He picked up on the second ring. 'Hi, darling, what's wrong?'

'Nothing. Can't I ring to say hello?'

'Of course you can, and it's good to hear your voice, you rarely call when you're away filming.'

'I know. I'm just feeling …' Claire didn't know what she was feeling. 'But you sound like you're busy.'

'I'm putting together an outline for something I'm working on, but I'm okay to talk.'

That was so typically Giles. Once he'd got his teeth into a story or even the idea of a story, he'd work all hours until he knew he had the outline on paper.

'No, it's okay. You keep on with what you're doing. I just wanted to hear your voice.'

He laughed. 'But you only left this morning.'

'I know. I'm …' she paused, 'Okay, I've committed to cooking on camera tomorrow night, and I'm having second thoughts about it,' she blurted.

He laughed. 'For a minute there I thought it was something serious.'

'It is! I've never cooked anything on camera before.'

'Alright, walk me through how you agreed to that,' he said.

Claire leant back into the mound of cushions

on the bed and detailed the events of the day. 'And somehow,' she finished, 'I found myself invited to their monthly club cook — which we'll now be filming. Ed, of course, thinks it's great.'

'I don't see a problem,' he said. 'Ed's not going to let you look ridiculous, and from what you've said, the other women sound as though they're going to be fine as well. I think you're worrying needlessly. Besides,' he added, 'you have celebrity cook-off the week after next, so you're going to need to get comfortable cooking in front of a camera and quickly. I'm with Ed; I think it'll make great television.' He paused, 'worrying about things like this isn't like you, Claire. Where's this coming from?'

'I know, I'm sorry. Maybe I'm just tired, and it's messing up my head.'

'I'm sure that's it. Fortunately, this is the last week of filming, and you can take it a bit easier.'

'In the lead up to Christmas? I doubt it. Have you seen what's already on the calendar — and we still need to decide what we're doing for Christmas? Did you think any more about that place in Edinburgh I suggested?'

He hesitated. 'I have thought about it and … we'll talk on Friday night about it, okay? You'll definitely be home in time to go out for dinner, won't you?'

'I sure will. I'll be going straight into the studio when I get back to London, but our booking isn't until eight. Why?'

'As I said this morning, I have something I want to talk to you about.' His voice trailed off.

Claire wished they could just have *the talk*. The waiting was frustrating.

'Now, darling,' he said, 'you get some sleep.'

Get some sleep…she wished. Claire lay on the bed for longer, still dressed, her mind wandering back to Owen.

Still wide awake, Claire got off the bed and opened her laptop. When Facebook was first a thing, Claire had searched for Owen, simply telling herself wanted to know what he was up to, to be reassured he was okay. Although plenty of Owen Gallaghers came up in her search, none of them were her Owen. From time to time over the years she'd done the same and had always come up empty-handed. Until now, however, she'd resisted the urge to google him. Now she did just that.

The image that stared back was definitely the Owen she knew, but it was an Owen who'd grown up very nicely indeed. He was dressed in his chef's whites; the sleeves rolled up to his elbows, his arms crossed in front of him. His hair had darkened to a deep rust and was styled as if he'd run his fingers through it absent-mindedly, the way he used to when he was thinking. The familiar deep brown eyes stared at the camera with an intensity she'd not seen before, and his expression was stern in that pose that publicists seem to like the fieriest and most intense chefs to have. The dimples she loved kissing were barely visible.

Claire flicked through the images and found them all to be similar – all serious, and all looking confident in a don't-mess-with-me type of way. The Owen she knew was a private person and would've hated all of that. People change though.

Most of the images were from at least three or four years ago. There was very little about his personal life – a couple of photos of him squiring an "it" girl with a "Hon" before her name to some opening or another – but nothing else. If he went to events like that it was not surprising they'd never crossed paths. Before she began doing this job, she never mixed in those circles – she still didn't, at least not to that extent.

She searched further and found some videos of segments he'd done on *Saturday Kitchen*. It seemed strange watching him on the screen; the smile she knew and had loved sneaking through as he bantered with James Martin, the host. Had Owen done the same – sought images and videos of her? Did he watch *Time for Tea*? Did seeing her on TV bring back memories of how they used to be? Did he see the magazine covers and wonder how things might have been different?

Buried in amongst it all was the story of his firing from *Belucci's*. Claire followed the links to another story where Bruno blamed the loss of one of his Michelin stars on the review by The Spoonman that Ed had mentioned. Knowing Belucci as Claire did now, she thought he would've made Owen the fall guy – Belucci usually liked to have someone to blame. Following more links, Claire found the review itself. Ouch. After that, there wasn't very much about Owen until he bought *The Lamb* in Brookford. In those articles, she learned he'd spent the intervening years in a couple of Michelin-starred gastropubs in Yorkshire – where presumably he'd been since leaving *Belucci's* – but again, there was nothing about his personal life.

Claire flicked back to the images. The Owen she knew had been full of life and purpose and had plans to change the world. This man looked as though the world he'd found had hardened him. Staring at his eyes in the photo sent a thrill of goosebumps up her arms. Shaking her head, she shut the laptop and changed for bed.

That night she dreamed of Owen, but it wasn't Owen the smiling boy she'd been in love with, it was this Owen – the Owen in the photographs on her laptop who was all man.

In every episode of *Time for Tea,* Claire would wander around the town, calling in at grocers, delis, cheese shops, butchers – any shop that looked interesting. The production team usually set this up in advance and it was part of the job Claire enjoyed – so much so that these days the crew knew to allow additional time as Claire invariably got caught up in conversations and completely lost in the moments.

For this episode, having dishes in mind and specific ingredients on her list gave the segment another, more meaningful dimension from the usual meet and greet. Despite having lingering doubts about preparing her contribution for the camera, this was shaping up to be the best episode they'd done.

Filming for the day was completed with Claire having afternoon tea in the lounge of her hotel. She was sitting in a wing-backed chair, a pot of tea and a plate of scones (she would've scored a solid nine out of ten), jam and cream in front of her, and a fire roaring in the background. Jimmy, the cameraman, filmed her checking off the ingredients list in front of her and flicking again through the cookbook, speculating aloud what the other ladies might cook.

Finally, she pushed the remainder of the scones aside, looked longingly at them and said to the camera, 'It's such a pity to leave these, but I have a feeling I'll be needing a good appetite tonight.' Then she smiled and tapped the cookbook on her lap. 'Wish me luck.'

As it happened, luck was something Claire didn't need – she did, however, regret not wearing jeans with a stretchier waist.

Tallis' kitchen was enormous. At one end of a large open-plan room, it had two full-sized ovens, a double-sized cooktop, and enough bench space to cater for a large party. At the other end of the room was a long, timber dining table with leather dining chairs. It was such an expansive space, but Tallis had made it appear cosy by filling the walls with art and other personal touches. A fire burned in the grate and in one corner stood a massive, heavily decorated Christmas tree. Against the glass of the door that led to the garden was pressed the noses of two Labradors. 'I think they want to say hello,' said Claire.

'They'll jump all over you,' Tallis warned.

'That's absolutely alright. Nigel, my cocker spaniel, is the same.'

'Well, maybe for a second.' As Tallis slid the door open the dogs charged through, competing with each other for Claire's attention.

'Meet Cocoa and Bailey,' said Tallis, laughing as she watched Claire squat down to more evenly share her cuddles between the two. 'Okay,' she said after the dogs had greeted Ed and the crew with the same level of enthusiasm they'd shown to Claire, 'Out you go.' She opened the door and despite their hopeful looks back at Claire, both dogs obeyed.

Claire straightened and brushed at her jeans and jumper.

'I'm sorry,' said Tallis. 'Their paws are always dirty.'

'It's honestly fine.' Claire said. 'They're lovely dogs – and this room is gorgeous.'

'Thank you. When the production team contacted us and let us know there'd be some filming in our houses, I thought I'd better get the tree earlier than I usually would. I knew it would be close to Christmas when the show went to air and that you'd be wanting some Christmas spirit,' said Tallis.

'Thank you, we'd arranged the decorations for the marquee on Thursday, but hadn't even considered your houses. This is a fabulous kitchen – do you entertain very much?'

'Sadly, no. Derek likes to go out when he's entertaining clients so mostly it's just the three of us – although more and more often these days it's the dogs and me.'

Although Tallis smiled, Claire glimpsed loneliness shadowing her face. 'Where's Adam tonight?'

'He's gone to Gail's to spend the evening with Anna, and Derek usually stays in Bristol during the week – the travel was getting him down, so he bought a flat near work.'

Claire nodded, but Tallis had already turned away.

'Can I pour you a glass of wine?' asked Tallis.

'That would be lovely, thank you. You were saying Derek spends most of his week in Bristol,' said Claire. 'What is it he does?'

'He has a construction company.' Tallis handed Claire her glass. 'Derek was always going to be one of those men who did well. He started doing conservatories and extensions, and now it's almost exclusively commercial.'

Claire was impressed. 'And he's self-made?'

'Absolutely. We've both come from fairly humble beginnings,' Tallis said with a wry smile. 'But Derek was determined to make good, and he has done.'

'You sound proud of him,' said Claire.

'I am proud of him. He's worked hard.'

'I imagine you've had more than a little to do with it.' Claire grinned.

Tallis laughed. 'I suppose I have; you know what they say: behind every successful man is a woman.'

'And behind every great woman is herself?' Claire raised her eyebrows.

Tallis' cheeks tinged a subtle pink. 'I don't know about that. I've never really done anything special, and these days Derek doesn't need me very often.' As if realising she'd given away too much she turned and looked through the bag of ingredients Claire had bought.

'By the looks of how beautifully styled your home is and the way you were talking about your son earlier, I'd say you've done something very special,' Claire said, her tone gentle. 'Ed was saying how your application for the show was the most comprehensive he'd seen, so I suspect you're only just getting started.'

'I don't know about that.' Tallis hesitated briefly and then said, 'Does it ever feel strange to do what you do? People must treat you differently.'

Claire nodded. 'I've been doing this show for a few years now, and it's the dream job that I never thought to dream about, yet still, I often feel as though I'm pretending and one day someone will wake up to that, and it'll be all over.' She walked over to the sideboard and ran her hand across the smooth oak. 'Sometimes it's very lonely, you know. My friends, the ones I had before all of this, have gone in different directions to me, and the people I meet now, well, they either treat me differently, or I feel that they are the real celebrities whereas I'm just someone who got lucky.' She laughed shortly. 'Why am I telling you this?'

Tallis didn't laugh. 'I know what you're talking about – with the in-between thing.'

'Perhaps we're more alike than you think?'

'Perhaps we are.' Tallis smiled now. 'I've done nothing like this before, and I know Derek doesn't like it, but, he's not here, is he?'

She may not have realised it, but as Tallis spoke her chin firmed, and she stood a little taller.

Claire smiled back and nodded slowly in understanding. 'I, for one, am delighted you did put that application in.'

'Okay, Claire, sorry to interrupt,' Ed said. 'We're set up here now. We'll film everyone as they arrive and then you can come back in with your groceries, and we can talk about what you'll be cooking, and then—'

'Stop.' Claire held her hand in front of his face and smiled to take the sting out of the gesture. 'We're going script-free tonight, guys. I'm fine with coming back in and greeting everyone as if I've just arrived, but how about we keep the cameras rolling through the cook and see what we've got to play with?' She turned to Tallis. 'Are you fine with that? We'll only be using about ten minutes of the footage, but I think it'll make it authentic and warm. It's also, in my experience, the best way to forget the cameras are there; and once you've forgotten about the cameras, everything feels so much more natural. Ed won't let anything that shouldn't go to air, go to air – that's not what this show is about.'

Tallis nodded. 'I trust you but let me talk to the others as well.' The doorbell rang. 'Speaking of which …'

As she went to answer the door, Claire turned to Ed. 'What about you? I know you prefer a run-sheet, but I think we should just fly by the seat of our pants tonight.'

He grinned. 'The usual procedures seem to have been overturned on this shoot, so go for it.'

Thankfully, everyone was keen to go ahead as Claire had suggested, and it wasn't long before they were all unpacking groceries, and the cameras were forgotten.

'Right,' said Gail. 'You're doing starters, Claire, so tell us, what are you cooking?'

'I can see mozzarella,' said Fee. 'I hope it's the mozzarella and crazy gremolata.'

Claire grinned. 'Good guess. I'm also doing the

tuna and beans. It sounds like nothing, but I hope it'll taste fabulous. I've got some baguettes we can dunk into the olive oil. I don't know about you, but I can't leave oil undunked. And the bakery in town was way too nice to walk out of empty-handed.'

'I'm doing a festive fusilli,' said Gail. 'Spiral pasta with semi-dried tomatoes, mascarpone and, wait for it, vodka!' She held up the bottle triumphantly.

'Caro and I are doing a *Pollo Alla Cacciatora*,' Fee announced, waving her hands around and pulling off a reasonably successful Italian accent.

'That's chicken cooked "the hunter's way",' Caro said. 'We're using thigh fillets to speed up the cooking process. We're also doing a holiday hotcake with eggnog cream. It's like a Christmas self-saucing pudding.'

'Oh, that sounds completely decadent,' said Claire. 'What about you, Tallis?'

'I'm preparing a butternut squash with pecans and blue cheese and, because I just happened to get some lovely scallops this morning, we've also got scallops and chorizo. But—' She looked around at everyone with a cheeky grin, 'to get this party started, a Christmas cocktail, from the book, of course, is in order. I give you Christmas in a Glass!' With that, she held up a bottle of prosecco and one of gingerbread flavoured syrup. 'Shall I do the honours?'

With glasses in hand, the five women clinked them together and chorused a "cheers." They slotted together in the kitchen as if they'd been cooking together as a team for years. As they chopped and sliced and stirred, they chatted in the comfortable way long-time friends did, and not as women who'd known each other for just over twenty-four hours.

True to the express promise of the cookbook, it wasn't long before everyone was sitting down to platters of food, which the crew eyed off hungrily. Tallis poured glasses of wine as they all took their places at the table.

Gail raised her glass. 'I'd like to raise a toast to all of us – old friends and new – and to this food which looks fan-bloody-tastic. Thanks to Tallis for hosting us tonight and to Claire for giving us an excuse to over cater and for suggesting we give our little group a proper name. So, for the first, but absolutely not the last time, here's to The Cotswolds Culinary and Cookbook Society. Yes, it's a mouthful, but a delicious one.'

They all raised their glasses. 'To the Cotswolds Culinary and Cookbook Society.'

Once the women started eating, Claire caught Ed's eye. He nodded. 'Okay guys, I think we've got all the footage we need,' he said. 'That was great – and we're hungry too!'

The crew joined them at the table, and it wasn't long before the food was demolished. When they still appeared to be ravenous, Tallis whipped up syllabub using cream she had in the fridge, liqueur and a packet of almond biscuits that she crumbled over the top. Claire caught Jimmy swiping his finger around the top of his glass to make sure he'd got every last bit.

'Why can't we end every shoot like this?' Jimmy said, with a cheeky grin.

With everyone pitching in, the cleaning and washing up was completed with a minimum of fuss, and it wasn't late when everyone began to leave. Tallis had walked Claire and Ed out to his car when he received a call.

'Sorry,' he said, 'It's the wife – I'd better take it.'

Tallis raised her eyebrows at Claire as he walked away from the car.

'We're not like that,' Claire answered the question Tallis hadn't asked. She wrapped her coat tighter and slid her hands into the pockets. 'We work closely together, and we're good friends, but there's been nothing more than that. Ed's happily married and has three very gorgeous children.'

'I'm sorry,' said Tallis. 'I shouldn't jump to conclusions.' She pulled the zip up on her jacket rather than meet Claire's eyes.

'It's fine. It's a simple mistake to make, and the boundaries can get blurred in this business.'

'Are you attached? I thought I'd seen pictures with you and someone.'

Tallis lowered her head as she said it. Claire was learning this was a defence every time Tallis felt she was blushing.

Tallis went on, 'I googled you.'

'Yes, I've been with my partner Giles for almost seven years. He's a freelance journalist – he does those big investigative pieces you see in the weekend lift-outs.'

'You're not married?'

'No, although I have a feeling he might be about to propose.' Claire wasn't sure why she'd told Tallis about that. There was something about Tallis that made her feel as though she'd known her forever and, more importantly, could trust her in a way Claire trusted very few people in her world. 'When we got together neither of us wanted to get married – he's a bit older and has been there before – but the way he's been talking I'm beginning to wonder whether he's changed his mind. We have dinner planned on Friday night, and he said yesterday that there's something particular he wants to ask me.'

'And you think it's a proposal?'

'I'm getting that idea.'

'How would you feel if it was?'

Claire shrugged. 'While it's not something we've spoken about, I think the time's right.' She let out a small laugh. 'I'm certainly going to dress up in case it is a proposal. Who knows, if he doesn't ask me, now the idea is in my head, I might just ask him.' She lowered her voice. 'I've said nothing to Ed though, so this is just between you and me.'

'Got it.' Tallis smiled and nodded her confirmation. 'We're all looking forward to Thursday and to meeting Owen Gallagher too. Gail did some googling, and she's extra keen to meet him if you know what I mean.' Tallis beamed and raised both eyebrows.

Claire was under no delusions as to what she meant. 'I'm looking forward to seeing him too. It's been years.'

'I wondered how well you knew him,' said Tallis, her gaze narrowed on Claire. 'You did very well to hide it, but you seemed very surprised to hear his name.'

'Aah. I guess it surprised me. Owen and I were friends when we were younger – it's fair to say we grew up together – but I last saw him when I was eighteen and haven't heard from him since. I had no idea he'd become a chef – or he'd come home to Brookford.' She made a mental note to ask Gracie why she hadn't mentioned it. 'I wish Ed would hurry,' she rubbed her hands together, 'it's cold out here. Oh, here he is now.' Tallis wouldn't have missed her clumsy change of subject, so Claire focussed her attention on Ed instead. 'Everything okay? Tallis and I were freezing out here.' She smiled to take the edge off her words.

'Sorry about that. Everything's fine at home – just the usual chaos and Allison wanted to say goodnight.' His eyes softened as he mentioned his wife.

'And so should we. Say goodnight, that is,' said Claire and kissed Tallis' cheek. 'Thank you for everything tonight. We've got a full day tomorrow, so I'll see you on Thursday. Call us if you need anything. I know you have Ed's number, but here's mine too.' There was gratitude in Tallis' smile as she accepted the card. 'And please, call me even if you're just having a slight attack of the wobblies; I know exactly how overwhelming all of this can be.'

Even as Claire said the words, she smiled at the irony of offering advice to Tallis when she was having an attack of the same wobblies at the thought of seeing Owen again. On the bright side, after having such a great time in the kitchen tonight she was no longer worried about the Christmas cook-off, it would be an absolute breeze.

CHAPTER SEVEN

Tallis had everyone organised early on Thursday morning, so by the time Claire arrived at Fountains Hall, the baking preparation was well underway.

'You ladies look like you have everything under control. The marquee looks fabulous, the weather is on our side, and the smells coming from this kitchen are fabulous,' Claire said.

Their slice of choice – a Bakewell tart – was out of the oven and set aside to cool.

'We'll drizzle a simple icing over the top and slice it into small squares,' said Caro. 'Trust me, this tart will taste nothing like the Bakewells you get in the supermarket.'

'I should hope not,' said Claire with a grin.

Tallis was taking the second of her Victoria Sponges out of the oven. They looked as light as a feather.

'Strawberry jam in the middle?' Claire asked.

'Naturally.' Tallis smiled back. 'Homemade, and we have local cream and a dusting of icing sugar for the top.'

Gail was in charge of the scones with the first batch already under a tea towel to stay fresh.

'What's your savoury choice?' asked Claire.

'I'm doing a pumpkin scone with a bit of a spice to it – some clove, nutmeg and cinnamon. The colour will be great, and it will taste of Christmas.'

'I'm looking forward to trying them.' She leaned closer and said just loud enough for the camera to catch, 'and I might just steal the recipe.'

Fee was mixing fillings for the sandwiches. 'We're doing smoked salmon and cream cheese – with a little dill in the cream cheese – and a classic cucumber with herbed lemon butter. I won't fill the sandwiches just yet – the last thing we want is curled corners – but I'll be ready to go with those shortly. In the meantime, we need to get the jam into little glass bowls for the tables. And we also need to get the cream ready and in the fridge.'

'Clotted?'

'Yes, we weren't going to, but Tallis has been practising, and this batch is perfect. You'll love it.'

'I'm sure that I will.'

Claire motioned for Jimmy, who'd been following as she spoke to each of the bakers, to turn the camera off. 'Grab a cuppa,' she said to him. 'We'll need you back in here soon enough.'

As Jimmy left the kitchen, Ed arrived, and with him was Owen Gallagher. If Claire had thought Owen looked hot in his chef's whites, he was even more good-looking dressed down in jeans, a navy woollen jumper and trainers. He was slim in the way that showed he spent a lot of time on his feet and was always on the go, but he filled out the jumper and his jeans in all the right places.

Her eyes finally found their way up to his, and that's when her tummy fell, and heat rushed to her cheeks. His face wore no expression, and his eyes bore into hers. It was as if they were the only two people left in the world, and everything else receded into the distance. A shiver ran up her spine.

Ed cleared his throat and brought her back to her senses.

'Owen.' Claire smiled and held her hand out to shake his. 'It's been such a long time.' Her outstretched hand hovered for a few uncomfortable minutes. Finally, he clasped it, the heat of his touch shocking her into meeting his eyes again.

'It's good to see you, Claire,' he said, smiling now. 'It's been how long?'

Owen continued to hold her hand, not shaking it, just holding it. The darkness faded from his eyes, and his laugh lines showed.

'Um wow, about ten years, maybe more?' Her head was whirling; her stomach churned. She hoped none of that showed in either her face or her voice. And still he held her hand.

'Definitely more. It was the summer we finished school.' He tilted his head slightly to the side. The dimples that hadn't been apparent in the very serious publicity photos Claire found online disrupted her heartbeat in a way it hadn't been disrupted for a very long time.

'And that was over seventeen years ago,' Owen confirmed.

Claire laughed, but it sounded forced and high-pitched even to her ears. Finally, he released her hand, and she rubbed it against the leg of her jeans as if she could wipe away the heat of his touch. He watched the movement, with a slight raising of his eyebrows that Claire pretended not to notice. 'That long? Well, we've certainly got some catching up to do.' She hoped her words sounded normal.

'We certainly do.'

Claire's eyes shot to his, but his smile hadn't quite made it as far as his eyes. She swallowed once and struggled to find a semblance of her usual control. 'And I'd love to hear about Brookford and *The Lamb* and how you've come to be back there,' she said with a forced smile, 'but now's probably not the time for that.' Okay, professional Claire was back. 'Thanks so much for taking the time to join us today. How about I introduce you to the bakers and Ed will fill you in on how things will run.'

Claire made the introductions automatically and then stepped back to watch Owen as he engaged easily with the women. Her heart was beating its way out of her chest; it amazed her no one else seemed to have heard it.

Gail was the first to take his attention and he listened with intent as she answered his questions. Then he'd moved onto Fee who, oh my god, yes, Fee was giggling like a teenager under his interest.

Claire's gaze wandered briefly from Owen to Tallis, who was watching her and raised the slightest *are you alright* eyebrow in her direction. If Tallis had noticed her discomfort, perhaps her cool, calm and collected act hadn't been as polished as she'd thought. Claire pursed her lips together and nodded once as Tallis returned her attention to Owen, smiling at a comment he made about her sponge. Seeing him now as he easily charmed the other women, Claire could almost pretend she hadn't seen the steely intensity when he'd first set eyes on her. If that look was any indication of how he felt about her, it certainly appeared he hadn't forgiven her – and she couldn't blame him. Despite the distance of time, she hadn't forgiven herself.

Thankful that everyone's attention was on Owen, Claire ducked her head and went outside, walking around to the back of the tearoom. The cold hit her face, and while she regretted not taking the time to grab her coat, she welcomed the fresh chill on her skin. Leaning back against the stone wall and looking across the grounds, she concentrated on breathing. Breathe in. Hold it. Breathe out. In. Hold. Out. As she exhaled, her heart rate – and the churn in her tummy – slowed. There was nothing to worry about. All she had to do was get through the next few hours. That's all. Then she'd never need to see him again. Unless she was in Brookford, but even then, she could avoid him if she tried – she wasn't in Brookford very often, anyway; it had been months and months since she last visited.

On Friday night, she'd be back home with Giles. He'd propose, and they'd be engaged, and she'd feel safe again. This strange feeling that everything was tumbling would be gone, and she'd be fine. That's all this reaction to Owen was, a symptom of whatever weird anxiety was going on in her head. She took another couple of deep breaths. Everything would be okay if she could just get through today.

As her breath quietened, she told herself she'd seen nothing in his manner other than the discomfort of meeting up with an old crush. It was always bound to be awkward between them, that's all. She was shivering because she was cold; there was nothing more to see here.

Then Owen strode around the corner of the building. With his hands in his pockets and shoulders hunched against the cold, he leant back on the same piece of wall as Claire, one foot resting on the stone behind him, just centimetres between their arms, the warmth from his body transferring to hers.

'You're looking good, Della,' he said,

She laughed shortly. 'No one's called me that in years. I'd almost forgotten you used to.'

'Only almost? I haven't forgotten anything about you.' He lazily stroked Claire's little finger.

He'd done that so many times before, and now in one move Owen undid all her hard work to get her breathing and heartbeat and tummy settled. Seeing their hands together opened the flood gate of memories of all the other times they'd held hands. Each of them came back one after another. She braved a glance at Owen's face, his eyes didn't meet hers, instead they were firmly focused on their linked hands. As if he realised what he was doing, he pulled his hand back from hers and closed his eyes briefly.

'I haven't forgotten anything,' he said again, but more softly this time, his eyes opening to meet hers.

Claire studied his face seeing everything she was feeling reflected in his. His lips were together in a hard, straight line, his eyes dark with sadness or hurt, perhaps both. They stared at each other for what seemed like minutes but must've only been one heartbeat, maybe two.

Owen blinked and this time when he opened his eyes the steel she'd seen earlier was back in them – the darkness of what she assumed were painful memories completely at odds with the gentle, almost reflexive touch of his hand. He shook his head and dropped his gaze from hers.

'I certainly haven't forgotten a single thing about our ending,' he said and pushed off the wall and away from her, leaving her colder than before. 'I only wish that I could forget,' his tone freezing her to the core.

'If you dislike me so much, why did you agree to do this today?' Claire almost hissed the words, confused at his sudden change in tone.

'Who said anything about disliking you?' He shook his head and rubbed at the back of his neck 'Trust me, I've tried. I'll see you inside.'

As Owen walked away, Claire pushed the back of her knuckles into her forehead in a bid to squash the memories that had been locked away for so long – and were now mounting a bid for freedom.

The image that loitered for the longest was the first time he'd held her hand. It was one of those bright blue days you get in early spring that made you feel as though summer was almost here and the jumpers could be packed away for the next six months, even though you knew in your heart that it was fleeting.

They'd gone walking through the wood that would be full of bluebells in a just a few weeks, and their hands had brushed. Accidentally at first, and then again, less accidentally. If Claire closed her eyes now, she could still feel the thrill that ran through her as first Owen's little finger hooked around hers, much as it had done today, and then he took her hand and held it. Neither of them had said anything. They'd just kept walking, their eyes on the path ahead, but both knowing inside that something had changed.

Then, a week later, he'd kissed her for the first time, and took their relationship to a new level. Claire squeezed her eyes shut and bought one last memory out of the box, the one that would push all the others back inside where they belonged. The one where she learnt that he'd left Brookford without saying goodbye. And her guilt at knowing she could've prevented it.

With fifteen minutes to go before the teas needed to be served, Claire made a final visit to the kitchen. Although there was plenty happening, there'd been no disasters, no messes, and very little in the way of chaos. In the marquee, the crew had set the tables. And in the kitchen, tea trays were filled and ready to go. Gail and Tallis had persuaded Anna and Adam to help serve the teas – and they'd roped in some of their friends. They were all dressed in jeans and Christmas jumpers, waiting for the go-ahead from the production team to begin serving.

Claire took a deep breath; it was showtime. 'Okay, ladies of The Cotswold Culinary and Cookbook Society, are you ready to go?'

Caro reached for Fee's hand, which grabbed Gail's and then Tallis' hand. They embraced and emerged from the group hug with broad smiles.

'We certainly are,' Fee confirmed.

'Let's do this!' said Gail.

With the cameras following, they walked the short distance from the tearoom's kitchen to the marquee where it appeared the entire population of Fenwyck had turned out for the occasion. Claire hid a smile knowing the high street would resemble a ghost town if anyone should drive through this afternoon.

'Good afternoon, ladies and gentlemen,' Claire began. 'Welcome to Fenwyck in the Cotswolds – and *Time for Tea.* Your afternoon tea today has been prepared by these fantastic women beside me: Tallis, Gail, Fee and Caro. I've been lucky enough to have a sneak preview of what's soon going to be gracing your tables, and I think you're in for a treat.' She paused briefly and smiled. 'As we all know, today isn't just about the food, it's also about communities like yours getting behind local causes, and I'm pleased to announce that Fenwyck has decided their charity of choice will be the Cotswolds Donkey and Farm Animal Sanctuary. The contributions you make today will help feed these animals – all of whom have been rescued from some very dire circumstances – over the winter months. Joining us today from the sanctuary is Esther and Barry Paxton. They're sitting just over there – stand up and give us a wave.' Claire waited as they did, then continued, 'and they'll both be available to talk later if you have questions or would like to know how you can help further.

'Our other special guest today is Owen Gallagher. Owen was born and bred here in the Cotswolds – just a few miles up the road in Brookford, where I also grew up.' Claire paused and forced a smile at Owen. 'After working in some of the best restaurants and gastropubs in the country, Owen has come home to Brookford, and you'll now find him on the pans at *The Lamb* in the high street. I'll get you to please welcome Owen.' She waited for the applause to end. 'Esther, Barry, Owen and I will decide today's dish of the day jointly and it will earn its maker a dinner for two in Owen's restaurant. So, without further ado, I'm going to hand over to Gail, Tallis, Caro and Fee to tell you a little bit about what you'll be eating today.'

Claire smiled in encouragement at the bakers and squeezed Tallis' hand. 'You've got this,' she mouthed and made her way to the table she was sharing with the guest judges.

Once settled with their teas, Claire relaxed into hostess mode and encouraged Esther and Barry to talk about their sanctuary and how they'd got started.

'When my parents passed away, I inherited the house and land, and Barry and I both decided to retire from our jobs and move back here to Fenwyck,' said Esther.

'Esther was a special education teacher, and I was a cabinet maker,' explained Barry.

'It seemed selfish of us to have all of this land

and not share it. At first, we had just one donkey and then another and another. Then someone had some ex-battery hens who needed a home, and it grew from there – we had the land to support them, and neither of us could say no, could we?'

Barry shook his head and placed his hand over Esther's. 'I've never been able to say no to Esther – in all the forty years we've been married.'

'Forty years? That's lovely,' said Claire. 'You must've been childhood sweethearts?'

'We were. We fell in love when we were sixteen.' Esther beamed at her husband. 'When we were eighteen, we separated briefly, partly because of family pressure but mostly because I thought I might've been missing out on something, but before too long we were back together again.'

'First loves rarely last,' said Owen with a sideways glance at Claire.

'It's lovely that your story is a happy one,' said Claire in haste.

'What about you, Claire? Have you got a partner?' asked Esther.

Owen turned to look at her, waiting for her answer. Firmly ignoring him she kept her focus on Esther. 'Yes. I'm dating a journalist. We've been together for almost seven years.'

'Should we hear wedding bells anytime soon?' asked Esther.

'Oh, I don't know about that,' she said, buttering the top half of a pumpkin scone.

'Perhaps he needs a nudge in the right direction. Sometimes us men don't know what's good for us, do we, Owen?' Barry winked.

Owen's return smile appeared strained. 'You could be right,' he said. 'Although sometimes women don't know what's good for them either – especially when they're young. You're fortunate Esther realised what she had in you, Barry.'

Owen's comment was clearly directed at her, and suddenly the conversation was taking an uncomfortable direction. 'I'm enjoying the spice in this pumpkin scone,' she said. 'The cinnamon really adds a certain something.'

Owen grinned at her poor attempt to change the subject.

Esther switched her focus to Owen. 'What about you, Owen? Is there a Mrs Gallagher?'

The sudden flash of sadness that crossed his face was gone almost as quickly as it had come. Was he thinking about his mother?

'No. Not anymore.'

Claire's eyes widened in surprise and met his briefly.

'Unfortunately, when I left my last job in London and went north to Yorkshire, my now ex-wife decided she preferred the city to my company.'

The pieces were starting to come together – Alex Spooner's review of Belucci's restaurant had cost Owen his marriage and his job.

Owen shrugged. 'It was sad, but these things happen.'

Sensing the need to get back on track with the filming schedule, Claire motioned to Jimmy to bring the camera over, and brought their focus back to the purpose of the afternoon. 'I think we need to discuss these fabulous dishes we've been tasting. I don't know about you, but I'm having a hard time choosing my favourite.'

'I'm torn between this Bakewell slice, the sponge cake, and the cucumber with lemon butter,' said Esther.

'For me, it's the pumpkin scones, the sponge, and the smoked salmon,' said Barry.

'My vote would go to the Bakewell slice,' said Owen. 'Although I haven't had a sponge cake this light since the last one my mother made.'

'No,' said Claire, 'nor have I.' Conscious of excluding Esther and Barry, she clarified, 'Owen's mother made the most amazing sponge cakes. She made jams as well. My mother doesn't enjoy cooking, so I always appreciated having tea at Owen's house. Everything I know about baking I learnt from her.'

'Is she still living?' asked Esther.

Owen shook his head. 'No. We lost her just before my final exams.'

Esther shook her head sadly. 'It's hard to lose your mother at any age, but so young …'

Claire didn't know what made her do it, but she rested her hand on his. 'Well, if we're all in agreement, I think any food that brings back memories such as that has to be our winner.'

'That's fine with me,' said Esther.

'I'm not arguing,' said Barry.

'The sponge it is.'

It was soon time to wind proceedings up, so Claire closed with the announcement of the dish of the day to a quietly pleased Tallis, thanked everyone for their support and wrapped the filming, leaving her free to mingle in the marquee. She stopped to chat with some of the growers and shop owners she'd met during the week, introduced herself to other villagers, agreeing that yes, the food was fantastic, the donkey sanctuary was a wonderful cause, and she'd definitely be back for another visit.

As she moved from table to table, she surreptitiously looked around for Owen. Surely he hadn't left without saying goodbye again. Bidding farewells to the last of the villagers, she made her way back towards the kitchen, wrapping her jacket around her tightly as she crossed the lawn between the marquee and the tearoom. In the doorway, she paused, hardly noticing when Ed stood next to her.

As if he knew the direction of her thoughts, he said, 'Owen had to leave to get ready for tonight's service. He told me to say goodbye and that he'd call by the hotel tomorrow morning and meet you for breakfast before you leave.'

'Oh. Okay.' Claire tried to hide her disappointment.

Ed stopped by the car and examined her face. 'Is there something going on here that I need to know? Some history between you two? I know you said the other day you were friends, but it was more than that, wasn't it? Don't tell me you were childhood sweethearts and he cheated on you and broke your heart?'

Claire forced a laugh into her voice. 'Wow, talk about imagination. It was nothing like that.'

'Are you sure? There was definitely some powerful chemistry between you two that I'm hoping to see come across on camera. Are you telling me I imagined that?'

'Maybe. Okay, we do have a history of sorts. We were best friends, and then we dated for a while. But he didn't cheat on me, and I didn't cheat on him. It just ended – like things do when you finish school and go your own way. I went to university in London, and he left to see the world.' Claire met and held his eyes. 'As I said, it just ended.'

'Did he break your heart?' he squeezed her shoulder, the kindness bringing a lump to Claire's throat.

'Yes,' she finally admitted. 'And I think I might have broken his.'

He nodded. 'I see. And you were both fine today?'

'We were. We're all grown up. He's been married and divorced, and I'm with Giles. It's all good.' She offered a sad smile. 'To be honest, seeing him again put things in perspective, you know? He's fine, I'm fine, we'd blown everything out of proportion all those years ago, and now it's all as it should be.'

'If you say so,' he said, still studying her face.

'Absolutely. Now, unless you need me for anything else, I'd better help clean-up.'

She walked away under the scrutiny of Ed, knowing he didn't believe a word of what she'd said. That was okay – nor did she.

CHAPTER EIGHT

The kitchen was soon looking more like its usual self, and by just after six, everyone had either gone or was preparing to do so. The Paxtons left with a wave and an invitation to visit anytime, and Lady Elliott had locked up the tearoom and was outside talking to Ed.

'Well that was fun, we really must do it again another time,' Lady Elliot gushed.

Tallis called Claire over to where the other women were gathered around their cars, the interior light from Tallis' vehicle illuminating them.

'We just want to thank you for choosing our little team,' Tallis said.

'We've all had the best time,' said Fee.

'And we hope that you'll continue to be a member of The Cotswolds Culinary and Cookbook Society,' said Gail.

'And that you stay in touch with us,' said Tallis.

Claire had only known these women for a few days yet had grown closer to them than she had to anyone in a long time. 'In order of your comments,' she said with a grin. 'You're very welcome. I'm very glad, absolutely and absolutely. Even if I can't be with you every month, I'd like to be with you in spirit for the monthly cook-off.'

Ed interrupted their moment. 'I'm sorry, ladies, I'm going to need to take Claire away, but just so you know, I haven't seen the footage in full yet, but I'm already sure this will be our best show ever. And it's all down to you four. So, thank you.'

Later that night in her hotel room, Claire tried not to think about Owen. She especially tried not to think about how her body had reacted when he'd touched her. She debated whether your skin has a memory like your muscles do and whether her reaction was simply her skin remembering how it used to feel when Owen touched her in the past. This was, she reasoned, all just a trick of the brain – that if he touched her again, she'd feel nothing. Then she tried not to think about that either.

The call from Barty was, therefore, a welcome interruption.

'I just wanted to check in and see how the week had gone?'

'Really well,' she said and told him about the women she'd met and Tuesday night's meeting of The Cotswolds Cookbook and Culinary Society.

'It sounds like it'll turn out to be a good episode. And you were obviously okay about cooking on camera, so you can now stop worrying about doing Celebrity

Christmas Cook-off.'

'I suppose,' she said. 'Maybe I was just worrying about nothing.'

'You don't sound convinced about that,' he said. 'In any case, it's something you'll need to get over yourself about – the network is getting closer to finding you a co-host for the other project we're talking about.'

'The one where I'm working beside a chef, and we're doing our versions of the same dish, but theirs is posh, and mine is not? We've been through the contracts for that, haven't we?' Her smile was wide as an idea struck her. 'How great would that name be for the show: *Posh or Not?* I might suggest it to Ed.'

'While it would fit the brief, I don't think they'll go for that. As for the contracts, yes, we've been through them, but until now there've been delays finding the right chef to partner you with.'

Claire nodded, even though Barty couldn't see. 'You said they've nearly decided. Who do they have in mind?'

'Bruno Belucci's name has come up.' Barty said the words so quickly, waiting for her to explode. He didn't need to wait for long.

'No way, Barty. No no no no no. I could never work with him. I hope you told them that.'

'Bruno's not too bad. He's a very experienced chef, and I think his people have been trying to find the right vehicle for him.'

'He might be experienced, but I couldn't work with him. You can't have forgotten how he made that pass at me and then got nasty when I said no.'

'That was a long time ago. You hadn't even begun filming *Time for Tea*, and you've now just finished your third season. You're much more experienced now.'

'Seriously? Are you going to dismiss it? Are you implying that if I'd been in the industry for longer, I wouldn't have reacted the way I did, or he wouldn't have tried it on in the first place? I don't care how long ago it was; he was out of line, Barty.'

'I'm not saying that he wasn't out of line, just —'

'Just what? I don't think he'd want to work with me either. Last time I saw him was at that awards dinner back in the summer, and he didn't hold back then either. He also snubbed Giles, and I don't recall that he was very friendly to you either.'

'He probably had no idea that Giles was your partner,' Barty's attempt to defend Belucci's behaviour was half-hearted at best. 'He certainly wouldn't have known that Giles is probably the most respected investigative journalist in the UK.'

'That's no excuse. Bruno was plain rude. After what he said about me, it would be hypocritical of him to take this job – why would he want to work with a home cook? It would be beneath him unless he thinks it would make him look fabulous and me inferior. No.' Claire shook her head. 'I won't cook beside someone who I know will be laughing at me, making judgements about what I'm doing and probably having a grope whenever he can. It's absolutely out of the question.'

'Okay, I get it. You don't want to work with Bruno. I have some meetings this week, and I'll ask them to keep looking.' He paused, 'are you sure that's the only problem you have with the project – the idea of working with Bruno? If there's anything else I need to know about, you'd better tell me before we sign the contracts – or are you planning on blocking every proposed co-host until the network gives up on the idea?'

'Of course not.'

'Are you sure? Remember this isn't live to air, there's plenty of editing and we'll make sure the chef you're working with is one who doesn't take himself that seriously and respects you rather than judges you.'

'That puts Bruno Belucci out of the running then.'

Barty continued as if he hadn't heard her. 'Besides, let's not forget this was your idea in the first place.'

Claire muttered something under her breath.

'What was that?'

A loud sigh escaped her lips as she collapsed back on her pillow. 'I just said I need to learn to keep my stupid ideas to myself – especially when I'm under the influence of cheap champagne.'

'It was hardly cheap, darling, and you hadn't had very much of it at all. I remember the occasion well. It was after the wrap party for season two, and we were watching a contestant on *MasterChef* who you felt was overly pretentious. You announced you didn't need to do unnecessary things to food or buy unnecessarily expensive produce to cook a fabulous meal. Then you said it would make great viewing if you were to get a home cook and a chef each to cook their version of the same dish and see which one tasted better. You might have even said something like "seriously, Barty, how much faffing around can you do with a roast chicken, anyway?"'

'Fine, it was my idea, I get it.' Claire absentmindedly twisted a piece of hair around her finger. 'I didn't expect them to go for it though, did I?'

'Okay, it's been a long week, and you're obviously not in the mood to talk about the new show. What's on the agenda for the weekend?'

Claire sat back up and plumped the pillows against the headboard of the bed. 'We're off to *Lily James* tomorrow night.'

Barty gave a low whistle. 'Nice. What's the occasion? No wait, don't tell me that Giles is finally going to pop the question?' When Claire didn't immediately answer, he added, 'really? You're not serious?'

Claire shrugged.

'Are you?'

'I'm shrugging. And why shouldn't he be ready? We've been together for seven years and living together for nearly five, you know.'

'Yes, I do know; I was there when it started, remember? I just didn't think that's the way you guys were heading.'

They'd met at a party Claire had attended with Barty. It had been the classic eyes meeting over a crowded room thing, and when Claire had gone outside for some air, Giles had followed. She'd been the one to say, 'do you want to get out of here?' and the rest had been history.

'Which other way could we possibly be heading?' Claire's tummy tightened at the possibility, and she held her breath as she waited for Barty to reassure her.

'I don't know, darling, and I'm not suggesting you're heading in a different direction. All I'm saying is I thought you and he had decided you would never get married and that you didn't want children.'

'We'd talked about that in the early days, but I was just twenty-eight, and I didn't think I wanted any of those things.'

'And now at the ripe old age of thirty-five, you've changed your mind. What's prompted that? Is it filming with all these country women who are mothers or grandmothers? Is your clock ticking?' He made a clucking noise like a hen.

Claire laughed. 'Stop it! No, it's got nothing to do with that, or maybe it has. I don't know. I just feel things are changing, and we've been together for ages; the only thing missing is the piece of paper.' The more

Claire had thought about the possibility of marriage, the more she wanted it.

'Is this fear talking? Is the idea of the new show freaking you out so much that you're trying to hold on to something normal and safe?'

'No. Maybe. I don't know.' A prickle of heat grew behind her eyes. 'I didn't think it was important, but now I do. Don't ask me why, but I just do.'

'Okay, all I know is he's said before that he likes things the way they are – as I thought you did. I can't see him wanting to make too many changes.'

'People can change their minds, you know.' Desperation had found its way into her voice. 'He's let slip a couple of times about how when you get older you change your view on the world and contemplate the things you said you'd never do. It's almost as if there's a decision he needs to make, and that's the only thing I think it could be. In fact, if he doesn't ask me, I might just ask him.' When Barty was silent, Claire asked, 'Don't you think I should get married?'

'You can do whatever you like.' He paused for a few seconds. 'I don't care whether you get married, or you don't get married, but if marriage is what you want, then I wish you joy.'

Claire laughed. 'Oh my god! You sound like something out of Jane Austen.' She pursed her lips and parodied him. 'If that's the way you feel, I wish you joy.'

He joined in. When the laughter died, he asked,

'What's Giles working on at the moment?'

'You know Giles, there's always some story or another he's chasing. Why? You're not usually interested in his work, and you know I can't talk about it.'

'No reason, I'm just wondering whether that's what he's contemplating, and it's got nothing to do with being ready to propose.'

The first tendrils of doubt wound through Claire's brain.

'Have you thought about what you'll do if he doesn't want to get married?'

'I don't want to think about it,' she admitted. 'But thanks for putting it into my mind,' she snapped.

'Right, so you're fine to catastrophise about everything that can go wrong on a cooking show, but you don't want to think about a possible adverse outcome in your private life.'

'You and I both know that if things go wrong on *Cook-off*, the whole of England will have seen it go wrong, whereas if I propose and Giles says no to me, no one else will know that I'm devastated. It's private. Besides, if that's the way it pans out it doesn't matter – I'm also supposed to be writing a review for *Lily James* so I can't see a downside.'

'Fair enough. Just while you're worrying about it though, it's not just the whole of England who'll see if you stuff up on *Cook-off*, quite a bit of Scotland, Wales and Northern Ireland will be watching it too.'

'Gee, thanks for that. How to make me feel better.'

His exhale was one of surrender. 'You know what? I'm not talking about this anymore tonight. We'll only go around and around in circles. You've had a good week, and the show is probably going to be the best one you've done. Now, get some sleep. You're going to want to look your best tomorrow night for Giles.'

Once she'd hung up on Barty, Claire's thoughts went straight back to Owen. What right did she have to be overthinking her reaction to one man when there was a possibility she could be marrying another? She loved Giles; she knew that she did. While she hadn't meant it when she said it to Barty, Claire decided that if Giles didn't propose, she would. To put things in perspective, Owen was someone she hadn't thought about in years, and she wouldn't have been thinking about him now if he hadn't touched her. She might even have been okay if that damned sponge cake hadn't brought up memories of his mother; and that in itself made her recall a time before she died when Claire could've put her hand over Owen's and known her comfort was all he needed to feel.

She still remembered the day he told her his mother was sick. It was the beginning of spring, and they'd walked up the hill towards Sapperton and were sitting on the grass. Owen was leaning back against a fence post, Claire sitting in between his outstretched legs, his arms wrapped around her, his chin on her head.

He said, 'Mum's sick. It's lung cancer, and that's so fucking unfair because she hasn't had a cigarette in her life.' And then his chest shuddered, and he was crying, so she held onto his hands and pulled his arms tightly around her. Owen lowered his head until it was next to hers, their cheeks together, their tears mingling.

By the time summer arrived, Mrs Gallagher was gone, and nothing was ever the same again.

CHAPTER NINE

Owen was already in the hotel's breakfast room reading a newspaper when Claire came downstairs the following morning. He had a coffee in front of him and a pot of tea on the table for her. Dressed as casually as he had been yesterday, he looked, despite having run service last night, much fresher than she felt.

When he saw her, he closed the newspaper and rose to kiss her cheek.

'No handshake today?' she quipped.

He grinned. 'No, I think we're more than a handshake, don't you?'

She nodded. 'Yes, we are.'

He held the chair out and gestured for her to sit. 'What are you eating?' he asked.

'I'll have a boiled egg and some toast. And you?'

'Just toast and coffee for me.'

Claire sank into the chair and slid her room key into her handbag as he placed the order.

'I'm sorry,' he said once they were alone again.

'You're sorry? What for?'

'Being a pratt yesterday. I wanted to throw you off your game, and that was unprofessional of me. I have no excuse other than I'd been wondering how it would be to see you again and when I did, I didn't deal with it well.'

Claire poured some tea. 'I was thrown too – I didn't know we'd booked you until Ed mentioned it the other day. I didn't even know you were a chef. It all came as a complete surprise to me.'

'I see. Would it have made a difference?'

She shrugged. 'Probably not.' She sipped at her tea and then blurted out the words she'd been determined not to say. 'It made me realise that I'd missed you. I'd missed us and how we used to be back in those days.'

'Yeah, me too.'

'It was fun back then. Until that last summer, everything was so idyllic. Sometimes I wonder whether I got that memory mixed up – how things sometimes look better from a distance. If I described our growing up to anyone else, it would sound like the growing up that no English child has had for real since the 1950s and maybe not even then.'

'Like something out of an Enid Blyton book – all adventures and endless summers and picnics with jam sandwiches at the bottom of the garden?'

She nodded at his description.

'I don't think you muddled the memories because mine are the same – at least until Mum got sick and then you and I fell apart. She died, and you betrayed me,' he said bleakly.

'I wasn't completely honest with you – that last time we spoke – but I'd say that betrayed is a strong word to use.'

He shrugged. 'It's how I felt.'

'You left before I could explain everything.' Claire combed her fingers through her hair. 'I've often wondered whether if I had, you would've stayed and done your final exams. Whether it would've changed anything.' She shrugged. 'You ran away and I thought I'd ruined your life.'

Owen slumped back in his seat. 'I don't know, Della. Maybe everything has turned out for the best. Look at us both – I have my restaurant, and you've got a TV show. If we'd stayed together, we wouldn't have done that.'

'Neither of us are doing what we said we would, though.'

'Does anyone?'

'Perhaps.' Claire leaned forward and set her jaw. 'Owen, how long did you spend hating me?'

He faltered. 'I only hated you because I loved you so much.'

Claire met his eyes. They reflected the sadness in her heart. 'How long, though?'

'It doesn't matter. One day I stopped, and I don't hate you anymore, I guess that's what's important.'

And by inference, he didn't love her either – not that she'd expected he would. They'd both moved on and they'd both grown up.

'And you were married?'

'Yes. To Julia Spencer-Brown.'

The "honourable" she'd seen in the photo. 'The daughter of the Earl?'

He nodded.

'Quite the catch.'

His lopsided smile made her heart miss a beat. 'For a boy from Brookford, absolutely. She thought I was going to be the next big celebrity chef; *I* thought I was going to be the next big celebrity chef. But when Belucci sacked me over a viper piece from The Spoonman, Julia decided she didn't want to be with someone who used to be the next big celebrity chef. She had no intention of moving to Yorkshire.'

'I googled you the other night and read about that. As I mentioned before, I didn't know you were a chef, and I didn't know you were in London. I thought I'd somehow know if you were near.' She said with a sad smile. 'That sounds ridiculous, doesn't it?'

'It does a little, but I think even if I didn't know you were in town, I thought somehow I'd know too.' He shrugged. 'So, we're both as ridiculous as each other. Seriously though, while you've been everywhere I looked for the last few years, there was no reason for you to know where I was and what I was doing – unless you were mixing in those circles and going to those restaurants.'

'Which, aside from the occasional launch I went to with Barty, I didn't.'

'Who's Barty?'

'Harris Bartholomew. He's my manager or agent; I never know the difference, though both terms sound like a bit of a—' She fought for the right term to use.

'They both sound like a bit of a wank.' Owen completed her sentence.

'Yes, they do.' Claire laughed. 'Barty and I have been friends for years, so when *Time for Tea* came up, and I needed someone to deal with all of that stuff, he volunteered himself. But back to your story, I read you went to Yorkshire for a while?'

'You *did* google me.'

Claire squirmed in her seat. 'I did. What about now that you're back in Brookford, have your own place and, if what I read is right, will soon have your own Michelin star to hang on the door? Would Julia come back to you then?'

He shook his head. 'I doubt it. For a start, I live above the restaurant, which means I live above a pub and she wouldn't like that, and not just because there's not enough room for her shoe collection. I wouldn't want her back now anyway. Love is supposed to be through the good and bad, you know.'

Had Owen directed his words towards her?

'I'm sorry, Dells. I wasn't having a go at you. I just meant it shouldn't have mattered to her where we were living as long as we were together.' He ran his fingers through his hair, and suddenly she wanted to do the same, to feel his hair under her fingers. She gave a slight shake of her head to clear the image, relieved when the waiter arrived with breakfast.

'How's your family?' he asked once the waiter had left them alone again.

Claire tapped the top of her egg with the back of her spoon. 'They're good. Gracie's married now – she and her husband Bill and their four-year-old son Milo live in Brookford – on a farm just outside the village.'

'Little Gracie all grown up,' he chuckled at the thought. 'She would've been, what, thirteen or fourteen when I last saw her?'

Claire did the numbers in her head. 'About that. Stephen went to Australia, met his wife Hayley and never came back. They have three children – Ava and Noah are six, and Cooper is four. Mum and Dad went over for their wedding and then retired there.'

'Have you been over to see them?'

'Giles and I went a couple of years ago. They're all in Sydney – on the North Shore, I think you call it. They're happy, so that's great. How's your father?'

Owen's face fell. 'He passed away about fifteen years back. A heart attack.'

'I'm so sorry.'

'Thanks. He was lost without Mum, so it was probably best he only had a couple of years without her. They were so close that sometimes I wondered why they had me. I knew they loved me, but they were so self-contained that they really didn't need me. After she died and I left, Dad moved down to Hastings to live with his sister.'

'Did you come back to England for the funeral?'

He nodded. 'Yes, it was a quiet one.'

The visions of Mr Gallagher at Owen's mother's funeral filtered through her mind. He'd been inconsolable – as was Owen – but while Owen had clung to her, Claire had never been able to shake the picture in her head of Mr Gallagher standing off to the side, isolated in his grief. Yet he'd still had room in his heart to feel sympathy for her on that day she turned up at his door asking for Owen, and he had to tell her that Owen had gone.

Pushing aside those memories, she continued. 'How did you end up working in restaurants? I take it you never went back to school to take your final exams?'

'No, I didn't. As you know, I'd bought a ticket to Vietnam and from there wandered around South East Asia. It was cheap to live, but I soon ran out of money so got jobs in bars and then kitchens – and it was in those kitchens I fell in love with food. It wasn't just the flavours of South East Asia that interested me, but the way food was so tightly embedded into the stories and the culture. I'd do a service until midnight, go home for a few hours' sleep, and then roll up to the fresh food markets before dawn. I'd grab another couple of hours' sleep and then be back for prep and service again. I did that for years, coming back here only for long enough to deal with visas.'

He paused and drained his coffee. 'I made my way to London about ten years ago and got a job at Nahm in Belgravia. Then I did a stint with Marco and worked my way up to sous chef before going to *Belucci's*. By then I'd done a couple of segments on *Saturday Kitchen*, and there was some talk of a spot on *Great British Menu* – which was when Spooner's review came out. I wasn't even in the kitchen the night Spooner apparently reviewed us – Bruno was running it – but he needed someone to take the fall for him and that someone was me. Part of me wondered whether Belucci was threatened by the media interest I was getting at the expense of himself, and Spooner gave him the excuse he'd needed to get rid of me.'

'I know Bruno Belucci, and I wouldn't be at all surprised if that were the case,' said Claire. 'Did you see The Spoonman's review of *Bella Donna* the other day? I wonder who he'll blame this time.'

'All I can say is Belucci was a bastard, but at least he was a bastard to your face. The Spoonman, whoever he is, is so much worse than that. He wields his poisonous pen behind a pseudonym, and no one knows who he is. He ruined my career for a time; he definitely ruined my marriage – although knowing Julia as I do now, who knows whether he just sped up the process. Either way, I would like to confront him and let him know just how many lives he's destroyed in the name of what I'm sure he thinks is just entertainment.'

'Don't you think people who are spending their hard-earned money deserve to know they're spending it somewhere where they'll get some value for money? Restaurants aren't cheap – especially Bruno Belucci's restaurants.'

He stared at her. 'Are you defending him? The Spoonman?'

Claire scrambled to put her thoughts into order. 'No, of course not. I don't believe they should only publish good reviews. Too many – especially of the uber-expensive, uber-hot places in town – are overly positive just because they have a name chef and are fashionable, or because the chef has paid for the critic to, shall we say, accentuate the positives and overlook the negatives. I don't care whether they've paid the reviewer in cash, free meals or by dinner reservations when no one else can get them, it's still a paid review.

'I'd read the glowing reviews for *Bella Donna* before I ate there and let me tell you, my experience was nothing like that. I disagree with the way Alex Spooner goes about it, but I do think reviews should be fair and accurate.' She paused. 'For example, take *The Lamb*, your place. There are some great restaurants in The

Cotswolds, we're spoiled for choice here, so people have decisions to make for where they'll be spending their money, right?'

'Right. It's why a review from a *trusted* critic can make or break you.' He raised his eyebrows as he emphasised the word "trusted".

'Exactly. You want them to eat at *The Lamb* because your food is excellent, and you want them to come back with their friends. You don't want them to visit because they've read a review you've paid a blogger to write, that's made your place out to be something it isn't. That, in my mind, is worse than an honestly written poor review. The whole point of the review system is to give people an idea of what to expect so they can make an informed decision about where they'll spend their money, right?'

'Absolutely. My ethos is seasonal British, so I'd get pissed off if someone came in expecting bells and whistles because that's not what I'm about. I want people to have done their research and have an idea about what to expect when they walk through my doors – and a well-written review does that.'

Claire nodded. 'Which is where the big-name critics come in. Most are fair, and because of that, they're respected. The Spoonman though, that's just theatre and clickbait.'

He nodded. 'I agree with you. What Spooner did to Belucci – and others – was to dramatise it until it was an entertainment piece rather than an authentic review. And that helps no one.'

She nodded and scraped her spoon around the eggshell to get the last of the egg. 'Yes, You're right. Having said all of that, they've asked me to review *Lily James* on Friday night.'

'Adrian Ritchie's new place?'

'Yes. I like Adrian, so I've told him I'll pay for the food myself and will write it up only if I enjoy the experience. If I write the review, the paper will pay for it; if I don't, I'm out of pocket.'

'Doesn't that tempt you to write something nice even if it wasn't?'

'Possibly, but that would make me no different to Spooner. Nicer, but no different – the review would still be false, but I suppose that comes down to my integrity. I'm fortunate I can afford to wear the cost of the meal myself if it doesn't work out – most people, when they're starting out writing reviews can't afford that luxury so would write it up regardless.' She poured more tea. 'Now I'm not saying that's the right way to do it either, but the system is definitely skewed towards sensationalising the ordinary. Nor am I saying Belucci didn't deserve what was written about *Bella Donna* – I just don't think it needed to be written in the way it was. I can't stand the man. He's arrogant and thinks he's god's gift to the kitchen and all women.'

'That sounds like you've had a personal run-in

with him.'

'I have. Belucci made a pass at me one time and then turned nasty when I said no.'

'Seriously?'

'Yes. I was at this launch with Barty when I was still writing my column, and he was still PR'ing – I used to write this column about the history of classic and regional dishes.'

'Yes, I know. I read every one and the way you wrote them, I could've been in the same room as you. It was fun – just the right amount of food history, a little humour and the recipes I could imagine you baking.'

She stared at him for a few loaded seconds and allowed the thrill of the knowledge he'd been thinking about her run through her body. 'Anyway, it was back then. Barty was working with this PR firm, and I got to be his plus one at events I otherwise wouldn't have got to go to – in fact, it was at one of those that I met Ed and got this gig. I also met Giles at one of them. Barty says that's why I owe him both my love life and my career.' She laughed, but Owen didn't join her. 'This launch was for a new place in Kensington that Bruno was a not so silent partner in. I can't even remember what it was called – not that it matters; it bombed pretty badly. Bruno grabbed me when I was on my way into the bathroom. It was all very unpleasant, and over before it started but I've never forgotten it. He's never mentioned it since, but he avoids me if he can or mouths off to anyone who'll listen to him about how I'm an imposter.'

'I don't imagine you would've forgotten it. I knew he was a twat, but I didn't know he was a lech as well – not that it surprises me.' Owen motioned to the waiter he'd like another coffee. 'How did you get started? I know about the column and that this show grew from that, but before?'

'My missing years?'

He smiled. 'Yeah.'

'Well, I did my exams, spent the loneliest and most miserable summer on record without you.'

He raised his eyebrows.

'It's true! I mooched about for months. Mum told me to just get on with it, and Stephen was so angry with you for leaving without saying goodbye. Gracie, of course, was wound up in herself and had no idea about any of it.'

'What about Jenna? She was your best friend.'

'I think Jenna was a little relieved it had happened to me rather than her and Chris. Once summer was over—'

'The loneliest most miserable summer on record?' He grinned.

'So now you're making fun of me?'

He shrugged one shoulder.

'After that, I went to London to uni – as I'd always planned. By third year I'd moved into a dodgy share house with Barty and too many other people. Then when we left uni and got jobs – Barty in this public relations firm and me at the paper – we moved out with another two of the women there, Martha and Freya. It was another dodgy place, but less dodgy than the first.

'I was going to be this investigative journalist and Barty would be the publicist to the stars – although he was, at the time, working for one of those firms that specialised in minor soapie stars and footballer's wives. Martha was an artist and Freya was an accountant, and the only one of us earning decent money. I was the only one who could cook – although at that stage I could only afford to cook scones, pasta and breakfast, so we ate mostly scones, pasta and breakfast. We even had a breakfast pasta.'

'What on earth is breakfast pasta – or shouldn't I ask?'

'For a start, it wasn't eaten at breakfast, but we called it breakfast pasta because it was essentially a marmite and cheese sandwich with pasta instead of bread.' When he continued to look confused, she clarified. 'You cook some marmite in a heap of butter, toss through the spaghetti, and smother it with grated parmesan. Martha and Barty both loved it with a squirt of ketchup too.'

'It sounds, um, interesting.'

'Okay, so maybe it won't be on the menu at *The Lamb*, but for a time it was my signature dish – and it was cheap. My job at the paper was entry-level, and I spent about a year fetching coffees and running copy and messages between departments before anyone gave me even the most boring of press releases to write up. Then I spent another year doing that before the woman who was writing the horoscopes resigned. She was also the agony aunt, so I inherited both jobs.'

'How old were you by then?'

'Twenty-three I suppose, with the life experience to match. So, I did those jobs and some other things like it and felt terrible about all of them, but when you're that age and being paid peanuts you can't really afford integrity, so I'd go home and bake. At least baking was honest, and the outcome was always a positive one that made me feel better about myself. Barty eventually complained about how it was making him fat, so I began taking what I'd baked into work – journalists are always hungry. The editor rewarded me with a proper story – reviewing London's best afternoon teas. It was great fun traipsing around London, from the Dorchester to Fortnum and Mason and everywhere in between, rating the tea, the scones, the cucumber sandwiches, the ambience. Duncan might've thrown it to me as a pity pitch, but the story ended up being unexpectedly popular.

'Out of this, and a discussion about what made one scone better than another, came a story about the history of the British scone and how the recipe had changed over the years.' Claire paused and sipped at her tea, smiling at the memory. 'It was meant to be a bit of fun, a one-off piece, but it attracted so much feedback it grew into a fortnightly column where I took British teatime classics, talked about their origins, and baked both an original recipe using traditional methods and an updated version.'

'You said you owed Barty your career and your love life. How is that?'

'As my career had finally begun to take off, so had Barty's. He'd progressed to a firm that managed some publicity for the BBC. Because we were living together and Barty always seemed to be single, I got to be his plus one. I met Giles at one of those parties and then a few years after that, soon after I'd moved in with Giles, Barty and I were at this launch for something that thankfully sank without a trace – what sort of twisted mind brings people from various reality TV shows, puts them into pairs and sends them to renovate a villa on Love Island?'

Owen laughed. 'You're not serious?'

'Sadly, I am. Anyway, after drinking way too much of the free champagne on offer, I got talking to someone about how viewers needed a break from nasty reality TV. I said that the world would be a kinder place if there were more scones and tea and if we celebrated ordinary people in ordinary villages more than we did. The person whose ear I bent that night was Ed's. He called Barty the next morning to get my number, and we talked some more.'

'And the rest, as they say, is history?'

'Something like that.' She let out a short laugh. 'It's hard to believe that was four years ago and we've just finished filming our third season.'

'It must've been strange at first – going from writing about food to being in front of the camera?'

'You have no idea! It overwhelmed me how quickly everything moved, and I struggled with the scripting. As I got increasingly flustered, I also became quite paranoid and thought everyone was wondering what someone like me was doing in front of the camera.'

'You mean instead of someone like Nigella?'

'Exactly. Then Ed took me aside and told me I was overthinking it all and to ignore the script and to pretend the cameras weren't running. He told me to imagine I was having a conversation with someone instead of talking to a camera.' She smiled at the memory. 'I got lucky.'

'And you've made the most of the opportunity,' said Owen. 'I enjoy watching the show, although I'll admit it was weird at first seeing you on screen and remembering—' He shook his head. What had he been about to say? Had seeing her on TV brought back the memories of how they used to touch each other, loved each other?

'You seem so natural on the show, and I saw

yesterday none of that is an act. That's why everyone enjoys it so much.'

His praise warmed her from the inside; she cleared her throat. 'Now that we've each caught up on the years between, what happens?'

He rubbed at his chin as he thought. 'Now we get back to our lives.'

'I guess.'

'You don't think?'

Claire raised her eyes to meet his. 'We haven't talked about the end.' His eyes darkened until she couldn't look at them anymore and had to turn away.

'You mean we haven't had the break-up chat, or closure … whatever it is you want to call it?'

She nodded.

'Is there any point, Della? We were eighteen; my mother died; my father flipped out because he couldn't deal with it. There was only you, and then you betrayed me.'

'You used that word earlier. I mightn't have been honest with you, but I don't believe I betrayed you,' she said.

'No, Della, you got scared. Admit it.'

'What did you expect? You presented me with two one-way tickets to Vietnam and told me we were going to run away together. You didn't ask me how I felt about it; you just assumed I'd be happy to go with you. I knew you were upset, and you wanted to leave

Brookford. I understood that. I told you I wanted to be with you, and I meant it. All I did was ask you to wait until we'd done our exams. It was important to me that I finished. You said you understood, and you'd think about it, and then you left without me. I was only asking you to wait for an extra couple of weeks – a month at the most. We'd been studying so hard. What did you expect me to do?'

'Stand by me. You promised you'd always love me, and it seems that was only as long as it suited your timetable. My exams were gone the minute Mum got sick. I barely retained anything I read – I thought you knew that.'

'I did, but I'd worked hard, Owen. I wasn't going to throw all of that away. One month, I said, and I'd leave with you. I asked you to wait for me. I understand you wanted me to come with you, and I've felt so guilty about that over the years – that I could've and should've talked you into staying and finishing school; but I don't know why you think I've betrayed you.' She shook her head in confusion. 'That's a big word, and I can't see how it applies to what I did. If anything, you're the one who betrayed me when you left town without a word or even a note. Do you know what that did to me?'

'You lied to me,' he glowered.

A snort of disbelief escaped her. 'About what?'

'You were seen.' When she continued to look blankly at him, he sighed. 'In Cirencester.'

Claire's tummy dropped and her heart pounded, but somehow she kept her eyes on his face.

'You told me you were going to Jenna's to help her with a question on the practice English paper, but you didn't, did you? I was there, Claire, in Cirencester that afternoon, and I saw you. You were hanging outside one of the cafés in the high street with some bloke. And then when I called you later to ask how it had gone with Jenna, you lied and said you'd got the paper done and Jenna was grateful for your help.' He shrugged. 'I knew then you'd cheated on me and that despite what you'd said about waiting, you had no intentions of coming with me, so I left anyway.'

Owen sent her a long and pained look. The hurt in his voice was as fresh as it must have been on that day all those years ago.

'Who was he, Claire? The bloke you lied to me to be with.'

'I can't remember his name.'

Owen shook his head, his mouth twisted in disgust.

'No.' She fought to bring her voice under control and sat on her hands so he couldn't see them tremble. 'It wasn't like that. He was a friend of Chris'. You're right; I lied to you about what I did that afternoon. I *was* with Jenna, but we weren't studying.'

'And I suppose if I spoke to Jenna now, she'd back you up? Not that I'd waste my time — you two were always covering for each other.' His lips were thin as he spat the words out.

'It's the truth – we were in Cirencester, we weren't studying, and we ran into Chris and whatever his friend's name was. You jumped to the conclusion that wasn't there.'

'What were you doing there that afternoon? What had Jenna dragged you into that you couldn't tell me about?'

She took a deep breath, and her eyes darted around the room searching for the answer he wanted to hear.

'No more lies, Claire.'

A little pulse beat in the side of his jaw. She wanted so badly to stroke it away. Taking another breath, she raised her eyes to the ceiling to delay her answer and hold off saying the words she'd hoped never to have to say to him.

'What were you doing in Cirencester that afternoon?' Owen insisted.

As Claire opened her mouth to tell him, the message tone on his phone sounded. He looked across at it briefly and then turned his attention back to Claire.

'Do you need to deal with that?' she asked.

He shook his head. 'It can wait.'

Then Claire's phone pinged with a message. Owen raised his eyebrows.

'Sorry, that's the ten-minute warning for my car. I'll have to go.' As she pulled her wallet from her handbag, she avoided his eyes.

'This isn't finished, Della.'

'I know, I—'

This time it was his phone ringing. He shook his head once and answered it. 'What?'

Claire's eyes widened at his impatience.

'What do you mean there's no salmon in the order? Christ!' He rubbed at his forehead. 'Okay, so what do they have? Right. Well, I'm just leaving Fenwyck now so should be no more than fifteen minutes.' He hung up and looked across at Claire. 'I'm sorry, but I'm going to have to run – that was Angie, my sous chef. We're trying out a new seafood supplier, and he's not only delivered late but forgot to include the salmon, which means I need to come up with a replacement dish just,' he looked at his watch, 'two hours before we begin lunch service.'

She nodded her head in understanding, and some of the tension dissolved. 'That's okay. You need to be there.'

As she placed some notes on the table to cover their breakfast, he shook his head. 'Let me get this,' he said. 'I'd hoped we'd have longer but…' He held his hands up in resignation.

'You have a restaurant to run,' she finished his sentence for him. 'I'm glad we talked though.'

'Me too.' He tilted his head slightly and studied her.

Claire shifted under his scrutiny.

'This conversation isn't over though.'

Claire swallowed hard. 'I know.'

'Next time you're in Brookford, call me, come for lunch, or dinner?'

Claire nodded again. He stood to take his wallet from the back pocket of his jeans and after placing some notes on the table, he handed her a card. 'You can reach me at these numbers.'

Claire fumbled in her handbag for her business card and handed it to him.

'I'll call you,' he said, the mood between them suddenly awkward.

'Or I'll call you.'

He smiled then and pulled her towards him. 'Goodbye, Della.'

His lips brushed hers so lightly that she couldn't catch hold of them.

'Take care,' she whispered.

And then he was gone.

She'd come so close to telling him. If Angie hadn't interrupted, she would've told him the truth, and if she'd done so, she doubted very much he'd ever want to speak to her again.

CHAPTER TEN

'You have the worst job in the world,' quipped Giles.

The host escorted them to their table at Lily James, slid their chairs out and took their coats before discreetly retreating.

'Don't I just?'

He looked around the room at the vintage mirrors, antique chandeliers and fairy lights. 'None of this should work,' he said.

'But somehow it does.'

Between the mirrors, there were remnants of wall colour – a distressed blue here, a washed-out cream over there, a faded floral wallpaper someplace else.

'Tell me again how you managed to get us in here at this time of the year?' asked Giles.

'The paper wanted to send someone out to do a review on this place, and Ade asked for me. He and I go way back.'

'It helps that you're the nicest person on British television, so of course he'd want a review from you.'

Claire peered at him across the table – although he

was smiling, it sounded as though there was an edge to his voice. 'Is everything alright, Giles?'

'Yes. I'm sorry, Claire, it's been a big week at work, and I've missed you.' He rested his hand over hers, and she settled back in her chair, letting out a huge breath. 'Plus,' he sat back and took a deep breath, 'there's something I've wanted to talk to you about.'

'Oh?' Her breath quickened. 'And you need us to be somewhere special for it?'

'Yes, no, well, I suppose it will help. The thing is … What I'm trying to say is …'

A waiter interrupted him. 'I'm sorry, sir, madam, my name is Jonathon, and I'll be your guide for your experience tonight. You might have noticed we haven't given you a menu yet?'

Giles and Claire nodded their confirmation.

'That's because our mission is to provide you with a dining experience that's tailored towards you – your tastes, your mood, what you feel like eating tonight, what might not be to your fancy this evening. Does that sound okay to you?' He waited for them to nod again before taking a pencil and notepad from his top pocket. 'First of all, are there any allergies or intolerances I need to take into consideration?'

They shook their heads, and he scribbled in the notepad.

'Any dislikes?'

'I'm not a fan of offal even though I know you're

not supposed to say that these days,' Claire screwed her nose. 'The whole nose to tail eating experience and all that.'

'But I'm fine with it,' said Giles.

'And okra, I don't fancy that either,' Claire said.

'I'm fine with that too,' said Giles.

'I also dislike mashed pumpkin – or worse, potato mashed with pumpkin.' She didn't bother mentioning she'd discovered she quite liked pumpkin mashed in scones.

'Somehow, darling, I don't think that would be an option here,' Giles said with a grin.

'I know, but I really don't like it.' Claire grinned back at him. 'And Jonathon here had asked …'

'Quite right, madam. Is there anything else?'

'No, that's all,' she assured him.

'And is there a special reason you're dining out tonight?'

'No, not at all,' said Giles.

She forced a smile as she tried not to look at Giles' face for some sign of what was going on; if it wasn't a proposal he was leading up to, what was it?

'Every night with Claire is special,' Giles was saying, his hand moving back to the centre of the table, his pinkie finger curling around hers.

The memory of how it had felt when Owen did the same yesterday flashed before her. Was it just yesterday?

Jonathon smiled back at them. 'Are you happy to leave the wine choice to us? Many of our guests prefer us to take the decision away from them so they can more fully enjoy their tasting journey.'

'That sounds fine.' Giles nodded in agreement.

'Very good. I'll leave you alone for now, but I'll be back to present you with your personalised experience soon. In the meantime, can I tempt you with an apéritif? Perhaps champagne or a classic martini? Or we have a very special play on an old-fashioned or a sloe gin negroni?'

Claire ordered the negroni and Giles started with the old-fashioned.

'How did the week go?' Giles asked once Jonathon had left them alone.

'It was great – Ed thinks it's going to be the best show ever. I went straight into editing when I got back this afternoon, and after looking at some footage, I'd have to agree with him. I can't remember the last time I've had so much fun on a shoot. And – you'll laugh at this – the guest judge happened to be an old boyfriend of mine from home. How random is that?'

Claire laughed to make it sound as though it was one of those things that happened every day and didn't matter at all, but Giles simply raised his eyebrows. 'Really? Who?'

'His name is Owen Gallagher. We grew up together.'

'Was he the high school sweetheart you mentioned you had?' he asked, a teasing note in his voice.

'Yes. I haven't seen him since we were both eighteen. He's moved back home and bought *The Lamb* at Brookford – that's the restaurant attached to the pub.'

'I hope he's made some improvements.' Giles grimaced at the memory of the only time he'd ventured into the pub.

'From all accounts it's unrecognisable. Owen said he'd cook us dinner if we're ever in town.'

Giles smiled but didn't respond to that.

'Apparently, he was working at *Belucci's* and got sacked as a result of a Spooner review,' she added.

'Really? I don't think I read that one. I thought *Bella Donna* was the only Belucci restaurant that Spooner had targeted. I think I would've remembered if there'd been another one.' He grinned at the thought of Bruno's discomfort.

'I read it the other night – it came out when we were on holiday just before we started filming the first season of *Time for Tea.*'

'That explains it then.'

'I still can't understand why I hadn't come across his name before this. He went to Yorkshire when Belucci sacked him, but even so.'

'Does it matter?' Giles crossed his arms, his eyes darting to the table beside them.

'No, I was just wondering. Anyway, that was my week. What was it you wanted to ask me?'

'It wasn't so much *ask* you, just I've got something I've been thinking about for a little while now that I'd like to talk to you about.'

'Oh, yes? It just so happens I have something I want to ask you too.' Claire held her breath for a few seconds. 'But you go first.'

'Okay.' He squirmed a little in his chair.

'I'm sorry to interrupt,' said Jonathon, placing drinks in front of them. 'Madam, sir, your personalised tasting.'

With a flourish, he presented them with a scroll which, at Jonathon's prompting, they unrolled. Inside the menu was handwritten in fountain pen on beautifully illustrated botanical paper. Rather than dishes, it appeared to be a collection of ingredients. At the bottom of Claire's menu was a message:

To my dear Claire,

Enjoy the journey …

Ade x

'I'll leave you with your drinks, and I'll be back soon to begin your experience,' said Jonathon.

'Which, by the looks of this, is celeriac, watercress and mushroom,' said Giles.

'It's probably a soup,' Claire said, 'or maybe a puree with the mushrooms dried to a dust and sprinkled over.'

'Or maybe it's a dip, and we'll get a packet of

crackers to go with it.'

Claire laughed at that, and Giles joined her.

Jonathon was back, this time with another waiter who carefully placed wide-brimmed white soup bowls in front of them.

'What we have here is a slow-roasted celeriac soup with a watercress puree swirled through the top and a mushroom and parsley tapenade. The celeriac has been roasted whole for four hours with olive oil and a little crushed coriander and sea salt. And your wine is a chenin blanc from the *Centre-Val de Loire*. Enjoy.'

The first sips of the soup were taken in reverential silence.

'Oh my,' sighed Claire.

'Indeed,' agreed Giles.

'And the wine is lovely too.'

'Although how you match wine with celeriac is beyond me.'

'But this isn't just any celeriac, they have lifted this celeriac to something way beyond the realms any ordinary celeriac could dare to dream of.'

'Is that what you're going to say about it when you write this up?' Giles asked.

'It certainly is.'

They didn't pick up their earlier conversation again until after Jonathan had whisked the soup plates away, and new cutlery for what was to come next placed in front of them – cauliflower, tahini, tamari.

'What did you want to talk to me about?' Claire prompted.

Giles took a deep breath. 'Back when we first met I was winning accolades for my work, and you were struggling to get your career started, but since then you've gone from strength to strength and me, well, I've really not moved.'

'But you're still getting more work than you can accept – and you're still winning awards.'

'Yes, but I'm bored, Claire. I want to do more. I've decided I want to write a book.'

'You always said you'd never be *that* journalist – the one that spent a year or more on one story. You said you needed the freedom to move and follow whatever piqued your interest.'

'I know, but as you get older, you change your mind about a lot of things you were previously so sure about.'

'But you've never said.'

He shook his head, 'Claire, I've been trying to tell you for months, but you're always so busy or running off to somewhere for a week. Anyway,' he said before she could respond to that, 'I've decided it's something I'd like to do.'

'It sounds like a great idea, you should. Presumably, you have an idea in mind?'

'Yes, I do. I want to widen the scope of my restaurant story and look at the nasty underbelly of these fine diners – the underpayment of staff, the exploitation and mental health of employees, in particular apprentices, and the harassment of women.'

'I hope you're not implying they're all like that?' Claire scanned the room as she spoke, fearful of their conversation being heard.

'Of course not, most are fine, and I'm sure your friend here is completely above board, but while I've been investigating the story, I've found quite a bit of corruption – so much that it's too big for one feature. There's a lot of money involved and getting the story out there – the whole story – would really shake up the system.'

Claire nodded, her eyes wide as she contemplated the potential fallout. 'Yes, it would certainly do that. Have you run it by any publishers?'

'I have – and I have some interest. The only catch is I need to have it written quickly. They're talking about having the first draft done in six months and having it on the stands by this time next year, and they're offering a sizeable advance.' He paused, 'I really want to do it.'

'You should absolutely do it then. What's stopping you?'

He fidgeted in his chair. 'That's where this gets complicated. Because the deadlines are so tight, I need to block everything out and just work on the book.'

'I understand that.'

'I've rented an apartment in Paris for the next twelve months, and I'll be working from there.'

Giles usually chose his words carefully, but he blurted these out.

'Being away will give me the perspective I need, and I'm close enough to come back to London if there are further leads to follow.'

'I suppose Nigel and I could spend a few months with you, but I can't see how I can commute from there once filming starts back in the spring. Maybe I could—'

'I'm sorry, Claire, but I was talking about moving there alone, so I can completely focus on my work.'

'Oh.' The information whirled in her head, and she struggled to catch the thoughts that had taken flight. Beneath it all was a pain that was spreading through her chest. Where had this come from?

'Is that all you have to say?'

'I don't know what to say, Giles. You've done this without talking it through with me, so it sounds as though there's nothing I can say.' Claire forced her face to remain expressionless, as though they were discussing next week's business rather than a decision that was threatening to tip her life upside down.

Jonathon's reappearance with yet another waiter bearing two plates of artfully arranged morsels and more wine was a welcome respite to the chaos that was reigning inside her head.

'What we have here is thrice cooked cauliflower. It's been blanched and then roasted whole and finally chargrilled. With that is a little watercress salad with some clementine, finished with a dressing of roast garlic and tahini and finally some pumpkin seeds which have been pan-fried in tamari. To go with it, we have a lovely fresh white wine from Gavi in north-western Italy. You should get the taste and fragrance of freshly chopped lemons with a floral note and a not quite dry finish.' He stepped back and smiled. 'Enjoy. I'll be back soon with the first of our ocean-inspired tastes.'

Claire sipped at the wine, but her mouth was full of something other than freshly chopped lemons and floral notes. 'I'm assuming that since you've mentioned you'll be locking yourself away that I won't be encouraged to visit?'

Giles looked down at his plate and forked a tiny floret of cauliflower through the dressing. 'I'm sorry, but I think that's best.'

She swallowed a mouthful of food too fast and choked on a pumpkin seed, so washed it down with more wine. 'Are you suggesting we break up?' Although she dreaded the answer, the question had to be asked. 'I thought you still loved me. Is this because I'm away a lot?'

'No, it's not because of that, although I think we might've lost our way a bit. I still love you, and maybe we need to take a break – at least while I'm doing this.'

Okay, so he wanted to swan off to Paris, write a book and then expect to pick up where he left off when he got back?

'Twelve months is a long break. It almost sounds permanent. What's prompted this Giles? I thought we were fine?' The hurt was painful in her chest. Anger threatened to spin out of control. Breath In. Out. In. Out.

'We were. We are. Fine, that is. I just need to concentrate on my career for a bit. I'm nearly forty-seven years old, and my currency as a freelance journalist is beginning to diminish. I see younger, fitter, hungrier men with substantially better social media skills leaving me behind. If I'm to survive, I need to adapt and to establish myself as an author and get myself on the talk show circuit.' He reached for her hand, squeezing it. 'I've watched your career grow while mine has languished and I can't deny that part of me envies you.' He forced a weak smile. 'Besides, it's not that you're at home very much these days. When you're filming, you're gone for a week at a time. Then there're the events and the openings, so even when you are in London, you're rarely at home. I don't think you'll even notice I'm gone.'

She snatched her hand back. 'This is my fault? You're blaming me because my career has taken off?'

'Of course, it isn't your fault. It has nothing to do with you or us – it's me. Call it a midlife crisis or whatever, but I need to do this. I'm sorry, Claire.'

'Fine, do it. I'm all for you writing a book about underpayments or whatever it is you want to pursue, but don't sit here and tell me you have to go to Paris to do that. You're going to Paris because you want to.'

They sat there staring at each other. Giles' mouth open as if he wanted to say something but didn't know how to get the right words out. Claire almost groaned in frustration when Jonathon reappeared with an explanation about the crab and pappardelle.

'To accompany this, we have a lively little—'

'Thanks, Jonathon,' Claire cut in before he could finish telling them about the wine. 'Please just pour it, and we'll see how we go with the tasting.' She forced a smile, so he knew she hadn't intended to hurt his feelings.

The pasta might have been silky perfect and the crab sweet, but it all tasted like sawdust to Claire as she ate in silence, stewing over what to say next. So much for her expectation of a proposal; the reality was very much the opposite. The stinging tears built behind her eyes, and she took another swallow of wine to keep them at bay. Giles watched her down the expensive wine but didn't comment.

'What was it you wanted to ask me?' Giles said as he pushed his plate away.

Claire took a deep breath and attempted to create an appropriate lie for him. Something that would leave her feeling a little less rejected. But it come out anyway. 'I was going to ask you to marry me.'

He jerked his head back and laughed. 'No, seriously,

Claire, what did you want to talk to me about.'

The punch of fresh hurt was a physical blow to her chest, and she hoped it didn't show on her face. 'That is what I wanted to talk to you about. I thought it would be nice, that it was about time. I thought since we'd been together for all this time you might think that too. In fact, I thought that was what you wanted to ask me tonight.'

He looked away. 'I'm sorry, Claire, I hadn't thought about it. I assumed we were both okay with the way things were.'

'Obviously, though, you weren't happy, or you wouldn't be renting an apartment in Paris and not telling me about it. That's not something someone who's perfectly happy with the way things are acts.' Her voice had risen in the middle of the sentence, but before it could get too far out of control, she deliberately lowered it until she was almost whispering.

'That's about writing a book – nothing else.' He paused as if considering how to say what he wanted to say next. 'When we first got together, we agreed on two things – do you remember?' He didn't wait for her response. 'We agreed that neither of us wanted children, and neither of us was interested in marriage.'

'I remember, Giles, but that was nearly seven years ago. I was twenty-eight and had just started out, and you'd already been married.'

'And been divorced.'

'I get that, but I'm not your ex-wife, and people change their minds.'

'I haven't changed mine.' His gaze was steady, but there was a tremor in his hand that told Claire he was having difficulty controlling his temper.

'You did about writing a book, and I have about wanting to be married.'

Jonathan was back with more food, more wine, and another explanation, but Claire couldn't listen to what he was saying. She nodded and smiled in the right places and pretended to be interested.

Neither of them mentioned Paris nor marriage for the remainder of the meal, and it wasn't until they were in the cab heading home that Claire asked the one question she somehow hadn't asked before. 'When are you going?'

'Seeing as how you've finished location filming for the year and won't need me to look after Nigel, I'll go next week.'

The implication being she'd only needed him around to look after Nigel when she was away. She bit down hard on the inside of her cheek and continued to look out the window as the lights of London went by. She usually loved this time of year; crowds aside, London was truly at its best in the lead up to Christmas.

'You'll be gone for Christmas?'

'Yes, I thought you could spend it with Gracie, Bill and Milo. You were only saying the other week it's been years since you had a family Christmas.'

'So that's all nice and tidy then,' she said bitterly.

We sound like two strangers making conversation rather than two people who had been together for years.

Giles turned his attention out the window of the cab.

'Is this it?' she whispered, the street lights illuminating the inside of the taxi. 'Are we over?' One tear and then another made their way down her cheek.

'I don't know. Perhaps. Do you want us to be over?'

Claire shrugged. 'Maybe, we're not going anywhere.'

He turned to face her and took her hand, raising it to his lips. 'We've had a good time, haven't we?'

'We have.' The tears continued to fall, silently, one after the other.

'Then let's not call it yet.'

There was hope in his voice, and she nodded once. 'Okay.'

When they got home, they each undressed in silence before getting into bed. Claire lay on her back and stared up at the ceiling. Beside her, Giles did the same. He turned on his side to look at her, reaching out to stroke the side of her face. She turned to face him and wriggled across the few inches until their bodies were touching. When she kissed him, it was tentative at first, and she pulled back to look into his eyes before he closed the distance and brought his lips back to hers.

Claire's body responded the way it had always done when he moved inside her, but it was different. Regardless of what had been said, this night together would be their last.

CHAPTER ELEVEN

Claire didn't think either of them slept. After they'd made love, Giles rolled onto his back and Claire to her side, facing away from him. In the early hours of the morning, Giles got out of bed and fumbled in the dark to get dressed. Claire kept her eyes closed and pretended to be asleep when he feathered a kiss on her forehead. It wasn't until their room fell silent and she heard the rustle in the linen press for a blanket and pillow for the couch, that she opened her eyes. The hours passed as she lay clinging to her usual side as if he were still in bed and she couldn't bear to let any part of her body touch his.

At around seven, Giles' call for Nigel and the closing of the door behind them was a signal to her exhausted mind to let go and fall into sleep.

A couple of hours later, the ringing of her phone woke her. Barty.

'Why didn't you mention that Owen Gallagher was on this week's show?'

'Good morning to you too.' Claire sat up and

stretched. Nigel was lying on his rug beside the bed – there was no sign of Giles.

'If Ed had told me that's who he'd planned, I would've tried to stop it.'

'Really? I was fine, he was fine, we were fine.' Claire idly scratched at the side of her nose and rolled her shoulders back. After lying in the same position all night, everything was feeling a little stiff and sore. At least the ache in her shoulders distracted her from the pain in her heart.

'It wasn't at all awkward?'

Claire had told Barty about Owen one drunken night years ago. Martha and Freya had moved out of the flat into a place of their own, and Barty and Claire celebrated being able to afford to keep the third bedroom empty by drinking way too many homemade cocktails. They'd argued about whether Barty got to use the spare bedroom as an office or if Claire could keep her growing pile of cookbooks in there. In the end, they'd decided they'd share it and toasted that decision with another drink.

Sometime around midnight, the conversation veered as conversations do at that time of the night to lost loves and first times and other things that in the sober light of day, Claire regretted speaking about – such as Owen. While she wasn't drunk enough to tell Barty the entire story, she vaguely recalled having told him about how she and Owen were each other's first and how he'd left without saying goodbye. In the years since that night, Barty had never brought the subject of Owen up, so Claire had been convinced he'd forgotten all about it. Apparently, that wasn't the case.

'Actually, it wasn't at all awkward.' She paused as Nigel jumped up onto the bed and nudged Giles' pillows into his preferred position. 'Okay, maybe just a little at first, but we talked, and it's all good.'

'He has a place in Brookford now, doesn't he?'

'Yes.' Claire was surprised that Barty had kept tabs on him.

'And you haven't run into him before?'

'No. What is this Barty? It's sounding very much like an inquisition. You know I haven't been home in ages.'

'Hmm. It's only that I worry about you. Did you know Belucci sacked him a few years ago? Poor bastard was on the pass when Alex Spooner dropped by. I heard his wife didn't hang around, either.'

'You're a lot better informed about him than I was,' she commented. 'But yes, he told me.'

'You know how it is; you hear things,' he dismissed. 'How was *Lily James* last night? Is it worth the hype? I haven't been able to get a booking yet, so I need to live vicariously through you, darling.'

'I think so,' she said carefully. 'The food was fabulous; at least what I tasted was pretty special.'

'I hear a but …'

'We're not engaged.'

'Aah.'

'He's going to Paris to write a book. He's rented an apartment, and he's leaving next week.'

'I'm so sorry, Claire.'

'Yeah, me too.'

'Is it over?'

'I don't know for sure – neither of us has said the words. He's calling it a break.' Her throat tightened, and that sting was back behind her eyes.

'And you?'

'I think I'm just a bit shell-shocked.'

Nigel was circling around and around on the pillow to make himself comfortable.

'Barty, I know you mean well, but do you mind if we talk about this later? I haven't had a lot of sleep, and I need to get my head around what's happened before I cry on your shoulder.'

'Of course, darling. You know I'm always there for you, don't you?'

'I do. Thanks for being such a good friend.'

'You're welcome.'

When he hung up, Claire leaned over and cuddled Nigel. This change – Giles not being here – would be as hard for her dog as it was going to be for her. He was only a few months old when Claire met Giles, so Giles had been around for almost all of Nigel's life. Watching Nigel sleeping peacefully on Giles' pillow,

Claire's heart sank. How was she going to manage it when they began filming next season's shows in the spring? Maybe she'd need to leave him with Gracie in Brookford during the week. As she was considering this, the phone rang again.

'Hi Gracie, I was just thinking about you,' Claire said when she answered the phone.

'Good thoughts?'

'Of course. I was thinking about when I brought Nigel home. Remember how you dragged me up to the farm shop on the Stroud Road because the spaniel up there had a litter?'

Gracie laughed. 'And Nigel was the only one left; yes, I remember. Anyway, I know you're probably on your way out somewhere glamorous for brunch or lunch or whatever it is they call it, but I just wanted to check if you and Giles are still spending Christmas in Edinburgh and when you'll be bringing Nigel to us.'

'I don't think we'll be going to Scotland after all.'

'Why not?'

Claire told her as much as she could say without bursting into tears. 'So, there we both were, making small talk for the next four courses. If it weren't so tragic it would've been ridiculous.' A small sob escaped. 'I don't even know if we've broken up – but it feels like it, and now he knows I want to get married and I know he doesn't, I suppose that we have. I'd forgotten what it's like to feel this shit about a man. Heartbreak is something that doesn't get easier with age.'

'No, I imagine it doesn't,' said Gracie. 'Come and see us. If you leave now, you'll be in time for a late lunch or at least afternoon tea. Stay the weekend. Actually, why don't you stay for the week? You don't want to be home watching Giles pack his bags and feeling sorry for yourself.'

Gracie was right – somehow it would seem less like it was happening if she weren't there watching it happen.

'It's a great thought, but I have to be in London on Monday to finish the editing and voiceover for this week's show, plus I'm booked to do a Christmas cook-off thing the week after next, so I'm going to have to get some practice in. I have no idea what the technical will be, but I know I need to prepare some party food and a yule log – which I'm dreading.'

'That won't be a problem. You'll need someone to test your food, and you can drive up and back to London on Monday – it's only a couple of hours – and then spend the rest of the week making a mess in my kitchen. Do the show and whatever else it is you have on and then come back here for Christmas. We'd love to have you, and it will do Nigel good to spend some time in the country.'

Claire didn't need much convincing. Giles came home as she was repacking the bag she'd half-unpacked the previous day.

'I thought you might need this,' he said, offering her a coffee, which Claire accepted, along with a bag of pastries, which made her stomach turn. Nigel's tail thumped against the bed in greeting.

'Where are you going?' he asked.

'To Gracie's. I thought it would be best for me not to be here while you're packing.' She carefully took the lid off the coffee to avoid spilling it.

He sat on the bed and watched her. She held the jumper she'd been folding against her chest and met his gaze. 'I love you, but I won't wait for you to come back,' she said.

'I know.'

'But then again, you mightn't come back.' She placed the jumper in her bag and rummaged in the drawers for some gloves and beanie, which she threw in too.

'There is that, I suppose,' he said.

Claire zipped up her bag. 'Okay, I'll be away then.'

Instead of picking up her bag she sat down on the bed beside it waiting for him to say something, to tell her he'd made a mistake, he wasn't going to Paris, he'd stay here, and they'd get married because he'd realised it was what he wanted too.

'I'll miss you,' he said.

'And I'll miss you too.'

They sat a moment longer, Giles on his side of the bed, Claire on hers, the bag in between.

'I love you,' he said and moved her bag onto the floor and shuffled across the bed to hug her, 'and I'm sorry I'm going away and I don't want to get married, but I need to do this.'

'Me too. I'm sorry for it all, but now I've decided I want marriage I can't just unthink that.' She pulled back from his embrace. 'If we're both sorry, why doesn't that make me feel better about it?'

He shrugged, a weak smile on his face that went nowhere near to reaching his eyes. 'No idea. But if it helps, I feel pretty shit about it all too.'

'No, it doesn't help – well, maybe just a bit. But I can't feel sorry for you.'

'I'm not asking you too.' After a brief pause, he said, 'you don't need to move out of here, you know.'

Claire startled; she'd almost forgotten Giles owned the flat they lived in – she and Nigel had moved in when his previous boarder had moved out.

'That didn't come out right,' he said. 'I meant to say I won't be here, and we haven't broken up.'

'Officially,' added Claire.

He shrugged one shoulder. 'All I'm saying is this is your home too.'

She nodded slowly and brushed a kiss on his lips. 'You'll be gone by the time I get back?'

He nodded.

'Okay. I hope the writing goes well.'

'Thanks.'

It all seemed very stilted and civilised when inside Claire wanted to throw things and scream at him for turning her world upside down – even though yelling wouldn't make her feel any better or change the situation.

She pulled away and stood up, pulling the sleeves of her jumper down so she could grab hold of them in her hands.

'Drive safely,' he said. 'Text me when you're there?'

'Sure.'

Claire called for Nigel, picked up her bag and left. Giles followed her to the door and watched as she packed the car, settled Nigel in his harness in the backseat, and buckled her seatbelt. He was still watching as she drove away.

Less than two hours later, Claire was nursing a cup of tea in Gracie's kitchen, having finished telling her the whole sorry tale.

'And what irritates me the most is that we were in the middle of seven of the most fabulous courses being dished up in London last night, and the last four might've been sawdust. We just sat there and smiled every time the waiter came by with more beautiful food and more beautiful wine. Some of the best food in recent memory on possibly the worst night I can remember. What an absolute waste. And somehow, I have to come up with a thousand words about how fabulous it was,' she sobbed.

Gracie gathered her in for a hug, and Claire bent down so she could envelop her into her softness. 'You're too short for proper hugs,' Claire complained in between sniffles.

'And you're too tall.'

At some point through her tears, Bill and Milo bustled into the kitchen, and upon seeing them, Bill then ushered his son out again.

Finally, when Claire was back in control, she sat back in her chair and reached for one of the pikelets Gracie had piled onto a plate. Smothering it in butter and some of Gracie's homemade jam, she took a bite and closed her eyes.

'Oh, these are good,' she said. 'They're like a great big, warm hug.'

'You always used to make them when we were kids, so when you called, I figured they'd be the best thing for a broken heart.'

'You were right.' Claire piled two more onto her plate.

'Milo loves them with marmite,' she said, 'and cheese.'

'Seriously? That kid has an interesting palate for a four-year-old. I must introduce him to my marmite spaghetti.'

'I don't think I want to be there when that happens.' Gracie laughed. 'It sounds revolting.'

'You'd be surprised.'

'Remember how you used to get up early on Saturday mornings in the winter and make a batch of these for the whole family.'

'And then eat most of them before you and Stephen surfaced. It served you right for sleeping in.'

'Do you still make them?'

'No, I can't remember when I last did. It's been years. Giles doesn't normally eat breakfast during the week, and he likes for us to go out for breakfast on the weekends.' She let out a short laugh. 'I mean, he used to like us to go out for breakfast on weekends.'

Gracie tilted her head to one side as she examined her sister. 'But you do still cook, right?'

Claire shook her head. 'Not really, well, not at all. I can't remember the last time I cooked at home. I certainly can't remember the last time I baked. I think I'm always too tired or we have somewhere to be, or we had a big lunch.'

'Okay, let me get this straight, you host a television show that's all about baking, and you don't do it yourself?'

Claire squirmed under her gaze. 'No. It sounds bad when you put it like that.'

'How do you relax then? You used to say that was always the way you made sense of the world. That when your hands were in flour, when you were weighing and measuring ingredients, all the pieces that were bothering you began to find their rightful places in your brain.'

'I know it did. It's been hard in the last couple of years to find time to bake. Instead, I walk; I take Nigel out every day when I'm at home.'

'What about friends? Do you go out with friends?'

Claire smothered another pikelet with butter.

'You do have friends, don't you?'

'We used to go out with Giles' crowd sometimes.'

'The ones you say are boring and fussy and look down their nose at everyone?'

'Yes. Those. But Giles has never been like that.'

'I don't know about that – he's always made me feel insignificant and young. What about your friends?'

'There's Barty, of course.'

'He's your agent – he has to be your friend.'

'He was my friend before he was my agent,' Claire pointed out.

'True, but I'm talking about your other friends, the ones you don't have to pay. Friends from work. What about the paper? You worked there for years.'

Claire shrugged. 'When I got *Time for Tea*, some of my friends from the paper got a bit, I don't know, envious, I think. I kept saying no to invites because I was busy and then they started to say no when I did ask; so they stopped asking and so did I.'

'What about your old housemates? Freya and … what was the other girl's name? They were together, weren't they?'

'Martha. And yes, they were together – still are. They've moved over to New Zealand. Martha's art has taken off, and Freya does something in finance. We stay in touch.'

'By stay in touch, I'm assuming that means you like each other's statuses on Facebook?'

'Something like that. I think I made some new friends last week – the bakers included me in their monthly cookbook club, and there's a couple of them in particular I think I could be friends with.'

'If you actually make an effort.'

'Yeah, I guess. I think I'd like to try, though. They were the first people I'd met in a long time who treated me as a home cook, just like them.'

'Well,' she mused, 'you are on the telly quite a bit, and magazines and what have you. But what about school friends? I see Jenna Michaels – Jenna Clarkson as she was – in the village from time to time. Do you stay in touch with her? Or Max Henderson? I know she was a bit younger, but you used to do some tutoring for her, didn't you? Did you know she stayed in Curlew Cottage – you know, the one we rent out from time to time – when she and her husband split?'

'We sort of stay in touch, but I didn't know she used the cottage. I didn't know you knew her.'

'I didn't recognise her to begin with,' conceded Gracie. 'And I keep forgetting to tell you that Owen Gallagher's back – and looking seriously hot. You were tight with him for a time, weren't you?'

'Yes, but—'

A boy-shaped tornado burst through the doors and landed on her lap, saving her from Gracie's inquisition.

'Aunty Bear! I is so so happy to see you.'

'And I'm very happy to see you too, Milo.' She hugged the squirming boy.

'What about Daddy? Are you happy to see him?'

'I am.' Claire stood and walked across to Bill, who'd followed his son and the two spaniels – Nigel and their Bella – into the room and kissed his cheek. He grinned when Milo tugged at Claire's sleeve.

'And Bella? Are you happy to see Bella?'

'I'm especially happy to see Bella.' Claire rubbed the dog's belly. Nigel jumped around, wanting his part of the action too.

'Daddy said we couldn't come in before because you were talking grown-up stuff with Mummy.'

'That's right.' Claire smiled her thanks at Bill.

'What was it about?'

'Um, we were talking about friends.'

'I'll be your friend, Aunty Bear.'

She ruffled his hair. 'You can be my best friend.'

'Mummy too?'

'And Mummy.'

'Daddy too?'

'Absolutely.'

'And Bella too?'

'Okay, young man,' said Gracie, scooping her son onto her lap. 'Do you want to put your wellingtons on, and we'll go for a walk down the lane with Aunty Claire and the dogs.'

CHAPTER TWELVE

Tallis called a special meeting of The Cotswolds Cookbook and Culinary Society and invited everyone to celebrate the screening of the Fenwyck episode of *Time for Tea*. Caro's husband, Malcolm, Caro's daughter and one of Fee's had said they'd be there. Anna and Adam were coming; even Derek would be home for the event.

Tallis was putting the final touches to the table when Derek phoned.

'I'm sorry, darling,' he said. 'Jerry is insisting – we're bidding for the new Boots store in the city centre and Jerry knows someone at the golf club who could help us get it over the line.'

Tallis stopped listening after that, a combination of anger and disappointment leaving a bitter taste in her mouth.

Adam came into the kitchen as she hung up the phone.

'Dad?'

Tallis nodded.

'He's not coming?'

Tallis shook her head.

Adam shrugged. 'Probably just as well, he didn't want you to do this anyway, so at least everyone who's here will be supportive of you and the others and not trying to make fun of it.'

Tallis smiled and impulsively hugged him. He tolerated it for a second or so more than he usually would before squirming out of her embrace.

'Yeah, okay, Mum. What's for eating?'

By seven-thirty everyone was groaning about having full tummies. Tallis had packed up the leftovers, and the kitchen was back to normal.

'Shhh everyone,' announced Gail. 'It's about to start.'

And there was Claire on the screen, walking towards the gate at Fountains Hall.

'Tonight, we have an episode that's close to my heart. Not only are we in Fenwyck – which is just a few miles from where I grew up – but our special guest judge is an old friend of mine, someone I haven't seen in a long time.'

Claire's smile was wistful, remembering something sweet.

'And if that isn't enough, I have some very special people to introduce you to today – and some delicious food to eat.'

As she spoke brief clips of the village, growers, Claire buying the ingredients for dinner and laughing with the shop keepers filled the screen.

'I'll even be joining in with a local book club with a difference – and will help cook my supper.'

A montage showed their cookbook club before the scene came back to Claire.

'Trust me, you don't want to miss that. Oh,' she paused, 'and if that's not enough to tempt you to stay around, there'll also be donkeys.' She smiled warmly at the camera, her remarkable eyes shining, and inclined her head slightly towards the house at the end of the drive. 'Come on, let me show you around Fenwyck … after all, life's always better after tea and scones.'

As the show's theme music began to play, the camera followed Claire as she walked up the drive.

'She's good at this, isn't she?' said Gail.

'She certainly is,' said Fee.

'And none of it's an act,' murmured Tallis.

'Be quiet,' said Anna, 'It's back on!'

After that, no one said very much; a giggle here, a laugh there. The room was quiet until the closing credits ran, and then it seemed like everyone was speaking at once.

'You were so good, Mum,' said Anna.

Caro and Fee were accepting hugs and congratulations from their daughters while Malcolm sat there almost thunderstruck. 'I didn't know you had it in you, love,' he said finally, his eyes shining with love and pride for his wife.

Even though all her friends were there, she was suddenly angry about the absence of Derek. She'd asked him to be there for her, to share in her achievement, for one night. What about all the nights she'd had to be there to support him? Sitting alone at a table when he was dragged off to see a business associate or left behind at the hotel with all the other wives while at a conference? All the times she gave up doing something she might've preferred to be doing because he'd asked her to. She'd asked him for just one night – and he hadn't been there.

Adam was by her side and kissed her cheek. 'You did good, Mum,' he said. 'You made all of this happen, you know.'

Despite feeling let down by her husband, Adam's support filled her heart. Her friends had wide smiles and were laughing and hugging each other. 'I did,' she said decisively. 'I did make it happen.'

'Don't sell yourself short, Mum,' he said, 'and don't let Dad get you down.'

She nodded once. Stuck behind the lump in her throat were the words she wanted to say. As he walked away to join Anna, Gail, Caro, and Fee took his place.

'Fenwyck looked good, didn't it?' said Tallis.

'The village should be proud,' added Caro.

'Bugger that,' said Fee, 'we should be proud – we did that.'

'And we wouldn't have done it without you,' added

Gail, winding her arm through Tallis'. 'We couldn't have done it without you organising us all.'

'Do you think Claire will stay in touch with us like she said she would?' asked Caro.

Tallis nodded. 'I do.'

'I do too,' said Gail. 'And if I'm any judge of the chemistry we saw on screen tonight, Claire might've got more than four new friends out of this week.'

Tallis' phone rang.

'Will that will be Derek?' asked Gail, 'wanting to see how it went.'

Tallis grinned when the caller ID flashed on her phone screen. 'Hi, we were just talking about you.' She mouthed "it's Claire" to the others.

'I just wanted to ring to say congratulations,' she said. 'It was by far the best episode we've ever done, and it was all down to you four.'

'We loved it too,' said Tallis. 'In fact, we're all here watching it together.'

'I hoped that you might be. I wish I were there with you all.'

'We held a special Christmas meeting for the occasion, but we were just saying if you're going to be around in the new year, we'd love you to join our January meeting – we're off to Italy with Jamie Oliver.'

'Italy with Jamie, how can I say no to that? That's usually a quiet time for me, so send me through the details, and I'll see what I can do. Anyway, I'll let you get back to your party, and I'll call you next week?'

'Sounds good. Everyone says, hello.'

'Say hello for me, okay?'

Was Tallis imagining it, or had Claire's voice cracked a little?

'I'll do that.' Tallis ended the call and placed her phone back on the table.

'That was nice of her to call,' Caro said. 'She's probably out at a studio party, and she thought of us.'

'I don't know about that,' said Tallis slowly. 'But yes, it was nice of her to think of us.'

Everyone who mattered agreed that the Fenwyck episode of *Time for Tea* was the best one ever – and a fitting end to the series for this year. The ratings were high, but it was the social media attention that made the studio sit up and take notice. Overwhelmingly the public loved the impromptu feast that Claire and the bakers had prepared, the cameras capturing the chatter but somehow not intruding. As Claire watched the episode again, she had to agree with Ed when he'd said it looked as though they'd all known each other for years.

The scene that brought tears to Claire's eyes and, it would seem, half of England's, was the one where they were discussing the dish of the day and Tallis' sponge cake had reminded Owen and Claire of Owen's mother. The camera had caught the tender moment where Claire had laid her hand over Owen's, then lingered on her gentle smile and the glitter of unshed tears in her eyes as she and Owen shared the memory.

Claire hadn't been at a studio party; she had instead watched the episode on Thursday night with Gracie and Bill, who curled up on their lounge, while she sat on a cushion on the floor, snuggled under a rug. The fire was burning in the corner, Nigel and Bella stretched out in front of it.

'That scene with you and Owen, where you put your hand over his. That was so lovely and so natural.' Gracie wiped away a tear.

'I'd forgotten the cameras were running, to be honest,' Claire said. 'It was that kind of shoot.'

'Are you sure there's nothing between you two? Because it sure looks as though there could be.'

Claire shook her head. 'No, there's nothing there. He was burnt badly by his ex-wife, so even if there was something between us, I think that would be a big obstacle to get over.'

'He is hot though. I don't remember him looking like that; I always thought he was a bit of a weed.' Gracie snuggled into her husband's side. 'In fact, if Bill wasn't as irresistible as he is, I could be tempted.'

'I think I'd have something to say about that,' Bill said with a mock-growl.

Gracie reached up and kissed him. 'You know I only have eyes for you my love.'

Claire smiled at their banter but couldn't help

replaying that scene with Owen in her head.

On Saturday Claire made the trip into Brookford to pick up some more flour to make yet another yule log. Essentially a yule log was a sponge cake baked in a swiss roll tin, filled, rolled up, and iced and decorated to look like a branch that had fallen in the forest. The hard part was getting the sponge right and being able to roll it without the cake cracking. Her last attempt had been an abject failure, and she was determined to nail it.

It was when she was coming out of the store that she ran into Owen. Literally.

'I'm so sorry,' he said, steadying her. 'I wasn't looking where I was going.' Without dropping his hands from her arms, he kissed her cheek.

'It's okay. I wasn't looking where I was going either.' Her cheeks were warm despite the chill.

Celia Marshall was still lingering at the counter and watched them with great interest. Owen must've noticed the same and with a smile back to Celia led Claire out of the store.

'Man, it's cold,' he said, rubbing his gloved hands together. 'What brings you here?'

Claire held up the flour she'd bought. 'I have the Christmas cook-off next week, so I'm practising. There's a yule log showstopper that's proving to be difficult.'

He laughed. 'They usually are. But Brookford?'

'I've been staying with Gracie for most of the past week – although I'm heading back to London tomorrow.'

'Is Giles with you?'

'No, that's well … he's moved to Paris.' She concentrated on the cobble outside the market hall where they stood.

'I'm assuming he's not there on holiday?'

She shook her head.

'I'm sorry, Della, that must have been tough.' While she couldn't see his eyes, there was sympathy in his voice.

'Yes, it was. Talk about high emotion – that closure thing with you on Friday morning and then the closure thing with him that night. Not one of the best days of my life.' She forced a short laugh and met his eyes. 'Did you watch the show?'

He nodded. 'Not live, but I watched it with the restaurant crew after we finished service. We did a good job.'

'We sure did. Best episode ever, the network is saying.' Claire hesitated before adding,

'Hey, do you have time for a coffee?'

He glanced at his watch. 'Sorry, Dells, I wish I did, but I still need to get a couple of things and then get back for lunch service. But we'll catch up next time you're in town?'

'Sure. I'll be back here for Christmas, so maybe then?'

'Yeah, that sounds good. Give me a call.' He kissed her cheek again and strode back into the store.

When he didn't turn back, she shook her head, frustrated at her own conceit; whatever chemistry she'd seen in that footage was obviously only for the cameras. It was clear Owen felt absolutely nothing for her anymore other than a fondness for an old friend. She should've felt relieved, but the dull ache inside her belly felt awfully like disappointment.

Once Claire was back in London, she sent flowers to each of the Fenwyck Four and called Tallis.

After they'd been chatting for a few minutes, Tallis said, 'Oh, I nearly forgot to ask. Are congratulations in order?'

Claire's slight hesitation was Tallis' answer.

'I'm so sorry.'

'Thanks. It turned out his news wasn't what I'd hoped it might be. In summary, he's gone to Paris; I'll be spending Christmas at Brookford with my sister and her family, and although we're still calling it a break, I think we both know it's over. And for something completely dismal, it ruined what would have been a memorable meal at *Lily James*.'

'I've read about that place — something about how it has more marriage proposals in a week than the Eiffel Tower does in a month. They're saying it's the most romantic restaurant in London.'

'Yes, well, sadly my proposal wasn't one of them. It is romantic though, dripping with the stuff – just not in the direction of our table.'

'On the upside, though, the food was good?'

'Incredibly so. That place is absolutely off the charts – but in a good way. The experience is like nothing else that's happening in London at the moment and the food, well, the courses I could taste, were next level. It's that whole new flexitarian approach where protein is almost a garnish to the vegetables – most of which are grown either in Ade's kitchen garden or locally. Anyway, enough about all of that, talk to me about something more uplifting and cheerful.'

'Gail and I are off to dinner at The Lamb next week.'

'You're not taking Derek?'

'No, I don't think he'd appreciate it, and it seems more appropriate for it to be us, if you know what I mean.'

'I do, and I think it's lovely. Owen will look after you for sure.'

'It's a pity you can't join us.'

'Unfortunately, I have to be in London – otherwise, I would've loved to be there.'

'Well, I'll let you go, but it was lovely talking to you. Merry Christmas.'

'And you too. See you soon.'

Claire spent the rest of Monday putting the

finishing touches to her review. She'd had to ring Ade a couple of times to check on some flavours he'd used but was satisfied she'd removed all the emotion of the evening and presented the restaurant in a way it deserved to be. Duncan, the food and lifestyle editor at the paper, called her once he'd approved the copy and confirmed it would be in the following weekend's lift-out.

'It's a good, balanced piece, Claire – I think Adrian will be happy with it.'

'I hope so. It might be a special occasion restaurant, but Ade should be proud of what he's done.'

'Have you got much work booked in over the next couple of months?' Duncan asked.

'I'll probably take a month or so off over Christmas, and we don't start filming until March. Other than that, I don't think Barty has firmed up my schedule yet.'

'I was hoping you'd say that. I want to talk with you about a couple of one-off profile pieces – up close and personal features with some of the hottest new chefs, that sort of thing. Are you interested?'

'Absolutely. Give Barty a call, and we can lock something in.'

'Will do. If I don't speak to you before, happy Christmas, Claire.'

'You too, Duncan.'

CHAPTER THIRTEEN

The Spoonman, by Alex Spooner

Lily James, Covent Garden

Meal for two, including drinks and service – ring your bank manager.

Adrian Ritchie's latest venture, Lily James, is booked out months in advance. It is, I'm assured by virtually every person I speak to, the hottest restaurant in London at the moment, which is why I was overjoyed to have obtained a booking for dinner just weeks before Christmas – and on a Friday night, no less.

I read recently that Lily James can now claim the mantle of being London's most romantic restaurant with more proposals of marriage per week than the Eiffel Tower is responsible for in a month. That's a lot of proposals and given the rose-tinted reviews praising the venue, one can only assume most of the recipients of these proposals said "yes".

It's fair to say I had high hopes for Lily James. I'd enjoyed an excellent meal at Ritchie's self-titled fine diner, Adrian's, and, although a little heavy on the spice, Ginger Flower, his Asian street food offering didn't disappoint either. Lily James was, however, a very different experience.

Ritchie has described the food on offer at Lily James as being Bespoke Botanical, but what, dear reader, is Bespoke Botanical, and why on earth should it matter? Lily James doesn't have diners, they have guests. Nor do they have waiters, they have someone to guide you through the Lily James experience. I know what you're thinking, and you'd be right.

Ritchie has said that one of his aims for Lily James is to provide a menu that's heavily based on plants, with as many as possible of those being sourced from Ritchie's kitchen gardens. That's the botanical part taken care of. As for the bespoke claim? Guests at Lily James are not presented with menus. Instead, a personalised experience is created for them. In reality, this is less exclusive than it sounds and, given I didn't see very much variance in what was being consumed at the surrounding tables, I'm led to the assumption it's more like a posh version of the alternate chicken and beef that we see at most wedding receptions. Perhaps not so bespoke after all.

The first of our seven courses were introduced imperially as "celeriac, watercress, mushroom". Our waiter, sorry, guide told us the celeriac had been roasted whole for many hours before, presumably, being thrown into a blender and turned into this rather bland looking – and tasting – soup. The only point of interest on the plate and, indeed, our taste buds, was a swirl of bright green puree and a dollop of what we were informed was a mushroom and parsley tapenade.

We spied some diners, sorry guests, with their eyes closed as they sipped their soups, but my dining companion commented that might not have been out of reverence but rather a desire to block out the forest floor muddiness of the tapenade.

Next, we had cauliflower – as did fifty percent of the room. The poor vegetable had been, we were informed, not just cooked, but cooked many times in many ways before finally being roasted. At this point I'll digress for a moment and consider the cauliflower, which surely must have the world's best PR team behind it as this humble and, let's face it, rather foul-smelling vegetable is finding its way onto menus masquerading as anything from rice to pizza to even (God forbid) steaks. On this occasion the cauliflower thankfully wasn't pretending to be anything other than itself.

There are occasions in life where one should show one's true colours, take off the mask one shows to the world. This, however, was one of those instances where the mask – a tahini dressing scattered with some pumpkin seeds toasted in tamari – was where the flavour and interest lay and was, therefore, best left on. It was the highlight in an otherwise dull dish. One has to feel some sympathy for the cauliflower after being subjected to so much to end up tasting just like cauliflower. Some festive colour was present in the form of a few segments of clementine and some torn watercress that we were informed was a salad.

When the third course arrived, my companion cheered. 'Finally,' he said, 'some carbs.' I couldn't have agreed more, and the pappardelle which was, we were assured, house made, was the highlight of the evening's menu, sorry, experience. Served with crab that had hailed from Cornwall, it didn't need the pesto they served it with. I would've been quite satisfied with the scattering of toasted hazelnuts and a drizzle of good olive oil, but that's just me.

Following this we were presented with, in order, fish – sustainable; lamb – Welsh, and served with the pumpkin salvaged after the seeds were used on the hapless cauliflower; and beef – Scottish. It all tasted perfectly pleasant, but when you're paying this much for a meal, sorry, experience, you want more than pleasant. You want to be wowed, and neither my dining companion nor I were.

Dessert was a nod to the season with a clementine and cardamom panna cotta. It was served with rhubarb which had been roasted and sprinkled with a line of nutty granola. It was a dish that I would very happily have devoured if served to me at breakfast, but as the finale to an experience such as this was purported to be, was nothing short of disappointing.

I haven't spoken about the décor yet – and that's because I truly don't know where to start. Is it romantic, bohemian, shabby chic, or something else entirely? Bo-ho-ro perhaps? Who knows? I certainly don't. And, to be honest, I don't care, although I wish the designer had made his or her mind up and settled on one style or another.

By all means, visit Lily James if you're intending on

proposing to the one you love most in the world. When he – or she – accepts, you'll be so overwhelmed with the love in the air that you won't taste the food or mind the expense. This isn't necessarily a bad thing.

CHAPTER FOURTEEN

The first sign of trouble came at ridiculous o'clock on Tuesday morning when a call from Duncan woke Claire.

'I'm pulling the review on *Lily James*,' he said.

'Why? I thought you liked the piece,' said Claire.

'You haven't read this morning's paper?'

'No.'

'Spooner got there first.'

'Damn!' Claire's tummy fell, and a quiet unease washed over her.

'Exactly. You'll say something stronger than that once you read it. This one will go viral – and not for any of the right reasons.'

'Poor Ade. Did you know?'

Duncan was supposedly the only person on the paper who communicated with Alex Spooner.

'You know the way it goes – I never know where he's going to be. The copy shows up, and we go with it.'

'But this will devastate Ade, and he doesn't deserve it.'

'I know it will – and you're right, he doesn't – but I can't argue with the readership spike every time one of these comes out. I'm sorry, Claire, but your balanced piece can't compare with the attention we get from The Spoonman.'

Once Duncan had rung off, Claire went online and found the review. It was as dreadful as she'd feared it would be. She contemplated texting Ade and decided against it; chaos would be reigning in his office and kitchen. Telling him that Duncan had pulled her review would be one piece of bad news too many for him to deal with today. Barty had said that Ade had been booked as a judge on cook-off, so although Claire would see him on Thursday, she still wanted to talk to him before then.

Her mind went back to that Monday morning two weeks ago – was it only two weeks ago? – when Giles was sitting here smirking at Spooner's take on *Bella Donna*. Whilst she'd felt that for once The Spoonman had got it right with *Bella Donna*, she still hadn't been able to laugh at it. After hearing Owen's story and knowing the consequences of what could happen when a Spoonman review went wrong, Claire could never read another one and laugh at it again. She'd never read one without wondering who'd been hurt in the background and hoped desperately that Ade wouldn't be one of those victims.

•

The anxiety stayed with Claire throughout Tuesday. She tried Ade's number twice, but when it rang out, left a message on his voicemail.

She woke with an unsettling heaviness on Wednesday and, after trying Ade's number again, distracted herself with a Christmas shopping trip. The crowds in Oxford Street were enough to drive anything but the survival of the fittest from her mind, but she couldn't deny Christmas was in the air and that made it bearable. Slade's "Merry Christmas Everybody" or Wizzard's "I Wish It Could Be Christmas Everyday" seemed to be playing in every shop. She peered into the windows of Fortnum & Mason and wandered through the ground floor food hall all decked out with Christmas goodies; even queueing to pay for her purchases she knew there was nowhere else she'd like to be at this time of the year.

On Thursday when she woke to steady rain, she feared the worst, but upon arriving at the studio for the first day of filming for *Celebrity Christmas Cook-off* the mood was upbeat, festive even, so Claire pushed the little voice with the negative thoughts back into the dark place where such voices belonged.

Her fellow participants were a varied bunch. There was Mimi, a singer in a girl band that was top of the pops about ten years ago and who'd moved into a new career as a social media influencer; Ian, a retired footballer who still thought he had all the moves; and Declan, a middle-aged Irish comedian whose off-screen persona was remarkably serious.

Mimi freely admitted to having never opened the oven in her house, while Ian seemed to have a good knowledge of simple, yet healthy meals. Declan, on the other hand, had been brought up by a single mother who'd taught him how to bake. He confided that he used to prepare dinner for his younger siblings. While Mimi and Ian flirted, Declan and Claire talked about scones.

Joining the usual judges, David and Anthea, was Adrian Ritchie. Claire took him aside to tell him how sorry she was about the Spooner piece.

'Thanks for saying that. Duncan sent me the review you wrote – it was an excellent piece. It's just a bugger about the timing.'

'Has it impacted your bookings?'

'No, thank goodness. Enough people who know about what we're offering have already been guests at *Lily James* and told their friends. We're booked steadily through to March, and I could count on one hand, and still have fingers left, the number of cancellations we've had since the review was published. While I'd love to give Alex Spooner a piece of my mind if I ever met him, I think the days where he can influence the life or death of a restaurant are over. We've been Instagrammed so many times that his words mean little.'

'The picture really does tell the story.'

'Absolutely. Perhaps if he'd visited in the first week, it would've been different. These days Spooner's about sensationalist clickbait and little more. To be honest, I think he's getting more and more dramatic because he knows his reach is narrower. It feels as though he's escalating into some grand statement that will be his last hurrah – and the sooner we're rid of him, the better.'

'I'm glad you feel that way,' said Claire. 'And I think you're right. It feels as though he's not even pretending to write a proper review these days. The last few reviews felt bitchy and quite personal – as though he's got an axe to grind.'

'Well, I can't think of who I've upset recently, so I've no idea about that. Between you and me he was spot on with *Bella Donna* – although I heard that Belucci has already sacked the poor bastard he hired as head chef for that place, even though sources tell me it was Belucci himself on the pass that night.'

'Well,' said Claire, 'from what I've heard it wouldn't be the first time that's happened.'

'Are you referring to Owen Gallagher?'

She nodded.

'I heard the same story; in fact, I even confronted Belucci with it one time.'

'Really? What did he say?'

'He blustered a bit, but he didn't deny it. The

problem is, not every young chef has the resilience to bounce back from something like that. Owen Gallagher has come back, and all respect to him. I always thought Bruno was threatened by Owen because the networks were sniffing around him. Spooner's piece just gave him the excuse he was looking for to get rid of the competition. If I were a conspiracy theorist – which I'm not, I'd even suggest that Belucci put Spooner up to it. But then no self-respecting restauranteur would even consider damaging his own business just as a reason to sack someone.'

Claire laughed and told him he was ridiculous, but she couldn't help but wonder whether he was onto something. Their conversation was cut short as they called everyone to take their places.

The celebrity's first challenge of the day was party food. They'd been given two hours to produce a platter comprising at least three items. Claire prepared a mezze plate with an aubergine, mint and yoghurt dip, Moroccan chicken lollipops, Middle Eastern spiced meatballs and some flatbread.

She'd practised her timing for the dishes at home, and thankfully the cook went as planned. David felt she could've seasoned her dip more, and Anthea thought she needed a dipping sauce for the chicken. Although they loved her flatbread and meatballs, Claire felt Declan had probably come out on top with his cocktail sausages, mini spicy lamb sausage rolls with tomato chutney, and a very retro devils on horseback. Mimi crashed and burned, and Ian's healthy alternative was middle of the pack with no disasters.

The second task of the day was the technical – a biscuit challenge. The celebrities had to bake and decorate twenty-four speculoos biscuits – a thin and aromatic biscuit from Belgium and the Netherlands. Claire breathed a sigh of relief – while she was messy with a piping bag, she'd made these before, albeit several years ago, so at least knew what they should look and taste like – unlike poor Mimi who had no idea and spent most of the time telling everyone just that.

At the end of the day, Claire's biscuits were judged to be the most authentic tasting but looked messy. Again, Declan's were good, although a little thick in parts. Ian's came out on top with good spicing and picture-perfect piping. Poor Mimi smiled and looked pretty when she presented her biscuits in their pink icing and silver-balled glory.

Later that evening, Barty rang to see how the day had gone.

'I've just finished running my bath, Barty. I have a wine and my book, and I was looking forward to sinking into it – I've been on my feet all day.'

'You can bathe and talk to me at the same time, can't you? I'll just pretend I don't know you're naked, although I'm sure I've seen it all before – glimpses at least.'

'Very funny. Give me a few seconds then.'

He waited while she settled in the bathtub, wine glass in reach and phone on speaker.

'How did it go?'

'Remarkably well. No problems at all today. You would've been told who else was on the show?'

'Yes. Is Mimi as clueless as she makes out?'

'Sadly, yes. But I'm sure she's a lovely girl at heart.'

'Naturally. How was poor Adrian? Battered and bruised after The Spoonman's review?'

'No, surprisingly. He was upbeat about the whole thing. He seems to think The Spoonman is losing his power and can no longer influence a restaurant's lifespan just through a clickbait headline.'

'Do you think he was just putting a brave face on it?'

'No, I think he meant it. As he said, he's only had a few cancellations, so it hasn't impacted his business at all. In fact, the more I think about it, I think he's right: I think Spooner knows he's lost his influence and is building up to something dramatic as a last hurrah.'

'Hmm. Who knows what he's thinking?'

'Exactly. Anyway, I have no idea what I was worried about, everything went well, and I'm feeling good about tomorrow's showstopper. I've practised the damned thing often enough.'

'That's good to hear. And Giles? Have you heard from him?'

'He texted to let me know he'd arrived and was settled – even gave me his new contact details – but other than that, nothing. I suppose when he says he was going to focus on the book, he really meant it. I'm okay about it though – obviously, I'm sad, but I'm coping. It helps that I'm busy. So, you don't need to worry that I'm going to end up crying into my marmite spaghetti on your posh couch anytime soon.'

'Just as well,' he said. 'You'd probably make a right mess, and that dog of yours would chew my designer cushions.'

'Yes, and I love you too, Barty. Thanks for checking in – I'll give you a ring tomorrow when I'm done.'

Although cold, Friday dawned clear with no rain forecasted. Claire entered the studio with confidence after the previous day had been successful in the kitchen. The niggling feeling of the last few days pushed well aside.

For their final challenge, the celebrities were asked to bake and decorate a yule log. Claire had her recipe, she had her plan, and she'd practised making both the log and the decorations. Everything should have gone perfectly.

An hour into the cook, the celebrities had done their on-camera chat with the judges about what they were making and where they saw the biggest challenges to be. Claire, Ian and Declan had their sponges in the oven and were working on the buttercream icing, although Mimi was still asking Ian what the recipe meant when it said to "fold in the flour".

'Didn't you do any practice?' asked Ian.

'I thought they might've allowed us to use a packet, didn't I?' Mimi replied.

Off set, David looked at his phone. He frowned, then his eyes darted to Claire, and he frowned again. He showed Anthea, who did the same. They stood with their heads together, whispering to each other; a shiver crept up Claire's spine. David beckoned Ade over, and the three of them stared intently at the phone. When he looked up from the screen, Ade's face was pure thunder.

Claire's stomach plummeted, and a breath hitched in her throat. *What was going on?*

To buy some time and a chance to get her breathing back on track, Claire squatted in front of the oven to check the progress of her cake.

Breathe in. Hold. Breathe out. Hold.

Adrian approached Claire's bench, David's phone in his hand. He shook his head to the cameraman as a sign that this wasn't to be filmed and showed her the text David had received.

England's darling of the bake, Claire Mansfield, revealed as Alex Spooner, the restaurant reviewer with the poisonous pen.

Claire's face burned, and her hands shook as she clicked on the link to the story which one tabloid had picked up from sources unnamed.

Although short, it was damning and named her as being Alex Spooner's alter-ego – the man or, as it turned out woman, most hated in the restaurant industry and responsible for the closure of many restaurants and the destroyer of dreams.

The article was a short one and finished by stating that although Ms Mansfield was not available for comment today, sources close to her have confirmed she was the notorious and, until now anonymous, Spoonman.

Oh Christ. Ade had disgust written all over his face. He bent low and hissed into her ear, 'You back-stabbing bitch.' He took a deep breath, shook his head, and left her squatting in front of the oven, struggling for both breath and control, her heart racing and her body shaking.

The rest of the bake was a disaster. Claire forgot about her sponge, and by the time she checked, it was overbaked and cracked when she attempted to roll it. Her chocolate didn't melt properly and ended up all grainy and dull. She'd neglected to sift the icing sugar, so that had little lumps in it, and the tempered chocolate she was going to use to decorate the log didn't work and bent rather than snapped.

Then to crown the whole mess, as Claire was placing the fork of the log onto the tray, she lost her grip, and it ended up on the floor. When she bent down to retrieve it, for one brief, mad moment, she contemplated staying down there and giving way to the tears that had been threatening to spill over ever since she read that text. The cameras were still rolling, so she swallowed hard, inhaled deeply and stood, wiped her hands against her apron and faked a "these things happen" smile.

The judging was lethal. David pointed out how the cake itself was overbaked and wondered what had happened to the tempered chocolate leaves, which were limp and dull rather than snappily glossy. Anthea tutted over the grainy chocolate in the icing and said it made it look grey rather than deeply brown – a yule log that had slipped into the fire and been pulled out again before it could provide any warmth. Claire didn't blame either David or Anthea for their comments. Although they'd never been the subject of a Spoonman review, they had friends who had been. As for Adrian, he took a bite of the log, scraped off some icing with a spoon, stared at Claire and pushed it away. 'This looks like it's been trampled on by heavy boots and belongs back on the forest floor,' he sneered.

Declan gasped, but she smiled and thanked the judges, somehow stopping the emotion from showing on her face and the tears from sneaking out of her eyes.

When it was all over, and Ian declared the winner – with Declan coming in very close behind him – Claire went straight to her locker in an attempt to make a quick getaway, but Ade caught her before she could make it out of the building.

He grabbed at her arm and swung her around to face him. 'How could you?'

'I didn't.'

'You didn't what?'

'I didn't write that review, Ade.'

'How did it work, Claire? Did you write that first review and then get offered more to write it as The Spoonman? Is that how you've managed it for the last few years? Smiling to our faces as if butter wouldn't melt in your mouth and then sticking the knives in our backs? I liked you, Claire. I thought you were the real deal.'

'I am. And I didn't write that review.'

'How am I meant to believe that? According to this, you've been lying to us all for years, and now you've been found out.'

'But—'

'No,' he said, holding a hand in front of her face. 'I don't want to hear any more lies. You're finished, Claire. No one will touch you after this.' He turned and left the room.

Claire made it to the relative privacy of a taxi before turning on her phone and seeing the extent of the damage. Multiple missed calls and messages – most from people she knew in the industry. She couldn't listen to any of them. Nor could she read the texts. She switched her phone to silent and curled into a ball in the taxi's corner.

CHAPTER FIFTEEN

She waited until she was home before calling Barty.

'What's the damage?' she demanded, her voice cracking, unable to make sense of what was happening.

'Not good,' he said. 'If I were you, I'd pack a bag for a week or so and get over to my place before the photographers surround yours.'

'Seriously? This surely can't be that big.'

'It is,' he barked. 'It's *that* big. They've wanted to know who The Spoonman is for years. And to find out it's you? The darling of the bake? The nicest person on British television? It's big. Don't worry though. All we need to do is call a press conference and tell them they got it wrong – you're not Alex Spooner. Once we do that, it'll all go away. In the meantime, get over to my house, and we can talk about who we'll use to refute the story. I think Miriam at *Hello* owes me a favour – and she's always liked you. We'll fix this, I promise.'

'What if we can't?' Claire said it so quietly that at first, she didn't think he'd heard her.

'What do you mean?'

'What if it was me? What if I was Alex Spooner?'

He was silent for a few minutes.

'Barty?'

'Are you saying what I think you're saying?'

'Yes,' she said in a small voice.

'Fuck!' Barty sighed before adding, 'Don't. Say. Anything. More.'

'But—'

'Claire! Shut the fuck up and get over to my house.'

It was that big – Barty had never raised his voice to her in the past, and it wasn't at all like him to swear either.

'Grab your passport and some summer clothes in case we need to send you to Australia for Christmas.'

'But surely—'

'Stop!'

Claire couldn't stop the gasp of shock that escaped her at his tone.

After a few seconds of silence, he said, 'This is what you pay me for, Claire. This is where I go to work, and you do as I tell you. Okay?'

'Okay,' she whispered.

'Good. I'll organise a car and will text you when we're on the way. In the meantime, don't take any other calls, and switch your phone to silent.' He hesitated. 'It's probably not a good idea to go onto social media either.'

'Oh no,' she groaned. 'What are they saying?'

'Nothing that'll do you any good to read. The car

will be there soon, so use the next thirty minutes to pack some clothes – and Claire?'

'What?' The words came out in a half sob as she waited for him to say everything was going to be fine, that this would all blow over, that they'd be able to laugh about it in a couple of days.

'Don't talk to anyone but me,' he cautioned. When she didn't respond, he said, 'Do you understand?'

'I'm nodding.'

'Alright then. Now get packing, and I'll see you soon.'

As soon as Barty rang off, her phone lit up with messages and calls from numbers she didn't recognise. She closed her eyes briefly and then, taking a deep breath, clicked the icon for her Facebook account. Notifications popped up and filled the screen. She closed the app and dropped the phone to the floor. It landed with a thud. It really was that bad.

But, she reasoned, it would all blow over in a few days. Surely. Now though, she needed to do as Barty said and pack some clothes. Shaking her head in resolution, she stood and moved into the bedroom, pulling clothes randomly from the wardrobe and drawers and throwing them into the suitcase.

He didn't mean it about going to Australia, did he? Claire was sure she'd be spending Christmas as planned with Gracie, Bill, Milo and the dogs. Just in case, she tossed in a few concessions to summer.

As she zipped up the bag, a blare of a car horn sent her into a panic. Hadn't Barty said he'd text? Her phone was still on the floor where she'd dropped it, and with the screen facing up, Claire grimaced at the number of new messages and missed calls that filled the screen. The horn blared again.

Outside there was a gaggle of photographers who all rushed forward as she opened the front door. She stood on the doorstep, unable to move as the media and paparazzi shone lights into her eyes and shoved microphones into her face.

'Why did you do it, Claire?'

'How does it feel to have your secret out in the open?'

'Did you know the whole of London's restaurant industry hates you right now?'

She stood mute, only blinking as flashes exploded in front of her. Eventually, Barty elbowed his way through the scrum and reached her side. Claire's heart pounded when he took her bag and wrapped his arm securely around her.

'I've got you, darling,' he whispered. 'Head down and walk. That's it, one foot in front of the other. We're nearly there.'

Barty's voice guided her, almost crooning instructions in her ear until she slid into the car and slammed the door. The car veered from the kerb, leaving the media throng behind, and she heaved a sigh of relief and curled into a Claire-shaped ball and rested against the door.

Barty said nothing during the drive to his riverside apartment, but when the car stopped outside his building their eyes met briefly. His were full of concern, and that warmed her heart.

Once inside, she stood at the windows in his living room and stared at the city across the river.

'Claire, sit down, you're making the place look untidy,' he joked.

'And we both know you like everything in its place,' she said, turning back to face him, managing a weak grin in return.

Barty's apartment was like he was – stylish and smooth, splashes of colour in cushions and paintings in contrast to the black leather, chrome and glass of his furnishings. He dressed in much the same way – favouring designer suits and separates with unexpected plumes of colour and patterns in linings, shirts and, when the occasion warranted, ties.

'I do,' he said, running his hand across his hair. 'Tea?'

'Please.'

As Barty busied himself in the sleek white kitchen whose only use had ever been to make tea and prepare drinks, she sat on the sofa and thumbed idly through an issue of *Tatler* arranged on the coffee table with other fashion and style magazines.

He placed the tea on a coaster on the table and walked to the same window Claire had been staring out.

'What you said on the phone,' he started, 'You said you were Alex Spooner.'

'Yes.'

Barty's shoulders rose as he took in a deep breath. His hands balled into fists briefly before he extended the fingers again, alternating between clenching and flexing almost as if he could control his hands, he'd be able to control his temper. It frightened Claire in a way nothing else today had done. In all the years she'd known Barty, she'd never seen him angry. Even when one of his reality TV clients went against his advice and ended up in the tabloids for all the wrong reasons, he'd be cutting, but sardonic at the same time. Never had she seen him like this.

'For fuck's sake, Claire, why didn't you tell me?' Barty spat the words out.

'I didn't think I'd need to.'

'You didn't think you'd need to? Surely you knew it would come out eventually?'

'It's been so long since I was Alex Spooner that I'd almost forgotten I ever was.'

'That's not an excuse ... hang on, did you say you're *not* Spooner after all?' Finally, he turned to face her.

'No,' she sighed. 'I used to be, but I'm not anymore. Remember when I was writing the horoscopes?'

'Yes. I thought it was hilarious, but what about it?'

'And every so often I'd have enough money to take us both out for dinner?'

He nodded. 'It was such a treat. Neither of us had any money to spare back in those days.'

'I could afford to buy dinner because I was writing those reviews as Alex Spooner. Someone else did it before me – they also wrote the horoscopes, I think. Duncan wanted to keep the name going, so we've all used the by-line "Alex Spooner".'

'How long ago are we talking about?'

'I stopped writing as Spooner when I got my regular column.'

'In other words, you haven't been Alex Spooner for years?'

'That's right. Another Spooner took my place on the reviews, and they started paying a real astrologer to write the horoscopes. I can't be sure, but I think it's changed again since then; the reviews are bitchier these days.'

'I see.'

Barty thrust his hands in his pockets and bit at his top lip, a mannerism Claire had always joked was his thinking face.

'I still don't understand why you didn't tell me,' said Barty.

'I signed a non-disclosure agreement – which I suppose I've just broken by telling you as much as I have.' Claire shrugged and concentrated on her tea.

'Did Giles know?'

Claire nodded. 'I'd already stopped when I met Giles, but yes, I told him; it was years ago.'

'But you couldn't tell me?'

She dropped her chin to her chest. How could she say she trusted Giles to keep quiet about it, but not Barty? Even though she was sure Barty wouldn't divulge a client's confidence, back then, it was a different story. Today, Barty still enjoyed a gossip and loved to entertain her with stories of what (and who) the latest B- or C- lister celebrity had been up to.

Barty might've been her best friend, but that didn't mean she'd have trusted him with information like that.

He studied her for a few seconds, his expression unreadable. 'Right, so you were Alex Spooner, and now you're not.'

She nodded.

'And then you stopped?'

'Yes. So, I can't come out and say I'm not Alex Spooner because while I'm not at the moment, I used to be, and because of the document I signed I can't talk about it.'

'I need time to think about this. Until then, I don't want you saying anything to anybody. Okay?'

Claire nodded, and finally the tears that had been waiting for an opening flowed freely down her cheeks.

'Oh, sweetie,' he said, sitting beside her and holding her close. 'We'll fix this.'

'How?'

'I don't know yet, but we will. Trust me, Claire; I'll get you through this.'

She burrowed further into his chest and sobbed, the arms around her tightening.

'What we need is some comfort carbs, wine, and Hugh Grant,' he said when her sobs subsided.

As Claire sat up, his arms dropped away. She wiped her eyes on the sleeve of her jumper and pulled a tissue from the box to blow her nose.

'Just not *Notting Hill*,' said Claire, smiling through the leftover tears. 'That's a little too close to home right now. And where do you intend to get carbs? I'd guess you don't have anything resembling food in that fridge.'

'I have olives, darling,' he said. 'How else can I make a martini? And I have a lot of menus from excellent restaurants who deliver.'

'Of course you do.'

'There'll be no marmite spaghetti in this apartment, thank you very much. We've both come too far for that.'

Claire laughed at the comical look on his face before sobering again. 'We've come a long way, haven't we Barty?'

'Yes, darling, we have. Now, wine - or would you prefer a martini?'

'Wine is fine thanks, Barty.'

As Barty fixed their drinks, Claire couldn't help but think that while they had come a long way, she'd managed in one day to fall all the way back down, and she didn't know whether she'd find a way to climb back up again.

CHAPTER SIXTEEN

'I don't believe it,' said Tallis, struggling to make sense of the breaking news about Claire.

'Neither do I. Something about it doesn't feel right,' said Gail.

'No, it doesn't, does it? Claire came across as warm and kind, and I don't know about you, but I'm sure that's who she is. She couldn't turn around and write the reviews that Alex Spooner writes.'

'You saw the way she was with the crew – respectful to everyone. There's no way she could be like that to people who work with her and for her and then be as nasty as Alex Spooner is.'

'There's something else too – something that's on the edge of my memory that I can't quite grab. Keep talking, and it might come to me,' said Tallis.

'Then there's Owen. I know you said Claire had said they were friends, but I saw something else between them when we were watching that footage. I wouldn't have been surprised to know they used to date or something. If that were the case, how could she have written what she did about him in that review on Belucci's? He got sacked over that.'

'That's it!' announced Tallis. 'That's what I was trying to remember. Claire told me she hadn't seen or heard from Owen since they were both eighteen. She also said she had no idea he'd become a chef. And if she didn't know he was a chef, how could she specifically refer to him in that review?'

'Did you believe her when she was telling you?'

'Absolutely. Claire had no reason to lie about it – especially not then. Plus, did you see her surprise when Ed announced who the judge would be?'

'Actually, you're right. I did notice that.'

'And there's more. When I was talking to her the other day, she told me how fabulous *Lily James* was and yet she supposedly wrote a negative review about it.' Even though Gail couldn't see her, Tallis frowned and shook her head. 'No, Gail, I don't believe one word of it. Claire did not write the reviews they're saying she wrote. I just can't understand why she's not refuting it.'

'I think you're right, Tallis, but what can we do about it?'

'I don't know yet, but I'm going to start with phoning her and letting her know she has our support.'

'It'll be interesting to hear what Owen has to say about it too,' said Gail. 'If he believes her, he might be prepared to help.'

'*If* he believes her. If anyone has reason to want to

know the identity of the person who had them sacked, then it's Owen. Also, we don't know the history of their relationship – if it ended badly, he might be more inclined *not* to believe in her, even if it just means he has someone he can blame.'

'Well,' said Gail, 'it's up to us to convince him then isn't it?'

Owen Gallagher was even more handsome in his chef's whites than he had been in the jeans and jumper he'd worn to the Fenwyck afternoon tea. While Tallis thought it, Gail voiced it.

'Just when you thought your hormones had gone into hibernation along comes someone like that to make them sit up and take notice,' she said.

Tallis giggled. 'Shush, he'll hear you.'

'I'm sorry, Tallis, but there are some things it's impossible to be quiet about, and Owen Gallagher is one of those things. Oh my god, he's coming over. What do we do? Stand up? Sit down? How does this meet the chef thing work?'

Before Tallis could answer, Owen was at their table.

'Stay where you are,' he said with a smile, before leaning down and kissing first Gail's then Tallis' cheek. 'It's good to see you both.'

'It's good to see you too, Owen. Thanks so much for having us here, we're both looking forward to our meal,' said Tallis when Gail seemed to have trouble getting her words out.

'You're very welcome. It was a fabulous tea you put on, so it's the least I can do.' He looked around at his full restaurant, even on a Thursday night. 'I'm sorry I can't stop for a chat now, but I wanted to say hello and tell you to enjoy your meal. I need to say a quick hello at a few other tables and then get back into the kitchen, but I'll be out to see you again later in the evening.' He left them to their menus and had a few words with every other diner on his way back to the kitchen.

'There's absolutely nothing pretentious about him, is there?' she murmured.

'What was that?' asked Gail.

'I was just saying that it's hard to fathom the man that just stopped to chat to us and has spared the time to make every single person in here feel welcome, with the review that The Spoonman wrote on *Belucci's*. What did it say again?'

They'd googled the Belucci review again before coming out that evening. It had only served to reinforce their belief that Claire hadn't written it.

'It said, "sadly Gallagher's arrogance and sizeable ego is not in proportion to his talent in the kitchen. If it had been, our meal might have been of average quality as opposed to merely edible." There was something else in there about him believing too much of his own press and a veiled comment regarding the high-handed treatment of staff and patrons.'

'Hmm,' Tallis mused. 'Reading it now, it sounds more like a hatchet job on Owen than on Belucci.'

'True. Belucci doesn't appear to have suffered any ill effects from the review at all.'

'Not that we know of, anyway. In any case, what are we eating? The waitress will be back soon for our orders. I'm thinking of the curried cauliflower or the mushroom ravioli to start and then the fish pie.'

'There's so much I want on here.' Gail pulled a coin out of her handbag. 'Okay, I'm tossing for it. Heads it's the rarebit and tails it's pork belly.'

Tallis and Gail chatted lightly over their meal – about village gossip, Caro's concern over her second daughter's marriage, Fee's forthcoming trip to York to spend Christmas with her son and his family, Anna, Adam, and how on earth a smoked haddock rarebit could be one of the best things Gail had ever tasted.

As Tallis wiped the last piece of creamy sauce from the edge of her pie dish with a piece of bread she'd been saving especially for that purpose, she sat back in her chair with a happy sigh. 'I think that has to be the best meal I've ever eaten,' she said.

'I think you could be right,' agreed Gail. 'I'm so full, but I've enjoyed every single mouthful.'

'I'm pleased to hear it,' said the waiter who smiled as he stacked the plates. 'I'd normally ask if you wanted to see the dessert menu, but Chef said to tell you he'll be out with something for you in ten minutes or so.

Can I fix you a coffee while you wait?'

Within the promised ten minutes, Owen had pulled up a chair at the table and placed squares of sticky toffee pudding with a salted caramel ice cream in front of each of them. 'I hope you don't mind me eating with you,' he said.

'Absolutely not,' said Gail. 'We both enjoyed our meals so very much.'

'Good.' He grinned. 'That's what I'm in this game for.'

'I have to ask,' said Tallis, 'how did you get the mushroom flavour into the pasta?'

Owen tapped his nose and looked around before leaning in, 'I could tell you, but …'

When Tallis and Gail laughed, he said, 'believe it or not, it's dried mushroom which I've ground to a powder and added to the dough.'

'It was amazing – and worked so well with that pulled pork filling,' said Tallis.

'I'm glad you liked it. Now, I hope you don't think I'm intruding where I shouldn't be, but have you heard from Claire?'

Tallis and Gail looked at each other.

'You don't seriously think she did what they're saying she did, do you?' he asked before either of them had a chance to respond.

'No, we don't,' said Gail, 'but we were concerned you would.'

'And we were trying to work out how we could convince you she didn't,' said Tallis.

'That's reasonable. If I were in your shoes, I'd think the same. After all, I was sacked after a Spooner review and being sacked caused my marriage to break up.'

Gail gasped at his admission.

Owen lifted one shoulder. 'Yes, it's true. I have a lot of reasons to detest Alex Spooner, and it would be very easy for me to grab hold of a name to blame; except this is Claire and I know she couldn't have written that review.'

'But you and she haven't seen each other for a long time; she might've changed,' said Tallis.

'True, but not that much – although I have to admit I wasn't proud of my first reaction when I heard the news. There were a few minutes after Angie told me when I did wonder. In fact, … here's Angie now and given she has *that* look on her face, I suspect I'm going to need to excuse myself for a few minutes.'

'Yes, sorry Chef, but you need to call this man back as soon as possible – something about some pheasants you might want to take off his hands.' She handed him the phone and a slip of paper.

Owen nodded, 'In that case, I'd better speak to him. I'm sorry ladies, but Angie can keep you company for a few minutes. Angie, meet Tallis and Gail. And Angie, this is the time where you need to ask Gail what spices she used in those pumpkin scones.' With another smile of apology, he took the phone and went back into the kitchen.

'I've heard so much about those scones – and your sponge cake, Tallis,' said Angie. 'In fact, that episode was the best one I've seen – and not just because Owen was in it.'

Little dots of pink appeared on Angie's pale cheeks, and Tallis struggled to hide her smile. She suspected Angie had more than a little crush on her boss.

'Owen was just saying you were the one to tell him the news about Claire being Alex Spooner?'

Gail didn't flinch when Tallis lightly kicked her under the table.

Angie looked around before answering. 'I don't think I'll ever forget the look on his face,' she said. 'It was like I'd sucked the life out of him. His eyes were dead. You know they used to date? It was back when they were teenagers, and he hasn't said anything to me about it, but this is a small village and word gets about.' Her face coloured again.

'What did he say?' asked Tallis.

'Absolutely nothing,' said Angie. 'That was the thing. He didn't say a word. He removed the tea towel he always has tucked into his apron, folded it up, put his knives back into their wrap, untied his apron and just walked out. Not a word. I took over prep for service, but he didn't come back for ages – it must have been an hour or so, and when he did, the rain had soaked him to the skin,' she added. 'I sent him upstairs to his flat to dry off. By the time he came back down, it was as if I'd never said anything.'

'Did you ask him if he was alright?' asked Gail.

She nodded, 'Yes, and he said he didn't care what anyone else said, but Claire hadn't done what they said she did, and he wouldn't stand for anyone saying anything different in his presence. Then he took over service as if nothing had happened.' She looked around again and Owen was walking back towards them. 'I wouldn't normally gossip, you know,' she said, 'it's just that Owen said you were friends with Claire and even though I've never met her she seems nice on the telly and I thought …'

Tallis smiled gently. 'It's okay, Angie, what you said won't go any further than us.'

When Owen rejoined them, Angie said, 'everything okay, Chef?'

'Yes, better than okay, we've got some pheasant coming in over the next few days, so I think it's as good a time as any for you to try out that special you've been practising.'

Angie's smile was wide. 'Thanks, I will.' Turning to Tallis and Gail, she said, 'it was lovely to talk to you, but I'll leave you with Owen and tell the others the good news.'

'Okay, let me guess,' said Owen, 'Angie mentioned Claire and I used to date?' His smile was wry.

Tallis nodded. 'Yes, she did, but she didn't mean anything by it.'

'I know, she wouldn't have, but she would've heard the gossip around town.' He let out a short laugh. 'We were close – best friends as kids, and then we dated from the time we were sixteen. It didn't end well, but if Claire wants to tell you about that, it's up to her. To be honest, I'm still not sure what happened.'

'You seemed to get on well in Fenwyck?' said Gail.

'We've talked,' he said, 'and we'll talk some more, maybe. Who knows, one day we'll be friends again.' He exhaled and scratched at the back of his head. 'She might be famous, but she's still the same person underneath.'

'Is your history the only reason you believe in her now?' asked Tallis.

Owen smiled. 'No, it's not the only reason, but what I'm interested in is why you two are so interested. I told Angie you were friends with Claire, but it's not like you've known her for very long.'

There was a faint challenge in his voice, and Tallis matched it. 'No, that's right, we haven't, but it feels like we have.'

'We clicked,' said Gail. 'That doesn't happen very often so when it does,' she shrugged, 'well, you have to go with it.'

'Fair enough. But in answer to your earlier question, the reason I believe in her now is that she had no idea I'd become a chef, so how could she have written that review about me? It's logical when you stop and think about it. And I'll be honest, I did have to stop and think about it – my first reaction wasn't one I was proud of.'

Tallis met his eyes which were filled with what could've been regret.

'That's what made us know for sure too,' said Tallis. 'She told me that night we all cooked together she had no idea you'd become a chef, and she spoke about you with kindness—'

'Which was more than I deserved,' interrupted Owen.

'I don't know about that, but she spoke of you fondly. Also, when I was talking to her early last week, she told me how she'd eaten at *Lily James*, and the experience had been a good one. She had no reason to lie to me on either of those occasions. That's how I know she didn't write that review about *Belucci's* and she didn't write the review on *Lily James*.'

'So, who did?' asked Gail.

'We don't know your industry, so we're hoping you might know?' said Tallis.

Owen shrugged one shoulder, his face serious. 'I have no idea, but I am concerned there's been nothing from her to refute the claims either. Have you spoken to her?'

Tallis shook her head. 'No. I've rung a few times and left some messages for her to call. I even tried Ed on the number he gave us. He said he hadn't heard from her either. He sounded strange though on the phone.'

'Yes, I tried calling her with no luck, and I spoke to Ed too,' said Owen. 'He's not saying much at all. I think the network is deciding what action they'll take – this scandal has definitely tainted her brand.'

'But if it's not true?' said Gail.

'*We* know it's not true, but no one in the industry is speaking up for her. To be honest, I'm not sure anyone would be prepared to listen to her right now – especially not those who've been at the other end of a Spooner review. Ed gave me her manager's number, and I've left some messages for him too.'

'Doesn't her sister live in Brookford?' asked Gail. 'Maybe we can get a message to Claire through her.'

'Yes, Claire told me Gracie lives just out of town. The last time I saw Gracie, she was very young, and I don't know her married name. I'll ask around the village, though. Gossip runs both ways, you know.'

'What else can we do?' asked Tallis.

'Keep trying to contact her,' said Owen. 'I'm hoping the silence from her camp is because she's lying low until the worst of the scandal is over.'

'Okay.' Tallis nodded. 'Christmas is only a few days away, so we'll leave it until after then.'

'Leave me your numbers and let's get back in touch in a couple of weeks,' said Owen. 'If we haven't heard anything by then, I'm going to start making some more calls.'

CHAPTER SEVENTEEN

For the week after the story broke, Claire remained holed up in Barty's apartment. Those first dreadful days had been a blur of misery and confusion; Claire didn't know what she would've done during that time if it hadn't been for Barty.

On that first terrible night, he held her each time the tears came. He'd poured her wine and ordered pasta she didn't eat, and then when the movie she hadn't been able to concentrate on finished, he insisted on giving her his bed to sleep in.

'I'll take the couch,' he said.

'That's ridiculous,' she replied. 'Your legs will hang off the end.'

'So will yours,' he'd pointed out.

She'd nodded mutely and waited as he retrieved the clothes he needed for the night and then shut the door and lay on her back as the horror of that moment when Ade showed her the text kept her awake.

Barty had kept the newspapers from her but had admitted they were all full of the story. She'd been grateful when he handed her a new phone with a new number so she could contact her family. Neither she nor Barty mentioned the possibility of her calling anyone else. Claire didn't imagine anyone else would want to be talking to her. When she said as much to Barty, he turned away and changed the subject.

She had somehow managed to hold it together when Barty told her the network had put her contract on hold and that *Time for Tea* would not be returning to screens in the coming year. She'd asked him about *Posh or Not*, and he'd shaken his head and said nothing. But when he'd said Duncan wasn't returning messages, Claire assumed she was cut from the paper as well.

For Duncan – the only person who could stand up and tell the world someone had made a mistake – to turn away from her, was the final nail in the coffin that was her career and her reputation.

She'd nodded sadly and excused herself to lie down. With the bedroom door closed, she allowed the tears that were never far from the surface to flow again.

One afternoon Barty came home to find her on the floor doubled over in pain, her face wet. He'd rushed to her side and bundled her into his arms. Her phone lay beside her; the screen opened at her Twitter page. He turned the phone off and rocked her until she was calm. After that, he either shut down or put her social media accounts into hibernation and for all intents and purposes, so was she.

Each night when he came back from the office, they'd drink wine and order in expensive food that neither of them ate much of. Barty would talk lightly about this reality star or that one, making her laugh at their demands and exploits, taking her mind off her troubles for the barest of instances until it was time for bed.

She'd lie there on her back listening to Barty's soft snoring and snuffling from the couch, but unable to sleep until the early hours – although even then it was sleep full of dreams repeating the disaster that had been *Celebrity Cook-off*. This time Owen was the judge, and when she presented her crumbled yule log, he threw it onto the ground and told her that's what she'd done to his life. Then he laughed, and everyone else laughed, and Bruno Belucci was there saying she was a fraud and now she'd been found out. Not that she'd seen the show when it had aired – Barty had spared her that additional humiliation.

When Barty's alarm sounded each morning, she'd get up and have a cup of tea with him before going back to bed for a few more hours of restless sleep and more dreams that she couldn't escape.

Barty had decided the best place for her would be somewhere where the scandal meant nothing and wanted her to go to her parents in Australia. She called Gracie and told her she wouldn't be coming to Brookford.

'I don't see why you still can't come to us,' Gracie
had said.

'I can't. It's all still too fresh, and if anyone gets wind
of me being with you, you'll get dragged into it all too.'

'Okay, I understand that I suppose, but no one will
find out. But what about your side of the story? Surely
they've made a mistake?'

There was hope in her voice, and Gracie needed
to hear her say the papers had gotten it wrong, that it
was all just a big mistake.

'Claire, it's not true, is it?'

'Some of it is. I was The Spoonman—'

Gracie gasped.

'For a time – a long time ago – way back before
I got my column. I was just starting, and I didn't have
a lot of choices. I wasn't proud of it, but I did it. So, I
can't stand there and say they're wrong when technically
speaking, they're right.'

'Surely though you didn't write any of those nasty
reviews?'

'No,' Claire said firmly, 'I absolutely didn't. Those
didn't start appearing until a few years ago – and they've
got steadily more sensational in the years since. Mine
were positively boring in contrast.'

Gracie was silent for a few seconds as if turning
this information around in her head.

'You know, when you think about it, it's just like
actresses who do lingerie shoots before they're famous

and then the pictures come out later and make it look like they've made a porno. You did what you had to do to pay the rent, and you're now being made to suffer for decisions made when you were poor.'

Claire's laugh came out of her nose like a snort. 'Actually G, that's not a bad analogy. I might just use that.'

'Go for it. Do you know who it is now?'

'No. I think Duncan is the only person who might know – and I'm not even sure he does.'

'Why doesn't he come out and stand up for you?'

Gracie had asked the same question that Claire had asked several times over the past few days. 'I don't know. Maybe because they want to milk the publicity that's out there at the moment. Maybe because the mood at present is one where no one's prepared to listen to my side of it. Everyone has someone they can hate right now – me – but if it comes out it wasn't me who wrote all of those vile, damaging pieces, then the question stands – who is the real Alex Spooner?'

'Christ, it's a mess and a half, Claire.'

'You can say that again.'

'What are you going to do?'

'All I can do is lie low for now. Long term? I have no idea. The problem is, I signed a confidentiality agreement all those years ago, and that means I can't talk about it, so please promise me you won't say anything to anyone. I get you'll probably tell Bill, but technically I shouldn't have even said anything to you.'

'Okay, but is there anything I can do?'

'Thanks, G, but there's nothing you can do at the moment except continue to look after Nigel for me.' Claire sent a silent message of thanks that she didn't need to show her face in Brookford right now – the idea of running into Owen was more than she could bear.

'You know Nigel's welcome to stay as long as you need him to.' Gracie hesitated briefly before asking, 'Have you heard from Giles?'

'No.' As she spoke, the pain that had been sitting around her heart rose into her throat. She'd asked Barty each afternoon whether he'd heard from anyone; but what she really wanted to ask was whether he'd heard from Giles. Each day he'd shake his head sadly and then ask her what she fancied to order in for dinner.

'I see,' said Gracie. 'What about anyone else?'

'No one.' Claire fixed a frozen smile, even though Gracie couldn't see it. 'At least I still have Barty.'

'That's it? One friend? And you pay him to like you. We went through this the other week.'

'That's not true. I'm not making any money for him at the moment, and he still likes me. I also have you.'

'I'm your sister, so I don't count.'

'Even though you're my sister, I don't have to like you. I know plenty of people who love their sisters because they have to but can't stand them.'

'Okay,' she said. 'You got me there.'

'To be honest, G, I don't know if I do have any

other friends anymore.'

'What about Jenna and other friends from school?'

'Other than Jenna, they've all moved away. I promised myself I'd call Jenna next time I'm in Brookford, but given I've ghosted her for such a long time, I wouldn't blame her if she didn't want to speak to me either. I was on my way to being friends with Tallis and Gail, but I doubt I'll hear from them again. I thought Ed, my producer, was my friend, but he's friends with too many people The Spoonman upset, so I'm sure he's disgusted with me too.'

'Have you even tried reaching out to any of these people?'

Claire shrugged. 'No, I'm too scared I'll be proven right.'

'What about Owen?'

'If I were Owen, I'd never talk to me again, either.'

'But you made up, didn't you? The other week?'

'Yes, we talked, sort of, and I think given time we might be friends again someday, but Owen got fired from a job a few years ago because of a Spooner review – and his wife left him because of it.'

'I'm sure there were more reasons the marriage didn't work.'

'Possibly, but as far as Owen is concerned, it was Alex Spooner's fault. That means now he thinks it was my fault.' As far as Owen was probably concerned, aside from being the heartless bitch who broke his heart, Claire was now also the poison pen who'd cost him his job, his marriage, and who'd certainly brought his career to a temporary halt. The tentative peace she thought they'd begun to find in Fenwyck would now be gone forever.

'I see.' Gracie hesitated before adding, 'I wasn't sure whether you'd want me to tell you this, but I ran into Owen in town the other day.'

Claire closed her eyes briefly. 'How was he?'

'He was looking good. He asked about you. He wanted to know how you were and said that if you needed someone to talk to, he'd be there.'

'That was nice of him to say so.' But Claire didn't believe it. Knowing how he'd suffered as a result of a Spooner review, she knew that no matter what he might've said to Gracie, she could expect no sympathy from that quarter.

Gracie didn't reply and stayed silent for a beat. 'You know, Bill and I were talking, and if you're not going straight back to London, Curlew Cottage is empty at the moment. We haven't bothered to advertise it over the winter, so if you wanted to stay there, you could – at least until you sort things out. We're in the farmhouse just down the lane if you need us, and Nigel can happily see Bella whenever he wants.' She paused again. 'I know it's not London, and it's certainly nothing flash, but maybe it might do you good and give you some breathing space.'

'I don't know ...'

'There's a cosy fire in the living room, a kitchen for

you to bake in, and lots of lovely quiet.'

It was a tempting offer. She'd only been in Curlew Cottage once before and struggled to remember the details. She did, however, recall the flagged stone floor throughout, the worn wooden table in the tiny kitchen and living area, the overgrown kitchen garden outside and the view across the valley. Maybe she could do it – for a little while anyway, just until she could get her thoughts in order.

'I'd pay your normal rent.'

'Of course you would. And you'll be doing us a favour – it's hardly ever let regularly over the winter.'

It would save her having to deal with her problems for a few more weeks and maybe give the gossip papers a chance to find someone new to bitch about. January was usually fertile ground for soap stars misbehaving on holidays – or compromising photos of footballers at Christmas parties.

'No one would need to know you were there,' said Gracie. 'You've got more chance of being seen at an airport than you do in a cottage in Brookford.' She pushed home her advantage. 'Come to us for Christmas as you planned. I'll stock the cottage with groceries, and there are plenty of walks you can do through the country for exercise – you couldn't do that in Sydney, it's too hot, and you know you don't like the heat …'

'I'll think about it,' said Claire, already knowing she'd say yes.

CHAPTER EIGHTEEN

Claire drove down to Brookford on Christmas Eve. She called in at the flat to pack a suitcase of warm clothes and load the car with some essentials. Being back in the flat was strange without Giles. She almost expected to see him tapping away on his laptop in the second bedroom that had doubled as his office, but the room was empty, and his desk was so clean it was easy to believe he was never coming back. Maybe he wasn't. Claire's cookbooks were piled high on the floor, gathering dust, but his shelves were empty.

As she was about to leave, she turned back and, on a whim, collected her old roasting tin and heavy stand mixer. She stacked her cake tins and baking trays into one box, and some of her favourite cookbooks into another and loaded them to the car. Who knew, maybe she'd get a chance to use them at Curlew Cottage; it wasn't as if she'd have anything else to spend her time on.

Before she left London, Barty handed back her old phone. In the week she'd been in hiding, the publicity had died down a little – thanks to a footballer misbehaving, a soapie star caught up in a cheating scandal, and another reported rift between the royal wives – and the messages and texts had stopped. That was the only piece of good news Barty had for her.

'I'm sorry, Claire,' he said. 'The network isn't budging. They are, apparently, in talks with Owen Gallagher though.'

'I'm glad something good has come out of this for someone. Owen was always going to be great on screen. What about Ed? Have you heard from him?'

He shook his head. 'Sorry, sweetie. I've kept an eye out for any texts or missed calls from people who you might've expected – or at least hoped – to be on your side and deleted everything else.'

'But apparently, they weren't on my side.'

'So it would seem.'

Claire's heart sank and she pushed her fingertips to the corner of her eyes.

'Come here,' he said and held his arms out. 'At least you can still rely on me.'

'I know. You and my family are pretty much all I have at the moment.' She pulled back from his hug. 'Barty, I'd like to find out whether I'm allowed to tell my side of the story.'

He sighed and shook his head slowly. 'I don't think that's a good idea. The newspapers have finally given up on you for now; you don't want to risk starting it all back up again.'

'Perhaps you're right. Maybe in a few weeks?'

'I think you should let it go. In a way, you've done the industry a favour as The Spoonman can't publish at the moment anyway.'

'Or if he does, everyone will know to come after me.'

'There is that.'

'And that's why I want to set the record straight. Will you at least think about it?'

He nodded. 'I'll think about it.'

'Thanks, Barty, for this.' She motioned to her phone, clean of anything that could upset her further, 'and for being here for me.'

'I'll always be here for you, darling.' He hugged her again.

Just for a minute, she wanted to stay in his embrace where everything was safe.

Claire had been back in Brookford for almost three weeks. In that time, she'd kept close to the cottage. Other than Gracie, Bill and Milo, she saw few people and filled her days with long walks down the lane and through the fields.

In the first few weeks, Gracie would get her whatever groceries she needed, but in the last few days, she'd begun venturing up to the farm shop on the road to Cirencester. When she was done walking, she sat by the fire and made cups of tea and read all the books on the shelves in the cottage and, as a result, was now an expert on the birds of The Cotswolds.

This morning, in the second week of January, she shivered as she stepped out of her back door, Nigel bounding along ahead of her before stopping at the garden gate and looking back, his tail wagging hard. 'Hurry up,' he seemed to be saying. 'It's cold out here.'

'Hang on,' Claire said as if he'd spoken. 'I can't move as fast as you can.'

She ruffled his head, unlatched the gate, and he was off down the road toward Gracie's, stopping to double back and make sure she was still following behind. After having her to himself again, Nigel was now reluctant to let her stray too far from his sight. She didn't want to think about how he'd be if she, or rather when she, moved back to London. Claire rubbed her gloved hands together and breathed into them, watching the little puff of breath hang in the air.

There'd been some snow overnight – not enough to settle, but in the places where the sun hadn't yet reached there were still little piles of icy white. As she did every morning on her way down the lane, she called in on Gracie.

'I'm heading into the village,' Gracie said. 'Did you want to come?'

'No,' said Claire. 'I don't need anything.'

'What about groceries? Do you want me to pick anything up for you?'

'Thanks, but I'll walk up to the farm shop this morning and get some meat and veggies. Or I might go into Cirencester this afternoon. I can get other supplies there.'

Gracie raised her eyebrows. 'Don't you think it's time you showed your face in the village? People know you're here – they've seen you at the farm shop. If you leave it too long, word will get around that you're snubbing the local shops and you think you're too good for the rest of us.'

'That's not true,' argued Claire.

'I know it isn't, but they don't.'

'I'll think about it.'

'See that you do.' Gracie's voice was stern, but the look in her eyes was one of concern.

Gracie and Bill had been lifesavers – giving her just the right amount of space and just the right amount of family involvement. Most importantly, they hadn't pried or tried to rush her.

The snow was falling lightly as Claire and Nigel let themselves back into the cottage after their walk. Claire restoked the fire, put the kettle on and checked the bookcase for something else to read. Unless she wanted to study the Ordnance Survey maps for ramblers or delve further into the migratory habits of the Garden Warbler or Little Ringed Plover, she'd exhausted the available choices. The cookbooks and baking trays were still in the boxes she'd brought up from London;

stacked next to the lounge. She'd stubbed her toe on the book box at least three times in the last week so, as a sign, started to unpack them.

By early afternoon, Claire had stored all the trays and tins in cupboards or on the dresser shelves, and the cookbooks filled the small bookcase. She'd hung her clothes in the small wardrobe and folded the rest into the drawers in her bedroom. The boxes and suitcase were stashed in the spare bedroom, and she sat curled up in a chair beside the fire reading *Nigella Express* and remembering that week in Fenwyck before everything went wrong.

In hindsight, Giles had given her plenty of indications he'd been working on something big and wasn't satisfied with the way his career was going. He'd also shown no sign of wanting more from their relationship than they already had. Anything else had been a construct of her imagination. She'd been so wrapped up in her career and what she wanted, that she hadn't stopped to think maybe he didn't want the same things. Regardless of the words they'd said to each other, it was clear the relationship was over. He had to have been aware of the publicity surrounding her before Christmas, and yet he'd chosen not to contact her to see if everything was alright. If that wasn't a sign they were finished, Claire didn't know what was.

While she still had no idea how she was going to approach finding work, she could do something about

Giles. Before she could chicken out, she dialled his number. He answered almost immediately.

'Claire. It's good to hear your voice. How long have you been back in London?'

'You knew I went away?'

'Of course,' he said. 'When the Spooner thing broke, I tried to call you, but you weren't answering your phone. I ended up ringing Barty, and he said you'd changed your number and were lying low with Gracie and Bill for a few weeks. He said you'd phone me when you got back. How was it?'

Barty hadn't mentioned that Giles had phoned. 'I'm still here, in fact, I think I'll stay for a few months – or at least until I know what I'm doing. How's the book going?'

'Good. It's been slow to start, but I think I've got the structure nailed now. I have to have a first draft done by the end of May – June at the latest.'

'Do you think you'll make it?'

'Yes, no problem. Tell me, what are you going to do about this Spooner situation? I haven't read anything where you've refuted the claims, but I suppose that's a bit tricky?'

'Barty thinks I should stay quiet and out of the public eye for now. He thinks it'll be best left as it is. He didn't say as much, but I think he doesn't think anyone will believe me.'

'I know Barty knows more about this sort of thing

than I do, and normally I'd tell you to follow his advice, but I don't think that's wise in this situation. Until you clear the air, whoever is writing as Alex Spooner can continue to do so and you'll be blamed for it. Do they know who leaked it?'

Claire hesitated for a second too long.

'Did you think it was me?'

'Not really. I mean, Barty might've mentioned it once … because we'd broken up, you know … but I didn't believe him.' She grimaced into the phone, glad he couldn't see her face.

After a brief silence, he said, 'Okay, I can't believe you could even consider I'd do that, but I can see how it might've looked, but I can assure you I've always kept that secret. To be honest, until I read about it, I'd completely forgotten you used to write as Alex Spooner.'

Giles' tone was even. 'I wouldn't do anything to hurt you, Claire. I can't believe Barty thought I might've.' He paused for a few seconds. 'Have we broken up? I know I said we were just on a break, but we aren't, are we?'

'No, Giles, I don't think we're on a break. It's not just Paris; it's that you organised it without talking to me. It was such a big decision to make, and you didn't even consult me. Then there's the whole question of marriage – now that I've decided it's important to me, I can't just forget that.'

'I know, Claire. And I'm sorry I don't want it. I love you, but …'

'Not enough to marry me.'

He said nothing to that. He didn't need to.

'It's okay, Giles, I'm okay about it.' As she said the words, she knew them to be true. She was okay – sad, but okay. 'You were always clear about what you did and didn't want, and it's not your fault I changed my mind.'

'Would it make it better if I told you that if I were ever going to change my mind about marriage, it would be for you?'

'No, not really,' she laughed ruefully, 'but thanks for saying it. I'll move my things out of the flat.'

'Take your time. Use it whenever you need to be in London. Also, I sent your last payment towards the mortgage back to your account – I'm fine to manage that. I'm also happy to talk financial settlements – after all, we've been together for quite a while.'

'No, Giles, the flat was yours, and I brought nothing into it other than mess and cookbooks. We didn't even have joint bank accounts.'

'If you're sure?'

'I am. I'm not exactly destitute; I was earning good money for the last few years and didn't have a lot to spend it on, so I'll be okay for a while.'

'What are you going to do now?' he asked.

'No idea.'

'What about writing a book of your own, a spin-off

from your column about regional teatime favourites? Naturally, with a catchier title than that.' He laughed shortly. 'A much catchier title.'

'That's not a bad idea.'

'Are you baking again?'

'No, not yet – although I did bring a lot of that stuff with me.'

'You know it always made you feel better – you used to say it made you feel centred and grounded. You said that when you had your hands in flour things that didn't make sense made sense.'

Claire smiled as the memory returned. It was early in their relationship and before she'd moved in with Giles. He'd come over to the house she shared with Barty to find the kitchen, and Nigel, almost covered in flour.

'What I want you to do when you hang up from me,' Giles said now, 'is go into the village and buy some butter, flour, milk and cheese and make yourself some cheese scones.' He paused for a second. 'That is what goes in them, isn't it?'

'It is. And maybe some mustard or cayenne pepper.'

'And then I want you to start writing again. It doesn't need to be the cookbook, maybe a blog, maybe just your own journal, but start writing. Make it like your column – I know how much you loved doing that – but find yourself again in it. Keep it anonymous for now if that helps and then when the time's right, talk about the real Spooner story.'

The words she wanted to say were stuck behind the lump in her throat. As much as she enjoyed doing *Time for Tea,* she truly missed writing. He knew her so well but had Claire really known him?

'Start with the scones,' he said. 'Write about them. Make it personal and pretend no one is reading.'

'No one will be reading.'

'Maybe not at first. But this isn't about that; it's about you.' He paused again. 'And don't hide away forever. Even if Barty doesn't want to get you an interview, talk to the people who matter the most to you – even if you think they've turned against you. Give them a chance to believe in you again.'

'But what if they don't?'

'Then, at least you'll know. Come on Claire, you were brave enough to propose to me –'

'But I didn't.'

'You sort of did, but at least you know, and I know, and we can be friends and move on. You need to do the same with people like Ed and Duncan. Even Adrian Ritchie and the women you met in Fenwyck. Phone them, talk to them, tell them what really happened. It's up to them how they behave after that, but at least you'll know.'

When she hung up from Giles, the weight of not knowing where their relationship stood had been lifted. It wasn't how she ever would've imagined they'd end. Not that she thought they were forever – she'd been jolted out of that sort of thinking when she was eighteen – but she'd assumed they'd last the distance, which was, she supposed, kind of the same thing.

The speed and relative ease of their ending made sense – they'd come together just as quickly and easily. There was no challenge, no barriers, no obstacles to get past. She'd moved in with him when his previous boarder moved out, and when it made sense to. There was never any negotiation or outlining the terms of cohabitation. Instead of paying rent, she paid into Giles' mortgage. It just happened. And they'd just reversed it in exactly the same way – relatively quickly and much less painfully than it should've been.

Claire gave Nigel a rawhide to chew on and told him to be good, picked up her keys and headed out to the supermarket in Cirencester for baking supplies; not Brookford, she still couldn't face potentially seeing Owen. She was nowhere near strong enough for that yet.

CHAPTER NINETEEN

Brookford Kitchen Diaries

A wonderful friend told me this morning that I should write a blog. There's been a lot going on in my life lately, and I'd just finished telling him I didn't know where to start to make things better.

'You need to write,' he said.

Sometimes I think he knows me better than I know myself. The important bits anyway: the way I like to take my tea back to bed so I can plan through the day, and the way I spread too much butter on everything. The Danish have a word for that — tandsmor. There's a little diagonal cross through the o that I don't know how to make on my laptop, so we'll just pretend that it's there. Tandsmor means tooth butter — when the butter is spread so thickly that your teeth leave marks in it. It's a joyous word, and that's what joy feels like to me — tooth marks in butter.

Anyway, my friend told me I needed to start writing again, and I needed to start baking again. It made sense to write about baking and to begin with scones. He said that too. I once told someone that if there were more tea and scones in the world, people would be nicer to each other. That it's impossible to be mean when you have tea and scones – especially good tea and scones. It stands to reason then that if you want to feel better about yourself, you should bake scones and eat them with lots of excellent butter.

That's why we'll be starting this blog with scones; not just any scones, but cheese scones with just a hint of cayenne pepper or mustard powder.

Why not plain scones? Mainly because when we talk about plain scones, we need to get into the jam and cream or cream and jam debate. Then there's the whole clotted cream thing, and soon enough it all gets out of control. We'll do plain scones when I'm feeling more up to talking about jam and cream and why I like to put my jam on first – unless the cream is clotted – and how there's no substitute for real clotted cream. There. I said it.

It's been so long since I made scones – plain or savoury – I had to stop for a while with my hands in the flour and think it through. It took me time too to even get my hands into the flour, and once I did, I remembered exactly why I needed to. My friend had told me it would make me feel better, and it did. Instantly. It was something I'd forgotten, but he'd remembered. Bless him. And once I remembered why I needed to have my hands in flour, I remembered how to make the scones.

My mind focused on the flour and the butter and how if

I rubbed the two together with the very tips of my fingers – the tips of my fingertips, if you like – it would turn from flour and chopped up butter into something that looked more like grains of sand. And if I added a shake of cayenne pepper to this mix and some grated cheese and milk and stirred it together with a knife, I'd get a scone dough. And if I took that scone dough and patted it out flat on my benchtop and cut it into rough triangles and then painted those triangles with milk and put them in a hot oven then, in fifteen minutes, I'd have light and fluffy cheese scones. Scones that I made myself from flour, butter, milk and cheese. Four ingredients – okay, five if you count the cayenne pepper – that had the power to change my mood completely.

I'd forgotten how baking can do that, and I'd forgotten just how good that transformation felt. I'd also forgotten how incredibly tasty cheese scones are with a lot of very good butter.

Claire read through the words again, attached a terrible photo of her cheese scones and her tiny and very messy kitchen, and pressed publish before she changed her mind.

Once Claire started baking again, she found she couldn't stop. Every day she'd get up and boil an egg for her breakfast, set off down the lane with Nigel for their walk, and then she'd come home and bake. It would be scones one day, pikelets another, or perhaps a loaf of bread or some rolls if she felt like it.

She'd keep some and take the rest down the lane to Gracie. It wasn't so much about the food as the ritual associated with it – a ritual that had become almost a mattress she could lean back on that would cushion her against any further blows. Following a recipe, a set of instructions, made her feel safe and in control.

As she baked, her spirit healed. Even cleaning the kitchen after her daily bake had become part of the rhythm as had her walk to the farm shop and the weekly trip into Cirencester for supplies.

And she blogged. Sometimes she'd write about the recipe she'd just baked, but other days she'd write about the memories that the baking was bringing up. Some were still too raw and too private to write about, but others brought back happier times.

One day she cooked marmite and cheese spaghetti for her lunch and on impulse took some down for Milo to try.

'He won't like it,' Gracie had said.

'Let him decide, hey?'

Milo plunged his fork into the bowl, looked at it critically, and took a huge bite. As he chewed, a smile lit his little face, and he nodded enthusiastically. 'Aunty Bear, I like!'

'As I suspected,' said Claire, 'a young man of taste.'

'Have you gone into the village yet?' was Gracie's comeback.

She shook her head. 'I'm not ready.'

The only real contact outside the little world Claire had created for herself and Nigel was Barty. He called every couple of days to check in on her. When Claire asked why he hadn't told her Giles had called, he sounded confused.

'I thought I did,' he said. 'He called the day after it hit the papers, and you weren't taking very much in at that point. I could've told you the world was caving in and it wouldn't have registered with you. There was a lot I was dealing with too, so if I didn't tell you he'd called, I apologise.'

Claire didn't even want to think back to the mess she'd been in for those first few days and admitted he was right – he probably had mentioned it, and she hadn't paid attention.

'How was he?' asked Barty.

'He sounded well. He's making steady progress on his book and seems to have settled in.'

'And you two?'

'We talked, and we've decided that we're finished. It was all very amicable, and I'm sad, but my heart isn't broken.'

'I'm pleased to hear it – not that you've broken up, but that you're alright about it. What have you been doing with yourself?'

'Baking mostly. And walking. It's helping.' Claire didn't know why she omitted to tell him about her blog. Even though *Brookford Kitchen Diaries* was out there in the public domain and she was getting more views each day, it was still anonymous. Somehow it felt important to maintain that anonymity – at least for now – to keep it a safe place for her to write. 'I've been thinking though, I'd like to tell my side of the Spooner story. You said you'd consider it – have you?'

'I have, and I don't think it's a good idea. I saw Bruno Belucci the other day, and he was still furious. I asked him what he'd say if it came out that you hadn't written those reviews and he said he'd think it was another lie.' He paused before saying, 'I'm sorry, Claire. They have a name, and that's all they care about. My advice to you would be to let it go.'

When she didn't reply, he said, 'I mean it, darling. Let it go. Find something else to do. If you need money, you can come to me.'

'Thanks, Barty, but financially I'm okay for a while.'

'Right then. Think of this as being a few months off after a ridiculously busy year, and we'll look again at the job situation in a month or so.'

'Last year was pretty mad, wasn't it?' She was desperately trying to turn this enforced break into a good idea rather than something she had no choice in.

'It was, darling. The break will do you a world of good.'

Barty would take her lack of argument as her agreement to his suggestion, but she also couldn't let it go.

•

One unusually blue Wednesday morning, early in February, Tallis was in the garden planting some borders that would hopefully bloom through the spring. A black and white cocker spaniel bounded into her yard and enthusiastically made friends with Cocoa and Bailey – who were, like most Labradors, always ready to make new friends.

Tallis sat back on her heels, taking in the doggy chaos. Claire lingered at the gate, tucking a piece of hair behind her ears as she watched the dogs darting around the garden.

'And that, I assume, is Nigel?' asked Tallis.

Claire nodded. 'I'm sorry to barge in,' she said. 'I know it's been a while, but I was sitting at home writing about pumpkin scones, and I couldn't help thinking about you and Gail and Caro and Fee.' She put her hands into her jeans pockets and hunched her shoulders up to ears in an exaggerated shrug. 'Did you know although scones probably date back to Scotland in the sixteenth century, the pumpkin scone is much more recent than that and was probably invented, if invented is the right word, in Queensland, Australia some four hundred years later?'

Tallis stood slowly, took off her gardening gloves, and smiled a wide and genuinely welcoming smile. 'I didn't know that.'

'Giles told me I should contact the people important to me, tell them the truth and at least then I'd know for sure what they thought of me and that would be better than spending my days wondering.' Claire swallowed once and then again. 'And you and Gail are two of those people,' she said and promptly fell apart.

As the tears flowed freely down her cheeks, Tallis threw the gloves aside and came over to hug her. 'My poor friend,' she said. 'You've been through the wars.' She held Claire until Nigel sneaked in to steal the garden gloves and run off with them.

Gloves retrieved and dogs under control, they sat in Tallis' kitchen drinking tea and eating chocolate chip cookies.

'These are the chocolatiest chocolate cookies I've ever eaten,' said Claire, breaking another one in half to nibble at the fudgy insides.

'I felt like baking them this morning, so I'm glad you dropped in,' Tallis said. 'I don't know who I would've fed them to otherwise. I would've had to eat the whole batch – so you've saved me from myself.'

'Derek isn't home tonight?'

'Hardly,' she scoffed. 'Adam will be though, and teenage boys have appetites that would make you cringe. So,' she said, pouring more tea, 'none of us believe what the papers are saying, so tell me what really happened.'

Claire's eyes welled again as she told her story. At the end of the telling, Tallis was silent for a few seconds. 'Why haven't you told the papers this?'

'I wanted to, but I signed a confidentiality clause. I shouldn't even be telling you any of this. Also, Barty, my manager, doesn't think anyone will believe me.'

'I believed you, but then we already had an inkling nothing was as they said.'

'Even Caro and Fee?' Claire leaned in a little further, eager to hear the answer.

Tallis' voice was gentle. 'Even Caro and Fee. Fee has been at me for weeks to call you and see if you were alright. I tried to call the day after the news hit but couldn't get through. I hoped you were lying low and would call us when you were ready – and here you are.' She smiled encouragingly, hoping Claire saw the support behind it.

'I haven't seen anyone,' Claire smiled wistfully. 'I've started baking and writing again. I'm doing a blog about baking – after all, what else would I write about?'

Tallis grinned at that.

'This morning, I wrote about pumpkin scones, and I thought of you all. How can I write about pumpkin scones without writing about The Cotswold Culinary and Cookbook Society and without using Gail's recipe?'

'Well, obviously, you can't.'

They chatted lightly for an hour, catching up on what everyone was up to. Tallis told Claire about the cruise Caro, and her husband were planning in the spring, Fee's daughter's pregnancy, and the new vet in town that Gail was pretending she wasn't attracted to.

Claire told her things were finished with Giles, but he'd given her the push to bake and write again.

'I'm back in Brookford,' she said. 'I've moved into a cottage on my sister's farm for a few months – it's small but perfect for now.'

'That's not even ten miles away,' said Tallis.

'We're practically neighbours.'

'Do you have any plans to go back to London?'

Claire's eyes dropped to the table. 'Not immediately, maybe not until I decide what's happening on the work front. There's nothing in the pipeline for now.'

'It must be nice being back home again though – in Brookford. Have you seen much of Owen?'

'No.' Claire broke another cookie in half before dividing it into quarters. 'But I saw him when I was down before Christmas – which reminds me, how was your dinner at The Lamb?'

Tallis smiled at the obvious change of subject. 'Gail and I both decided it was probably the best meal we've eaten. Everything was perfect – but also no frills, bells or whistles. Owen brought our desserts out and sat and talked to us as we ate. He's such a lovely man and so good looking.'

Claire's head jerked up.

'We talked about you. He wanted to know if we'd heard from you.' Tallis poured some more tea, risking a side glance at Claire.

'Don't you go looking for anything that's not there.'

Claire warned, her smile softening her words. 'Owen and I were over by the time we were both eighteen. There's nothing there now – no matter what you two might believe. I can't imagine what he thinks of me now.'

Tallis laughed at that. 'Okay, I'll consider myself told, but I still think you should talk to him. I think you'd be surprised at what he has to say about it all.' She lowered her voice. 'He cares about you, Claire.'

'Tallis …'

Tallis held up her hands in mock surrender. 'Okay, I won't say anything more about it. On a different subject, though, we're having this month's club meeting on Saturday. We're cooking from Nigella's *Feast*. Are you in?'

Claire nodded, 'I sure am, and I just so happened to bring my copy of that book from London with me. There are some brownies in there that are better than sex.' She grinned, 'well at least better-than-average sex or even no sex.'

Tallis laughed. 'Perfect. We're meeting here at ten in the morning.' She paused and smiled at Claire. 'The others will be so happy – and relieved to see you. I'll tell them you're on pudding.'

As soon as Tallis waved Claire and Nigel on their way, she rushed back inside and dialled a number. The phone only rang twice before it was picked up. She could hear the noise of a busy kitchen in the background.

'Owen, it's Tallis. I know you're probably in the middle of service, but I thought I'd let you know Claire dropped around today.'

'Okay, can you just hang on a sec while I find somewhere quiet? Angie? Can you run the pass for a couple of minutes? Right, I'm back. How is she?'

'She was putting on a brave face, but she's quite fragile – definitely not the woman who was here in December.'

'She's been through a lot since then,' said Owen. 'Did she tell you what the story was?'

'Yes. She didn't write those reviews, but she did write as Alex Spooner some years ago when she was first starting out. She's anxious about what you think of her.'

Owen was silent for a beat, then two. 'I know. I've seen her sister in town, and she won't tell me anything other than Claire doesn't want to see me. I can understand why she'd be worried, but she'd have to know I couldn't believe that of her?'

Tallis said nothing.

'Wouldn't she?'

'I'm sorry, Owen, I have no idea what went on between the two of you back then, but it was obvious to me that she wouldn't know – until you tell her. Anyway, she's coming here for lunch on Saturday, so I'll check back in with you after.'

'Did she say where she was living?'

Tallis hesitated again. 'She's in a cottage on her sister's farm, but don't go barging in there until after we talk to her on Saturday.' When he didn't respond, she prompted, 'Okay?'

'Okay,' he said. 'But we all need to talk and figure out what we're going to do about this.'

'Agreed. I'll call you on Saturday.'

Tallis hung up and rummaged through the kitchen drawers for a notebook and a pen. Then she began to write. The problem as she saw it wasn't just that Claire wasn't Alex Spooner, it was broader than that.

She drew a line down the middle of the page, and then one across, forming four boxes. In the first, she wrote:

Who knew that Claire used to be The Spoonman?

In the second: who leaked the information?

In the third: who wants The Spoonman to be Claire?

And in the fourth: who is the real Spoonman?

As images and words jumbled in her head, she underlined each sentence. Twice.

Okay, Tallis, think.

Who knew Claire used to be The Spoonman?

Her editor knew.

Giles?

Her manager?

The leaker … or was that leakee?

Did it naturally follow that the person who'd leaked the story knew Claire used to be The Spoonman? Or did they have some other score to settle?

Maybe it was someone unconnected to Claire

who'd been told the secret one drunken night and had held on to it until the information was worth something. Why they leaked it was another question, closely related to the third that Tallis had written down but different again:

To settle a score with Claire.

To embarrass her.

To damage her reputation.

None of these possibilities made sense. Tallis might not have known Claire for long, but she didn't strike her as the kind of woman who'd trodden on others to get to where she was.

Adam and Anna wandered into the kitchen as she stared at the words she'd written, tapping her pen against her forehead.

'What are you doing, Mum?' Adam kissed the top of her head lightly and pulled the notebook to one side. 'Is this about Claire Mansfield?' he asked.

'Yes, I'm trying to make sense of why someone would leak the information.' Tallis pulled the notebook back in front of her.

'Because they want her job,' suggested Anna.

'Because someone knows who the real Spoonman is and that person's identity needs to be protected,' said Adam.

'Because the real Spoonman wants Claire to be blamed,' said Anna.

Tallis feverishly scribbled on her notepad as Adam

and Anna threw suggestions around.

'But if everyone knows it's Claire, it would make it difficult for The Spoonman to write more reviews unless they knew Claire had visited that restaurant,' said Tallis.

'Which would mean it would need to be someone she knew,' said Adam.

Tallis scribbled another point in her notepad. 'She might not have written those reviews, but someone she knows wants the world to think she has.'

Adam nodded, but Anna spoke. 'Nothing else makes sense.'

'It doesn't, does it? Anna, what's your mother doing after work today?'

Anna grinned. 'Coming around here to help you solve a mystery?'

'Right answer.'

CHAPTER TWENTY

The following morning Claire and Nigel did their usual walk down the lane, stopping by the donkeys to say good morning, standing back while the geese were herded into a paddock by children from the neighbouring farm, bending down to take a photo of some snowdrops peeking through the leaves that had fallen a few months ago in autumn.

Dropping in at Gracie's house, Claire handed over the basket she'd been carrying.

'What have we got today?' Gracie asked, peering under the tea towel that Claire had thrown over the basket as protection.

'A focaccia with mushroom and rosemary,' she said. 'Something a bit different, I thought.'

'It smells amazing. You should let me pay you for these, or at least buy some ingredients.'

Claire shook her head. 'Absolutely not. Despite what you've said, you could get more rent for Curlew if you advertised it, so I know you're doing me a favour. Anyway, I need someone to cook for, so you're doing me an extra favour.'

Gracie grinned. 'When you put it like that.' She took the focaccia out of the basket and gave the basket back to Claire.

'I thought Nigel and I might walk into the village this afternoon and pick up a few things,' said Claire.

Gracie turned away, but not before Claire caught a glimpse of her smile.

'That sounds like a good idea. I'm sure Celia in the supermarket would be grateful for your business.'

It seemed strange to be back in the village where she'd grown up. It should've felt different from how it had felt when she was here before Christmas, but it wasn't. Claire's whole life might've changed, but the village hadn't; why would it?

Walking down the high street, she hadn't wanted to run into Owen; she also hadn't wanted to see the disapproving or disappointed looks on the faces of the people who'd watched her grow up and who'd been so proud of her success. Their opinions shouldn't have mattered, but they did. Even though she knew few of them personally, the people of Brookford were her people.

She called in at the general store and bought some flour from Celia and picked up a pork pie from Bob in the butchers. She peered through the window of the deli, impressed with the array of cheeses.

Mrs Smith, who'd run the bookshop for as long as Claire could remember, waved as she flicked through the paperbacks in the racks on the footpath. 'I'd heard you'd come home, dear,' she said, making her way to the open door of her shop.

'Yes, I'm back.'

'You're at Curlew Cottage then? That must be nice with Gracie and her Bill just down the lane. That Milo is as cute as a button.'

'Yes,' Claire agreed, 'it's good to be home.' She checked her watch. 'I'm going to have to run, but I'll come back and see you soon – I need something new to read, but I've already got things to carry home.' She held up the bag of groceries.

Mrs Smith's gaze went across the road to the pub. 'You'll be going in to see Owen then?'

Claire shook her head. 'Maybe next time I'm in town.'

'Don't be leaving it too long,' she said. 'It's good to have you both back home where you belong.' She smiled and went back inside.

Claire and Nigel carried on down the high street, past the market cross and the bakery, stopping only when they reached the banks of the river. When Nigel strained at his leash, no longer happy to sit and watch the ducks swimming under the old arched stone bridge, Claire pulled on the lead firmly, and they walked across the bridge and up the slight hill to where the church stood.

Brookford's church was like many in this part of The Cotswolds: a wool church, built on the back of fortunes made from the wool and woollen mill trades. Begun in Norman times, the spire dated from the sixteenth century, and the inside had been extensively renovated in the late 1800s. That wasn't what she'd come to see though. Even though she hadn't been here for a few years, she knew exactly where she was headed and found the headstone quickly, away from other graves, under a yew tree.

Mona Gallagher

Keith's wife

Owen's mother

Much loved, always missed

Claire smiled ruefully. She was always going to end up here today. She squatted down and gently brushed the headstone, clearing away some moss that had grown. In those months between Owen leaving town and her going to London, Claire had come here regularly. She'd made a point in the years since of visiting Owen's mother every time she was back in Brookford.

'Hi, Mrs G,' she said. 'I'm sorry it's taken me such a long time to come and see you again.' She sat cross-legged on the ground in front of the headstone, Nigel immediately flopping beside her. 'There's been a lot happening, and I've been, well, I haven't wanted to see anyone. But enough about me; I saw Owen before Christmas. He's a chef now, and he's doing so well – he's probably been up to see you and fill you in. Anyway, I'm sure you'd be so proud of him. You know, we both thought of you when we had this amazing sponge cake – it was almost, but not quite as good as yours.' She exhaled, a tear tracking its way down her face. 'I think about those days a lot – when we were young and fearless, knowing nothing could touch us. It seems so long ago.'

Beside her Nigel had risen to his feet and barked; the bark followed, as it often did with Nigel, a tentative wag of the tail.

'I think about those days too.'

His voice sent a rush of heat to her cheeks, embarrassed at being caught talking to his mother's headstone. Or was the heat nothing to do with embarrassment?

'Owen. Um, I didn't expect to see you here.' She swiped at her eyes and untucked her legs, losing her balance as she tried to stand. Owen's hand was there to steady her, but she ignored it. Ducking her head to hide the heat spreading across her cheeks, she brushed her hands at the back of her jeans.

'I saw you walk past, and I hoped you might call in,' he said. Claire lifted her head to meet the question in his tone. He went on, 'But when I saw you weren't stopping, I wondered if you'd come here.' He paused and met her gaze with a crooked smile that had both dimples showing. 'I gave up waiting for you to come to me.' He bent down to ruffle Nigel's head. 'What's your name, fella?'

'It's Nigel.'

'And he can speak too?' He grinned at Claire. 'Please tell me he's not named after Nigel Slater.'

'I won't tell you that, but let's just say if Nigel were a girl, he'd be Nigella.'

He tilted his head back and laughed. 'Too funny, Dells.' He shrugged his shoulders against the cold, shoving his hands deep into the pockets of his jeans. 'Do you come here often?' he asked.

Claire's raised her eyebrows at his absurd question and again as a flush crept across his cheeks.

'Oh man, that came out wrong!'

She nodded, her smile wry.

'I meant to ask, do you often visit – Mum, I mean?'

'I used to come up here every time I came home – it's been a while though.' She rubbed at the back of her head and rearranged her scarf. 'It must've looked so weird, me sitting here talking to her.'

'Not at all,' he said. 'I did the same last time I was here.' He bit at his top lip and bent to brush away some non-existent dirt on top of the stone. 'It was the day the news about you broke.'

Claire hoped he didn't hear the gasp she attempted to muffle behind her hand.

'I had to get out of the kitchen, and I came here. I hadn't been, not since I left town, but something brought me up here.' He straightened and faced her. 'I was so angry with you.' He scraped the dirt with the toe of his shoe before raising his eyes to hers. 'I remember when that review first came out, the one on *Belucci's*, I was furious then – with Spooner, with Belucci, and with Julia for walking out; but none of it compared to how I felt when I heard that news before Christmas. It felt like I'd been punched.' He kicked at a tussock of grass.

Claire swallowed hard, and although every nerve in her body was screaming at her to run, she didn't move.

'I didn't know how you could do that to me, after what we'd been to each other.' His short laugh sounded more like a snort of derision. 'Even by the normal standards of revenge, it had been a good one – you'd broken my heart when I was eighteen and then came back to finish the job.'

'I—'

'Let me finish, please, Claire.'

She nodded once, her throat full.

'That day in Fenwyck, you'd smiled at me when you saw me; god, I'd even felt your hand tremble when I'd been a pratt and hadn't been able to resist touching you. I'd believed you when you said you hadn't cheated on me, and I trusted you'd tell me the whole story one day, and yet all the time, you'd written that review.'

Claire pinched hard on the webbing between her thumb and forefinger, willing the hot tears that were burning behind her eyes to stay where they were.

'So, I came up here. I don't know why – maybe I wanted a sign. It was cold and raining, and I hadn't even stopped to get a jacket. I closed my eyes, and I saw you on the day we buried Mum.' Owen's eyes were full, and he didn't stop the single tear that escaped. 'You held onto me so tightly, and you promised me you wouldn't hurt me, and you wouldn't leave me. Do you remember?'

She nodded, unable to speak, her tears falling as the memory carried her back to that awful day.

'But I left you when I thought you'd broken that promise. When I opened my eyes again, a shower of drips fell on me from that branch.' He pointed to the limb of the tree, 'and it was like Mum was there, and she was telling me to calm down and think things through. That's when I reminded myself that I'd believed the worst of you for so many years because I hadn't stopped to consider there could be another explanation for what I'd seen that day in Cirencester. You'd kept your promise to me, but I hadn't kept mine to you. I knew in my heart you couldn't have written that review about me and yet here I was doing exactly what I'd done all those years ago.' His breath hitched. 'I was judging you.'

Claire's eyes widened at his admission.

'It wasn't until I got back to the restaurant and went upstairs to change that I realised what had been nagging at me – somebody had directed that review at me personally, yet you had no idea I'd become a chef.'

Owen's intense scrutiny caused her legs to give way. Reluctantly, she grabbed at his arm to steady. He slid his arm around her waist and guided her the few paces to a bench seat and gently lowered her. They sat side by side, their shoulders brushing. Nigel followed them and placed his head on her knee and looked up with his liquid black eyes.

'What if I'd lied?'

'Oh, Della, you've never been a good liar – I wish I'd remembered that all those years ago – and you had no reason to lie to me when we talked that last morning in Fenwyck. There was no likelihood the secret would ever come out. I was totally convinced when you said you didn't know I was in London, so how then could you have written something like, and I'll quote, "Bruno Belucci has taken a gamble with trusting relatively unknown Owen Gallagher with his flagship. It's a gamble that has backfired in a spectacular way." You didn't write that, Della.'

She shook her head. 'No, I didn't. I'm not entirely innocent, though; I was Alex Spooner for a time – when I first started at the paper.'

'Tallis told me.'

'I see.'

'Yes, because she cares about you and she knows that I do too.'

Claire averted her eyes from his gaze.

'Was that one of the jobs you told me you'd done

that you weren't proud of?' he asked.

'Yes. I hated it – but I was I prepared to do whatever I needed to do to get to my by-line, and it worked. When I started writing my regular column, I had a good reason to stop being The Spoonman.'

'Do you know who did it after you?'

'No. I have no idea.'

'How then—' Owen pulled his phone from the pocket on his chef's coat, looked at the screen and grimaced, 'I'm sorry, Della, I have to take this.'

Claire nodded and watched as he stood and paced; the phone pressed to his ear.

'Is it that time already? Sorry Angie, I completely forgot he was dropping by. Make him coffee, and I'll be there in ten minutes. Thanks.'

Claire stood too and slipped the bag of groceries and Nigel's lead into her hand. 'We'd better be getting back too,' she said. 'It'll be dark before I know it.'

'I'll walk with you as far as *The Lamb*,' Owen said. 'You're what, a couple of miles out of town? A cottage on your sister's farm?'

'How did you know where I was living? Gracie said she hadn't told you.'

'She didn't. She kept your secret. Tallis, however, didn't. When I saw her and Gail before Christmas, I asked them to let me know if they'd heard from you, and Tallis phoned me after you'd been to see her yesterday.' He grinned again. 'Don't look at me like that. All she told me was that you were living on a cottage at Gracie's farm. As for where that was, well, this is a small village.'

'It certainly is.'

When they arrived at *The Lamb*, Owen took her arm and brushed a kiss on her cheek.

'Are you going to be okay walking the rest of the way?'

'I'll be fine. Nigel and I walk a lot.'

'If you're sure?' He ruffled the dog's head.

'I am, but thank you.'

'I'll see you round, Della.'

'You will.' Claire had no idea what made her do it, but when he turned to head inside, she stopped him. 'Drop around sometime,' she said. 'If you want to, of course. I'll bake something. I bake a lot these days.' She lowered her eyes, heat in her face.

'I might just do that,' he said.

When their eyes met, his grin was wide, and she smiled back. Then, with a wave, he turned and strode through the door of *The Lamb*. She watched him until someone bumped into her with a muffled apology.

Shaking her head at her impulsive invitation, she said to Nigel, 'Come on, fella, let's see if we can't get home while there's still light to see our way.'

Despite what Tallis had said, Claire still had some concerns about her reception from Fee, Caro and Gail, but needn't have worried as the members of The

Cotswold Culinary and Cookbook Society all greeted her warmly. Tallis had already updated them with Claire's side of the story and they each hurried to tell her they hadn't believed what had been reported.

'I said to Fee there would be something else behind it.' Caro said.

Fee continued, 'There's no way you could've written those awful reviews like they said you did. We all agreed on that. We've just been waiting for you to come back to us so we could tell you so.'

At Fee's words, tears of gratitude pooled behind Claire's eyes. Unable to speak, she gripped Fee's and Caro's hands in a show of thanks.

'Owen said there had to be more to the story,' said Gail.

Claire tried to ignore the way her heartbeat reacted to Owen's name.

'The night we had dinner at The Lamb,' Gail related, 'the story had broken only a few days before. We'd tried contacting you but couldn't. He'd called your manager and left messages but hadn't heard anything.'

'Barty had my phone and wasn't even listening to the messages. He said he deleted anything from numbers he didn't recognise.' Claire unpacked her bag of groceries but didn't miss Tallis, Fee and Gail exchange glances across the kitchen.

'What did Owen say?' asked Claire.

'He said he didn't believe the story – that there

were inconsistencies in what was being reported. He also said when the two of you talked, you told him you didn't even know he'd been working in London until you googled him,' said Gail.

'It's true; I didn't know. When Ed told me we had Owen Gallagher as a guest judge, I wondered whether there could be a coincidence – the Owen I used to know could burn toast.'

'That's what he said,' said Gail, whose grin was the same as the one on Tallis' and Fee's face. 'He said there was no way you could've written it – and he was very adamant about that.'

Caro finally picked up on it too. 'Do I sense a romantic involvement?'

'No,' said Claire. 'We dated when we were kids – that's all. These two,' she pointed to Tallis and Gail, 'are just trying to do some matchmaking and need to leave it alone.' Claire raised her eyebrows at them, and Gail adopted a "who me?" face. 'And you're just as bad.' She directed a mock glare at Fee.

'Seriously though,' said Tallis, 'as I said the other day, you need to speak to him.'

'After all,' said Caro, 'we hardly know you, but we all trusted you.'

Another lump rose in Claire's throat, and she struggled to speak. 'And I'm so grateful for that. I've spoken to him – yesterday – and all of this chat isn't getting anything cooked. What's on our menu today?

I'm doing the snow-flecked brownies.'

'Whoa,' said Tallis. 'Hold up there. You spoke to him yesterday?'

'I went into Brookford yesterday afternoon and ran into him.'

'And?' prompted Gail.

'And that's what he said to me – what he'd told you.' She smirked. 'That's all. He's okay, I'm more relieved than I can say, and now I just want to forget all about it for a few hours and cook some yummy food.'

Tallis watched her closely for a few seconds and then nodded slowly. 'Fair enough. I know Gail is doing a mushroom and pasta bake and I'm doing these fiddly stuffed potato patties – with a green Fattoush salad if I get time. By the way, I told the others about your blog, Claire, and we all think it's fantastic.'

'I love the blog,' said Gail.

'Are you going to blog our club meeting today?' asked Fee. 'Oh, and I'm doing Massacre in A Snowstorm.'

'I thought I might if it's alright with you all,' said Claire. 'I won't show any photos of us, and I'll use our first names only. And what's that about a massacre?'

'It's meringues and cream and pomegranates.' Fee had a wicked grin on her face. 'When you see it, you'll know what I'm talking about. What about you, Caro?'

'I think blogging our club meetings is a great idea.'

'And what are you cooking?' asked Gail.

'Some lamb meatballs and couscous.'

After they all finished eating and then tidied the kitchen, the five women sat and talked until well into the afternoon. Caro and Fee were the first to leave.

'Next month we're going to France with Rick Stein,' said Fee as she made her way to the door.

'I'll look forward to that,' said Claire with a grin. 'Spring in France is always a good idea, and it's not every day you get to travel there with Rick.'

Once they'd gone, Tallis put the kettle back on. 'Sit down, Claire,' she said. 'There's something Gail and I would like to talk to you about.'

'It sounds serious.' Claire forced a grin, but inside a brief tremor of fear flipped her tummy.

'It's nothing to worry about,' said Gail. 'We've been thinking about how we can help sort this mess out for you.'

'Guys, I appreciate the thought, but—'

'No buts, Claire,' said Gail. 'I hear what you said about respecting your manager's opinion, but I think he's wrong. So does Tallis. People would believe you – Owen did, and he has more reasons to want someone to blame than most other people. Secondly, while the real Spooner is out there, nothing is stopping him—'

'Or her.' Claire reminded them.

'Or her,' said Gail with a grin, 'from publishing more reviews.'

'It should be easy enough to prove it wasn't you

– all we need to do is show you haven't eaten at all the restaurants The Spoonman has reviewed,' Tallis said.

Claire pondered that for a few seconds. 'I wouldn't know – but then I haven't read all the reviews so can't say for sure.' She smiled and then laughed as another thought occurred to her. 'Although I've often said I'm not entirely convinced The Spoonman has eaten at all the restaurants he—'

'Or she,' interjected Gail.

'Or she,' Claire smiled at the correction, 'has written reviews for.'

Tallis wrote something in her notebook. 'Okay, who else could know about you being Alex Spooner once upon a time?'

'I've thought this through, and Giles is the only person I've ever told – and that was after I'd stopped being The Spoonman. I half wondered whether it was him who'd leaked to the press, but he said he'd always kept my secret. I should've known better – journalists never reveal their sources, and ours wasn't a bad break-up, as far as break-ups go. Duncan, my editor, knew, but I couldn't say for sure he wouldn't tell anyone.'

'Were you living with anyone else when you were writing as Spooner?' Gail asked.

'I was sharing with two other girls and Barty back then, and neither Martha nor Freya would've had any idea, and they live in New Zealand now. It horrified Barty when I told him – and that was only after the news had broken. No, it hasn't come from any of them.'

'Hmm.' Tallis looked at the notes she'd made. 'Let's take the last two reviews – *Bella Donna* and *Lily James*. I know you ate at *Lily James*, but what about *Bella Donna*?'

'Yes, I've eaten at both. I was at *Lily James* on the night Giles and I broke up – not that we actually broke up on that night, but we might as well have done. As for *Bella Donna*? Aside from the fact that Bruno Belucci is an arrogant so and so who thinks he's god's gift to chefdom, he deserved a bad review for *Bella Donna*, just not a Spoonman review – no one deserves one of those.'

'You don't like him?' asked Gail. 'I always thought he came across as looking all suave and Italian when I've seen him on TV, a little aloof and brooding perhaps, but that's also sort of attractive.' She added the last with a blush.

Claire raised her eyebrows. 'You're welcome to him. I can't stand the man. It's not just what he did to Owen; he also made a pass at me once – and got angry when I said no. Apparently, he was in the running to be my co-host on this new show that isn't happening anymore. I'm not glad about the show being canned, but I am thankful that Bruno would never work with me after this. It surprised me he wanted to in the first place.'

Gail and Tallis exchanged glances. 'I wouldn't be too vocal about that if I were you,' said Gail.

'No,' agreed Tallis. 'What you just said then could easily be construed as a motive.'

'You're right. I hadn't thought about it that way.'

'Maybe we need to think on this a bit more,' said Tallis, closing her notepad and resting her pen on top.

'Anyway,' Claire said, getting to her feet and whistling for Nigel, 'I'd better be getting back to Brookford. Thanks for caring and please let me know if you come up with anything else.'

'We certainly will,' said Tallis. 'I know this is supposed to be about you, but I enjoy playing a detective, and I don't exactly have a lot on my plate at the moment.'

'The Cotswolds Culinary and Cookbook Society and Detective Agency,' quipped Gail.

'On that note, I'm definitely leaving,' Claire said with a laugh.

As Claire drove home, she mused at Tallis' and Gail's investigative efforts. They meant well, but Claire feared this mystery was one that wouldn't be easily solved.

CHAPTER TWENTY-ONE

Tallis smiled as she applied her makeup. It had been too long since the three of them had been out for Sunday lunch together. All too often if Derek was home, Adam was not; and if Adam was out, she and Derek would eat out at a large country hotel – even though Tallis would've preferred a village pub. She'd say something like, 'why can't we eat at *The Pheasant* in Fenwyck, or *The Angel* in Burford, or even *The Snooty Fox* in Tetbury? It doesn't have to be somewhere posh, does it?'

'I want to show you off,' he'd say.

It wasn't her he wanted to show off, rather he wanted to be seen in these places.

So out they'd go, to some village where there were more antique shops than there were permanent residents. They'd sit in a smart hotel restaurant where Derek would speak a little too loudly, where he'd make too big a deal of buying her expensive wine, following which he'd wonder aloud what each of the other patrons did for a living and whether they had second homes in the village and lived in London, while Tallis sat there feeling uncomfortable and as if she didn't belong.

This weekend things had been different. Derek had another client dinner that had kept him in Bristol until Saturday morning and upon arriving home had gone straight to his Saturday golf game while Tallis and the other members of the cookbook club prepared lunch. None of that was unusual.

What *had* been unusual was that he'd come home from golf and wanted to eat dinner in and then watch a movie – her choice. What had been even more unusual was that after they finished watching the movie, he'd wanted to make love. Tallis couldn't remember when that had last happened. With Derek spending most of his time in Bristol, neither he nor Tallis were used to sharing a bed, so when he was home, Derek had taken to sleeping in the guest room – something that suited Tallis.

When Derek had first begun staying in Bristol, she thought she'd miss him more than she did – she thought she'd miss sex more than she did – but as a month turned into two months and then three and then became a year, she'd found she barely even thought about it anymore, let alone missed it. Even so, the lovemaking had been nice. It had also been nice going to sleep afterwards with his body beside her. Nicer still was when she woke during the night to find he'd moved back to the guest room.

The nice feeling had persisted this morning when he offered to make her a cup of tea, and then he announced he'd made a booking for them all to go for lunch.

'I was going over to Anna's though,' said Adam, a surly look on his face.

It was a look she saw too often when Derek was home, and hardly at all when he wasn't. It was almost enough to mar the feeling of niceness that Tallis was trying to hold onto, so she ignored it.

'I think your mother would like it if we all went out together,' said Derek, smiling across the breakfast table at her.

'I would,' she said. 'It's been such a long time since we did.'

Adam searched her face and then nodded reluctantly. 'Okay, Mum, if it would make you happy. I'll let Anna know.'

'Thank you, darling,' she said. Then asked Derek, 'Where have you booked?'

'*The Lamb* in Brookford. I thought I'd see what all the fuss is about.'

Tallis smiled, although inwardly she cringed. Derek might be her husband, but that didn't mean she was blind to his faults – even if there were times she pretended to be. When he showed off in front of people she didn't know, it no longer mattered, but when he played the big man in front of people she liked and respected, it was harder to hide her embarrassment. And while she didn't know him well, she knew enough of Owen to know she both liked and respected him.

'Earth to Tallis.' Derek clicked his fingers in front of her eyes.

'That sounds nice,' she said. 'Although I'm happy to cook a roast at home too.'

'No,' said Derek. 'You deserve to be spoilt.'

She applied her lipstick and declared herself ready to enjoy the meal out with her family. Derek was Derek, and she loved him, and was sure somewhere underneath the designer leisurewear was still the lad she'd fallen for all those years ago.

'I'm glad I booked,' said Derek when they walked into *The Lamb*. 'There isn't a spare table in here.'

The waiter directed them to their table and announced the Sunday menu was limited – just two choices and a vegetarian option for starters, with either of two roasts, fish or roasted cauliflower for mains, and either crumble or sticky date for pudding.

'This is a different menu to the one you had when you came here,' Derek grumbled after the waiter took their drink orders.

'It's Sunday lunch,' Tallis reminded him. 'I'm trying to decide between the beef and the lamb – although,' she said watching meals being placed in front of the other diners, 'just give me a plate of those Yorkshire puddings and some gravy and I'll be a happy woman.'

As fabulous as the "Yorkies" were, Tallis was even happier that Derek had found nothing to fault with his meal. And Adam, who tended not to say a lot when at the table with Derek, was unusually talkative and full of discussions about courses he was interested in applying for when he finished school later in the year.

'I'm leaning towards law,' he said, 'so that means London—'

'What's wrong with Bristol University?' asked Derek. 'You can flat with me. It'll be like two lads hanging out.'

Derek slapped Adam on the back, and he cringed.

'I want to specialise in human rights law, and London's the best place for that,' said Adam.

'Is there any money in that?' Derek frowned. 'Isn't that just about do-gooders defending lost causes?'

Adam's face turned from excitement to annoyance.

'Where is Anna looking to study?' asked Tallis, steering the conversation.

'She hasn't decided,' he said. 'She's thinking about graphic design or maybe literature or—'

Tallis frowned at Derek's snort, but Owen's arrival at the table saved her from having to make a response.

'Tallis,' he said, leaning down to kiss her cheek. 'Marty recognised you from when you were here before Christmas.' He nodded toward the waiter who had served them. 'It's good to see you. And you too, Adam.' He shook Adam's hand.

Tallis returned his warm smile. 'Owen, this is my husband, Derek.'

'Pleased to meet you.' Owen reached across the table to shake Derek's hand.

'You too,' said Derek. 'It's a nice place you've got yourself here.'

'Thanks. I hope you enjoyed your lunch.'

'We did,' said Adam. 'Those Yorkies were next level.'

'I'm pleased to hear it.' Owen said grinning, then turned to Tallis. 'How was lunch yesterday?'

'Great. The food was fabulous as always and the company even better.' She paused briefly, 'Claire mentioned she saw you the other day.'

He looked away momentarily, but not before a smile crossed his face. 'Yes, we talked. She said I could call in any time, so I think I might drop by after service today.'

Tallis pinched her lips together to hide her smile. 'I think that would be a lovely idea,' she said.

'Well, I'd better be getting back, but thanks for coming in and good to meet you, Derek.' He kissed Tallis' cheek again and went back into the kitchen, stopping to greet the diners on some other tables.

Tallis brought her attention back to her family; Derek was staring with his mouth open, and Adam was grinning. 'I didn't know you knew him that well, Mum,' he said.

'My sponge cake made quite the impression.'

'It must have done,' said Derek, who didn't look at all pleased at this turn of events.

Tallis wasn't surprised. He was used to her sitting back while he was the centre of attention.

'And the Claire you mentioned? Was that the woman from the TV?'

'Yes, she was over for lunch yesterday with the others.'

'You all seem very pally.' He forced a smile.

'I suppose that we are.'

He raised his eyebrows but said nothing more, and Tallis guided the conversation into a discussion about what everyone's movements were for the week.

More than once on the short drive home, Derek flicked his eyes from the road to her. Tallis smiled inwardly at the thought of him trying to rationalise the picture of his stay-at-home wife with the woman who casually had celebrities as friends.

Once at home, Adam changed his clothes and rushed straight back out again on his bike. 'Off to Anna's,' he called. 'I'll see you later.'

'Are you going to say goodbye to your father? He won't be here when you get back.'

'Sorry, Dad, see you next weekend.'

And then he was off, and they were alone.

'I don't have to go back tonight,' Derek said. 'Not if you don't want me to.'

Tallis attempted to hide her surprise. 'It's up to you. I know you like to avoid the Monday morning commute. Let me know if you decide to stay though, and I'll cook something for supper.'

'Whatever you're having will be fine with me,' he said.

Tallis widened her eyes in surprise; it wasn't like him to be so agreeable. 'I normally have a bowl of soup or a toastie,' she said, 'but I'm happy to prepare something for you.'

He opened his mouth to say something more when his phone rang. Fishing it out of his pocket, he glanced at the screen. 'I have to take this,' he said.

Tallis watched as he slid open the back door and went into the garden, his phone pressed against his ear, pushing Cocoa away when he would have jumped against him. She shrugged and walked into the laundry to sort through the washing piled high on the bench. She rubbed at her arms against the chill and slid the window shut, but hesitated when Derek's voice filtered into the room. Not wanting him to think she was eavesdropping, she moved back out of sight and pressed against the wall so he wouldn't be able to see her if he turned around.

'Sweetheart, I'm sorry we argued yesterday morning too.'

'Of course, I haven't changed my mind, but we have to—'

'I understand,' he said. 'But you were the one who said it was over.'

'No, she has no idea, I've made sure of that this weekend.'

Tallis' hand flew to her mouth to catch the gasp that would've escaped otherwise. Unable to move, she stayed rooted in position, her heart beating loudly against the hand pressed to her chest.

'I miss you too,' he said.

Derek's voice grew fainter until all she could hear was the pounding in her ears. Letting out the breath she'd held for too long, she slid down the wall until she sat crumpled on the floor, then pressed her hands into her face. There it was – the proof of what she'd often suspected but hadn't wanted to acknowledge.

What to do, what to do. Think Tallis. Oh god, Adam. Adam couldn't know. She couldn't do anything that would affect Adam's study. It was too important he got into university, and she would not have Derek jeopardise that. No, nothing could get in the way of that. She dragged in a shaky breath and gripped her hands to stop them from trembling.

The front door slammed shut, and Derek called for her. He couldn't find her here; he'd know she'd heard him and that she knew. She whipped around the corner into the powder room and flushed the toilet.

'Sorry,' she said as she walked back into the kitchen. 'Did you want me for anything?'

'Yes.' He turned away and clicked open his briefcase. 'I'm sorry, darling, but I have to get back tonight. I'd forgotten I have an early meeting tomorrow and I can't risk getting stuck in traffic.'

Tallis forced a look of disappointment as he turned back and smiled. If she hadn't heard what she had, she would've believed him. 'That's okay. Maybe next weekend you can get home on Friday, and we can spend a little longer together.'

He kissed her lips quickly. 'I'd rather stay here with you now.'

'I know you would,' she lied.

When he left an hour later, she kissed him goodbye and told him to drive carefully, and that she'd see him next weekend. Back into the kitchen, she picked up his coffee mug and regarded it for a few seconds before hurling it into the floor. As it shattered into hundreds of pieces, so did her soul. All she wanted to do was cry, but the tears wouldn't come.

In her heart, Tallis knew her marriage was over; it had been over for some time, but Derek had been so attentive this weekend, allowing her to hope they could find a way back. Knowing that he'd slept with her only because she, whoever *she* was, had broken it off – whatever *it* was – and he probably thought he might need to ensure she, Tallis, was still there for him as his Plan B, there was no way back.

She'd suspected Derek had, from time to time, been unfaithful over the years. She'd never known for sure, and that suited her. If it was just a suspicion, she didn't need to do anything or say anything. If it was just a suspicion, things could continue as they always had.

Other people suspected too. On more than a few occasions, Gail lowered her eyes or looked away when she'd mentioned that Derek was working late, or couldn't come home until Saturday, or had a business trip that didn't involve her. And Caro had sent a warning look to Fee one time when Fee would've said something, but Tallis had pretended she hadn't noticed. If she noticed she'd have to acknowledge Derek's infidelity, and if she acknowledged it, it made it real and something that required a solution.

But who could it be? Derek's type were flashy blondes who wore super-high heels and squeezed into those tight-fitting dresses that showed off their assets – all of them. It would have to be someone younger – much younger than Derek's forty-five. As she cleaned up the broken china, she racked her brains. In cases like this, it would typically be the assistant or the secretary. Rosemary, Derek's assistant – although she was more of a business manager – had been working for him for as long as he'd had the business. As lovely as she was, Rosemary was too comfortably built for Derek to see her as anything other than part of the furniture. Plus, she'd been to school with him so was outside the age bracket Tallis was considering.

There was that newish receptionist … What was her name? Shelby? She was blonde and slim and giggly. Tallis emptied the dustpan with the broken mug into the bin. It could be her, but what on earth would a woman like that see in a man like Derek? She straightened and scratched idly at the back of her head. Who was she kidding? It could be someone she'd never met: a business associate, a sales rep from one of his suppliers, a client, the wife of a client, a woman he'd met at the golf club. It could be anyone.

Tallis sat back onto a chair at the counter in her empty kitchen in her empty house. She got up again and let the dogs in. They jumped around her in joy for a few seconds before running around sniffing at what might have changed in the few hours since they were last here.

It didn't matter who the other woman was; for Adam's sake, she'd grit her teeth and paste on a smile and would let this one run its course the way the ones before had run. The alternative was to confront Derek and risk everything – and she didn't want that. She had no money of her own and after being out of the workforce for so long, no means of earning any. No, she'd carry on as normal, she had to – for both her and Adam's sake – at least until Adam finished school. In the meantime, there was another puzzle she could try to solve.

Tallis pulled out a notebook and her laptop and begun searching for The Spoonman's reviews. She noted the name of the restaurant, the name of the chef and the date the review had been published. If there was a pattern there, Tallis intended to find it.

CHAPTER TWENTY-TWO

Claire had just pulled a tray of pumpkin scones out of the oven when there was a knock at the cottage door. Nigel went from flop dog to watchdog almost immediately. She wiped away the condensation filmed over the kitchen window. There was a car parked next to hers she didn't recognise.

Given that Gracie usually knocked once and then walked straight in, Claire opened the door with some trepidation, automatically brushing the flour away from the front of her jumper.

Standing on the step with his hands in his pockets and hunched in against the wind was Owen.

The corner of his mouth turned up slightly and he cleared his throat. 'You did say I could drop by,' he said, bending down to ruffle Nigel's head.

'I did, didn't I?'

Owen and his dimples standing at her door sent the butterflies in her tummy free-flying through her body.

He shrugged his shoulders and shivered. 'Are you going to let me in to get warm or do you want to have this conversation out here in the cold? I'm fine either way, but I'd just like to know whether I need to get another jacket from the car.' His smile was wide and disarming.

'You'd better come in.' Claire held the door open.

He wiped his boots on the mat and stepped into the cottage. Instantly, the already cosy room felt smaller.

Owen sniffed the air and then turned with a grin. 'It smells as though I've timed this visit perfectly. Scones?'

'Yes, Gail's pumpkin ones. Tea? Or would you prefer coffee?'

'Tea is fine, thanks.' He walked across to the fire and picked up another log. 'Do you want me to stoke this?'

'Yes, if you wouldn't mind.' She turned away and grimaced at the lameness of the conversation.

'It's a cute little place.'

'Thanks. I like it, and you've pretty much seen all of it. There are two bedrooms beyond that door and a bathroom off the kitchen, and that's it. It's a bit confusing too – the front door comes in from the back and straight into the kitchen, and the back door between the two bedrooms, opens up into the kitchen garden which is sort of at the front.' She was rambling –anything to make this feel even a little bit normal.

'Are you here for a while?' he asked as he poked at the coals with a fire iron.

'I'm not sure yet. It depends …'

'On when you go back to work?' he said, turning around to face her.

She nodded. 'Amongst other things.'

Claire poured the tea and placed the scones on a plate, motioning for him to sit at the table.

He took a scone, buttered it and managed to place half of it in his mouth, closing his eyes to savour the spice. 'This is good.' He sipped his tea. 'I saw Tallis earlier. She came into *The Lamb* for lunch with her family.'

'Oh, really? I've met Adam, but I've never met her husband – what's he like?'

Owen hesitated, chewing thoughtfully on the other half of his scone.

'He's just that type, you know? Come from nothing, done well and now wants to make sure everyone knows it.' He grinned as he cut another scone in half, the food loosening his tongue. 'He seemed put out when I kissed Tallis hello. I got the impression he likes to have Tallis where she belongs – either at home or looking nice on his arm. I think he's the one who likes to be noticed and having me treat her as a friend threw him a bit.'

'Hmm, I wondered if it might be something like that. There were a couple of times yesterday when his name came up, and Gail raised her eyebrows at Fee – I don't think Tallis noticed, but I did. I wouldn't be surprised if the others aren't convinced all of his business dinners are actually business related.'

'You haven't asked them?'

Claire shook her head. 'I don't know them well enough yet, and if Tallis doesn't want to talk about it, well, I'm sure she has her reasons.'

'And what about the subject you've been avoiding?' His gaze was intense.

Claire was sure he was going to bring up the conversation they'd had in Fenwyck. She forced her eyes away from his and concentrated on buttering another scone.

'The one where you tell me why you haven't phoned Ed Wilson back yet,' he said.

'Ed?'

'You seem surprised; what did you think I was going to talk about?'

'It doesn't matter. I haven't had a call from Ed to return.'

It was his turn to look confused. 'But he called you – he told me so. He said you didn't pick up, so he left some messages. He's another one who cares about you and who doesn't want to believe what he's heard.'

'After the story broke, I went and stayed at Barty's for a few days. I gave him my phone and I think he deleted everything that came through. If Ed called, I didn't know about it.'

'That explains it then. Ed sounded worried for you.'

She shrugged. 'He hasn't tried to get in touch with me since.'

'That surprises me,' said Owen. 'Once I told him

what I suspected – that I thought they'd sold you out – he was furious on your behalf.' He picked up another scone and layered on the butter. 'These are excellent. You should call him Dells – he's looking for any reason to believe you. Call your editor, too. You need to find out who's done this to you.'

Claire gave a short laugh. 'You're as bad as Gail and Tallis. They didn't say as much, but I got the impression they think it's personal.'

'I have no doubt they're right. I think it's personal too. I just don't know who or why – and as much as we can try to figure it out, we need your help for that.'

'Don't tell me they've roped you into their little investigation?'

'Absolutely.' His gaze softened. 'Della, they care about you, I care about you. Let us help you.'

As Claire searched his eyes, the same stirrings she'd felt that day in Fenwyck returned. He said he cared, but it was the caring that comes from a historic friendship rather than anything romantic – on his side at least.

She brushed at her eyes, and he placed his hand over hers.

'There's a way back from this that'll make you even more popular than you were before,' said Owen.

'I've seen the other side of the celebrity thing now, and I don't know if I could do it again.'

'You could – *especially* now you've seen the other side.'

Claire pulled her hand out from under his and stood to reboil the kettle.

'Ed's approached me about something new,' he said. 'Something that would mean we'd be working together.'

'Don't be ridiculous, Owen. You're a chef; I'm a home cook – we couldn't be further apart.'

'Hear me out, Della.'

She turned back to face him, frowning. 'Hang on, is he talking to you about that project where we each cook the same meal or ingredient from a different angle?'

He nodded.

'*Posh or Not* I was calling it.'

'That's what he's calling it too.'

'I thought they'd shelved the idea.'

He lifted one shoulder. 'Ed mentioned they had problems finding you a co-host.'

'Yes. Can you believe they were looking at Bruno Belucci? As if I could work with him.'

Claire didn't miss the little smile that played around Owen's face.

'When did they approach you?' asked Claire.

'Almost straight after we finished filming at Fenwyck.'

'Interesting.'

He laughed at the look on her face.

'What's so funny?'

'You are Della. You're wondering how to ask me

if I'm sure they're still interested now they've dropped you.'

She wrinkled her nose as she thought of an appropriate response.

'The answer is that I am sure they're still interested – and I was talking to Ed on Friday. He still wants you Dells.'

'I don't think so,' she said.

'He does. I got the impression he's prepared to wait until you're ready.'

She was shaking her head before he'd even finished the sentence. 'No Owen, not after what happened on *Celebrity Cook-off*. Please don't talk any more about it.'

'But I think—'

'No. I mean it – I really don't want to talk about it.'

He nodded slowly. 'Okay. But do two things for me?'

'It depends on what they are.'

He grinned. 'Let me cook you lunch one day this week …'

She smiled back at him. 'Given that Gail and Tallis were telling me it was possibly the best meal of their lives, how can I say no to that? And the other?'

'Call Ed. Please.'

'I don't know …'

'Della, there are more people than you'd expect who want to believe in you, and the longer you stay silent, the harder it'll be for you.'

'But Barty said—'

'You said that Barty's an old friend and your manager?'

'Yes, we shared a house for a few years.'

Owen's eyebrows shot up.

'Not like that. Just housemates.'

'Okay, he'd have a vested interest in looking after you. What did he say?'

'He said that people were so relieved to have identified The Spoonman at last and have someone to direct their anger towards, that opening the whole thing up again would just cause me more angst.' She shook her head again. 'I'm sick of talking about it. When do you want to cook for me?'

He grinned at her obvious change of subject. 'Why don't you come over on Wednesday. Come late, say around one-thirty and then I can eat with you.'

'Sounds good to me.' The sparkle in his eyes was playing havoc with her senses. It would do her good to get out and about with people again; with the way she was reacting to Owen, she'd been on her own for too long.

'Have I told you about my blog?'

'No,' he smiled at her attempt to talk about something else. 'Why don't you tell me about it now?'

For the next hour or so they talked about her blog and argued about the differences between "cheffy" techniques and the corners you cut when you want food quickly and whether the expensive produce was truly worth it.

'Take marmite and cheese spaghetti, for example,' Claire said. 'Simple, quick, nothing posh.'

'No,' he said, shaking his head and laughing. 'Never, I can't believe you're even suggesting it!'

As they laughed and bantered, it took Claire back to the days when they were in their teens and would argue about bands and football clubs and books. The days before he held her hand, the days before he kissed her and the days before everything changed between them.

They swapped tea for beer and wine; Owen stoked the fire again, and Nigel lay snoring on the sofa.

The light outside was growing dimmer when Owen said, 'Before when I asked about the elephant in the room, you thought I was going to ask you about that day in Cirencester, didn't you?' When she said nothing, he added. 'You never told me what you and Jenna were there for.'

She took a deep breath, her heart hammering inside her chest, and stood to take the empty cups to the sink. 'Do you want another beer?'

'No, I don't, but I want the truth this time.'

'I think I'll have another wine. Are you sure I can't get you—'

'No more lies, Claire. What's so bad that you can't tell me?'

A little pulse beat in the side of his jaw. She wanted

so badly to stroke it away. She poured another glass of wine and sat back down at the table with him. Taking another breath, she raised her eyes to the ceiling, delaying her answer and putting off saying the words she'd hoped never to have to say to him.

'What were you doing in Cirencester that afternoon?' he asked again.

Swallowing hard, she met his gaze. 'We were there to buy a pregnancy test. We couldn't buy one in Brookford without the whole village knowing about it, so we went to Cirencester.' She scoffed. 'Who do you think buys them in Brookford? Certainly not anyone who lives there. Maybe people from Cirencester or Stroud.'

He didn't laugh. 'For Jenna? Is that why Chris was there?'

From the look on his face before he asked the question, he knew what her answer would be, but he needed to hear her say it.

She shook her head. 'No, Owen, we were buying it for me.' Claire watched as his gaze dropped from hers, his face paled, his hand rubbing at his forehead almost as if he could make the words sink in. As if he hadn't understood what they meant.

'Oh Christ, Della.' He scratched absently at the back of his head and finally met her eyes. 'Were you?'

She nodded, her eyes glittering. 'Yes. I didn't take the test until the next day. And then I went to your house to tell you, but your father said you'd left that morning. I asked him if you'd left a note for me or said anything, and he said you hadn't. He said you'd left no way of being contacted.' A tear ran down her cheek and she let it go.

'And the baby?'

Claire turned her back so he wouldn't see her tears. 'I lost it only a few days later. Jenna was the only one who knew. I think she's still the only one who knows any of it happened.' She stood and went to the sink, looking out through the gloom. 'And then I sat my exams, and I went to uni like I'd planned, as if nothing had happened.'

Owen's chair scraped against the stone floor, and a moment later his hand gently rested on her shoulder. He turned her away from the window and pulled her against his body for the hug she would've given anything and everything in the world for all those years ago.

'I'm so sorry, Della. For the baby, for you having to go through it alone, for not believing you. I'm sorry for everything.'

Claire cried into his chest; the tears she'd thought long gone but were just waiting for him. He held her until she was spent.

'I'm sorry,' she said, rubbing at the front of his jumper. 'I've made a mess of you.'

'Della, sweetheart, I think I managed that all on my own a long time ago.' When she would have moved out of his arms, he held her tighter. 'I was so angry with you I wasn't thinking straight. We'd had that awful fight the day before about waiting and staying and exams and everything, I thought you were looking for reasons *not* to leave with me, that you'd only said you'd think about it to keep me happy.' He paused, then sighed. 'That last night, after I'd seen you in Cirencester, I thought if I asked where you were and you lied to me, then I'd know you'd lied about everything else,' He looked with intent. 'But you hadn't lied about anything else, had you?'

'No. I hadn't. I wanted to be with you, but I also wanted to do my exams. You'd been so upset and lost since your mother died, and I had no idea how to deal with it. How could I? And then when I realised I might be pregnant, it scared me, and I didn't know how to tell you without messing you up even more. I decided to wait until I did the test before I said anything to you. Jenna was the only one I told – she came with me. We hadn't planned to meet up with Chris and his friend, but once we had, it was difficult to get away.' She cupped his face and pulled his head so she could rest her forehead against his. 'Oh, Gallagher, we were so young it was never going to end well. Maybe we should think ourselves lucky it finished before we had time to ruin each other's lives completely.' She smiled weakly and pulled away, picking up her wineglass and draining it. 'Are you sure you don't want one?' She held up her empty glass.

'Maybe I'd better,' he said.

Nigel had woken, stretched and padded across to the door. 'I'll let him out first,' Owen said.

Claire nodded; the dog's ablutions were a timely excuse for Owen to get some fresh air after the bombshell she'd dropped on him.

While he was outside, she washed and dried the few dishes they'd used, put more wood on the fire, and poured them both a glass of the red wine she'd been drinking.

It wasn't long before the door opened and Nigel came tearing through, wagging his tail and jumping all over her as if he hadn't seen her for days. Owen took a little longer, stamping his feet on the mat, hanging his jacket back up on the hook at the door.

He went and stood by the fire, holding his hands in front of him. After a few minutes, he came back to where Claire was waiting in the kitchen and took the glass she offered him.

'I'm sorry I wasn't there,' he said. 'And I'm sorry I ran away. I know there's no way I can make any of that up to you now, but—'

Claire rested her hand on his arm. 'Please don't, Owen. I don't need you to beat yourself up about this. It happened a long time ago. I could've told you the truth that day and I didn't. This is on me as much as it's on you.'

He nodded slowly and scratched at his head. 'It's the thought of you at my father's house. I'd never thought about that before. I'd never wondered how you'd feel, how you did feel when you found out I'd left. I thought I was the only one who was hurting.'

'Stephen said I was a right misery guts that summer. He wanted to punch you, but you weren't there.'

Owen chuckled at her attempt to lighten the mood. 'There were so many times I wanted to come back and get you. Then when Dad said you'd gone to London, I knew you were okay. When he left to live with my aunt, I didn't hear anything else until I saw your name in the paper and then saw you on TV. By then I'd convinced myself I'd done us both a favour.'

'Who knows?' Claire shrugged. 'Maybe you did.'

He nodded. 'Where do we go from here?'

'We start again? As friends?'

Their eyes met and that shiver of awareness spread through her again.

'That sounds good,' he said. 'To start with.'

Claire broke their stare first. 'Do you want to stay for dinner?'

He checked his watch. 'No, I'd better be going.' He put his glass on the sink before turning back towards her. Just when she thought (hoped) he was going to kiss her, he wrapped his arms around her waist and kissed the top of her head.

'Thank you, Della,' he said.

'What for?'

'For telling me.'

She nodded into his chest, the wool of his jumper scratchy against her cheek.

He pulled away and lightly brushed his lips to hers. 'I'll see you on Wednesday.'

'Yes, I'll see you then.'

After he left, the cottage was too quiet and, for the first time since she'd moved in, Claire felt lonely. At the same time, she also felt lighter – in telling Owen, the little hole in her heart that had been a part of her for so long was finally beginning to heal.

CHAPTER TWENTY-THREE

On Monday morning Claire left Nigel with Gracie and, with the car full of empty boxes, drove to London to pack up the rest of her things. She boxed up books and music, emptied drawers and her side of the closet into bin bags, and debated over which keepsakes to take. In the end, she took only what she'd brought into the flat and left almost everything she and Giles had purchased together. She had no need for any of it – she certainly had no space for it. When or if he came back, he could review what was left, and they'd talk about it then.

She met Barty for dinner on Monday night at a pub near his place on the river. He had her in fits of laughter at the stories of one of his clients – a twenty-something soapie star – and her exploits with a popular, but married, football star.

'I tell you, Claire, it was a tabloid's dream come true. Cassie Costello, blonde, bubbly, and extremely well-endowed – she would've been a page three girl just a generation ago – caught *inflagrante delicto* with Ranold Ewer, the striker with some club or another, you know I don't keep up with football, darling, in the disabled toilets of a nightclub during a drug bust. She still doesn't understand what the fuss was about. Ranold's wife is threatening to divorce him publicly, and Cassie is sporting a rock (so big it has to be fake) that her boyfriend, the lead singer with that boy band, Yes Please, has given her. It's the story that keeps on giving. I'm just waiting for the next instalment when we get to negotiations about prenup agreements.'

'At least she's keeping you busy.' Claire laughed.

'Sometimes I'm convinced she thinks she's my only client.'

'Don't we all?'

'Except you, darling, you've always been very low maintenance. I've recently taken on Bruno Belucci and—'

'You're joking! Seriously? I'm surprised he's signed with you when he knows you represent me.'

'It certainly was an unexpected call, but beggars can't be choosers, darling, and until we get you back to work, needs must and all that. Bruno is a good client to have on my books.'

'The implication, of course, being I'm not at the moment.'

Barty shrugged. 'I'm not going to sugar-coat it, Claire, but yes.'

Claire took a large mouthful of her beer. 'Speaking of which, have you had any thoughts about turning that situation around?'

'I've put a few feelers out,' he said, 'but nothing I'm prepared to talk about until it firms up.' He leaned forward and held her gaze. 'I meant what I said before; if you're strapped for cash, I can help – you can even move back in with me if you'd like to. You can't stay in the backwoods forever.'

'Thanks, Barty, I appreciate the offer, but I'll be fine for a while yet.'

He nodded and sat back in his chair. 'What about Brookford? Have you gotten involved with village life yet?'

There was something in the tone of his voice that made Claire wonder whether there was something else he wanted to know. Whether she'd seen Owen, perhaps? His face was impassive. She must've imagined it, so skirted around the subject.

'Not quite, although I now feel as though I'm nearly ready to do something again – I'm getting bored baking scones and walking country lanes.'

'Okay, leave it with me and I'll see what I can do, but I'm not promising anything spectacular.'

'I know, I just want to get back to work. Have you thought any more about a tell-all with a friendly journalist?'

'I have. At the moment you staying silent is helping the noise die down. If what I'm hoping comes to fruition, we'll time an interview to come out about a month before we start promotion so we can maximise the sympathy and human-interest angle.'

'That makes sense, but I'm not interested in sympathy. I just want to set the record straight, so I can walk into restaurants in London without worrying about what's being done to my food in the background.'

'I hear you. Give me another month or so and I think we'll be on track. It'll also give me time to try and clear it with Duncan – he wants to hold you to the non-disclosure agreement you signed so we'll have to tread carefully around that. Can you hold out that long?'

Claire lifted a shoulder in resignation. 'It doesn't seem as though I have any other choice.'

The next morning, before Claire loaded the car to return to Brookford, she texted Ed, deliberating over the right tone so if he didn't want to talk, it would read as if it was of no consequence.

Hey Ed, I'm in town for a few hours so if you're free and decaffeinated, we could rectify that situation.

Her phone rang almost immediately.

'Claire Mansfield! Well, it's about bloody time you came back from whatever rock you've been hiding under. Where are you?'

'I'm at the flat at the moment but heading back to Brookford this afternoon.'

'Any chance of you dragging that cute arse of yours into town?'

'I'm not coming into the studio,' she warned.

'No, I understand, but how about that Italian café we both love in Soho?'

Ed was leaning against the counter when Claire arrived in the café, an empty espresso cup in front of him. He held up two fingers to Lorenzo behind the bar and motioned towards one of the red laminate-covered tables.

'You're looking good, Claire,' he said. 'Too skinny, and your hair's a mess, but you look good.'

'Now that's a back-handed compliment if ever I heard one.'

'I was beginning to wonder if you'd ever call me back.'

'Call you back?'

'Yes, I called after the news hit. Barty answered and said you'd gone into hiding and didn't know when you'd be back, but he'd tell you I called.' He watched as her eyes dropped to the table. 'He didn't tell you I called, did he?'

'No, I think he probably forgot – or he might've said, and I didn't take it in. I wasn't thinking straight or listening well at all.'

'And let me guess, because I haven't called since then you've been thinking I'd given up on you too.'

She nodded.

'I hadn't given up on you, but when I didn't hear from you, well, I had to wonder.'

'Whether there was any truth in it?'

He nodded. 'But I was talking to Owen Gallagher about *Posh or Not* – did he tell you?'

'I saw him the other day, and he tried to tell me about it, but I didn't want to hear, although I love that's what you're calling it now.'

'You know, as a title it just might stick; I do want to talk to you about it, but maybe not today. I make no guarantees about tomorrow or the day after.'

As the second round of caffeine hit Ed's bloodstream, his speech sped up. It was one of the things Claire always loved about working with Ed. When he slowed down, it was almost as if he was a toy gradually running out of battery, and when you plied him with caffeine, you could stand back and watch as he came back to life.

'When I told Owen I was wondering about whether you'd done what they said you had – don't look at me like that, you'd hate it if I wasn't honest – he pretty much told me what I could do with his job offer if I were stupid enough to believe the total shite that had been reported about you.

'From what I can understand he's been telling the same thing to anyone who'll listen to him – and as he's getting to be more and more the flavour of the month, more and more people are listening to him. It helped everyone knows he got fired because of The Spoonman and therefore has more reason to hate you than pretty much anyone else.'

Claire opened her mouth to speak, but he still hadn't finished.

'We ran into Adrian Ritchie – Owen and I, that is – and your name came up. Ade went ballistic and started saying how you'd fooled everyone and how you made out you were everyone's friend, but you were really a backstabbing bitch.'

Claire couldn't stop the gasp from escaping.

He continued, 'I think he thought because Spooner had burnt Owen, he could say what he wanted, and Owen would agree with him, but Owen stayed calm and put him right back in his place. He said he'd known you since you were kids and he didn't believe what had been reported. Owen knew you couldn't have done it, and it was all utter bollocks. By the time he was done, I think Adrian felt pretty badly about the way he treated you on *Cook-off*, but he wasn't to know, was he?'

'Is that you finished?' Claire asked with a smile.

'It is. Can you tell me what the real story is?'

'I'm not supposed to, but I will.'

At the end of the telling, he had the same reaction as everyone else did.

'Now the story is out there, I wouldn't think the paper can hold you to that confidentiality clause – not unless they can prove you breached it in the first place and, let's face it Claire, the likelihood of that is pretty slim. I think Barty's playing it smart by saying nothing.

Do you have any idea who's behind it?'

'No. At first I wondered whether it might've been Giles – mainly because of the timing – I suppose you heard we broke up?'

He nodded. 'I did and I was sorry to hear it. I wondered whether it was because of the story.'

'No, we broke up before that – when I got back from Fenwyck.'

'Regardless of how you guys broke up – and no, I don't want the details – that's not his style. Besides, my understanding is Giles is working on something big – I don't suppose you can tell me about that?'

Claire shook her head.

Ed continued, 'So he'll have something of his own to promote soon, and they're talking a documentary as well. He's not going to risk that on a cheap shot at his ex-girlfriend.'

'I agree.' She hesitated before adding, 'Barty mentioned this morning that he's talking to some people about something for me. Is it you he's talking to?'

Ed shook his head. 'No, but that doesn't mean he's not talking to another production company. I do, however, want to talk to Barty about the same thing I've been talking to Owen about, so if he's already in conversation about something else, I'd like to get into his ear first.'

'Please don't, Ed. Not yet. I don't know that I can deal with the rejection again.'

'I understand, but soon, hey?'

Claire nodded. 'Soon. Maybe.'

On the drive back to Brookford, Claire pondered what she'd learnt. Ed believed her, and he potentially had work for her. Just a week ago she would've thought that was impossible, but now, things were beginning to look up. And tomorrow she was having lunch with Owen; not that it was a date, she reminded herself, but not fast enough to check the flutter in her tummy and the smile she wore as she drove west on the motorway.

CHAPTER TWENTY-FOUR

On Wednesday the air was crisp and the sky blue – a perfect late winter day. Claire's morning walk was a wonderland of frost with tiny crystals of ice that had formed on the spiderwebs, the grass, the stray hairs from the donkeys in the paddock down the road, glistening in the weak sunlight. Nigel's breaths were little puffs of white air, and as they walked, Claire pretended she was a child again by seeing how long she could breathe out for and then watch her breath hang in the air.

She'd baked a black seeded bread – darkly sweet from treacle and cocoa – as an offering for Owen. Although taking food to Owen was like taking ice to Santa Claus. She justified by saying if the recipe worked and if Owen liked it, it would be the subject of tomorrow's blog.

The kneading, waiting, knock back, waiting, baking time gave her ample occasion to worry about what to wear. While she told herself this was just lunch with an old friend, she wanted to look better than she had on Sunday when he'd called by – although anything would be an improvement on the old flour-covered jumper and shapeless leggings with sheepskin boots.

She pulled on her usual skinny jeans and tucked them into knee-high flat black boots, a dark red jumper and a tweedy jacket. It was dressy enough for lunch out, but still country chic. Not wanting Owen to think she'd gone to too much trouble on his account, she applied the bare essentials of make-up and let her hair fall over her shoulders in loose waves. The colour needed touching up, but all things considered, she was happy with her reflection in the mirror.

She debated leaving Nigel with Gracie and decided he could come into town too, but rather than walk as they had done last time, they'd drive.

'I'm glad you're here,' Owen said and kissed her cheek. 'I wondered whether you'd cancel.'

'No.' Claire smiled, shaking her head. 'I've been looking forward to it. I hope it's okay I brought Nigel.'

'Absolutely,' he said, reaching down to scratch behind Nigel's ears. 'We're dog friendly in here. What's that you have there?'

Claire handed the basket with the fresh loaf to him. 'I know bringing food to you is probably pointless, but I baked this earlier today and I thought ...' She shrugged awkwardly and unbuttoned her jacket, smoothing down the front of her jumper. 'Anyway, I have no idea if it's any good or not, so you're my guinea pig.'

He opened the tea towel wrapped around the loaf

and inhaled deeply. 'It smells amazing. Sweet, but at the same time yeasty and earthy. I'll cut some later so we can try it together.'

The smile he gave her made her heart skip. She laid a hand against her chest, hoping it would control the chaos within.

Owen placed his hand under Claire's elbow and led her into the dining room.

'Wow,' she said, her eyes darting around the room, 'you have made some changes here.'

It didn't seem that many years ago they were all – the gang from school – celebrating their eighteenth birthdays in here. In those days, the floors had been covered with some multi-coloured carpet that held generations of spills. The fireplace had been festooned with heavy horse brasses, and the low beams had been painted black. Now it was unrecognisable.

Owen had stripped the carpet back to reveal a beautifully textured hardwood floor. He'd also sanded the black paint from the old ceiling beams, removed the whitewashed plasterwork from the original stone walls behind the bar and the fireplace, and painted the windowed front wall in a soft dove-blue that was almost, but not quite grey. He'd replaced the old bar with a wooden countertop, and underneath that were timber planks painted in the same pale blue-grey.

They had knocked the old 1960s mantelpiece to make a feature of the stone surrounds, and above where the mantel used to be now hung a striking oil painting of a sheep, just the head and chest, on a bright blue background. Under the bay windows on the street side were bench seats covered in an aubergine, teal and cream pattern, and filled with striped cushions in similar colours.

'It looks fabulous – nothing like I remember,' admired Claire.

'Hopefully, the menu will be nothing like that either – although we still do pub favourites in the main bar and the beer garden.'

'I remember the restaurant used to serve the same food as in the pub, but with table service.'

He smiled at the memory. 'Now I have two completely different menus.'

Claire raised her eyebrows in a silent question when Owen guided her to a table set with four places. Nigel had already found himself a comfortable spot near the fireplace.

'Tallis phoned me yesterday,' he said. 'She and Gail have discovered something they wanted to run by us, so I invited them to join us – I think it's something you need to hear.'

Any fragment of hope Claire might've been clinging to regarding the possibility of a rekindled romance was dashed. While the barest touch or glance from Owen made her heart beat faster, it was clear he didn't feel the same.

As she took her seat, she smiled up at him. 'Of course, that's fine.'

'That's great. They should be here soon, but in the meantime, I'll arrange a drink for you. Is white wine okay?'

She nodded. 'I'm driving, but that sounds nice.'

Tallis and Gail arrived soon after, and Owen greeted them in the same friendly manner he'd done with Claire.

'I hope you don't mind, but I've already told the kitchen what we'll be eating today, so I'll get things rolling and will be out shortly.' As he left, he gave Claire another of those completely disarming smiles.

'Now that's an offer I don't get every day,' Gail declared. 'A man offering to feed me.'

'Me neither,' said Tallis.

Claire had picked up a menu from one of the other tables. 'I'm glad he's making the decisions, I don't think I'd be capable of narrowing down my choices,' she said, hoping the warmth of the fire hid the heat in her cheeks. 'Everything looks great on this menu.'

Tallis and Gail looked at her and grinned.

'Is that a blush I can see?' asked Gail.

Claire shook her head in a mock scolding and fanned her face with the menu. 'Don't go there.'

'But did you see the way he looked at you just then?' asked Gail.

'It would be enough to melt the hardest of hearts,' said Tallis.

'You two have both been reading too many romances,' Claire said. 'Besides, he said you'd discovered something?'

'Yes,' confirmed Gail, 'but I want to enjoy lunch first – we need full bellies for this.'

'That sounds ominous.' Despite her smile, a tendril of dread twisted its way into Claire's head.

Owen chose that moment to come out with their first course, placing bowls of soup accompanied by a croquette in front of everyone. He relaxed into the chair next to Claire and laid the napkin over his lap.

'What are we eating?' Claire asked to distract from the heat of his thigh, which was just centimetres from her leg.

'This is a soup of white onion with thyme. The onions have been cooked super slowly so as not to colour, but to maximise the sweetness. Normally with onion soup, you'll have a crudité or toast with gruyere, but we serve it with a cheddar croquette instead.'

'Same same but different?' said Claire, avoiding his gaze.

'It looks and smells amazing,' said Tallis.

All four were silent as they tasted the soup, but Gail soon got the conversation started again. 'Is it strange owning a restaurant in the village you grew up in?'

Owen nodded. 'It is a little. When I first heard that *The Lamb* was on the market, I wondered how I'd fit in being back in Brookford. Even though I had no ties here, it still seemed like a homecoming of sorts. Then there was the worry people would resent the changes I was making to the old place and the menu.'

'Have you done a lot of redecorating?' asked Tallis.

'You can answer that,' Owen said, grinning at Claire.

'It's almost unrecognisable,' gushed Claire. 'I was last here for a funeral.' At Owen's questioning look, she added, 'Horrie – Max Henderson's grandfather. Do you remember Max?'

Owen nodded his understanding. 'I do. What's Max up to these days?'

'She's in New Zealand now. Last I heard she was pregnant, although I suppose she's had the baby – and probably another one – since then. Jenna would know, but I haven't spoken to her in ages either.'

'You've lost touch?'

Claire understood the surprise in his voice. For most of their childhood, they were inseparable, the three musketeers – Owen, Claire and Jenna.

Claire shook her head slightly to bring her thoughts back to the present day. 'You know how it is, life and all that. Besides, you're one to talk – none of us had heard a thing from you since you left.' Claire held Owen's gaze for a beat. 'I'm sorry,' she said to Gail and Tallis, 'I'm rude talking about people who you don't know. Let's just say when I was here for Horrie's wake, nothing had changed from when we were coming in for a sneaky lager when we were teenagers.' She smiled and wiped a piece of croquette around the bowl. 'After tasting this soup, I can say the food is also unrecognisable – and that's a wonderful thing.'

One of the waiters came and took the empty plates away, looking to Owen for approval to start on the main course. 'Thanks, Stu, that would be great.'

'Claire said you used to burn toast; surely she was exaggerating?' Tallis directed her question to Owen.

'No, not at all. I wasn't at all interested; my mother was an amazing cook, so there was no need for me to learn. Della here used to bake a lot. Self-saucing puddings, pikelets, and scones, of course.'

'I had a little more incentive to learn,' said Claire, dragging her focus away from Owen's closeness and back to the conversation. 'My mother wasn't anywhere near as good a cook as Mrs G was.'

'I've been meaning to ask,' said Gail. 'Owen calls you Della – what's that about?'

'You tell it,' Claire said, grinning at Owen.

'She went through this stage where she wanted cookbooks for every birthday and Christmas and just loved Delia Smith. She used to say that she wanted to be Delia when she grew up and write cookbooks and make TV shows about them, just like Delia did. Everything she cooked back then was from a Delia book. It would be "Delia says this, or Delia says you have to do it like that". I used to tease her about it all the time. Saint Delia, I used to say.'

'Don't knock Delia,' said Claire in a mock warning.

He answered her smile with one of his own. 'I took to calling her Delia, but it was just one syllable too many for me, and I shortened it to Della or Dells.'

When his eyes darkened, Claire found it hard to breathe.

'It was always my name for her; in fact, I'm surprised she didn't name her dog Delia.' He moved his leg under the table.

A wave of heat rushed through her core and up to her face when his calf rested against hers. She dropped her eyes to the table to hide her confusion, but when raised them, Gail and Tallis were trying to hide their smiles.

'I still have them all, you know. The cookbooks that is.' Claire attempted to cover her embarrassment. 'And a lot more besides. I brought them all back from London with me yesterday, but goodness knows where I'll put them in the cottage. At the moment they're piled up in the back room.'

'And you've done what you said you wanted to do,' exclaimed Tallis.

'I suppose that I have, although it was a dream I'd grown out of by the time I'd reached my mid-teens, and had decided instead I'd do journalism.'

'If his name for you was Della, what was yours for him?' asked Gail, a cheeky look on her face.

'He was always just Gallagher to me.'

The waiter delivered the mains – a haddock and leek cake served with a poached egg, spinach and a hollandaise sauce. It was simple, yet perfectly executed and very good.

As they ate, Owen's leg remained against Claire's. Although their bodies were barely touching, the electricity crackling between them was intense. She imagined if the lights were suddenly to go out, the sparks between them would light up the sky like fireworks.

Claire declined a pudding – declaring that as wonderful as they all sounded, she couldn't have managed another bite – and opted instead for an espresso, but Gail and Tallis shared a treacle tart to which Owen had added thyme as a herby twist and served with clotted cream.

When Owen got up from the table to get the tart and coffees, Claire was both sorry and relieved at the same time. The moment he'd gone, Gail and Tallis began giggling.

'Oh, for god's sake, you're both carrying on like teenagers,' Claire chided.

'Speaking like carrying on like teenagers, you should see the looks you two are giving each other. There's enough energy in the air to heat my house until spring.' said Tallis. 'And my house takes a lot of heating.'

'Aww and now she's blushing.' Gail teased. 'I think

we should say our piece and leave these two to it.'

'Don't be silly,' Claire muttered. 'There's nothing there.'

'I wouldn't count on that,' said Tallis.

Owen was soon back with coffees and the treacle tart. As he handed Claire her coffee, his hand brushed against hers, lingering longer than necessary. Her eyes darted to his. The smile spreading across his face confirmed he knew precisely the effect his proximity was having on her. Thankfully Gail and Tallis were in raptures of their own and missed the exchange.

'That was a fabulous meal, Owen,' said Claire to regain her composure. 'I can understand why the word around town is that you'll have your own Michelin star before too long.'

'I'm not sure I'll ever eat anything as fabulous as that tart again,' said Gail.

Tallis dabbed the corner of her lips with her napkin. 'Just beautiful. Remind me never to invite him to one of our monthly cooks!'

Owen laughed. 'You're all very welcome, but I think now that we've eaten, we should talk about what you've discovered.'

CHAPTER TWENTY-FIVE

When Tallis took the notepad from her bag, Claire grinned and said, 'you have come prepared,' but as the notepad was followed by a folder full of plastic sleeves Claire's smile faded.

'What is that?' Claire asked, already fearing the answer.

'It's every review that The Spoonman has written in the last five years,' said Tallis matter-of-factly.

'I can see that, but why?'

'So we can see if there's any pattern,' replied Gail. 'The way we figure it, if we can find a pattern, we can find a motive, and if we can find a motive, we can find our man.'

'Or woman,' reminded Tallis.

'And have you found a pattern?' asked Claire.

'We think we have,' said Gail. 'Until about four years ago, Alex Spooner's reviews were tongue in cheek but essentially harmless. Some were good, some were bad, but all had an element of amusement to them. Then something changed.'

'Perhaps that's when someone else began to write the reviews,' suggested Claire.

'Yes, we thought that too; we think we've pinpointed when the change occurred but will need you to confirm if you've eaten at any of these restaurants. Okay?'

'Sure,' said Claire. 'But I doubt I have.' She peered across the table at the list in front of Tallis. 'Okay, what's first on that list of yours?'

'*The Bridge?*' asked Tallis. 'It's under London Bridge.'

'There's a pub under there I've gone to a few times that does a fabulous ploughman's platter, but no, I don't know *The Bridge.*'

'*The Royal on Mayfair?*'

'Nope. No … oh, hang on, yes, I have. I went with Giles. We'd only just moved in together. Everything was happening at that time – Giles and I moved in together, and soon after that, I met Ed and then *Time for Tea* got started.'

'*Lulu and Patsy?*'

'Yes. For someone's birthday. I loved the name, but the food and the occasion were otherwise forgettable.'

'*Scarborough Fair?*'

'Giles took me there for my birthday, so it must've been March. And we'd begun filming, so it must've been four years ago. Very average service. I remember the waitress flirted with Giles all night, and we had quite a row about it on the way home.'

'*Y Not?*'

'Appalling name, good starters, boring mains and wine was an ingredient in every dish on the menu.'

'Everything?' asked Owen.

'Unfortunately, yes.'

'Who did you go there with?' asked Gail.

'Giles. I remember he was distracted that night because one of the leads for the story he was working on had fallen through, and he was in a hurry to get home.'

'Is there anything else you can remember about the night?' asked Tallis.

'No. I ran into Barty there, though.' Claire screwed her nose up as she thought. 'Yes, that's right, we ran into Barty. Giles was being a pain in the neck about work and wanted to leave. Barty said he'd look after me and make sure I got home okay, so we stayed and had dessert – which was unforgettable for all the wrong reasons – and then we went somewhere else for a drink after.'

'*Belucci's?*'

'Yep. Was this the review you took the fall for?' Claire asked Owen.

He nodded. 'It sure was.'

'I remember Giles and I took Barty there for his birthday. The meal was excellent, and for once Giles was nice to Barty.' Claire paused and took a sip from her water glass. 'I never understood why they didn't get on. Anyway, it was a good night.'

'I must've been on the pass that night,' said Owen with a grin.

'Do you remember when that was?' asked Tallis, writing something in her notebook.

'Yes, Barty's birthday is in late July, and Giles and I went away on holidays at the beginning of August.'

'And the review was out in mid-August,' said Owen. 'I'll never forget that day. Belucci went mental.' He laughed ruefully and gave a little shake of his head.

'I still can't believe you were probably in that kitchen and I never even knew,' said Claire. Their eyes met. Had he felt her presence that night?

Tallis cleared her throat to bring them both back to attention. 'What about *Ziggy's*?'

'Fabulous meal. Ziggy, the chef, and I dated briefly when I started at the paper. It was years ago, and he was an apprentice back then. It didn't last long, maybe a few months – his hours were dreadful. *Ziggy's* was his first restaurant, and he invited Giles and me after we ran into him one morning at brunch.'

As Tallis and Gail took Claire through The Spoonman's reviews, it became clear that although there was no pattern to when a Spooner review would be published, Claire had eaten at every single restaurant reviewed in the last four years.

'It's as we thought,' said Gail. 'The style of the reviews began to change with the *Royal on Mayfair* piece, the Scarborough Fair review was the first really nasty one, and Belucci's was the first personal one.' She looked across at Tallis as if unsure how to continue.

'What else have you noticed?' asked Claire. 'Just say it.'

Tallis hesitated briefly. 'Before you moved in with Giles, there's no correlation between you and the restaurants that were reviewed, and once you started on *Time for Tea*, the tone of the reviews changed.' Tallis looked Claire straight in the eye. 'Are you sure that Giles didn't write them?'

'Absolutely positive,' said Claire. 'There are several restaurants on this list I don't think Giles had eaten at and even if he had been commissioned to write a review – and trust me, Giles would consider that beneath him – he'd never review a place he hadn't experienced himself. It's a journalistic integrity thing with him. And, before you ask the next question, Giles and I ended on a reasonably good note. He'd gain nothing from leaking the story.' Her tone was defensive, but it was obvious from the way Gail and Owen looked away that they also believed he might've been involved.

'You said he and Barty didn't get on; was that because Giles was jealous?' asked Tallis.

'No, not at all. Giles understood that we were friends, and I've often thought the animosity between them was on Barty's side more than Giles. I think Barty was worried, at least at first, that Giles could put a stop to our friendship.'

'I see. Did Giles know that you dated Ziggy?' Tallis made another note in her book.

Claire shook her head. 'We never really discussed past relationships – at least, not in specifics.' She couldn't look at Owen as she said it. 'I knew he'd been married once before – and given that he was forty when we met, I would've been concerned if he hadn't had any emotional baggage – and he knew there'd been someone serious in my life when I was younger and that I'd dated since then. But we agreed early on there was no point in rehashing our pasts.' She gave a short laugh. 'I told Giles about Ziggy after we'd met him at brunch that morning.' A further thought occurred. 'He didn't even know that Owen and I dated. I didn't tell him that until after Fenwyck – and whoever wrote that review on Belucci had something against Owen. So no, it couldn't have been Giles. Besides, Giles has never eaten at *Bella Donna*, or—' she ran her finger down the list of restaurants that had been subject to The Spoonman's treatment over the last few years, 'half of the restaurants on this list.' She sighed. 'But I have eaten at every single one of them. It doesn't look good, does it?'

No one said anything to that.

'Okay,' said Owen. 'It's not Giles. Let's look at this in another way. Who did you eat there with? Is there any pattern there?'

'I'm not sure. Often, I'd meet Barty for a lunch, or sometimes Ed or Duncan. A couple of times I took

Gracie as a special treat if she was in town.'

They spent the next few minutes with Claire going through each of the restaurants on the list and noting who she'd eaten with, although some she couldn't remember. 'I'd need to check my diaries; I'm pretty sure they're in one of the boxes I packed from the flat.'

Tallis noted it all down. 'I'll put this all into some sort of order when I get home. What about other people who you're close to? Would anyone else have eaten at these restaurants around the same time period?'

'I have no idea. Possibly.'

Owen took a deep breath. 'Okay, I'll ask: I know that he's your friend and your manager, but what about Barty?'

Claire shook her head emphatically. 'Barty? No. Absolutely not. He might've eaten at most of these restaurants, but then he rarely eats at home and is the type who'll go to the opening of an envelope. It's not about the food for him – he's all about fashion and just wants to be seen in the right places. Besides, me being out of work does him no good at all. If I'm not earning, then nor is he. Plus, he told me he hadn't been able to get a booking at *Lily James* and also, don't forget, he had no idea I'd been writing as Alex Spooner until I told him, and that was after the news broke.'

'Okay,' said Tallis, 'it can't be Barty.'

'Speaking of *Lily James*,' started Gail. 'Is there any history between you and that chef?'

'Adrian Ritchie? Why do you ask?'

'Because it's just occurred to me that although most of them are bitchy, the nastiest of these have been reserved for people with whom you have some sort of history.' She counted them off on her fingers. 'There was *Ziggy's*, and you dated Ziggy; *Belucci's*, and you dated Owen; *Bella Donna*, and Bruno Belucci had tried it on with you and also deliberately snubbed you. The review of *Lily James* is as bitchy as each of these, so it occurred to me you might also have had a history there too.'

Claire contemplated what Gail had said. 'When you put it like that, it makes it sound personal.'

'Della, I think it is personal,' Owen said, his tone gentle. 'Is there anything between you and Ade?'

Claire stared at him for a few seconds. 'Ade and me? We're friends. We kissed once at a launch for something or other that Barty dragged me to. It was before Ade was married to Imogen and well before I met Giles. It was one kiss, we'd both had too much to drink, and it didn't go any further.' Claire dropped her gaze to the table. 'As far as I'm aware, no one else knows that it happened.' Claire bit at the inside of her top lip as she thought it through. 'No one could ever say I had a reason for wanting to ruin Ade – he's one of the good guys and unlikely to have upset anyone. He has that whole Australian laid-back-I-really-should-be-surfing vibe happening. I don't think that one has anything to do with me.'

Owen rubbed at his chin thoughtfully. 'No, it

doesn't sound as though it would have.'

'Perhaps our theory is wrong?' suggested Gail.

'Also,' said Claire, 'Even if Ade had told someone about that kiss, *Bella Donna* doesn't fit the pattern as there was never anything between Bruno and me. It supports a vendetta that I might have had, but also one that someone else might be harbouring. I suspect if you want to find people who have something against Bruno you wouldn't need to look too far.' As she spoke, there was something at the edge of her consciousness, something someone had said, something just out of reach.

Tallis put her pen down and cupped her chin in her hand, her eyes flicking from the fire to the beams in the ceiling. 'Maybe we're on the wrong track, but it doesn't feel like it. I think it's more likely we haven't found the link yet. Or the motive.' She dropped her hand back to the table. 'That's what we need to concentrate on – the motive.'

'Maybe there isn't a motive. Maybe the reviews are completely random, and someone found out I used to be The Spoonman and thought they could make some money from the tabloids.'

She looked across at Gail who shrugged unconvincingly and Owen who gave a slight shake of his head.

'Sorry, Della, I don't believe that for one second.'

'Nor do I,' said Tallis. 'Also, it worries me how Barty doesn't want to set the story straight for you. I know he has his reasons, but to me they don't add up.'

'Were you two ever together?' asked Gail.

'Heavens no. There was a drunken kiss one night that we both laughed about later and vowed we'd never repeat.' Claire laughed at what she'd said. 'First, a drunken kiss with Ade and now Barty, plus I dated Ziggy, what must you be thinking of me?' She directed the question to Gail and Tallis, but she intended it for Owen.

'That you had a healthy social life before you met Giles,' said Gail with a straight face. 'And a thing for chefs.'

'Oh, ha-ha. No, other than that, there's been nothing between Barty and me. We've never really discussed it, but I think he's gay. For all Barty's social butterfly act, he's a very private person – even with me. He does care about me though, and I suspect that's why he doesn't want to arrange a tell-all story – in case it backfires, and he has to pick up the pieces. I saw him the other day, and he said he has some irons in the fire for me at the moment and if any of them come off, then he'll look at scheduling an interview for before the publicity kicks off.'

'Do you know what he's talking about?' asked Owen.

'No, he wouldn't tell me. He said he doesn't want me to get my hopes up in case it doesn't come off, but he's asked me to hang out for another month or so. I asked Ed if he'd heard anything and he hadn't.'

'That surprises me,' said Owen. 'Someone would've been bound to talk. Do you think he's telling you the truth and not just throwing you a line to make you feel better?'

'He said he'd arrange that interview as soon as the time is right, and I believe him. I have no reason not to, and he has no reason to lie to me.' Claire held Owen's stare, and this time it was his eyes that dropped first.

'Right,' said Tallis, packing her folder back into her bag. 'I think that's enough for this afternoon. I want to read through the reviews in some more depth. There's an idea niggling at the back of my brain, but I want to test it out before I say anything else.'

Claire nodded her understanding. 'Okay. I'll see you two in a couple of weeks?'

'Yes,' said Gail. 'Rick Stein's *France*. You're on pudding again.'

'And I know exactly what I'm cooking too.' Claire grinned.

Once Gail and Tallis had left, Claire picked up the empty coffee cups and took them into the kitchen, which was empty save for a gangly young guy at one bench prepping vegetables.

'That's Joey,' said Owen, who'd come up behind her. 'He's the apprentice. Hey Joey,' he called. Joey removed his earphones and waved across at them. 'This is my friend Claire.'

'Nice to meet you, Claire.' He grinned and popped

his earphones in and got back to his work.

'He seems keen.' Claire struggled to concentrate on the conversation with Owen standing so close that his breath was tickling the back of her neck. Was it her imagination, or had he come even closer? If she arched backwards, would she come into contact with the rest of his body?

'He is. He reminds me a lot of me when I was his age.' His hand rested lightly on Claire's hip, and heat burned through the fabric of her jeans. There was a smile in his voice as he said it. Removing his hand from her hip he stepped aside and took the coffee cups from her hand. 'I'll put these in the dishwasher he said.' Claire immediately missed his presence.

'It's a tough one,' Owen was saying as he wiped at a smudge on one of the benches. 'He's here because he wants to be, and I pay him accordingly, but there are a lot of restaurants who wouldn't pay him for the extra hours. Apprentices are churned and burned way too often. There's the argument that the hours ensure only those with absolute passion get through, but there's a fine line between that and exploitation.'

'Where's everyone else?'

'Gone home for an hour or so. They'll have done most of their prep for tonight already and will be back later to get ready for dinner service.' His voice grew fainter as he opened the door to the cool room. 'Hopefully,' he added, popping his head back around the door and grinning cheekily.

'You do this every day?' she asked when he reappeared.

'No. On Sunday we keep it simple and do a Sunday roast for lunch. We're not open Sunday evening or Monday, but we also do food in the front bar and the beer garden every day out of the pub kitchen – mostly pub classics. You'd like it, I think.' He picked up what Claire assumed was a runsheet from one of the benches and ran his finger down the list, nodding slightly.

'Are the long hours worth it?'

He lifted his head, his eyes crinkling at the sides. 'You certainly don't do this for the money,' he said. 'Although I hope one day this place will be a success. I've cut back from what I used to do – especially now that things are running well here. I try and get to the gym or out for a run in the mornings, and I'm usually at the restaurant from nine to oversee service prep. I like to do the pass for both lunch and dinner service and spend the afternoons on paperwork and whatever else needs doing. I have a head chef running the pub kitchen who knows what he's doing so that doesn't need a lot of oversight.'

'When do you eat?'

'I eat lunch after service finishes – and dinner with the rest of the staff at around ten.'

He put the runsheet down and lifted his head to smile at her. 'You'd like the pub, I think. How about I take you on Sunday night?'

'I'd like that – if you're not exhausted.'

He didn't answer immediately, but his eyes held hers as he walked back to the doorway where she stood. 'No,' he said, 'I won't be too tired.' Owen lifted a strand of Claire's hair and tucked it behind her ear, the backs of his fingers lightly grazing the side of her neck. She closed her eyes and struggled to breathe normally.

'I think I should go,' she said, unable to move from the doorway, not wanting to break the spell he had her under.

'Stay,' he whispered, leaning forward so his words tickled her ear.

She held her breath for a heartbeat, waiting for a kiss, for him to take the lobe of her ear and lightly nip it, for his fingers to trail down her neck again, for his lips to follow.

'Please,' he murmured.

His eyes were dark, his gaze intense. How would his lips feel on hers? Would they be soft as they used to be, or hard and insistent like the man he'd become? He swallowed hard and squeezed his eyes shut. When he opened them again, he smiled and stepped back. 'Let's go through and have another coffee,' he said.

'I'll just go to the …' Claire pointed toward the bathrooms with a wayward swing of her hand.

If she'd hoped the cold water she'd splashed on the back of her hands when she was in the bathroom had cooled her body, then seeing Owen standing behind the bar operating the coffee machine showed how far wrong that idea was.

'I really should go,' she said.

'Why? Do you have anywhere else you need to be?'

'No, but …'

'Sit down,' he said, 'and drink this.' He handed her a coffee and sat down at the table opposite her. On the table was the loaf of bread she'd brought him and a dish of butter. 'You can't leave before we've tried this,' he said.

Owen sliced the bread and slathered butter on both slices – thick, the way she liked it. As if by mutual agreement, they both bit into their bread at the same time. For a first effort, it was good. Dense, yet fluffy, dark, rich, and complex. It tasted as it smelled – and that was a wonderful thing.

'This is excellent,' said Owen. 'I could serve bread as good as this in here. The seeds – are they caraway and fennel?'

'Yes.'

'There's something else in here I'm not quite sure of. It's sweet, but at the same time, not.' He lifted his gaze to the ceiling as if looking for the right descriptive words. 'What's in it?'

'Would you believe treacle, coffee and chocolate?'

'Really? I would never have picked it – but it's certainly delicious.'

'So was lunch. Thanks again for that,' said Claire.

He waved her thanks away. 'It was my pleasure.'

When Owen smiled, that now familiar, yet completely inconvenient heat rushed through her.

'I had something I wanted to talk to you about too,' he announced, wiping a smear of butter from the corner of his lip.

'Oh?'

'Yes.' He took a sip of his coffee. 'It's about *Posh or Not.*'

'Owen, no—'

'Please hear me out, Dells. Then, if you're still not interested, I promise I'll leave it alone. I can't make any promises for Ed, but you won't hear any more about it from me. Okay?'

'You promise?'

'You have my word.'

She nodded. 'Go on then.'

'Ed really wants you – and so do I.'

Those last few words sent her pulse racing again, and she shook her head to clear the image of him wanting her.

As if he could read her thoughts, he grinned. 'To do the show, that is.'

Claire nodded and grimaced in embarrassment. 'So he said.' At the look on his face, she gave in. 'Okay, tell me what he's told you about it.'

'You know the premise; they take one restaurant

chef – that would be me; and a home cook – you. Each week we're provided with a theme or a core ingredient, and we prepare two versions. I'll do the cheffy version, and you'd do a more express style. Just as good, but different.'

'Yours is posh, and mine is not.' She returned his smile.

'Of course, they're relying on some friendly banter, and there's no denying there's chemistry between us. That'll translate brilliantly to the screen.'

Claire's stomach plummeted in disappointment. This whole thing, the calf action at lunch, the glances, the touches, it was all to prove they'd be great together on TV.

'You're right,' she said, trying to keep her tone cheerful. 'We would be good together *on screen*.' She emphasised the last two words.

'Does that mean you're interested?'

Claire sipped at her coffee as she thought it through. She'd been excited when they were talking about it last year, but to have Owen involved? She'd be cooking her kind of food, and he'd be cooking his – which was amazing. Most importantly, it wasn't live to air, so there'd be no chance of the humiliation she'd suffered the last time she cooked on national television.

'We'd film here, in Brookford,' he said, sensing her growing interest. 'Each of us cooking in this kitchen and serving guests in this room – friends, family, locals.'

He put his hand over hers. 'Think about it, Della. You and me cooking together, laughing together, arguing the way we were on Sunday. Me using posh ingredients, you telling me exactly why they're pointless. Me doing the poncy cheffy thing and you breaking the processes down into something that anyone can do at home and then sitting around waiting for me to finish.'

'You don't do the poncy cheffy thing,' Claire joked.

'Maybe not, but you get the idea. Ed said you'd pretty much signed up before—'

'Before everything went wrong.'

'Yes. Are you interested?'

She slid her hand out from under his. 'Yes, I think so. What about The Spoonman, though? How are we going to get around that? My credibility is so bad at the moment I wouldn't have thought the network would want to touch me again.'

'That's where Barty has done you a favour. You've conducted yourself with dignity the whole time when you could've been denying it to anyone who'd listen. It is, however, one of the reasons we have to find a way of proving you couldn't have written those reviews. It would be best if we could expose who it was and why, but I'd settle for proving that it wasn't you and finding out who leaked it.' He paused. 'This is going to sound selfish, but once we get started on this, we won't be able to afford the scandal if it takes off again.'

'I understand.'

'You need to be prepared that the person responsible for this is someone who is – or was – close to you. For that reason, I don't think you should talk to anyone about this yet.'

Claire lifted her head and met his eyes. That intense look was back in them, and it took her breath away. 'Not even Barty?'

He shook his head. 'No, not even Barty. Not until we talk to Ed and sort the details. The last thing I want to do is hurt you – I did that when I left you to deal with something on your own you shouldn't have had to deal with. I won't do it again, Della. Please trust me on this.'

She swallowed hard and nodded, feeling a heat behind her eyes. 'Alright.' She looked away, blinking, and slung her handbag over her shoulder. 'And now I really have to go. If I can rouse my dog, that is.'

'Okay. But you'll have dinner with me on Sunday?'

She nodded. 'I'll be here.'

'No, I'll come and get you.'

'That's ridiculous,' she said. 'You're right here. Why would you come and get me?'

He smiled. 'When I take a woman on a date, it's only good manners to pick her up and take her back home again. My mother taught me that much.'

'And this would be a date?'

'Yes, Della, it would be a date.'

It also sounded very much like a promise – and one that had every nerve in her body tingling.

CHAPTER TWENTY-SIX

Owen had reported the outcome of their discussions to Ed, who wasted no time in phoning Claire early the following morning and talking through the proposal in more depth.

'I know we'd got close to a deal late last year, but I'm more excited about it this time around,' she said. 'And not just because I'm unemployed at the moment.' What she didn't tell Ed was that a good proportion of her excitement also came from knowing she'd be working with Owen.

'I am too,' said Ed. 'This is a perfect vehicle for you, and Owen is the perfect co-host. To be honest, we wouldn't have even considered him if it hadn't been for the Fenwyck show. We're going to need to get moving if we want to start filming before summer, so I'll come down on Monday, and we'll go through more of the details with you and Owen. I know Owen has asked we keep this to ourselves at the moment – and I'm sure he has his reasons – but we're going to need to get Barty and the lawyers involved sooner rather than later.'

There was a question in his voice that Claire didn't know how to answer. She didn't understand the need for secrecy – at least not from Barty. 'I think he's just worried that Barty might not want me to take on something this big so soon after the scandal,' she said. 'You know how Barty worries about me.'

'That would be it,' said Ed. 'He certainly takes his responsibilities where you're concerned seriously.'

Claire didn't know how to answer that.

Claire spent the next few days walking, baking and writing her blog. She was getting a small following, although thankfully, mainly because she hadn't posted a photo of herself, nobody seemed to have connected Claire from *Brookford Kitchen Diaries* with Claire Mansfield, host of *Time for Tea*. As a result, it still felt as though she was writing for herself.

As she baked, Claire continued to heal, and as she wrote about the baking, she healed some more. Despite telling the Fenwyck ladies she'd blog their club meeting, she hadn't yet done so – mainly due to a concern that someone would read it and put two and two together. Although she'd have to face the public sooner rather than later – especially if *Posh or Not* came off – for now, she was enjoying the anonymity.

The blog was filling the space her column had left, and Claire found she was taking *Brookford Kitchen Diaries* in a similar direction to that. Last week the subject had been Victoria Sponge Cakes, and this week she was planning to write about Bakewell tarts and what went into making a great one – and that meant having to bake a few of them.

Gracie had commented a few times about how she was putting on weight and, while she hadn't yet complained about the daily delivery of scones or loaves, if she began experimenting with multiple versions of teatime classics, she'd need to find someone else to give them to. Perhaps Owen …

On Friday morning Claire and Nigel drove the short distance into Brookford.

Owen was out the front of *The Lamb picking herbs from a hanging basket;* she waved and was rewarded with a grin. She made a long-overdue appointment at the hairdressers for the following day – it was so she could put her best professional foot forward with Ed at Monday's meeting, and it had absolutely nothing to do with wanting to look good for her date with Owen on Sunday night.

In all the years she'd been away, Claire had thought London was where she belonged. But now she was back in Brookford, it felt like the right place for her to be. Or maybe it was knowing Owen was back here too that made everything feel right.

There was one person with whom she still hadn't reconnected – Jenna. Claire had told Owen that they'd drifted out of touch – and that was true. Claire had gone to university in London, and Jenna had stayed in

Brookford and married Chris. While their lives were very different, the real reason for their estrangement was her miscarriage. Claire had sworn Jenna to secrecy and then, at the end of the summer, walked away almost without looking back. In hindsight, Jenna represented a part of her life that Claire had tried to forget. Neither of them had ever talked about what happened that terrifying night. So, when Jenna came out of the general store as she was leaving the hairdressers, Claire crossed the road to greet her.

At first, Jenna seemed surprised to see her and Claire wondered whether it was surprise at seeing her in Brookford, or surprise that she was going out of her way to say hello. She feared it was the latter.

'You're looking well,' Claire said. 'Oh my god, is this Aiden?' Standing beside Jenna was a tall, thin boy who was the image of Chris when he was young.

'It certainly is. Aiden, this is Claire – Claire and I were best friends in school.' Aiden shrugged. To Claire, she said, 'I heard you were back in town. How long are you staying?'

'Indefinitely at this stage.' There had been an implied criticism in Jenna's voice, and she didn't blame her for that. 'You probably heard things imploded in London. I don't have any plans to go back soon and to be honest, it's nice to be home.'

Jenna nodded slowly and searched Claire's face, looking for a meaning behind her words. 'Owen is back too. Have you seen him?' Bored with the conversation, Aiden wandered off to join a group of boys kicking a football.

'I have. He's done an amazing job with *The Lamb* – it's nothing like the dive we used to get wasted in.'

'I wouldn't know, we haven't been into the restaurant side.'

'I'm sure he'd like to see you,' Claire said.

'And you two are talking again?'

'We are.'

'Did you tell him?'

'I did.' Unexpectedly, Claire's eyes filled with tears as the devastation of her miscarriage surged forward. She blinked hard to stop them from leaking out. 'God, I'm sorry,' she said.

Jenna's face softened, and she was suddenly the Jenna of old. 'It still hurts?'

'I'm sorry,' Claire said again. 'This is so silly. It was such a long time ago.'

'Have you ever told anyone?'

Claire shook her head and dabbed the corner of her eye. 'Until I told Owen the other day, you were the only person in the world who knew. I tried to forget about it. For a while, I managed to convince myself it hadn't happened, and then I saw Owen before Christmas, and it all came flooding back.'

Jenna nodded. 'I tried to forget about it too. I was so scared that night – there was so much blood.

I remember I was staying at your place because your parents had gone to Cheltenham for some party. Stephen was out, and Gracie was in bed. I wanted to call for help, but you wouldn't let me.'

'And then we went to Cirencester to the doctors the next day so no one here would know.' Claire kicked at a cobblestone with her boot.

'Why didn't we make more of an effort to stay in touch, Claire?' Jenna's words were soft.

Claire let the question hang between them for a few seconds. 'Honestly? I think because we both wanted to forget that night.'

'You're right. You know, I've never even told Chris.' She hesitated before asking, 'How was Owen when you told him?'

'Upset. He told me he'd left because he saw me that day in Cirencester – when we bought the test – and thought I was there with someone else. It was all such a mess.'

'But you're okay now?'

'You know, I think we are. Have you spoken to Owen?'

'I've avoided him,' Jenna admitted. 'I had no idea why he left, so it seemed safer not to talk to him. I have to say though, he's grown up to be seriously hot. Who would've thought it? Do you think you'll get together again?'

'I wouldn't think so,' Claire said, her face growing

uncomfortably warm.

'But you'd like to, right?' She laughed as if they were still sixteen.

'Maybe,' Claire conceded. Impulsively she added, 'Why don't the four of us get together some night – at the pub maybe? You and Chris and me and …'

'You and Owen?' she finished, raising her eyebrows.

'Yes, but not like that, not with us together, but both of us there.'

'Together.' Jenna smiled at Claire's discomfort.

'You know what I mean.'

'That would be great. Just like old times.' Jenna's face fell. 'The thing is though, I don't think Chris and I belong with you and Owen anymore.'

'Why not?'

'You really don't know?'

Claire shook her head.

'You're famous—'

'Very much for the wrong reasons at the moment.' Claire attempted a laugh.

'And Owen has seen the world and is back with his own restaurant. What did Chris and I do? Stay in Brookford and have a few kids.'

'I envy you that,' Claire admitted. 'I've never been married, and my attempt at motherhood didn't end so well. As for Owen, he hasn't exactly had an easy ride of it either. Give us a chance to show you that underneath we're still the same people – even though I know I haven't acted like it over the last few years.'

'You can't take all the blame for that,' Jenna said. 'But yes, okay, if you're going to be staying for a while, we'll get together.'

'Do you mean it?' Claire asked.

'Yes. Let me talk to Chris, and we'll make the arrangements.'

They swapped phone numbers and promised to catch up in the next few weeks. When Claire let it slip she was seeing Owen on Sunday night, a cheeky grin spread across Jenna's face, and again it was like the years in between had never happened.

Sunday evening seemed to be the night the locals brought their dogs to The Lamb. Nigel was settled in front of the fireplace between a collie and a Labrador. Claire watched Owen as he returned with two pints of ale.

'What was making you smile just then?' he asked.

'I saw Jenna the other day. It was weird at first, and then it was almost as if the clock had stopped and we were eighteen again. It's like that now – being back here, and in this pub with you, I feel young again.'

'And in love?'

Claire smiled and sipped her wine, trying to hide her grin. 'It was a long time ago.'

'Yet right now it feels like yesterday,' he said.

She nodded. 'It does.'

'It also feels different, though.'

Yes, it felt different. Back then, he was in love with her, and now they were – Claire didn't know what they were. 'We're different people now,' she said. 'We've grown up.'

'That wasn't what I was going to say, but yes, we have.' He tilted his head a little to the side as he watched her. 'Don't you want to know what I meant?'

Claire shrugged as if she didn't care.

'I was going to say that back then I thought I was in love, and I wanted you as any eighteen-year-old boy wants his girlfriend.'

'But now you don't?'

Owen shook his head slightly. 'The way I feel about you right now goes beyond wanting.' He stared, watching for a reaction.

Claire swallowed hard and bit her lip. Could he see inside where her heart wanted to take flight?

'Yes,' she breathed, bringing her eyes to his. 'I feel it too.'

He nodded and smiled slowly. 'I hoped you'd say that.'

'I don't know that it's the wisest thing to go back, though,' she whispered.

His eyes seemed almost black, with little glints in them from the fire beside where they sat. The light bounced off his hair, and without thinking, Claire pushed her fingers through its softness. His head rested in her palm for a moment before he kissed her wrist, all the while looking into her eyes. It was a ridiculously sexy moment that simultaneously thrilled and scared her. Making love to him now would be very different from how it had been back then, and yet she wanted it so much.

He placed her hand back on the table. 'I think I'd better order some dinner before we forget we need to eat.'

While he was gone, every reason why it wasn't a good idea for them to go back presented themselves. Not least that it was only a few months since she was sure enough of Giles and their future to contemplate marriage.

'Tell me what's going through your head,' Owen said when he settled back in beside her, so close that under the table, their knees were touching. 'I can see it whirring away behind your eyes.'

'I'm scared,' Claire admitted. 'I'm not long out of a relationship, and the rest of my life isn't exactly stable, so my decision-making abilities would have to be suspect too.'

'I'd expect you would be scared – and just so you know, so am I. It's happened quickly, this thing that's between us, so maybe we should slow down just a little, to let us get to know each other properly again.'

'I'd like that. As long as it doesn't mean you stop touching me.'

'Oh, Della sweetheart, I'm worried if I touch you the way I really want to touch you, I'll never want to stop.'

'Would that be a bad thing?' Although it was all too fast, at that moment, Claire couldn't think of anything she'd like more.

He shook his head and bought her hand to his lips, kissing her sensitive palm. 'Not in the least. But nor would it be, as you said, the wisest thing we could do.'

'Why?'

'Am I telling you this? Why aren't I playing the game?'

Claire nodded.

'Because I get the feeling, you have no idea who you can trust at the moment, and I think you need to know you can feel safe with someone.'

'And that person is you?'

'That person is me. Neither of us were as honest with each other as we should've been back then – that doesn't mean we can't be now. Okay?'

'Okay.'

The waiter arrived with their dinner; Claire grinned when Owen quickly released her hand. 'Alright there, Chef?' she asked, trying to hide a smile as she placed their plates on the table.

'Well, that's one way of making sure the news spreads around town,' he said wryly once the girl had left.

Claire lifted one shoulder and grinned. 'Two old friends out for dinner. What's there to gossip about?'

'But we're not just two old friends, are we?'

'No,' she admitted, cutting into her pie. 'If we're getting to know one another again,' Claire said, 'tell me about Julia.'

'Where do you want me to start?'

'At the beginning? How did you meet?'

Owen replaced his cutlery neatly beside his plate. 'Julia came into Marco's one night with her crowd. It was her birthday. I had to take out the birthday cake, and she asked my name.' His smile was wry. 'I'd never met anyone like her. She knew what she wanted and wasn't at all afraid to go after it. She decided in that minute she wanted me, and I was dazzled by her. I was poor, she was not, yet it didn't seem to worry her. Then Bruno Belucci sought me out to replace his head chef, and I thought I'd made it. One night she suggested we get married, and before I knew it, that's exactly what we were – married. We married in the registry office and then had a massive reception in Chelsea that she'd invited all her friends to. I felt as though I was on show, but she'd convinced me I was the next big thing and she wanted everyone to know it too.

'We'd only been married a few months when Spooner's review came out. I was out of a job, but almost immediately was offered something in Yorkshire. It was another head chef role and a chance to cook the food I wanted to cook, so I jumped at it. Julia and I had a huge row, and she said she wasn't going to Yorkshire. She reminded me she was the one who controlled our financial lives and assured me she could talk someone else in London into taking me on, the way she'd talked Belucci into hiring me.'

Claire couldn't help the gasp of disbelief that escaped her lips.

'I know. She virtually said I owed it to her, that she hadn't invested so much time into me to have me piss it away in Yorkshire. It was her or Yorkshire — I couldn't have both.'

'Oh, Owen. I'm so sorry.'

'Yes, so was I. I haven't seen her since. It was probably the quickest divorce on record, I didn't want anything of hers — and everything I owned at the time fitted into the back of my car.' He lifted a shoulder, raising his eyebrows. 'And that was Julia. What about you and love? I know you briefly dated Ziggy, snogged Adrian Ritchie and Barty, and haven't long finished with Giles. Are there any others I need to know about?'

'Very funny. You're not going to have me believe that the entirety of your love life in the last sixteen or seventeen years has been one short-lived marriage?'

'Good point.'

'As for me, yes, I dated. In the interest of full disclosure, there was another chef — Jimmy Gillespie. You'd think I would've learnt after Ziggy — the hours those guys keep is ridiculous, but then you'd know all about that.'

'I certainly do.'

'Anyway, it didn't last long, and we're still friendly. Jimmy even invited me to the opening of his restaurant a couple of years ago – *GiGi*. He had a bit of a stutter after a Spooner review but seemed to have recovered, and I believe is doing well now.'

'Hang on, *GiGi* was on that list Tallis showed us the other day.'

'So it was. I didn't connect the dots at the time.'

'That's another link in the chain. That makes five places where you've had a personal connection to the restaurant: *Belucci's* with me, *Ziggy's*, *GiGi's*, *Lily James* and *Bella Donna*.'

'Trust me, I never snogged Bruno Belucci. I have no personal connection with the man.'

'No, but he's treated you badly.'

'That would give me a reason to savage *Bella Donna* – not that I would've needed a reason to do that – but it doesn't give me a reason for *Belucci's*.'

'I think that one was because of your connection to me.'

'But no one knew about that,' she said.

'Good point. Or it could be another reason entirely. I think we need to go back through that list of Tallis' and check out the ownership of each of the restaurants on the list.'

'To see if there are any others on the list who I've slept with?' Her eyes blazed.

'I didn't mean it to sound like that. I only meant to say we needed to see if there was a connection.'

At least he had the grace to look contrite, but before Claire could say more, someone slapped Owen on the back; Owen looked around and grinned widely. 'Chris Michaels! And Jenna! This is a surprise.'

Jenna's eyes met Claire's, and she smiled apologetically. 'I told Chris you guys were going to be here tonight and—'

'And I suggested we come down and have a few pints for old time's sake,' finished Chris, coming around to Claire's side of the table to kiss her cheek. 'Unless this was—' He looked across at his wife. 'Were these guys on a date?'

'You didn't exactly give me a chance to explain that they were.' Jenna shrugged.

'It doesn't matter, does it, Gallagher?' said Claire, glad to have them interrupt what could have descended into an argument. 'Pull some chairs up and join us.' She smiled at Chris. 'You haven't changed at all.'

'Except I've got a lot less hair these days,' he said, rubbing at his head. 'Whereas Gallagher, the lucky bastard, seems to have managed to keep all of his.'

'I'll get some more drinks.' Owen laughed, rising to his feet.

'It's my shout,' said Chris, joining him. Their good-natured banter mingled with the other patrons as they left to go to the bar.

'Are you sure we're not interrupting?' asked Jenna.

Claire shook her head. 'It's fine,' she smiled to put Jenna at ease. 'It'll be fun to catch up. Just like old times.'

It wasn't long before the four of them were laughing and joking in the way they did when they were eighteen with plans and dreams; and when both couples were wildly in love. If any of them had been told back then how life would become complicated, none of them would've believed it.

'How come you've never done an episode of *Time for Tea* in Brookford?' asked Jenna. 'I know you were back briefly for Horrie's funeral and come by from time to time to see Gracie. Other than that, we were beginning to think you didn't want anything else to do with Brookford.'

Her smile took some of the sting from her words and Claire inwardly winced.

Across the table, Owen, who still had to drive Claire home, was nursing a soda water, while Chris, fuelled with the certainty ale brings with it, was predicting the winner of the Champions League. As Claire glanced at Owen, he met her eyes and smiled before turning his attention back to Chris. Their eyes had held for less than a heartbeat, yet the message in them warmed Claire in a way the fire never could.

'The only reason we didn't do an episode here is

that we haven't had any bakers from Brookford apply to be on the show. That's what determined where we went,' Claire told Jenna. 'Some of the towns we've visited would never have been on my list, but each of them had something special.'

Jenna tilted her head slightly. 'That sounds awfully past tense. Aren't you doing any more shows? I thought last season was the most successful yet?'

Claire lifted one shoulder and traced lines in the condensation on her beer glass. 'No. The show is being rested for this year.'

'The scandal that broke just before Christmas?'

Claire nodded. Jenna watched her closely, but their eyes didn't meet. 'Yes. Let's just say my brand is a little tarnished at the moment.'

'I saw Bruno Belucci on one of the morning shows only last week, and he seemed pretty convinced you wrote the reviews. He's saying he'll probably have to close his restaurant.' She paused before adding, 'But you didn't write it, did you?'

Claire shook her head. 'No, I didn't. But he wants someone to blame, and I suppose I'm that person. Mind you, I suspect anyone who's eaten there and knows even the smallest amount about food would cheer that closure. I might not have written the review, but I've eaten there, and it wasn't good. Nice bathrooms though.' Her attempted cheeky grin seemed to convince Jenna.

Jenna laughed. 'Well, you can't discount the attraction of a well-designed bathroom.'

Soon after, the waiter called last drinks, and they said their goodbyes. Claire whistled for Nigel, who lifted his head and slowly got to his feet, stretching luxuriously. His canine companions raised their ears as if to acknowledge his departure and settled back down to wait for their respective masters.

Neither Claire nor Owen had much to say on the brief trip back to Curlew Cottage. The closeness in the car and the dark of the night made Claire as aware of him as she had been earlier in the evening before Chris and Jenna interrupted them. When she risked a look sideways at him, his jaw was firm. Claire wanted to reach out a hand and place it on his thigh, but she didn't know how he'd react – or maybe it was because she knew exactly how he'd react, and as much as she wanted that, she wasn't sure she was ready for it.

'Are you coming in?' Claire asked, opening the front door and smiling as Nigel bounced around them.

'Only to see you inside,' he said. 'But I'm not staying.'

She nodded. 'Okay.'

He followed her into the cottage, shutting the door behind him and moved closer, his eyes dark with intent, his dimples showing. 'But that doesn't mean I'm going to leave without kissing you – if that's okay with you, that is.'

She nodded again. His hands were warm and soft, and he pulled her towards him. When they were just centimetres apart, he cupped her cheeks. She stilled as Owen closed the gap and gently tasted her lips.

He pulled back slightly and looked so deeply into her eyes that Claire thought her heart would stop. 'Oh, Della,' he said, 'I've missed you.'

Claire brought his head back to hers so he could kiss her properly. So familiar, but at the same time, so very different. He walked her back until she was against the door, her legs opening to allow him to stand between them, his body pushing into hers, his hands reaching under her jumper, his lips trailing down the length of her neck and back to her mouth. She moaned when his hand found its way into her bra.

His hand stilled on her breast, their bodies pressed together, his forehead resting on hers, both of them panting for breath.

'Tell me to go,' he said.

'I don't want you to go.'

'Please, Dells, tell me to go. We can't do this yet.'

'I know. It's too soon.'

'Then tell me to go.'

'Go home,' she whispered.

He swallowed hard and wrenched himself away, dragging his hand away from her breast and straightening her jumper, tucking her hair behind her ears. 'I want you so badly, but not yet, my darling.'

The tenderness in his words sent a rush of emotion through Claire that was so strong it took away all power of speech. She nodded once and closed the gap between them again, kissing him firmly before pushing him away.

'I'll see you tomorrow,' Owen said when he opened the door, lingering for another kiss.

'Tomorrow?'

'Ed,' he reminded her.

'Tomorrow then.' He kissed her once more, and reluctantly closed the door behind himself.

Claire hurried across to the kitchen window and rubbed at the condensation so she could watch him get in his car. He waved once and drove back up the dark lane. She followed the red tail lights until they disappeared.

CHAPTER TWENTY-SEVEN

Claire barely slept – and when she did, she dreamed of Owen. If she could attribute the way she felt about him to muscle memory or nostalgia, then last night's kiss had thrown her into confusion. That kiss last night was a kiss like none other before it. As Claire cradled her mug of tea the next morning, her lips – and other parts of her body – still tingled with the memory of that kiss.

Claire shook her head to bring her mind back to the business of the day and the meeting with Ed. She was ready to go back to work and wanted this job badly, but it worried her what Jenna had said last night about how Belucci was still talking about the Spooner scandal to anyone who'd listen. The network was taking a huge risk by bringing her on board for this project, and Claire hoped what Belucci was still saying wouldn't influence them against her. For now, though, there were scones to bake. Scones would make it all better; they always did.

When Claire arrived at *The Lamb*, Ed was already there, fully caffeinated and sipping on what Claire guessed was probably his second or third coffee. He greeted her with a hug and introduced her to his team. Claire had already met Jody, his production assistant, and Elle, the administrative assistant; but Clark – from the legal team – was a new face for her.

'Don't worry so much about these guys today, Claire. They're here to take notes and remind me what I said and didn't say.'

'That's fine. I bought plenty of scones for everyone anyway.' She looked around the room. 'Where's Owen?'

'In the kitchen,' said Ed. 'You might want to put him on notice that we're right to start.'

'Okay.' Claire made a production out of placing her basket on a table so Ed couldn't see the blush that had risen to her cheeks. 'I'll go in and let him know we're all here.'

'You do that,' said Ed absently, already reaching into the basket for a scone.

Owen was sitting on one of the stainless-steel benches. The restaurant was closed, so he was dressed in jeans and a wool jumper. Today's was an olive green that made his hair look redder and his eyes browner, and Claire wanted nothing more than to snuggle into his warmth.

'Hey,' she said in a husky tone as she leant against the door frame.

'Hey yourself.' He straightened and smiled but made no move to close the distance between them.

'What are you doing out here?'

'Waiting for you and worrying that you're going to walk through that door and declare last night's kiss – the one that kept me awake for the rest of the night – was a mistake and can't happen again.'

'Aah.' Claire sauntered towards him until she was standing almost between his legs, 'And what if I said that I laid awake most of the night worrying that you were going to say the same?'

In one swift move his arm was around her waist. 'I'd say that we were both worrying needlessly.'

Claire ran her fingers through his hair, linking them behind his head and gradually lowered his lips to hers. When she pulled back, his eyes had darkened.

He stroked her cheek. 'I could get used to good morning kisses like this.'

A thrill rushed through her as she imagined waking up beside him. His dimples deepened as he watched her face before kissing her again.

'We'd better get out there.' Claire gasped as he lay a trail of kisses down her throat.

Owen lifted his head reluctantly. 'We had, but you're going to need to give me a few minutes.' He slid down from the counter and pulled her hips into his so she could tell exactly why.

'Off to the cool room with you,' she joked and pressed her body even closer.

He squeezed his eyes closed. 'What are you doing to me, Della?'

'I could ask the same of you,' she whispered and gently pushed him away. 'Go, make yourself respectable, and I'll see you out there.'

He grinned, kissed her once more, hard, on the lips and nudged her out the door into the restaurant.

'Everything alright?' asked Ed, his gaze narrowing as she arrived back to the table.

'Absolutely,' said Claire, paying more attention to pulling a chair out from the table than was required.

He handed her some paperwork. 'We'll need this for later,' he said. 'It's a mock-up of what we'd like the season to look like. You might as well have a glance through it while we wait for Owen.'

Owen joined them a short time later, smiling at Claire before heading behind the bar to make coffee.

Ed nodded slowly, scrutinising Claire's cheeks and Owen's smile. 'I sure hope this translates to the camera.'

'What?' Claire asked.

'This energy you two have happening. If you haven't shagged yet, don't – wait until after we've finished filming.'

'Seriously?' said Claire. 'You just said that?'

'If that's the case, you'd better get the formalities dealt with quickly and those cameras rolling,' said Owen from behind the coffee machine.

'Oh god,' Claire groaned, 'you're both as bad as each other.' She pulled the cloth off the top of her basket to lift out the plate of scones. 'Here, have a scone. Oh, I see you already have.'

Clark brushed at a crumb on his pants, and Jody smiled.

'And very good they are too.' Ed shrugged nonchalantly.

'You even remembered to bring jam and cream,' said Elle.

Once everyone had coffees and more scones, Ed finally got down to talking business.

'As you'd probably recall, we were quite a way down the track with the contract negotiations with Barty when things were put on hold in December.'

Claire shook her head. 'Yes and no. Barty told me we'd agreed on terms and had no issues with the contract. But he also said the project was being stalled due to problems with finding a male presenter.'

'Yes, there were problems with that. You know Bruno Belucci wanted to do it? His people were pushing for him.'

'I heard and ugh.'

Ed laughed. 'Yeah, I thought you might've had that reaction. Then we were in talks with Adrian Ritchie's people, but Barty said he thought your styles might be too different. While the premise of the show rests on you cooking side by side with a chef, for it to work, we needed a chef whose food was approachable and not beyond the scope of viewers. Belucci was never going to work; the guy might look good—'

'That's a matter of opinion,' said Claire.

'In the focus groups we held, the women loved his look, but whenever he's done *Saturday Kitchen* he's come across as being arrogant – viewers feel that he's talking down to them. As for Ade, he's the complete package in terms of looks and presentation, but with all of his gels and dusts and sprays, his food is unachievable for the home viewer. I'd say that's what Barty meant when he said that your styles were too different. What we want to see is, for example, a home cook's version of roast chicken and one that would be served up in a restaurant like this, not one that's called something like Essence of Roast Dinner and has the carrot in a dust, or worse, an ice cream, and the gravy in little frozen balls of gel. And that's where Owen came in.' He paused and bit into his scone. 'These are good, Claire. Where was I?'

'With Owen,' Claire said.

'Yes. Owen's food is perfect – seasonal British classics using British ingredients and elevated to restaurant standards – and his camera presence isn't bad either, so my wife tells me. She said more than that, but we don't need to feed his ego. I don't see it myself.' He shrugged, and Claire and Owen laughed as they were supposed to.

'One of the reasons we asked Owen to do *Time for Tea* was because I wanted to see how you interacted with each other. I had no idea you were teenage sweethearts or something – that was just an added bonus as far as the chemistry went – but when we watched the footage, we knew we had the right person, so we approached him almost immediately.

'Then the Spooner thing broke, and the network wanted to shelve the entire project. At the very least we thought we'd need to find two new hosts – you were damaged and even if we took a risk on you—'

Claire winced as Ed, as always, told it as it was.

'We figured there was no way Owen would want to work with you now he knew who'd written the review that got him fired.' Ed paused and looked across at Owen. 'Instead, he was so far on your side – to the extent he said if we didn't have you onboard, we didn't have him either.'

Claire's eyes burned, and she couldn't risk a glance at Owen.

Ed trained his gaze on Claire. 'I'll be straight with you, Claire—'

'When have you ever been anything but?'

'True.' He paused briefly. 'We know there's more to the Spooner story than what we're hearing, there are people who are worried about what that's done to your brand, so tell me now: are we likely to have any trouble from The Spoonman?'

'I don't know,' Claire answered honestly. 'I don't read any of the magazines or watch the talk shows, but a friend of mine said she'd seen Bruno blaming the demise of *Bella Donna* on me.'

'I heard that too,' said Ed. 'I think if we can get you to tell your story to a friendly journalist – well, as much as you're allowed to tell – and we get some of the chefs who you've *apparently* damaged to stand up for you too, enough people will want to believe you rather than Bruno Belucci. He can say what he wants, but if no one is listening ...' He lifted one shoulder.

For the first time since that awful moment back in December when the story broke, Claire thought she might just get her life back. 'I know you're talking about Owen, but who else?'

'How about Adrian Ritchie for starters?' said Owen. 'He feels awful for his part in what happened on *Cook-off*.'

'Oh, I don't know, that yule log was pretty bad.' Claire attempted a laugh.

'You know what I mean, Della,' he murmured. 'The way he treated you made that so much worse; he humiliated you on national television.'

Claire shifted in her chair. 'I don't blame him for that.'

'Maybe not,' said Owen, 'but he feels badly about it.'

'Well, he doesn't need to.' She buttered another scone, unable to meet Owen's eyes, and forced her mind back into business mode. 'Barty told me he's in discussions with people about something new for me, so he'll need to be brought into the loop sooner rather than later.'

Ed nodded. 'I don't know who he's talking to and as I said to you the other day, I haven't heard anything. But yes, the point of today was to see if you're in; if this is something that you'd like to do. I know I'd normally take it to Barty but seeing as how I was catching up with Owen anyway, it's a two birds thing.'

'The short answer to that is yes, I'm in. I was interested in the project last year, but with Owen on board I think it's really exciting.' Her cheeks were burning as she realised how that must have sounded. 'It's also something that if it works, we can build on for future seasons. I just want to clarify what you mean by the weekly themes though.' Claire picked up the paperwork Ed had given her when she first sat down. 'Take episode one, for example – roast chicken. Owen might do the roast chicken he'd have on the menu here with a fancy jus, and I might take an express option and do a tray-bake roast – for those nights where you want roast chicken but don't have the time to do it properly, don't want any of the washing up, and want something you can throw into a tray and into an oven and let it do its thing while you have a bath. Is that how you're thinking?'

'That's exactly the approach we wanted to take,' said Ed. 'Owen will do the posh version, and you'll do the simpler version.'

'That makes sense. What else is on this list? Comfort Food, Date Night, Family Budget Favourites.'

She turned to Owen, 'I'd like to see you do that.'

Owen grinned and just like that they were in a world of their own again.

'Come to think on it,' said Ed, watching them. 'Maybe you two should shag and get it out of your systems before the cameras start rolling or we won't get anything done.'

'There's an idea,' said Owen.

'And for Christ's sake, don't break up before we finish the series. On second thoughts I'm not sure the shagging is a good idea. I can't have a heart-broken host trying to poison her co-host – or vice versa.'

Claire shook her head in mock censure. 'Let's keep this to business. As I was saying, there's also One-Pot Wonders, Taking It Outside …' She looked up at Ed. 'I hope you're referring to picnic or barbecue food?'

He nodded.

'Okay, but who wrote these titles? What else? Breakfast, Sunday Night Supper, and Getting Your Hands Dirty – which is another one I'd like to see you get your cheffy head around, Owen.'

'Not a problem at all,' he said. 'I'm up for it.'

Claire rolled her eyes at the double entendre.

'We need to speak about how the competition part will work,' said Ed.

At the mention of the word "competition", Claire faltered and panic set in. 'What competition?'

'Don't worry,' Ed said. 'It's all quite lighthearted.

We'll film the episodes here at *The Lamb*, and there'll be a group of diners – we're thinking about six people – to act as a judging panel. There'll be a different group each week. You'll each serve your dish for tasting, and they'll choose which one they enjoyed the most. Instead of a score, you'll get a cloche at the end of the service with the name of the panel's favourite dish in it. We're not going live, and none of us wants to see anyone embarrassed. We'll keep a tally, but it's more about bragging rights than the competition as such.'

Claire was relieved. 'I'm cool with that. Owen?'

'Yes, it all sounds fine to me. My lawyer has looked over the contract, and we're right to go.'

'Good. That just leaves you, Claire. Are you okay if I approach Barty now?'

'I am. Let Barty know you've spoken to me. He'll have a little tantrum at being left out, but that's how it goes. So long as the dollars we were talking about last year haven't changed, and the contract is the same, there shouldn't be a problem.'

'Good,' said Ed. 'We'll use the slots we already had booked in for *Time for Tea* so have been working away in the background to be ready to start filming in the first week in May with an air date in the middle of September. I'd suggest you two get together regularly in the meantime and do some practice and planning. We'll be photographing each completed dish with a view to publishing a companion cookbook – which will need to be ready for release on the day after the last episode – so whatever you cook had better be perfect. Claire, you're used to working with a recipe, but Owen, that'll be a challenge for you.'

Owen nodded. 'I understand. I guess that's where the practice comes in.'

'Exactly. It might seem like you have plenty of time, but trust me, you don't. By next week I'd like to have both contracts signed – Claire, would you be able to get up to London later this week if we can agree on terms?'

'Yes. That's not a problem.'

'For now, though, I'm going to need each of you to sign a non-disclosure agreement. We can't have a word of this getting out before we're ready to start marketing.' He looked across at Claire. 'We'll also talk to publicity about booking in an interview to tell your side of The Spoonman story, so you'd better get in touch with the paper and find out exactly what you're allowed to say.'

'I will,' she said.

'Good,' said Ed. 'We'll schedule a production meeting for every Monday morning going forward – with the first one for Monday after next. Don't worry, you won't need to come to London – we'll dial you in. I'll have Jody set it up and send through the agendas for each.'

Once Ed and his team left, Claire began stacking

the empty cups and scone plates and took them into the kitchen. Owen followed with the remaining crockery and packed them in one of the dishwashers.

'What do you think?' Owen asked once they had put the room back to rights.

'I'm really excited.'

'About the show, I meant,' he said with a wicked smile.

'Ha ha. Seriously though, I think this will be a great opportunity for us both – but I also think it'll be fun.'

'Yeah, me too.' He leaned back against the kitchen counter. 'What do you want to do now? I have the rest of the day off and, if you don't have anything else planned, I'd like to spend it with you.'

She peered through the window to the clear, blue sky. 'It's beautiful out there now. Why don't we drop by my place and pick up Nigel and go to a pub somewhere for lunch? We can chat about some ideas for that first episode and how my roast chicken will kick your arse.'

'Plus, if we're out in public, I have no choice but to keep my hands off you.'

'We're not in public now.'

'No, we're not. And I've been very much looking forward to kissing you again. It's been hours since the last kiss.'

'According to the clock on the oven it's been at least two,' said Claire, linking her arms around his waist.

'That's two hours too long.'

CHAPTER TWENTY-EIGHT

After dropping into Curlew Cottage to pick up Nigel, Claire and Owen drove up to Broadway for lunch, laughing when the pub they chose offered a two-course fixed-price lunch deal comprising the soup of the day and their roast of the day – which was chicken.

Over lunch they tossed around ideas and flavour combinations, bouncing off each other in the way they used to do, Nigel snoring peacefully under the table. Some episode themes were going to present Owen with more of a challenge than they'd be for Claire – like One-Pot Wonders or Comfort Food – while others like Date Night would require Claire to think more creatively.

'Did it take you long to get used to the cameras?' asked Owen as they lingered over coffee.

Claire chuckled. 'Sometimes I think I'm still not used to it. At first, I thought they'd send me on a How to Be A Presenter on TV course, but apparently they don't exist. Mind you, I also thought I'd have someone to do my hair and make-up, but that also doesn't happen on *Time for Tea*. At first, they gave me scripts that I memorised, but none of it sounded – or felt – natural. Then one day they filmed me chatting to one of the local growers without me knowing it was happening and decided I was best without a script, so that's the way we've gone ever since. It makes it easier in that I'm genuinely interested in the people we meet.' She held his eyes. 'In all seriousness, though, that's going to be the main thing you might have issues with. While you and I will be making a cooking program, the production team is making TV. It's not how or what we cook that will bring viewers to us, but how we interact with each other. While they're not after a conflict, they do want sparks, banter and friendly competition. They want a story that can be told in ten seconds and there'll be times when the producers will push for that, for a reaction – even if you're in the middle of reducing a sauce.'

Owen's brows furrowed. 'In other words, Ed wasn't entirely joking when he told us not to sleep together yet.'

Claire dropped her eyes to the table and nodded.

'I see. Do you agree with that?'

She wrinkled her nose and considered her choice of words before raising her eyes. 'Ed was speaking with his producer's hat on. If I were in Ed's shoes doing his job, I'd probably give us exactly the same advice. What will attract people to watch will be the premise of the show, and what will keep them watching will be our chemistry. Unresolved sexual tension – the whole "are they or aren't they" thing – is priceless. It would be Ed's worst nightmare if something went wrong between us and that tension was replaced with awkwardness.' She paused slightly. 'There's another thing – Ed didn't say as much and wouldn't, but I'd like to bet one of the reasons the network is taking another chance on me is because I haven't refuted the Spooner story and they know you were the subject of a Spooner review. Regardless of what Ed says now, I wouldn't be surprised if he uses that in the pre-launch publicity. I certainly would.'

He let out a short laugh. 'They'll use anything, won't they? I thought Ed was one of the good guys.'

Claire rushed to defend her friend. 'He is, but he also has a job to do. It's a fine line for him to walk, but I trust him. Besides,' she continued, 'as much as I want to, you know—' The blood rushed to her face, 'be with you, I'm not long out of a relationship, and I want to be sure.'

He studied her face for a heartbeat, maybe two. 'You want to be sure we're not just taking a little skip down memory lane?'

She nodded. 'I suppose that's what I mean, and we do have a lot of work to do over the next few months. I just don't think we need the distraction.'

'And I'd be a distraction?'

Her heart clenched at the tone in his voice. Smiling gently, she said, 'Gallagher, you're one hell of a distraction. I'm just saying you were right last night when you said we need to slow things down and get to know each other again.'

He groaned as Claire used his own words against him. 'I knew I'd regret saying that.'

'My life was completely turned upside down, and I still don't know which way is up. And now you're here, and I don't want to grab hold of that in case it's just about going back to when life was easy. When we do get together, I want it to be because I'm choosing you even though it might not be easy. Does that make sense?'

'Yes. Unfortunately, it does.' He sighed heavily. 'In other words, no more kissing, no more touching, and back to the friend zone.'

'For now, anyway.' Claire forced the words, even though her heart and her body were screaming not to. 'Besides, we'll be seeing so much of each other over the next six months you'll probably end up sick of me.'

'Oh, Dells, I doubt that very much. But we've been apart for seventeen years, what's another few months? Just so you know, I don't intend to give up on you this time and I won't make it easy for you to give up on me. But that means you'll guide me – you'll be the one who has to make the next move.'

Claire didn't know whether it was the promise in his words or the intent in his eyes that sent a charged thrill up her spine.

•

After lunch they walked through Broadway, admiring the honey-coloured stone houses with their picture-perfect gardens that would be a riot of colour when spring arrived. Some already showed the promise of warmer weather, with little clumps of jonquils here and there. With Nigel on one side and Owen on the other, Claire didn't think she could remember a more perfect afternoon out.

As they meandered along the footpath, a couple gave Claire a sideways glance and whispered to each other behind their hands.

'Does that happen a lot?' Owen asked when Claire returned the smile of a fellow dog walker. 'The looks from other people.'

'No, not that often. I think I've got one of those faces that looks familiar, but it's not like I'm a real celebrity.'

'Sweetheart, they only need to see those spectacular eyes of yours to know who you are.' They'd stopped to pick up after Nigel. 'Even if you are picking up dog shit.' He grinned as she tied the plastic bag off. 'Now there's a photo for the front page of the tabloids.'

Claire giggled at that. 'The first time anyone recognised me, I was in Tesco. About four episodes of the first series of *Time for Tea* had aired, and I'd rushed out of the flat to get more flour for a piece I was writing for Duncan. You saw the state of me after I'd been baking the other day?'

He smiled and nodded.

'I looked like that: Black leggings, a sweatshirt, trainers, my hair up in a ponytail, no make-up, and flour all over me. Someone called my name, and I looked around automatically. It was weird, but it hadn't occurred to me that anyone would ever recognise me. Anyway, the picture found its way onto social media and then into the papers. I thought the whole thing was a bit of a laugh, but Barty, oh my goodness, Barty had a right cow about it. I got a lecture from him about making sure I didn't leave the house looking anything less than, as he put it, appropriately dressed. "Darling," he'd said, "I know you're the girl next door, but please for the love of Christ, at least make sure your jeans are clean and you have a bra on."'

Owen laughed as she parodied Barty's voice. 'Seriously though,' she said, 'I've been fortunate. Because my image has been the girl next door and I always wear jeans on the show, people don't expect to see me glammed up, and most of the time I'm left alone. At least, that's how it was until the Spooner scandal.'

He circled his arm around her shoulder and pulled her into his side. 'And that's how it will be again, I'm sure of it.'

Barty phoned as they approached the car. Owen took Nigel's lead from Claire and went across the road into the deli to give her some privacy.

'Where are you?' he asked, after exchanging the usual pleasantries.

'In Broadway. I'm okay to talk though.'

'Good. I had a call from Ed Wilson a little while ago. He told me he'd been in Brookford talking to you about this new show. Are you sure it's something you want to do?'

'Absolutely. Besides, we discussed it late last year when the idea first came up. You were right behind the idea then.'

'Yes, but Owen Gallagher is untried. I know he's your old boyfriend, but he has no on-screen presence.'

'That's unfair, Barty. Owen had great feedback after his appearance on *Time for Tea*, and he's not exactly a newbie – he's been on *Saturday Kitchen*, and I know they were looking at him for *Great British Menu*. He'll be fine, and his food is not so fancy as to be out of the reach of a home cook. I think Owen is a perfect choice.'

He was silent for a few seconds. 'Have you been seeing a bit of him then?'

She didn't know why, but something made her hold back on revealing the extent of their relationship. 'A little. I've also caught up with the ladies from Fenwyck and am reconnecting with other friends from high school too.'

'You're sounding a bit too comfortable out there, Claire. At this rate, you'll never want to come home.'

He said it as if he couldn't contemplate the idea of staying in the country when there was a life to be lived in London.

'I'm beginning to wonder whether London *is* home,' she admitted.

'Now you're being silly. That's what I mean when I say I'm not sure this is such a good vehicle for you.'

'You thought it was good late last year. You said it was a good deal and that it was a great next step for me. What's changed?'

'I wasn't going to say this, but I'm concerned about the impact the Spooner scandal has had on your reputation, and I don't want to see you hurt as a result.'

'We discussed this Barty; we'll schedule an interview before beginning the publicity and paint me as the injured party. It'll be fine. Besides, I have to go back to work at some stage, and this is being filmed in Brookford so it couldn't be more perfect.' She paced around the car, stopping to lean against the bonnet when her animated hand gestures attracted attention from passers-by.

'There are other options.'

'Like what? You tell me you're talking to people about other ideas, but you won't tell me who or what.'

He was silent for a moment. 'You sound like you don't trust me, Claire. Where's that coming from?' he bit back.

Owen and Nigel were back, Nigel pulling ahead

on his lead for the last few metres before jumping up against her and then, at her signal, sitting quietly at her feet. Owen unlocked the car for Nigel to hop in before coming to lean against the car beside her.

She shook her head. 'Of course, I trust you. I'm just saying if you want me to make an informed decision about which project I'm to work on, I need some facts to make that call. And that means more information than you telling me you have other things on the go that you can't talk about yet. I want to go back to work, Barty, and I want to rebuild my career. This offer is perfect. It's working with a team I'm familiar with, and like, the money is right, the location is right, and the idea is a good one.

'Most importantly, the offer is here, now, on the table ready to be signed, so unless you have a better idea, I want to sign it.' She paused for a second or two to let those words sink in. 'You spent a long time at the end of last year convincing me of all the reasons why I should do it. I don't understand why you no longer think it's the "right vehicle" for me.' She rolled her eyes at Owen, who smiled patiently. 'And unless you can give me a great reason why I shouldn't, I plan on being in your office sometime this week to sign that contract.'

'Okay,' he conceded. 'You want to do it. I get that, but I'll bring the contract to you. I want to meet Owen and see where you'll be filming before I let you sign.'

Claire took a deep breath. 'Before you let me sign?'

she said slowly. Beside her, Owen raised his eyebrows. 'I'm sorry, Barty, you might be my manager, but you don't get to tell me what I can and can't do. You can advise me, you can guide me, but you don't own me, and you don't get to dictate to me.'

She waited a few seconds for him to react.

'Maybe that wasn't the best choice of words,' he said in a soothing tone, 'and I'm sorry if I upset you. You know I care about you and just want to see you make the best decisions for you. Mostly though, I don't want you to get hurt by rushing into anything.'

Although he was talking about work, there was an inclination he was referring to something else. He couldn't possibly know about Owen.

'I understand that Barty, but the fact is, I *was* hurt, and now I need to do everything in my power to repair that. Being here has been a good way for me to begin healing, and this show will help rebuild my professional life.'

'In that case, I'll see you during the week. How does Wednesday sound?'

'Wednesday?' Claire glanced at Owen, who nodded. 'That sounds good. Come to my place first, I'll email you the directions, and we can talk. Then we can go into Brookford to *The Lamb* once Owen has finished lunch service and you can do your meet and greet.'

'Can we make it in the morning? I have to be back in town for something in the afternoon,' he said. After a second or so of silence, he added, 'And I'm sorry if I upset you.'

'It's fine,' she said. 'I've already forgotten it.'

But she hadn't. As Claire placed her phone back inside her bag, she replayed the conversation in her head.

'Are you alright?' asked Owen.

'Yes.' Although Barty had her best interests at heart, something was niggling. She shook her head slightly to clear it.

Owen frowned. 'Are you sure?'

'No, I'm not sure. There's something … I don't know … It's probably nothing. In fact, I'm sure it's nothing.'

It was probably nothing.

CHAPTER TWENTY-NINE

For the hour it took to drive home, Claire tried to put her conversation with Barty out of her head and regain the easy banter she'd had with Owen before Barty called.

After one too many minutes of silence, Owen said, 'there's something bothering you, isn't there?'

She hesitated, looking out the window.

'Talk to me, Dells. It might help you work it through.'

Claire sighed in resignation. 'It wasn't anything Barty said – or maybe it was. I think he's been lying to me.' She took a deep breath and gathered her thoughts. 'Both Giles and Ed had told me they'd called and spoken to Barty, yet he didn't tell me. He says he *did* tell me about their calls and it probably didn't register with me, but I don't think he did. I think Barty wanted me to believe they hadn't cared enough to call. Now I'm wondering about whether he's also telling the truth about having other projects on the go. For some reason, he doesn't want me to do this, yet last year he did – in fact, he spent ages convincing me I should.'

'Why do you think he's lied about it?'

'I don't know for sure he is, I just have this feeling. It makes no sense for him not to want me to work. After all, if I work, he earns money. I don't understand what's changed since the last time this was on the table.' She sighed heavily. 'Well, there's one big thing that's changed – and that's the goodwill I have in the industry and with the public. That's what I can't get my head around – given that's an issue, I would've thought Barty would jump at any opportunity at the moment, and this is a good one. Instead, he's umming and aaahing and saying he doesn't think it's right for me.'

'Don't forget, the other thing that's changed is the co-host situation. You told me the last you'd heard about it, Barty had mentioned they were talking to Bruno Belucci, yet Ed told you that Adrian Ritchie was in consideration. Why do you think Barty didn't tell you that?'

'I have no idea, but I think you've just hit on what's been knocking in my brain – Barty has taken Bruno on as a client. He told me when I called in to see him the other week. It would absolutely be in his interest to have both of us on the same show. And Adrian pulled out once I was exposed as The Spoonman. I assumed that Belucci had already been discounted … maybe I was wrong.'

'Why don't you ring Ed and check,' he suggested.

Ed picked up on the first ring.

'Just so you know I'm in the car and have you on hands-free,' she said.

'No problems. Is Owen there?'

'He is, so be nice.'

Ed chuckled. 'I'll try but can't guarantee anything. Has Barty called you?' he asked. 'He didn't sound anywhere near as pleased as I would've thought he would be when we spoke.'

'Yes,' said Claire. 'I haven't long got off the phone to him. Don't worry about him, I'm committed to this project, and he's bringing the contract out on Wednesday. Hey, this is probably a stupid question, but when did Ade pull out of contention? Was it after the Spooner story?'

'Yes. Although, as I said to you earlier, we weren't convinced he was the right fit for you.'

The niggle was still there. 'Earlier today you mentioned Barty had said he thought Ade's style was wrong for the show – when was that?'

'Should I be reading anything into these questions, Claire?' he asked.

'I'm not sure yet.'

'Okay, Barty came back to us at the end of November and said you had some concerns about working with Ade. He also suggested Bruno Belucci – which really surprised me as I didn't think you got on with him at all. When I mentioned that to Barty, he said it would make for some interesting dynamics on the show.'

'It would certainly do that,' Claire agreed.

'Bruno wasn't even on our radar anymore – we'd done some polling on him, and it wasn't good, so we were still holding out for Ade. Then when the Spooner story hit, Ade said he didn't want to be associated with any project that involved you. By that stage, we'd already seen the footage out of Fenwyck and had approached Owen. At about the same time, Bruno contacted me directly and said he was still interested, but I told him we had shelved the show.'

'Didn't you think that was strange? That Ade wouldn't want to be involved with any project that I was working on, yet Belucci, who I'd apparently written about twice, had no such qualms?'

'Yes, it did, but to be honest, I didn't take him seriously.'

'Perhaps he thought a way of getting the public to like him was to show on national television that he'd forgiven me, that he was the bigger man.'

'You could have something there. After the Spooner story broke, he became a victim, and that brought with it more public sympathy than he could've earned in any other way.' Ed hesitated before adding, 'If you asked me why Barty isn't keen now, I'd say it's because it now involves Owen. When he found out Owen had done *Time for Tea* and I hadn't run it past him, he tore strips off me.'

'Really? You didn't tell me that.' She turned to look at Owen, eyebrows raised. 'You'd never cleared guests with him before, so why would you think you needed to do it then?'

'Exactly. If I didn't know better, I would've said he was carrying on like a jealous boyfriend.'

'But there's never been anything between us,' Claire protested.

'So you've said. Anyway, I have to keep moving,' said Ed. 'Let me know how you go on Wednesday.'

'I will. Thanks, Ed.'

'No problems. Have fun you two.'

'We will,' said Owen, taking his eyes from the road and meeting hers for half a second.

'Say it, Della,' Owen said, finally breaking the silence that had lingered. 'It won't be real until you say it out loud, so say it.'

'Barty lied to me,' she whispered, knowing exactly what Owen was referring to. 'He lied about Ade and Bruno, and I think he's lied to me about the other work he says he has for me. If he's lied to me about that, what else has he lied to me about? How long has Bruno been his client? Is that why he was pushing so hard for Bruno?' She hesitated, knowing that as soon as her next words were out in the open, she could never take them back. 'I think Barty was involved with leaking the story.'

Owen took one hand off the steering wheel and rested it on her thigh. 'I think you're right. Now we just need to know why.'

At home, Nigel bounded out of the car the moment the door was opened and bolted into the garden, to bark at the donkeys on the other side of the fence.

'Are you coming in?' Claire asked tentatively.

He nodded. 'Yes, I can get the fire going for you. It'll be freezing inside.'

Once inside, they each hung their jackets on the hook by the door. The cottage had been closed up all day, and there was a definite chill in the air.

'Do you want tea?' Claire asked, grimacing at the stilted conversation and the similarities to the first time he was here.

'No thanks,' he said as he poked at the kindling and paper to encourage the flames. 'But I'll take a glass of wine if you have one on offer.'

'I can do that.'

Claire poured wine into two glasses and handed him his before walking back into the kitchen and leaning against the table to watch him lift another log into the fireplace.

'Boys and fires,' she commented lightly.

'We do like to play with it,' he said, a wicked look on his face as he glanced up, the light of the fire in the background making his hair look alive.

Staying out of his arms was going to take some doing.

Owen stood and replaced the screen in front of the fireplace. 'That should burn for a while,' he said as he turned and smiled the same smile that had taken her breath away earlier.

'Are you hungry?' she asked, her mouth suddenly dry.

'Yes, but somehow I don't think what I really want is on offer at the moment.'

Claire's breath caught. She opened the fridge to look inside, even though she knew the contents by heart. 'No, but I can do you a pasta. Carbonara alright with you?'

'Sounds good. You're not a cream-in-your-carbonara woman though, are you?'

'No. Would that be a deal-breaker?'

'No, but it would mean that carbonara making duties would fall to me.'

'God, Gallagher, you're such a chef.'

He came up behind her, lingered for a second before pulling her against him. 'But all of those years of practice have made me good with my hands.'

Claire closed her eyes briefly as his warmth seeped through her. She sucked in a breath and lightly slapped his hands away before they could reach her breasts and make her forget all about the friend zone. 'There'll be none of that. Can you let Nigel back in please?'

He cursed lightly under his breath and stepped away, let the dog in, and made himself comfortable at the table to watch her cook.

'I know you probably don't want to talk about Barty, but you know we have to.'

She didn't pretend not to know what he was talking about. 'Yes, I know we do. He'll be here on Wednesday, and I need to decide how I'm going to play it.' She filled a large saucepan with water and put it on to boil, adding a generous pinch of salt.

'Do you think he knew you were Spooner?'

Claire nodded and began chopping pancetta. 'I do, even though he put on an Oscar-worthy act when I told him. I can't believe he was the one who leaked it, but I think he's responsible for it. Barty used to be a massive gossip, he still is, and I think he might've told someone I used to be Spooner, and it's come from that. He could've found something on my laptop at home that would've given it away, although why he never said so at the time, I don't know. That's not at all like him, but I think that's the real reason he hasn't wanted to set up an interview for me to tell my side of the story – in case they can trace the story back to him. No matter how long ago it was, if he was the source, he'll be in a deep pile of shit with his clients – none of them would ever trust him again. That's why I think it was accidental – there's no other reason he'd deliberately betray me like that; I'm his best friend. He saw what it did to me.'

Even saying the words out loud brought back the memories of that awful day back in December. The disgust in Ade's eyes and the humiliation on national television. Opening her social media accounts to see the hundreds of comments and the scathing headlines had bought her to tears. And lying awake all night knowing that tomorrow there'd be more of the same, wondering if she could ever show her face in public again. No, there was nothing that could've motivated Barty to put her through that – and no way he could sit back and watch while she was going through it.

'Maybe it wasn't him?' she said hopefully, tipping the pancetta into a frypan. 'Perhaps we're mistaken, and there's a reasonable explanation for everything. I trusted him – I've always trusted him. I thought when all of this blew up that he was the only person I *could* trust. If it is him, all I know is that I know nothing, and I can't trust anyone.'

Owen would've heard what she really wanted to say: *how can I let myself fall into a relationship with you when I don't even know if I can trust my closest friend?*

She risked a glance at him. He nodded once to let her know he understood. 'It's okay, Della. I get it.'

She offered him a sad smile.

'Let's think about this logically. If, as you say, there's no clear motivation for Barty to leak the information, is there anyone else it could be?'

She shook her head as she moved the pancetta

about in the pan. 'The only other people who knew were Giles and Duncan. Of those two, Giles would be the most obvious choice. He's a journalist himself, so if he wanted to drop something like that onto someone's desk, he'd know how to do it and who to drop it to. The problem with that theory is our split wasn't a nasty one. Mostly, though, his journalistic integrity is a deal-breaker for him. If it were to come out that he'd leaked something like The Spoonman story to a tabloid, it would shoot his credibility to pieces. There would be no coming back from that for him. Plus, Ed mentioned he's looking to get a deal for a documentary off the back of his book. He wouldn't risk it, even if he had a problem with our break-up. But that doesn't mean there's not someone out there who wants me to think it was Giles. After all, Giles and I are the only ones who know that our split was okay.'

She poured some vermouth into the pan and watched as it bubbled away into a bacony syrup.

'Vermouth?'

'I know it's not traditional, but it's a Nigella thing.'

'Naturally. What about Duncan, your editor? He knew it was you.'

'Yes, but he has even less motivation than Giles. When a Spooner review is published, the digital read rate spikes. The great ones get shared around social media, which leads to a bigger ongoing readership. Part of the deal with Alex Spooner is that no one knew who it was. They were the culinary man or woman of mystery. You've seen the logo – a simple black spoon. Once they exposed me as being *that* person, the mystery would be gone. Chefs would know who I was and would cringe when I walked in or refuse to take my booking. There'd never be another Spooner piece again.'

Claire set the pancetta aside, plunged some spaghetti into boiling salted water and began grating parmesan.

'If it was Barty, he's taken a massive risk, but maybe he thought he could control that risk by controlling me. No, I still think it was accidental, and he's now in damage control. As long as I didn't start talking too much about how it wasn't me, questions wouldn't be asked. And he stopped me from saying too much by telling me no one would believe me. It's why I didn't call Ed, or you, or anyone else earlier than I did. What he hadn't banked on was that you'd put two and two together and get a different number – and that you'd start telling people. And that presented him with a problem because you of all people were supposed to hate me.'

Owen sipped his wine as she cracked one egg into a bowl and separated the other, adding the yolk to the whole egg and popping the white into a cup in the fridge. She grated over some nutmeg, added a little pepper and whisked it all together with a fork.

'Perhaps we need to look at this differently,' said Owen. 'I know you discounted it before, but what if it wasn't accidental? What could be his motivation? One of them might be Bruno Belucci and whatever is in the background for him.'

'It would need to be more than a couple of Belucci cookbooks for Barty to risk the income he gets from me.'

'Exactly, and there would be other ways of doing that that wouldn't have exposed or hurt you as much as this did. I think this is about you. And it's about me.'

Stirring the cheese into the eggy mix, she paused and considered what he'd said. 'I don't know why.'

'I think Barty is in love with you – or,' he added as Claire was about to interrupt him, 'at the very least he wants to keep you for himself. And one of the best ways of doing that is to take enough away from you so you need to lean on him and depend on him.'

She thought back to the number of times he'd offered her financial help, refuge, told her he'd always be there for her to lean on. 'But he's never … no.' She shook her head. 'Absolutely not. He's never given any indication of that.'

'Did he know about our history?'

She nodded. 'Some of it. He didn't know about the baby – no one knew about that. But he knew we were in love and that you broke my heart.'

'That would explain why he went ballistic when

Ed used me on *Time for Tea*. This all happened after that went to air. No one seeing that footage could've denied the chemistry between us.'

'And I told him we'd talked and were okay.' Claire returned the pancetta pan to the heat and added some butter to it. Then she turned the pasta off and drained it into a colander before tossing it into the pan with the pancetta and butter. 'Hold that thought,' she said, 'and can you grab me a couple of bowls from the cupboard?' She pointed him in the right direction.

As he set the table and poured more wine, Claire took the pan off the hob and stirred through the egg and cheese mix until every strand of pasta was gleaming and creamy. She divided it between the bowls and sat back at the table.

'This is the best comfort food in the world,' Owen declared.

'Just total bliss. I'm thinking of using this recipe when we do the Date Night episode.'

'Carbonara? Really?'

'Uh-huh.' She slurped at her spaghetti, using her finger to catch the little creamy drips on her chin and then licking it off.

Owen watched her, a pained look on his face. 'Christ, Della, if you want me to keep my distance, enough with the finger licking.'

'Ha ha. Seriously though, I don't know whether it was Nigel or Nigella—'

'Slater or Lawson?' he grinned.

'I'd need to check. Anyway, one of them wrote that this was the kind of dish you'd make for that first night – something you can eat in bed or, rather, take back to bed, to fuel you up for the next round.' She tilted her head to the side as she thought it through. 'Or was it to give you something to work off? Yes, that story would make it perfect for Date Night.'

'I'm not sure I'll ever be able to eat it again without thinking about that and wondering what it would be like to take you, and the pan, right now to bed. Remind me never to put it on the menu, or I'll be walking around the kitchen with a hard-on.'

'Now, there's an image.' She grinned. 'That would certainly give Ed the chemistry he's wanting.'

She sobered as she returned to the conversation they'd been having before dinner. 'If Ed had already begun speaking to you about this project, and Barty knew that, if what you say is true – and I still don't believe your theory – Barty would want to stop us working together, even if it meant stopping the project completely. He knew what happened to you after Spooner's review of Belucci, and he knew that any tentative reconciliation we'd reached would be permanently damaged if it came out that I was to blame for that. That's the only motivation that fits – and even that's far-flung.'

'Perhaps. Let's take this back a step and think

about what we can prove. You said Barty mentioned the paper wanted to hold you to the confidentiality clause?'

Claire nodded.

'That's an easy one to prove – Ed's asked you to give your editor a call and ask him how much you can legally tell the press. Given that the information is out there already, I'd be shocked if they hold you to that. If you can prove Barty's lied to you about that, you'll know he's probably lied about other things.'

'What worries me is that if Barty has leaked the information, there's a possibility he knows who the real Spooner is, and if he thinks I'm on to him, he might let that person know.'

'And you think they might try to discredit you further before you can set the record straight.'

'Yes. And if you're right and this is about keeping us apart – and I don't think it is –the next big Spooner review will target *The Lamb*. But if I let Barty think the network wants to play up the possible conflict between us by me not saying anything more to the press and that I'm not interested in you, that would buy us time to try and figure out who's behind it all.'

'That sounds like a plan, but we need to be careful. When you spoke to Barty earlier, did you tell him where you were today?'

She nodded. 'But I didn't tell him who I was with.'

'Good. Let him think you've met someone. I

might drop something into the conversation as well. That way he'll get the idea you and I are friends, and I'm teasing you about someone you don't want to talk about. If he's operating from a position of jealousy, we can close that down. Let's keep it light and friendly, sign your contracts, and then we'll get back together with Tallis and Gail and go through that list of theirs again. It's one thing thinking we know who leaked it, but we need to find out who's behind it – and for that we need support.'

'Do you think there's something in the reviews we're missing?'

'I do.' He slurped a piece of spaghetti between his lips. 'Man, this is so good.'

Claire twirled more of the creamy pasta onto her fork. 'Yes, this is definitely what I'm cooking for Date Night,' she said, grinning when Owen groaned.

CHAPTER THIRTY

Even though she and Owen had agreed not to take their relationship further just yet, Claire's heart was flying. The sky was bluer than it had ever been, the air had the barest whiff of a touch of spring in it, and life was good. Even when she and Nigel passed the children and their gaggle of geese, Nigel resisted the urge to "help" them – whereas usually, he'd be in the middle of the feathery, honking chaos pretending he couldn't hear her calling him back. Today he wagged his tail hopefully but stayed beside her. Yes, it was a good day.

The good day feeling lasted until she got back to Curlew Cottage and began going through her diaries.

'I'm emailing through the dates I ate at each of the restaurants on your list,' she said to Tallis, holding her phone between her ear and shoulder. 'And who I ate with.'

'Was there any pattern there?'

'No, it was as I thought – sometimes Giles, sometimes Barty, sometimes Gracie, sometimes Ed. I tried to remember what I'd eaten, but unless it's memorable, one meal blurs into the other.'

'That's okay,' said Tallis. 'I've been through the reviews again, and I'm quite sure I can pinpoint when this Spooner began writing reviews, but there are some other inconsistencies that I can't quite put my finger on. I'll put the dates into my table and see if that helps.'

'Before you do, I'd forgotten all about *GiGi* when we first went through the list. It was only when I was talking to Owen the other night that I remembered I dated Jimmy Gillespie briefly too.'

Tallis exhaled. 'Another one with a personal connection to you.'

'Yes, I know. Also, I think Barty was indirectly responsible for leaking the story, but I don't know how to prove it yet.'

She walked Tallis through her reasoning, sharing the information she'd gained from Ed, Owen, and Barty himself.

Tallis hesitated before asking, 'Do you think he could also be Spooner?'

'I wondered about that,' said Claire, 'but he hasn't eaten at some of the restaurants on the list.'

'Are you sure?'

'Yes. Barty said he couldn't get a booking at *Lily James*, and he never liked Jimmy, so said he wouldn't be eating at *GiGi* on principle. As for *Ziggy's*, he made a point of telling me he hadn't been. Besides, he's neither a writer nor an eater. It's about being seen for Barty.'

'Okay. What's your next move?'

'I'm going to call my editor and ask about the confidentiality clause. In fact, I'm going to do that as soon as I hang up from you – before I lose my nerve. Although I'll be honest, Tallis, there's a huge part of me that doesn't want to hear what I think Duncan will tell me.'

'You think he'll contradict what Barty told you?'

'Yes, I do, and this isn't something I want to be right about. He's my best friend, and even if it was accidental, I have to know.'

'Yes,' she agreed, 'you do need to know. And on that note, I'll talk to you later.'

Tallis rang off, and Claire sat looking at her phone long after it was silent. Knowing was one thing, but deciding what to do about it was entirely another. Part of her hoped Duncan would tell her the paper was upholding the contract she'd signed. It would mean they'd need to rethink the publicity for the show, but that was a small price to pay to know for sure her best friend hadn't betrayed her.

Usually talking to Duncan involved a complicated dance of texts, missed messages and call backs, so it surprised Claire when he picked up almost immediately. After exchanging the briefest of pleasantries – which from anyone else would be rude, but from a man as busy as Duncan was generous – Claire got down to the reason for her call.

'I want to do an interview to set the story straight.'

'Sounds fair. I'm surprised it's taken you that long.'

'The non-disclosure agreement—' she started.

'What good is a NDA when someone's already breached the confidential information that you're trying to protect?' he said. 'Then there's the issue we can't use a Spooner piece anymore, anyway. No one upstairs is happy about that.'

'Is it likely another review will come through?'

'He's already asked if we'll take another one. Or then again it could be a she, who can tell?'

'You don't know for sure?'

'No, this Spooner has always remained anonymous. The email address is for Alex Spooner, and we pay directly into a company account.'

'If that's the case, it wouldn't be too difficult to find out who it is.'

'True. Any half-arsed reporter could find out who was behind both the email and the account. It's not a great look if anyone finds out we've been investigating ourselves. But if an investigative journalist wanted to chase the money, I suppose that would be a different story.'

There was a leading edge to Duncan's tone that Claire didn't understand. It was almost as if he wanted to make a suggestion to her without saying the words.

'What about telling me the company name?' Claire asked.

'You disclosing information that's already known to the general public might not be breaching an agreement that's no longer worth the paper it's written on, but me providing you with confidential information would absolutely be a breach.'

'Yeah, yeah, I get it. So, I'm allowed to say I used to be Spooner, and I'm allowed to say how long I did it for?'

'Yes.'

'And you'll stand behind me on that?'

'Absolutely. I'll send you an email confirming it if you like. As I said though, I'm surprised it's taken you this long. When I saw Barty, I told him the same.'

'When did you see him?'

'A while back – probably early January. Why?'

Claire could tell that his nose for news was twitching and said nothing else. 'No reason, he just didn't mention it, that's all. I'd better let you get on with it.'

'Once you've cleared the air, give me a call. We'll pick up on the previous arrangement we had – maybe a monthly column?'

'Thanks, Duncan, I'll think about it. Hold on,' she said before he could hang up. 'You mentioned that Spooner had approached you to do another review?'

'Yes. Only yesterday. We turned it down – it's all a bit hot at the moment.'

'What was the name of the restaurant?'

'A place called *The Lamb* somewhere in The Cotswolds. To be honest, I've never heard of it, so I probably wouldn't have taken it even if things were different. Do you know it?'

'Yes, Duncan, I do.'

When Duncan rang off, Claire stayed where she was. A sob that started deep in her chest rose to her throat, cutting off her ability to breathe. There was no longer any denying it. Barty was involved in this whole mess, and none of it was accidental. He'd been lying to her the entire time. Of all the hurt she'd had over the past few months, nothing came close to the pain that doubled her over. Nothing.

Nigel padded across and rested his head on her knee, his liquid eyes looking into hers. Claire held his head into her chest. Then she cried for the loss of a friend. She'd thought no matter what happened, she'd trust Barty to do the right thing by her and for her, and now? How could she ever trust anyone after this?

It was only later that afternoon, when she'd lit the fire and poured a glass of wine and stopped to think, that anger seeped through the sadness. At first, it was just a bitter taste at the back of her throat, a fluttering in her chest, but soon it had developed into a torrent of heat that pushed away the self-pity and cleared the fog in her brain.

Oh, God. Owen. How was she going to tell Owen? No, even though Duncan wasn't going to publish it, she couldn't tell him, not until after they'd seen Barty. Barty had to believe she didn't suspect his involvement – at least not until she knew both the extent to which he was involved and until she had enough proof to confront him and be certain it wouldn't backfire on either her or Owen.

Barty was all smiles when he arrived at the cottage. Claire had baked a batch of scones, not that Barty did more than nibble around the edges of one while he entertained her with tales of his more C-listed clients. While she smiled and laughed as she always had done, it was all an act and every smile hurt. If she hadn't known differently, she would never have believed that under the smiles and banter, Barty had been behind her humiliation and the destruction of her career.

'What about Bruno?' she asked. 'How's he going?'

'He's much more demanding than you ever were, darling, but if I can keep him focused on his deadlines, he has a cookbook coming out in time for Christmas, and between you and me he's in line for something big in the States. I think he's going to be the new Gordon – you heard that here first.' He tapped his nose twice to indicate the confidential nature of the information.

'Except that we still have the original Gordon, who's much less unpleasant than Bruno Belucci.'

Barty shrugged. 'As long as he gets the deal, I don't care how awful the man is.' He looked around the tiny cottage. 'Seriously, darling, when are you coming home?'

'I am home. I really like it here.'

He wrinkled up his nose. 'But this is so tiny. I think your entire cottage would fit into my living room.'

Normally a comment like this would have Claire rolling her eyes at him, but today it was all she could do not to snap at him. 'We can't all have a view of the Thames,' she said. 'I think this is cosy and cute. I don't have much stuff, so it's perfect.'

'But you could buy yourself something much nicer, somewhere closer to civilisation.'

She forced a laugh. 'Don't come over all "it's too far from Harrods, dah-ling" on me. We both know I don't care about any of that.'

'But I miss you, Claire. If you're going to persist in doing this ridiculous project, I think I'll talk to Ed and insist that it's filmed in London.'

Anger simmered through her, building with force. She'd agreed to play it cool. 'You'll do no such thing,' she scolded him. 'I'm not ready to be back in London yet.'

He nodded. 'So you've said, but if you're worried about having nowhere to live you can move in with me if you like.'

'As if you could deal with Nigel in your apartment,' she laughed, even though Nigel wasn't part of the invitation. 'Besides, I'm not sure Nigel will adjust to life in the city again now. He's been spoilt here.' Before he could say anything to that, she added, 'We probably should be going if we're to get into the village before lunch service starts. You did still want to meet Owen, didn't you?'

'I certainly do. Are you really sure about working with him – given your history, that is?'

'We're fine. We were kids when we dated – and you know what it's like when you're that age and everything is built up to be bigger and more important and way more dramatic than it needs to be. Besides, I like his style of cooking, and it will work well against mine.'

'If you're sure.'

'I am. Did you bring the contract?'

He patted his computer bag – a soft leather satchel that must have cost him a fortune.

'Very nice,' Claire commented. 'And, by the looks of it, expensive.'

'It was a gift.' He shifted in his chair and tapped his fingers on the table.

Barty was rarely mysterious about anything, so Claire pushed him harder. 'Lucky you. Is it from someone special? Anyone I need to know about?'

'No, of course not,' he said too emphatically. 'It was just something to say thank you – from a client.'

He picked up his teaspoon and tapped that on the table and the penny dropped. 'Oh my god – it's from Bruno Belucci! Really? For the cookbook or the American show?'

'Alright yes, it's from Bruno. And it's nothing like that – it's more of a thank you – for taking him on when others wouldn't.'

Barty had been about to say something else when Claire interrupted. 'And there's a good reason why he's had trouble finding representation – he's upset nearly everyone else.'

'I know you don't like him and, as you know, the feeling is mutual. He's not that bad once you get to know him; in fact, I'd say he's quite insecure underneath the bluster.'

'I'll take your word for it, but let's get moving, hey? Can I bring Nigel?' At the mention of Nigel, and Barty's subsequent expression, she continued, 'Let me guess your car has just been detailed. That's fine, he'll be fine alone for a couple of hours.'

'Is that your sister's house down the lane?' Barty asked as she locked the door.

'Yes. It's been great having someone I can really trust living so close.' Was it her imagination, or did Barty's eyes narrow when she said that?

As they drove into Brookford, Claire pointed out places of interest – the farm shop, the path through the wood that would be full of bluebells by the end of April, the road to Stroud, the road to Cirencester, the pub she'd been meaning to call into for Sunday lunch.

'You seem to be keeping yourself busy,' he mused. 'Do you go to the village a lot?'

'For some things. When I first arrived, I bought everything I needed in Cirencester, but Gracie reminded me I needed to show my face in the village as well.' Claire deliberately looked out the window as she spoke.

'And Owen? Have you seen much of him?'

'Of late, a little. He's busy though – I'd forgotten what dreadful hours chefs keep, it's no wonder so many of them end up single.'

'What about Owen? Is he single?'

Claire smiled out the window, grateful Barty couldn't see her face. 'I haven't seen him with anyone, and I have no idea how he'd have time for a relationship.'

'I guess he was probably burned badly when his wife left him, but women like Julia don't belong in Yorkshire or, for that matter, somewhere like Brookford.'

'I didn't realise that you knew her.' She turned to face him and resisted the urge to ask more about her.

'Yes, she's a friend of Bruno's – or rather, her father is. I think he might be a silent partner in *Belucci's*, but don't quote me on that.' He glanced at her and then said, 'I don't know what I'm talking about … but whatever the connection is, they move in the same circles.'

'And now, so do you,' she said with a grin. 'You were made for that life, Barty. It's what you've always wanted.'

Barty blushed. 'It doesn't mean I'm leaving you behind,' he said, almost apologetically. 'In fact, I'd like to take you with me – into that circle.'

Claire shook her head. 'I'm happy as I am, but thanks for thinking of me. Oh, look at that, we're here already. And there's a car park right out front. How lucky are we?'

Owen must've seen the car pull up and came out to greet them. He kissed Claire's cheek and then held his hand out to shake Barty's. 'Owen Gallagher, and you must be Barty. I've heard a lot about you. It's great to finally meet you in person.'

Barty shook his hand. 'All good, I hope?'

'Absolutely. Any reason it shouldn't be?'

Claire sent Owen a warning look, but his grin was pure innocence.

'Anyway, let me show you around. I know it's too early for lunch, and Claire said you needed to get back to London, but I thought we could have a snack before you have to leave.'

Barty nodded and didn't say too much as Owen gave him the tour. Once they'd sat down in the restaurant, that all changed.

'It's a nice set-up you've got here, Owen,' he said. 'But I'd like to bet you miss London and the energy there.'

'I do miss that – and now I have this place running as I'd like it to it's perhaps time to start looking back to the city for my next venture. I'll see how this show goes and decide after that,' he said.

Claire tried not to show her surprise, but the slight

pressure from Owen's foot against hers told her what he was saying was part of his tactic.

'Claire will no doubt miss you when you've gone,' he said.

Owen grinned. 'I doubt that very much. She has plenty to keep her busy. Other friends, if you know what I mean.'

Claire groaned and buried her face in her hands. 'Did you ask her what she was up to on Monday afternoon?' he asked Barty.

All the heat in Claire's body ran to her face like a wildfire.

'After Ed and the team left, I asked her if she wanted to take some time and do some planning for the first episode. Ed had mentioned that he'd like to get a good start on outlining. Instead of doing that she was in Broadway – and I don't think there was very much business going on.' He smirked and raised his eyebrows.

'Really, Gallagher? What are you, sixteen again? I told you the other day, it's none of your business who I'm seeing.' Claire let out a loud sigh, and Owen shrugged his shoulders.

Barty's laugh was high-pitched. 'Is this anyone I know? Or should know?'

'Oh god, Barty – not you too. It's too new for me to talk about,' she said. 'You know how it finished with Giles, so I'm taking my time with this one.'

Owen coughed, and Claire glared at him and then shook her head. 'Don't pay any attention to him – he's being juvenile. Obviously, some things don't change.'

Barty's smile was tight. 'I know you think I'm overreacting, but you need to be super careful at the moment. Once you sign this contract if anything unsavoury comes out, they can cut you like that.' He clicked his fingers. 'The Spoonman story did you enough damage; I'd hate for someone who you've only just met to make things worse.'

His sincerity was almost enough to have her believing she was wrong about his involvement.

'That's a great point, Barty,' said Owen. 'I've told her to be careful – she doesn't want to end up in something she has problems getting out of. I said, "Claire, whatever you do, don't agree to any photos."'

'Okay, that's enough! This conversation is over. If you think I'd be that stupid, you obviously don't know me very well.'

Claire scowled at Owen, and he put his hands up in mock surrender. 'I know when to shut up, so I'll just go back to the kitchen where I belong. In all seriousness, we're trying out a new celeriac soup on the specials today that I thought we could have while we talk business. I'll be right back.'

Once he left, Barty turned back to Claire. 'I understand why you're angry, but I'm only taking an interest in your love-life because I care about you.

Okay?'

She nodded.

'I have to admit, I was worried you might fall for Owen again – and that would be the last thing you'd need on this job. Can you imagine how uncomfortable it would be working with someone after you've broken up with them?'

'And you're not worried anymore?'

'No. The guy might be a good cook – although that remains to be seen, but you've got to admit, he's not your type. He's got that brooding, intense thing going on for his publicity photos, but under that, he's a bit of a pratt, don't you think?' He didn't give her time to answer before saying, 'I still think Bruno would've been a good match for you in the role, but now the American thing is on, that doesn't matter anymore.'

'Then it's worked out for the best for us all. Why don't you give me that contract and I'll get it signed before Owen gets back.'

He brought the paper out from his bag, little stickers showing where Claire needed to sign.

'I know I read this through last year, but has it changed?'

'No. The money is the same, and the conditions are the same. The main one you need to know about is that the production company has the right to terminate the contract if they feel you've done anything to bring their brand into disrepute.' He pointed out the main clauses to her. 'Normally I wouldn't need to point that out, but in light of recent events …' He shrugged his shoulders. 'If you're sure you want to do this, sign away.'

'I am sure,' she said and took the pen he offered her.

Owen returned to their table as Claire finished signing the documents. 'I know it's early,' he said, 'but this calls for champagne.' He signalled to his barman who, judging by the speed with which he produced three glasses of champagne, had been pre-warned. 'To us,' he toasted, 'and the start of a productive and successful working relationship.'

Although Barty didn't say much after that, he admitted, once he and Claire were back in the car, that the celeriac and almond soup Owen had served them was good. 'And with that slice of toasted sourdough and goat's cheese, it was a perfect light meal. The man might behave like an idiot, but there's no denying he can cook.'

'And you're fine with me doing the show with him now?'

'I suppose so,' he grumbled. 'Now, the other thing I couldn't talk to you about – and, before you ask, still can't – has gone cold, so you're far better off grabbing the work when it comes up. This is an opportunity for a second chance for you, Claire, so don't waste it.'

'Trust me, I don't intend to take it for granted.'

•

Later that afternoon, Claire was reading through cookbooks looking for inspiration for their outdoor episode when Owen knocked on the kitchen window. Claire waved at him and gestured that the door was open.

He kissed her lightly on the forehead; no sign of the pent-up passion of the other day. 'I thought I'd drop around before evening service,' he said.

She smiled and closed the cookbook. 'Tea?'

'Yes, please. I was hoping there might be something else on offer too.'

For a second, she misunderstood his meaning and heat rose to her cheeks.

'I was talking about food,' he said, grinning wickedly. 'I missed the staff lunch.'

'Of course.' Claire took a quick breath. 'There's some fresh bread in the tin in the corner; butter and cheese in the fridge. You should find some pickle in there too. Help yourself while I make us tea.'

Despite the size of the kitchen, Owen managed not to get in Claire's way as she made tea and he sliced bread and cheese for sandwiches. 'Can I make you one?' he asked.

She nodded, and he got on with the task.

'We didn't have a chance to talk this morning, but did you call your editor?' he asked as he placed the sandwiches on the table.

'Yes.' Her smile fell. 'He told me I'm no longer bound by the confidentiality agreement. And he followed that up with a confirmation email from the legal team advising me what I could and couldn't speak about. He also said he'd told Barty that too – back at the beginning of January.'

He placed a hand over hers. 'I'm so sorry, Dells.'

'Yeah, me too. I can't hide from it anymore – I still don't know for sure he leaked it, but given the effort he's making to shut it down, I'd say that's a likely conclusion.'

Owen chewed thoughtfully on his sandwich. 'Barty cornered me when you were using the bathroom.'

'Oh?'

'He asked if you were still keen to do an interview telling your side of the story. I told him that Ed had mentioned it was a good idea to get all of that out into the open before we started the publicity, but we were also considering the option of playing up the potential conflict between us. He asked what I meant about that, and I said people would love the thought of us working together when, as far as the general public knew, a review you'd written had seen me fired from a job. He seemed to relax when I said that, but he also said that if I had any influence over you or Ed, I should use it to talk you out of doing a tell-all interview.'

'Did you ask him why?'

'Of course. He told me he'd had an informal

meeting with Duncan who'd said if you spoke up, the paper would be forced to act on the non-disclosure agreement. I asked him if there was any wriggle room in it and he said he'd been through the contract closely and didn't believe so.'

'I'd long finished being Spooner before Barty began acting for me, so he's never seen that contract,' she conceded.

'I didn't think so.'

Claire raised her eyes to his. 'There's more. Duncan told me Alex Spooner had approached the paper and asked if they wanted a new review.'

'And?'

'Duncan said no, it was all a little too hot at the moment. To be honest, I think he's giving me the opportunity of telling my side first.'

'That's good of him, I suppose.'

She got up from her seat and walked across to the sink and looked out the window. A grey cloud had moved in front of the sun, causing the light to dim. Then she turned to face Owen and said, 'The review he offered Duncan was on *The Lamb*.'

Owen stalled mid-bite and stared at her. Her tummy dipped in fear. She swallowed hard to dislodge the lump in her throat. 'Say something, please.'

He placed his half-eaten sandwich on the plate and rubbed both hands across his face.

'Owen?'

'When did you find out?' He spoke slowly and deliberately, almost as if there was a full stop between each word.

'Yesterday, when I spoke to Duncan.' Her heart pounded as Owen raised his eyebrows. 'I didn't want to say anything to you in case it altered the way you approached Barty today.'

'Damn right it would have changed my attitude.' He stood and slammed his chair back into its place, knocking it against the table and causing it to wobble on the stone floor. 'Fuck!'

Claire flinched.

Owen squeezed his eyes shut and drew in a deep breath before releasing it. 'Oh Christ, Della, I'm sorry,' he said. 'You thought I'd begin thinking it really was you? We've been working together to prove that it's not.'

She shook her head miserably. 'I know you don't think that, but if that review had come out and your business was ruined because of me and the show was canned…'

He walked around to where she stood and pulled her into his arms. 'But it won't be published – although if it had been, I suspect that's exactly what I was supposed to think.' His arms tightened around her.

Her relief washed the fear away. 'Why does he hate me so much?' she wailed into Owen's chest.

'Spooner? I don't know, Della, I really don't. But I

promise you we'll fix this.'

'How?'

'I have no idea just yet, but I promise you that together we'll get to the bottom of it.' He kissed the top of her head. 'And then we'll talk about us.'

'I don't know, Owen. I don't know what to think anymore.' *I don't know who to trust.* His body tensed as the words left her mouth.

'It's okay, Della. I'm not going anywhere this time.'

His words should've relaxed her, but they didn't.

'Trust me,' he said as if he could read her mind.

She pulled back and studied his face, so familiar but at the same time so new to her. He'd asked her to trust him, but he'd run out on her before.

'I was young and stupid,' he said. 'I'm not either of those things anymore.'

She tilted her head to one side; her brow raised quizzically, his arms still around her.

'I mightn't be able to read everything that's in your mind, but I know you, Dells, better than anyone else. And,' he put a finger to her lips as she would've interrupted him, 'I know that you're scared, and I don't blame you. If I were in your shoes, I wouldn't know who to trust either.' He kissed her forehead and pressed her head back into the crook of his neck where it seemed to fit perfectly. 'I might've left you behind once before, but that's not going to happen again. You *can* trust me.'

She nodded once and allowed her body to relax into his. 'Owen,' she said after a few seconds. 'You think Barty is Alex Spooner, don't you?'

The vein in Owen's neck pulsed against her cheek as the silence lingered.

'Yes,' he finally said. 'I do. And I don't think it's because he hates you. In fact, I think it's the exact opposite of that.'

CHAPTER THIRTY-ONE

Over in Fenwyck, Tallis was waiting for Gail and Anna to arrive for dinner. She was filling in time by going through the Spooner reviews for what felt like the hundredth time. There were still some inconsistencies in the language of the reviews that had her confused. Then something that Claire had said came back to her.

'It's almost as if Spooner hadn't even eaten there,' she said aloud to the dogs.

As she pondered the possibilities that thought raised, her phone rang. Derek. She picked up with some trepidation. Derek hadn't made it home last weekend – a golf trip with clients – so Tallis hadn't seen him since she'd overheard his conversation almost two weeks ago. 'Is everything okay?' she asked him.

'Why wouldn't it be?'

'No reason,' she said. 'It's just you rarely call during the week.'

'Fair enough. But I have a treat for you. Pack your bags and your glad rags; we're off to London on Friday morning. I have some meetings to do and a dinner I'd like you by my side for.'

Tallis ignored the impulse to say she could think of plenty of other things she'd prefer to be doing rather than dressing up to entertain Derek's business associates.

'And as an extra special treat for you—'

Tallis grimaced; she wasn't a five-year-old who needed to be bribed with sweets.

'You can go shopping or lunching – whatever is you girls like to do.'

Maybe he thought she was seventeen and needed to be bribed with an open credit card and new clothes.

'We'll come home Sunday morning,' he said, oblivious to Tallis' silence. 'How does that sound?'

Tallis skimmed her eyes over the list of restaurants on the kitchen bench where she sat. A couple of days in London might be just what she needed to make sense of her suspicions – even if it meant she had to spend the evenings playing the happy wife by his side.

'That sounds lovely, Derek,' she said.

'Be ready first thing Friday morning.' And then he hung up.

Great. Knowing Derek, that could mean any time between seven and ten in the morning.

On the spreadsheet in front of her, Tallis had drawn up five columns. In these, she'd placed the names of the restaurants she believed the current Spooner had reviewed, the date of the review, the date Claire had eaten at each, and the names of those who'd eaten at each with Claire. In the fifth column, Tallis had placed an asterisk next to the nastiest and most personal of the reviews. Just five restaurants had this mark: *Belucci's, Ziggy's, GiGi, Bella Donna,* and *Lily James.*

While there was no pattern with the frequency the newspaper published the reviews, Claire had eaten at each of them within eight weeks of their publication. There was something else though, and it was just out of her grasp.

Gail and Anna appeared at the back door, and Tallis motioned to them to come in.

She kissed Gail on the cheek, but after a quick wave, Anna was already on her way up to Adam's room. Gail and Tallis exchanged looks.

'Should we be stopping that?' Gail asked.

'I think that bird has flown,' said Tallis, shrugging a shoulder, her gaze in the direction of where they'd gone.

'You've had "the talk" with Adam?' Gail asked.

'Absolutely. And I've stocked the bottom drawer in his bathroom with essentials.'

Gail laughed. 'Me too – with both the talk and the bottom drawer full of condoms. On the upside, at least neither of them has an excuse for not being covered, so to speak. I don't suppose there's much more we can do about it?'

'Somehow I think they'll be doing it anyway, and I don't know about you, but I'm glad it's somewhere safe.'

Gail nodded. 'You're right, of course.' She noticed the spreadsheets on the bench. 'Operation Spoonman?'

'Uh-huh. Something is lurking at the edge of my brain that I can't quite grasp. Wine first though, I think.'

Gail grinned and nodded. 'Absolutely. Pour away, and then we can see if we can't talk it through and jolt that thought from wherever it's hiding.'

After pouring them each a glass of wine, Tallis pulled her spreadsheet closer so they could both see. 'Okay, I've popped a mark next to the bitchiest of the reviews.'

'Yes, I can see that. Do these have anything in common?'

'Yes. Claire has had a personal relationship with the head chef in each of these restaurants.'

'Are we calling a drunken snog a personal relationship?' Gail giggled. 'Because if that's the case …'

Tallis grinned back. 'In this case, yes, we're counting it.'

'Okay, but she didn't know Owen worked for Belucci, or are you suggesting you no longer believe that?'

'Absolutely not. I do believe it. It's just that …' She took a sip of the wine. 'Keep talking. I've almost got the little beggar.' When Gail raised her eyebrows, she added, 'that lurking thought. I can almost see it.'

Gail studied the spreadsheet and thought some

more. 'Okay, Belucci made a pass at her, and she dislikes him. Can we class that as a personal relationship?'

Tallis looked unsure. 'Maybe not. The other thing they all have in common, again except for Belucci's two restaurants, is that Barty hasn't eaten at any of them.' She furrowed her brow. 'There was something that Claire said … What was it? It wasn't so much he hadn't eaten at the other restaurants on the list, but she remembers him telling her expressly that he *hadn't* eaten at *these*.'

Tallis had already told Gail about Claire's suspicions concerning Barty, and now she said, 'Normally you'd talk about somewhere you'd eaten at, not somewhere you hadn't. It strikes me as odd he'd make a point of telling her that.'

'That's it! That's what I've been missing! On the face of it, *Belucci's* and *Bella Donna* don't fit the personal relationship theory, and they're also the only ones Barty has eaten at—'

'But?'

'We know that Claire didn't know Owen was working at *Belucci's*, but what if Spooner *thought* Claire knew Owen was there?'

Gail clicked her fingers. 'And the only person who knew about Claire's relationship with Owen was Barty.'

'Exactly.'

They looked at each other and said simultaneously, 'Barty didn't just leak the Spooner story, he is Spooner.'

'*Bella Donna* doesn't fit the theory though,' said Gail.

'It does if you consider Barty may have thought he was protecting – or avenging – Claire.'

'Okay,' Gail nodded slowly. 'That makes sense. Let's say Barty is Alex Spooner, what do we do now? Should we tell Claire?'

Tallis shook her head. 'No. Not yet. She sounded so defeated when I spoke to her the other day. I don't think we should say anything about this until we find a way of proving it.'

'And how do you suggest we go about doing that?'

'As it happens, I have to go to London on Friday with Derek. He's told me to spoil myself with lunches and shopping – the things that women like to do.'

Gail's face spread into a grin. 'And you're thinking there are a few restaurants in London that you'd like to try?'

'And a few chefs I'm going to see if I can talk to. While it won't help us understand why Barty would do it – especially now that Bruno Belucci is one of his clients too – if we can prove he's lied about eating there and clarify some dates, we might have enough to confront him.'

'It has to be money or sex; it's always money or sex,' said Gail.

'What is?'

'Why people do things you wouldn't expect them

to do.'

'So, we need to figure out what it is for Barty – money or sex,' said Tallis thoughtfully.

'My money is on the sex,' said Gail. 'Although that didn't come out quite right, did it?'

'It certainly didn't.' Tallis laughed. 'Sex certainly makes more sense than money does. There's no monetary reason why he'd sell Claire out when he doesn't earn if she doesn't earn.'

'Plus, if it ever got out he'd leaked confidential information about clients his career would be over too.'

'Exactly. So, sex it is. And on that note, I think it's time for dinner. Do you want to get our hormonal offspring to come downstairs?'

'Oh god, do I have to?'

The look of horror on Gail's face made Tallis laugh.

Gail clomped noisily up the stairs, shouting, 'I'm coming up, and I'm approximately ten seconds away from opening this bedroom door.'

Tallis laughed even harder.

Tallis still hadn't decided if she was going to say anything to Derek about his affair. When Derek announced he had calls he needed to make during the drive, she sighed with relief. Those calls took them through until Tallis was required to help direct them to their hotel near London Bridge.

After checking in, Derek said, 'I have some people to see, but I expect you want to do some shopping?'

Tallis forced a smile. 'I thought I'd have some lunch and maybe a wander,' she said.

'Don't eat too much.' He laughed. 'Why don't you buy something new for tomorrow night?'

It was an order rather than a suggestion. Before she could answer, he kissed her cheek and left.

Tallis wandered out of the hotel and down past The Shard into Borough Markets. She'd never been before and would've been happy to wander the aisles tasting cheeses and charcuterie and filling a basket with the most wonderful looking vegetables, but with a lunch booking at *Ziggy's*, she looked longingly at the food stalls and resolutely walked past. Next time.

Located in what was probably an old vault or storeroom under London Bridge, Ziggy's had a cosy, almost Victorian feel to it. A smiling Italian waiter led Tallis to a corner booth, and she wondered, not for the first time, how a smile and a *"Ciao Signora"* could make one feel so welcome.

Tallis ordered an artichoke salad to start followed by orecchiette with turnip tops, chilli and anchovies, although the way her waiter repeated it back it all sounded so much more than turnip tops. Maybe when Adam went away to university, she should learn a language.

'*Orecchiette alle cime di rapa, molto bene* Signora. And to drink? Some wine, perhaps?'

'A glass of sangiovese please,' she said. Then, taking a deep breath, she added, 'Is Ziggy in the kitchen today?'

'*Si Signora.* Do you know him?'

'No, but my friend Claire Mansfield does, and she asked me to say hello from her.' Tallis crossed her fingers under the table as she told the lie.

The waiter's eyebrows went up. 'I'll tell him,' he said.

Tallis was finishing her pasta when a tall man in chef's whites with a mass of wild dark hair stopped at her table.

'I'm Ziggy,' he said. 'And you're friends with Claire?'

Ziggy's eyes were fixed on Tallis. They were so dark they were almost black. A zing of sensation shot through her body. Well, that hadn't happened for a long time, so long she hadn't expected it to happen again; it was nice to know it still could.

'I am,' said Tallis, willing her hormones to behave themselves. 'Claire said you were a wizard with pasta – she was right. I'm Tallis.'

Without asking, he slid into the booth opposite her and leaned forward. 'How is she?'

'She's doing well; she's living back in Brookford.'

'I'm glad,' he said. 'I worried about her after I read that *cazzate*. Claire as The Spoonman?' He shook his head. 'No, I don't believe it.'

'You don't believe that she wrote those reviews?'

'Certainly not.'

'How can you be so sure?'

He looked squarely at her, his dark eyes flashing. 'I thought you said you were a friend? You're not a *giornalista*, are you?'

'Absolutely not! I really am a friend – we met when Claire did *Time for Tea* in Fenwyck, and I'm trying to help her get to the bottom of this.'

He nodded slowly. '*Capisco*, I see. You'll be wanting to speak to Jimmy Gillespie too then.'

'He doesn't believe it either?'

'No – and for the same reason I don't.'

'Which is?'

He shrugged as if it were a question she shouldn't need to ask. 'Because we know Claire and know this isn't her, but also because the food in The Spoonman's review is not the food that I fed Claire – and the same applies to *Jimmy*.'

Her scepticism must have shown on her face because he said, 'When you're feeding someone you love, you remember what you fed them.' He paused. 'Jimmy would say the same – he told me as much when the story broke. He said to me, "Ziggy, Claire didn't write the review, I would never have served her Jerusalem artichoke soup." And I said to him I didn't serve the *strozzapreti* as *cacio e pepe*. It's good, you understand, but not special enough for Claire and not at that time of the year.'

'You both know about each other?'

He seemed puzzled by her question. 'Of course!' Then he sighed wistfully. 'Me and Claire, it was not meant to be.'

They talked some more, Tallis made some notes, and Ziggy made a call. 'Jimmy says he'll see you this afternoon before service.'

'I really appreciate this Ziggy.' Tallis stood to leave and pay the bill.

Ziggy waved it away. 'No, this is on me – you're working to clear her name, and when the time is right, I'll stand up for her too.'

'She'd appreciate that. At the moment it seems as though every time the gossip dies down, it's reignited by Bruno Belucci.'

Ziggy snorted and said something in Italian that Tallis assumed was not complimentary.

'You don't like Belucci?'

'He's a nasty man. Smiles for the cameras but he treats his apprentices like shit – I should know, he did it to me, but I had my revenge when I opened this place. He said it would never work and, well, look at it. Even a review from The Spoonman couldn't keep me down.'

That same zing whizzed through her veins when he smiled again.

'Tell Claire to see me next time she's in town. You come back too?'

Tallis was glad of the dim lighting when her face burned under his attention. He kissed each cheek. '*Arrivederci,* Tallis.'

Back at the hotel, Tallis had dressed and was applying her make-up in the mirror above the desk when Derek let himself into their room.

'Is that new?' he asked

'No, it's something I've had for a while.'

'Well, it looks nice.'

When Derek closed the bathroom door behind him, Tallis grimaced at her reflection and the lameness of their conversation. She always thought not knowing for sure whether he was cheating on her was worse than actually knowing, but that wasn't the case. Knowing was far worse – knowing meant a decision needed to be made and action taken. Knowing felt like a continual burning deep in her gut and a pain that never quite went away. She'd say something to him, she decided, tonight when it was just the two of them out for dinner. Then if things became nasty, she could hop on a train tomorrow morning, leaving him to attend the conference dinner on his own. Yes, that's what she'd do. And she'd make it clear to Derek that Adam wasn't to know until after he finished his exams.

Decision made, Tallis smoothed her dress, dabbed on some lip gloss and put her earrings in.

Derek came out of the bathroom, a towel wrapped

around his waist, or rather, she thought unkindly, around his stomach which was surely larger than it used to be. He dropped the towel and stepped over it to rifle through his bags for underwear. Tallis turned away from the sight of him and couldn't help wondering what Ziggy would look like naked. The same warmth she'd experienced earlier this afternoon filled her body. His stomach would be flat, and his arms and chest firm, not sunken and white and flabby like her husband's. Even though she should push the idea away, she played with it some more in her head, why not?

'I hope you don't mind,' Derek was saying, 'but Rosemary and Martin will be joining us for dinner tonight?'

'Of course not,' Tallis said, half relieved it would put the conversation they needed to have off until later. Perhaps she could find a minute to ask Rosemary if she knew anything about it – after all, she worked more closely with him than anyone else.

Tallis did just that after dinner. Derek insisted they finish the evening with whisky and cocktails, so they'd gone from the restaurant to a bar in The Shard. While Derek ordered the drinks, Tallis excused herself to visit the bathroom. After hesitating briefly, Rosemary accompanied her.

Both women were touching up their lipstick at the mirror when Tallis said, 'I think Derek is having an affair. I overheard him on the phone the other day.'

Rosemary leaned forward and wiped at a smudge at the corner of her mouth. 'Are you sure?'

Tallis nodded. 'Yes.'

Rosemary turned and leaned against the counter, pinching her lips together. 'Have you said anything to him?'

'No,' she said, 'not yet, but I was wondering if you … well if you know anything? I know you work closely with him, and I understand that my even asking puts you in an awkward position.'

Rosemary sighed heavily. 'It is awkward.'

Tallis turned from the mirror and faced her.

'But yes, I think there was someone,' she said, 'but I also think it's over.'

'I see.'

Rosemary patted Tallis' arm. 'He wouldn't leave you, Tallis. You're too important to him.'

Tallis noted wryly that she wasn't important enough to stop him from having an affair.

'Do you know who it was? And please don't tell me it was a cliché like Shelby.' She forced a short laugh even though there was nothing funny about the conversation and put her lipstick back in her bag.

'No,' said Rosemary, 'it wasn't Shelby. I don't know for sure, but I think it was the wife of one of our suppliers.'

'I see. And it's over?' Tallis asked.

'I believe so.'

Tallis snapped her handbag shut. 'Thank you for telling me,' she said.

'I'm sorry that you knew,' said Rosemary.

'Would it have made it alright if I hadn't?' Tallis held Rosemary's gaze until the other woman looked away.

'No, of course not. But you wouldn't have been hurt by it.'

Tallis shrugged and despite the seriousness of the conversation, smiled at Rosemary. 'We'd better be getting back out there,' she said.

So, it was true, and the affair was over. Did that change anything or everything? Tallis needed to think that through, but for the rest of the evening she smiled, and she chatted, and even though she caught Rosemary glancing at her from time to time, she was sure Derek was none the wiser.

As they were leaving, the heel of her sandal caught in a tuft of carpet and Tallis stumbled against a low lounge. Straightening, she apologised to the occupants and had a double-take – it was Claire's manager, Barty, and Bruno Belucci – familiar from the research she and Gail had done. They were with a willowy blonde in strappy heels and a jade green halter-neck jumpsuit. Barty looked up and nodded acceptance of her apology, but then turned away almost immediately.

Surreptitiously, she took her phone from her bag

and snapped a photo she was sure would be blurred, before hurrying to join the others. It probably meant nothing, but Barty with Bruno? Maybe Claire would know the woman they were with. Tallis made a mental note to ask.

CHAPTER THIRTY-TWO

Brookford had turned on one of those gloriously sunny weekends you get every so often in the early spring. The days were blue and mild, and signs of new life were on the trees and in the fields; wild daffodils had sprung up here and there, and a tall glass on Claire's kitchen table held a few. In the paddock behind Curlew Cottage, lambs gambolled in the sunshine, and even Nigel pranced about at Claire's side as they walked.

For the first time since arriving, she'd been able to open the cottage up and let the air blow through. She'd spent Saturday weeding and digging over the neglected kitchen garden at the back of the cottage and had invited Bill, Gracie and Milo around for an early supper. While she hadn't made any changes for the first month that she was living there, she'd begun to add some of her own touches; books in the bookshelf, throws over the lounge, a brightly patterned tablecloth she'd bought one summer holiday in Provence. Although the changes were small, the cottage looked more like a home and less like a holiday rental.

'The cottage is looking good,' Bill said, not having been inside the cottage since Claire moved in. 'Homely.'

'Thanks,' said Claire. 'I'm really comfortable here.'

'I'm not complaining – you know I'll never knock back an opportunity to be fed by someone else – but to what do we owe this unexpected treat?' asked Gracie.

'It's my way of saying thank you. I've been so grateful for the use of this cottage and being here has helped in more ways than you can know.'

Gracie's face fell. 'I hope this isn't your way of saying you're going back to London. I have to admit I hoped you might want to stay around for longer, especially now.' She looked across at Bill and gave him a knowing grin. Bill shook his head in mock exasperation.

'I think I might take Milo out to look at the garden,' he said.

'What do you mean?' asked Claire when they'd left.

'Well, let's just say I've seen Owen Gallagher's car here on more than one occasion – and that included Monday night.'

Claire shrugged nonchalantly. 'So, he stayed for dinner.'

'You cooked dinner for a chef? What on earth do you cook for someone like Owen?'

'Pasta, I cooked him carbonara.'

'And?'

'It was good.'

'Really good?'

'Really really good. One of the best I've done.'

'I'm not talking about the carbonara,' Gracie scoffed. 'How was the date?'

'It wasn't a date.' As Gracie was about to open her mouth and say something else, Claire grinned. 'The date was Sunday night.'

Gracie squealed and clapped her hands. 'Claire Bear's got a boyfriend. Claire Bear's got a boyfriend.'

'Oh my god you're juvenile,' Claire chided, unable to hide the smile on her face.

'Are you shagging yet?'

She shook her head. 'No, we're not.'

A look of pure disbelief came over her face. 'Seriously? Why not? He's so hot and you've been there before.'

'Which is why I'm being careful about going there again.'

'Okay, I get that, but you have snogged?'

Claire blushed, which was all the answer Gracie needed to run around the room doing her version of a praise-the-lord-hallelujah chorus.

'It's not the first time I've had a boyfriend, you know. And besides, he's not really my boyfriend.'

'Of course he is. And it's the first time you've had someone I like!'

'Giles wasn't that bad. He was a nice man.'

She screwed her face into a *"are you kidding"* look. 'Giles might've been nice, but he was also boring. Owen is anything but boring. He's intense and seriously hot.'

'I didn't know you knew him that well.'

'We bumped into each other a few times when you were locked away, too scared to go into town in case you ran into him.'

Claire's eyes widened.

'I'm not stupid, Claire. I knew he was the real reason you didn't want to go into the village.'

'Well, it's early days, and we're taking it slowly.'

'You'll make this work though,' Gracie said.

'We'll see.'

'Claire and Owen sitting in a tree, k-i-s-s-i-n-g …' she started chanting.

'Oh please.' Claire pretended to be annoyed.

'Anyway,' said Gracie, 'I hoped you'd stay around now that you and Owen are doing whatever it is you say you're not doing.'

'What's Aunty Bear doing?' asked Milo, who'd come back in with Bill and Nigel.

Bill grinned and Gracie looked to the ceiling for inspiration. 'Aunty Claire has a new friend.'

'That's nice,' said Milo. 'Do you have sleepovers?'

'Well, Aunty Claire, do you have sleepovers?' mocked Gracie.

'No, we don't,' she said, turning to scowl at Gracie who was grinning like a Cheshire cat. 'I told you it's not like that.'

'So you did.'

'Come on, Milo,' said Bill. 'Let's see what's on TV while Mummy and Aunty Claire get dinner ready.'

Claire had taken the opportunity of dinner guests to practice some recipes for the show and had prepared a roast chicken tray bake with a lemon drizzle cake for pudding. Although the tiny kitchen seemed even smaller when presented with the challenge of feeding extra people, before too long Claire had plates on the table, bottoms on chairs, wine in glasses and a tray containing golden-roasted mustardy chicken thighs ready to serve.

Claire waited until everyone was eating before bringing up the subject she'd touched on before dinner.

'As I was saying before, I'm grateful to you both for allowing me to stay here, and I was wondering if we could formalise the arrangement by way of a longer-term lease.'

'You're staying?' A wide smile spread across Gracie's face.

'Yes, I'm staying – if that's okay with you?'

'Absolutely,' said Bill. 'It suits us to have the cottage occupied and someone looking after it.'

'What are you going to do though?' asked Gracie.

'I've just signed a contract for something new. I can't tell you any details yet, but I'll be working here in Brookford.'

If it was at all possible, Gracie's smile grew wider. 'That's fabulous news! I'm assuming we can't say anything?'

'Not yet. We're in pre-production but should be in a position to make an announcement soon.'

'And it's with Owen?' Gracie waggled her eyebrows.

'Oh puh-leeese,' Claire said. 'You're so immature.'

'That's a funny thing you're doing with your eyebrows, Mummy.' Milo giggled. 'Can you do it again?'

Claire tried in vain to keep a straight face as Gracie attempted to do the eyebrow thing without laughing. Before long Milo was in fits of giggles, which made the adults laugh. As she sat back and watched her family chatter and eat at her little table, Claire wondered what she would've missed out on if she hadn't come back to Brookford – and admitted she never would've come back if it hadn't been for the Spooner scandal. From the biggest disaster in her life, from absolute rock-bottom, somehow, she'd found her way back home.

Although things were coming together, she wouldn't feel secure or be able to completely trust anyone again until she'd gotten to the bottom of why Barty had done what he'd done. It was time to bring this to a head and move on. And to do that she needed Owen, Tallis and Gail.

'We think Barty is Alex Spooner,' said Tallis almost as soon as she and Gail stepped inside the cottage late the following afternoon.

'And we think we know why,' added Gail, 'but we're not entirely sure.'

'I agree with you,' said Owen, who'd arrived at the same time as Gail and Tallis.

'And I think you should all come inside,' said Claire. 'I have tea and scones.'

'Because everything is better with tea and scones,' chorused the three of them.

'They smell great,' said Tallis. 'What's in them?'

'Rosemary, oregano and a little thyme. I think they would be great with a chive yoghurt cream and some smoked salmon or shaved ham.' Claire made a mental note of the combination for her blog. 'For a picnic, perhaps.'

'Or a garden party,' suggested Tallis.

Once everyone had buttered scones and full teacups, Claire called the meeting to order. 'Thanks, everyone, for coming at such short notice.'

'I've been in London for the past few days and arrived back this morning. Your text meant I could put the washing off until tomorrow,' said Tallis.

'I was glad to get away from Anna,' said Gail. 'She and Adam are supposed to be studying for exams – I just hope that's what they're doing.'

Owen sent Claire a loaded look that Gail intercepted. 'I don't want to know what you two got up to at the same age,' she warned.

'No, I don't think you do,' he winked at Claire, and suddenly her cheeks were on fire. He went on, 'As for me, I came over straight after lunch service and missed staff lunch, so I'm glad that scones are on offer. I don't suppose you have any bread and cheese as well?'

'Help yourself; you know where everything is.' Claire rolled her eyes at the look Gail and Tallis shared. 'As I was saying, thanks for coming over – even if some of you are just here for the food.'

Owen shrugged, grinned wickedly and said, 'that's not the only thing I'm here for, but it's a good start.'

Claire shook her head in mock exasperation. 'Before we start, we'll recap what's happened over the last week.'

'I think we can see what's happened over the last week,' said Gail. 'Owen looks very much at home here.'

Claire didn't bother to hide her blush. 'Owen and I have been working on something new – oh my god, Gail, get your mind out of the gutter!'

Gail tried to cover her chuckle by sipping tea.

'As I was saying, we've been working on something we can't talk about just yet.' She looked at Owen, who nodded approval for her to continue. 'And through that, we've caught Barty out on a few lies.'

'Like what?' asked Tallis.

'He tried to manipulate me into working with Bruno Belucci.'

'How did he do that?' asked Gail.

'He told me the network wanted Bruno for the role of co-host for a show we were looking at doing, but Ed told me that Bruno's people had been pushing the network to consider Bruno. Ed said the network wanted Adrian Ritchie, but Barty had attempted to talk them out of that, but he hadn't run that past me at all.'

'You said Barty had taken on the management of Belucci – do you think this happened before the Spooner story came out?' asked Tallis.

'Barty hinted he'd taken Bruno on because I wasn't earning, but yes, I think he's been Bruno's manager for a lot longer than that. Also, Ade immediately pulled out of the project when the Spooner story broke – he said he couldn't and wouldn't work with me, yet Bruno was still pushing for the job. That's what got me thinking – Ade didn't want to be involved with any project I was working on, yet Belucci, who I'd apparently written about twice, had no such qualms. Why would he do that?' Claire looked around the table. 'He'd do it to further his career and make himself look good – that goes without saying. But he'd also do it if he knew for sure I *wasn't* The Spoonman – and there are only a few ways he could know that.' She gestured to Owen to take over.

'If a) he was Alex Spooner, b) he knew who the real Spoonman was, c) he'd leaked the information or d) he knew who'd leaked the information.' Owen counted the options off on his fingers.

'And given he wouldn't exactly be writing bad reviews about his own restaurants, that just left the last three options.'

'What about you telling your side of the story?'

Gail asked. 'Barty wasn't keen for that to happen, was he?'

'No, he wasn't. In fact, he asked Owen to talk me out of it as he, Barty, had spoken to the paper and they'd indicated they'd enforce the contract.'

'And we know that wasn't true,' said Tallis.

'Far from it. So, I wondered, why would Barty not want me to do that interview?' Claire continued.

'Because,' said Owen, 'either a) he's worried the name of the leaker would come out, b) the name of the real Spoonman would come out and c) he knows the identity of both and has reasons to keep it quiet.'

'If I go to the media with a story proving I didn't write those reviews, the journalist who broke it in the first place will be asked some tough questions about their sources and how the information was verified, and that would lead back to, for want of a better term, the leaker. If that person is, as we suspect it is, Barty, his career will be over. If, however, I keep quiet about my side of the story, none of those potentially awkward questions will be asked, and I just have to ride it out.'

'Okay,' said Tallis, 'let's park all of this for now.'

Claire smiled as Gail raised her eyebrows at Tallis' use of the word "park".

'In terms of linking Barty to the leak, we need to work out how he knew about Claire's time as The Spoonman,' Tallis said, leaning forward in her chair.

Claire shrugged. 'There are only three ways that I

can think of …'

'Over to me?' asked Owen.

Claire nodded.

'You two make a great tag team,' said Gail.

'We do, don't we?' said Owen. 'If a) he saw something lying around the house or on Claire's laptop while they were living together, b) she let it slip when they had a drunken confessional session one night, or c) Duncan let it slip during a drunken confessional. Actually,' he grinned, 'I just made up that last one about Barty and Duncan and a drunken confessional because we needed a third option. However, it's unlikely given that Duncan and Barty don't have a relationship – business or otherwise.'

'But if Barty is Alex Spooner, they'd have a business relationship,' pointed out Tallis.

Claire shook her head. 'Duncan told me the other day he doesn't know who this Spooner is. He receives the copy on an email from Alex Spooner, and they make the payment to a company name. As he said, it would be easy enough for any, in his words, half-arsed decent reporter to find out, but no one has been bothered to do so.' She bit her lip as she considered another possibility. 'I think Barty saw something on my laptop or in my notebook while I was writing as Spooner and then put two and two together. Also, I might've said something that night we both drank too much.'

'Did you though?' asked Owen. 'Both drink too much?'

'I absolutely did. There's no way I would've told him about you or anything else if I hadn't.'

'What did he tell you in return? Did he disclose anything you didn't already know?' quizzed Owen.

A few seconds passed before she shook her head. 'No, he didn't. Come to think on it, he's never told me anything about himself that wasn't public knowledge. I've always said he's a terrible gossip, but on reflection, he only tells me things he thinks will amuse me.'

'And we're right back to the main reason he wouldn't want anyone to find out he'd leaked the Spooner story – how can you trust a manager who betrays your confidence?' said Tallis.

'Do we even know who the first person was to pick it up and run with it?' Owen looked at Claire.

She shrugged. 'Not a clue. I remember one of the judges had received a text and showed it to Ade.'

'I wonder who they received it from?'

'Does it matter?'

'Yes, Dells, it does. We might know that Barty is behind the leak and we have a few theories why – which we'll get to soon. But until we find where it originated, we can't link it categorically to Barty.'

'You're right. I could ask Giles if he can find out.' She slapped her forehead. 'That's what Duncan was trying to tell me the other day! He said that finding out who's behind the company he deposits Spooner's money to isn't something he could investigate – it would be the same as investigating themselves – but he said it's something another investigative journalist wouldn't have an issue with. He seemed to emphasise the words "investigative journalist".' As the light went on in her brain, a smile spread across her face. 'He was trying to tell me I should get Giles to look into it. It doesn't matter how Barty managed to get the story out; if we can prove he's behind the company name, we have him. I can't believe I hadn't thought of that.'

'Would Giles do that for you?' asked Owen.

Claire nodded. 'Yes, I'm sure of it. In fact, I'll text him now.'

'While you're at it,' said Tallis, 'why don't you see if we can't prove something else. Barty told Claire that he hadn't been able to get a booking at Lily James. Why don't you get Adrian to check his reservations and see whether that's the truth? I tried to get into there when I was in London but couldn't get either a booking or past his front of house to talk to Adrian Ritchie.'

Claire's eyes widened. 'You went to *Lily James*?'

Tallis looked satisfied. 'Derek had, after all, told me to shop and lunch. I might not have been able to see Adrian Ritchie, but I got to *Ziggy's* and *GiGi*.'

'And?'

'Firstly, you have excellent taste in men.'

An uncomfortable warmth spread through Claire,

and she averted her gaze from Owen.

'Once I mentioned your name, both Ziggy and Jimmy were happy to talk to me. Neither of them believed it could be you either.'

'Really?'

'Yes, and not just because they knew you,' gushed Tallis, looking even more pleased with herself than she had done before. After a dramatic pause, she continued, 'I originally had the idea of proving Barty had eaten there after expressly telling you he hadn't, but as it turned out I didn't need to even mention his name. Jimmy said he knew it couldn't have been you because the review made special mention of the Jerusalem artichoke soup and he said you didn't have the soup when you visited. Apparently, he has a photographic memory when it comes to things like that.'

Claire held her breath. 'And Ziggy?'

'He was confused too. The way he recalls it is you and Giles ate there when he was still trialling some of his recipes.'

'That's right, we did.'

'He said you had a—' she consulted her notes. 'I have no idea if I'm pronouncing it right, lemon *strozzapreti*.' She looked up from the page.

Claire nodded. 'That's right, I recall that dish. It was light and summery and perfect for one of the hottest days we'd had that summer. In fact, I think Ziggy's air-conditioning had been playing up.' Her head tilted back as she replayed the memory. 'Ziggy told us *strozzapreti* – it's long hand-rolled pasta that looks a little like a corkscrew – dated back hundreds of years to a time when the priests were rich and the people poor. Apparently, every roll of the pasta was supposed to signify a curse and a hope that the priest would choke on the pasta.' At the surprised look on the other's faces, she added, 'I remember because Giles said in the taxi home that he couldn't understand me going out with anyone who could have an entire conversation about the history of a particular pasta shape.'

'He has a point,' said Gail.

'Oh, I don't know,' said Owen. 'Pasta is a pretty interesting subject.'

'I've seen Ziggy, and I'm not at all surprised you went out with him,' said Tallis. 'Those eyes! When he looks at you, you'd think you were the only woman in the world. And he could give me the entire history of every single pasta shape in that accent of his, and I'd listen.' She fanned her face dramatically as the others laughed. 'Anyway,' she said, looking at her notes again. 'Apparently, your dish was served with cherry tomatoes, yellow courgettes, enoki mushrooms and basil.'

'Do all you chefs remember what people eat?' Gail asked.

Owen nodded. 'We do if it's someone we care about or someone we want to impress. Then we remember everything.'

'The point is,' said Tallis, 'that *strozzapreti* was a "special". By the following month, Ziggy was serving it as *cacio e pepe*.'

'It's like pared-down macaroni cheese,' Claire explained when Gail raised a questioning brow. 'The sauce is just quality cheese – pecorino, parmesan or something like it – and black pepper. Super simple, yet perfect at the same time.'

'Add some guanciale – that's a salt-cured pork jowl – and you have *pasta alla gricia*,' Owen explained, 'which is like a pared-back carbonara.'

'And also simply perfect,' said Claire.

'And quick,' added Owen. 'Because sometimes you don't want to wait for the full carbonara experience.'

His words were loaded with meaning, and Claire shifted in her chair.

Gail sighed theatrically. 'If you're both quite finished?'

'Yes,' said Claire. 'Sorry. I'm guessing Spooner visited the following month?'

'According to the date of his review, yes. Yet he wrote about how it didn't taste as if it had either *cacio* or *pepe* anywhere in it.'

'Which it didn't,' said Claire.

'Which leads me to the other thing we wanted to talk to you about,' said Gail. 'We don't think Alex Spooner even ate at some of the restaurants he reviewed.'

'Excuse me?'

Tallis shuffled through her paperwork. 'I went online to see what other critics and bloggers had said about these restaurants. That's when I realised there were similarities in phrasing and menu descriptions between some of those pieces and the Spooner reviews.'

'Maybe it was the opposite way around?' Claire suggested. 'Especially in the case of the food bloggers.'

'No.' Tallis shook her head. 'You know how each of the reviews has the month he dined on it? Well, some of the blog posts I read were dated before the date that Alex Spooner said he'd visited.' When Claire continued to look blank, she continued. 'You gave me the idea – you said that sometimes you weren't convinced Spooner had even eaten at the restaurant.'

'I know I said that, but I was only joking.'

'The thing is, I think he's taken some of his material from food blogs and other reviews. Were you in the habit of telling Barty what you ate?'

Claire nodded. 'Yes. He'd ask how the meal was, and I'd say something like "I had the pork belly, and it was amazing."'

'And all he'd need to do would be to check the menu for the detail,' said Owen.

'Unless the chef had been slack and hadn't updated his website,' added Gail.

'In which case you'd get the previous month's specials,' finished Owen.

Tallis nodded slowly. 'Precisely. Finally, there's the date itself.'

'You'll need a drumroll for this part,' said Gail, not attempting to curb her excitement. 'So, I compared the review dates with the dates you gave me, and they don't all match.' Her grin was triumphant.

'Really? Show me that.'

Claire tentatively took the paperwork from Tallis and read through it. Her hand flew to her mouth to smother a sob of relief. 'This is the first piece of real evidence we've had. I can prove it wasn't me.'

Owen put his hand over hers and smiled. 'You can. Finally.'

She beamed back at him and then turned her gaze onto Tallis and Gail. 'Thank you.'

Tallis nodded once in acknowledgement. 'There's no need for that and to be honest, I'm quite enjoying putting my brain to use.'

Claire pulled her hand away and pushed her chair back. 'I don't know about you lot, but I think we need wine.'

CHAPTER THIRTY-THREE

'Okay, if we accept that it's Barty, let's talk motivations,' started Claire.

'Sex and money,' said Gail. 'It's always sex and money.'

Owen grinned. 'It certainly is.'

'If we look at the money side first, there's no clear motivation for Barty to do it. Damaging your career hits his bank account too. You were at the peak of your popularity when the story broke, so that's a huge impact if that income was to dry up,' said Tallis.

'Unless it was replaced by something or someone even more lucrative,' finished Gail. 'Like Bruno Belucci.'

'Barty said he's been contracted to do a couple of cookbooks,' Claire said, sitting back down after having poured wine for everyone. 'The first is due out at Christmas. Plus, Barty told me Bruno's about to sign something big in the States. He's marketing him as the next Gordon.'

'What's wrong with the old one?' asked Owen.

Claire shrugged. 'I asked the same question. An

American signing would be lucrative. I also got the impression Barty is a little dazzled by the company he's keeping at the moment – the circles that Bruno moves in are very influential.'

'New Gordon or not,' said Owen, 'you were established and in demand as far as new shows go. *Time for Tea* would've been renewed, and there were other projects in the works too. Bruno, on the other hand, was only beginning his television career – in fact, I think it's fair to say, he wasn't generating any income for Barty at the time.'

'Nor was there any guarantee he'd make it big enough to replace the income Barty was making from Claire,' added Tallis. 'It doesn't make sense for him to stop all of that.'

'What does make sense,' began Owen, getting up to stoke the fire. 'Is that Barty did it for completely different reasons.' He turned back to the women seated around the table but didn't meet anyone's eyes. 'I think he did it because he's in love with Claire.'

'But—' started Claire.

'Della,' said Owen, sitting back beside her. 'Think about it. You told Barty how I'd broken your heart. He knew you'd dated Jimmy and Ziggy, and he also knew how badly Bruno had treated you.'

'But Ade? He had no idea what had happened between Ade and me.'

'No,' said Tallis. 'I've been thinking about that. I

suspect that one was about money – if he discredited Adrian through a poor review, it cleared the way for Bruno to get the job as your co-host. If he was already in it that far, why not take it that extra step?'

'But why leak it to the papers?'

'Aah,' said Owen. 'That question's simpler. He saw the chemistry between you and me on the Fenwyck episode.' He smiled a lop-sided dimply smile. 'Anyone watching that had to know it was only a matter of time before we got together again. Plus, who did you run to when it all happened?'

'Barty,' said Claire sadly.

'Yes,' said Tallis. 'Barty. You said yourself he took care of you, kept your phone away from you, made sure no one else could support you.'

'And made sure I wasn't able to contact anyone.' Claire felt the burn of tears behind her eyes and blinked a few times to keep them where they were.

'And convinced you that no one would believe your side of the story,' added Tallis.

'It might've worked if Gracie hadn't offered you this cottage.' Owen wrapped his arm around Claire and pulled her close.

Claire didn't miss the smile that passed between Gail and Tallis. Owen's warmth was so familiar, and she relaxed into it, taking the comfort it provided.

'It must have thrown him when you came here instead of staying in London with him,' added Owen.

Claire nodded. 'Yes, I expect it did.' She straightened in her chair, and Owen's arm slipped from her shoulder. She took a sip of wine. 'He's never said anything or shown any sign. He was my best friend,' she whispered.

Suddenly cold, Claire stood and walked the few steps to the fire and held her hands in front of it. 'He was my best friend,' she said again, louder this time. 'Who does something like this to their best friend?' The anger from the previous day rose again, and she turned to face the others. 'If he's in love with me, he has a strange way of showing it,' she said, digging her nails into her palms.

Owen pushed his chair back and stood to take her in his arms. She burrowed in for a few seconds and then pulled back. 'It's okay,' she said, kissing him lightly on the lips. 'I'm at the point now where I'm more angry than upset,' she said with a sad smile. 'What I want now is to finish this.' She pulled away from him but held his hand and led him back to the table.

Tallis' furrowed her eyebrows as she looked back through her notes.

'What's wrong?' asked Claire.

'We're still missing something,' she said.

'I don't know,' said Owen. 'As far as I'm concerned, we have what we need. It's just a pity we haven't been able to tie Bruno Belucci to it.'

'That's it!' Claire slapped the table. 'Yes,' Claire

said again, 'that's it. On the first day of filming *Celebrity Christmas Cook-off*, Ade and I were talking about The Spoonman's review – obviously, this was before the story broke – and Ade said something about how he'd heard that Bruno had fired his head chef over the review on *Bella Donna* and I said something about how it wouldn't be the first time. I was referring to you, of course,' she said, looking fondly at Owen. 'Then Ade said he'd confronted Bruno about that and he'd always thought Bruno was looking for a reason to get rid of you, his competition. He even said he wouldn't have been surprised if Bruno had put The Spoonman up to writing that review. What if he did?'

'At the cost of his own restaurant?' asked Gail in disbelief.

Owen was thoughtful. 'It makes sense in a weird sort of way – it was unusual for Alex Spooner to review a restaurant that was as well established as *Belucci's* was and it didn't really, from what I could understand, affect his numbers at all.'

Claire was silent for a few seconds. 'Tallis, have you got any sticky notes in that bag of yours?'

'Sure. Do you need a marker pen too?'

'If you've got one.'

Tallis rummaged through her bag and handed Claire the stationery. 'Okay, everyone up, let's clean the table off.'

Tallis grinned. 'Am I sensing a brainstorming

session?'

'You are,' said Claire. 'What if this isn't about me at all? No,' she said, holding a hand up as Owen would have interrupted. 'I get that Barty might've had motivations where I'm concerned, but what if this is about Bruno? Let's see if we can't make some connections.'

On the sticky yellow paper, she wrote the names of all the restaurants that Spooner had written the nastiest of the reviews in order: *Scarborough Fair, Y Not, Belucci's, Ziggy's, GiGi, Bella Donna,* and *Lily James.*

'Scarborough Fair and Y Not?' said Gail

'We've only been concentrating on the ones that had me in common, but what if this started back at *Scarborough Fair?* We originally discounted that one because it didn't have the bitchy feel of the later reviews, but it was nasty. We'll google that in a minute, but let's go through the motivations for the others.'

'Starting with *Belucci's,*' said Owen. 'If what you're saying is right, he wanted to get rid of me.'

'Jealousy is a curse,' said Gail.

'I also heard that he lost a Michelin star that year – if he knew that was on the cards, he could blame you for it and not put his investors offside,' suggested Claire, another thought she couldn't quite grab hold of lurking in the corner of her brain. She pasted the two stickers on the table below *Belucci's.* She wrote "investors" on one sticker and placed it below the other she'd written "Owen – jealousy".

'That means he lost one star at the same time Jimmy won his,' said Tallis.

'Bruno wouldn't have liked that,' said Owen. 'That could've been the motivation for the attack on GiGi.'

'I'd say so,' said Tallis. 'Although Jimmy also said that one night Bruno turned up at GiGi for dinner with someone or another – I'll have to look the details up, I've it written in here,' she held up her notebook, 'and there was a queue and the Maitre'd wouldn't let him jump it. Apparently, he did the whole "don't you know who I am" thing.'

'That would annoy Bruno,' said Claire, writing on more stickers. 'Oh, to have been a fly on the wall.'

'*Lily James*?' said Gail. 'Are we going with Bruno wanting the co-hosting job?'

Claire nodded and wrote that on a Post-it Note, sticking it in place below *Lily James*.

'If he was jealous of Owen, it stands to reason he'd also be jealous of Adrian Ritchie,' said Gail. 'He looks like he'd be just as comfortable on the front cover of *GQ* as he would a surfing magazine.'

Claire nodded and wrote jealousy on another sticker.

'You also said he confronted Bruno about how he'd fired me,' said Owen. 'Bruno doesn't like anyone questioning him.'

Claire wrote that on another sticker.

'The same could be said for Ziggy,' said Tallis. 'He told me how Bruno churns and burns his apprentices and how he told him, Ziggy, that is, that he'd never amount to anything and that his restaurant would fail.' She paused, 'Jealousy again.'

'If memory serves me correctly,' said Owen, 'Ziggy was pretty vocal about Bruno's treatment of his apprentices. There were rumours that Bruno was underpaying them but had threatened everyone that they'd never work again if they spoke out.'

An alarm bell was beginning to ring in Claire's ears.

'Tallis, can you please check to see if the chef at *Scarborough Fair* ever worked for Bruno?'

'Sure.'

While Tallis followed a trail in google, Claire poured everyone more wine; Gail put her hand over her glass, 'not for me, I'm on driving duty.'

'I can't find anything that links the chef at *Scarborough Fair*, someone named Will Rowland, with Bruno. After the Spoonman review, there's just one other story about *Scarborough Fair,* and it's about how the investor had pulled out and the restaurant subsequently closed.'

Claire looked to the ceiling as she moved the puzzle pieces in her brain. 'Does it say who the investor was?'

Tallis looked up, surprise on her face. 'Actually, it does. It's SB Catering Pty Limited.'

'That's it!' said Claire and wrote a name on another sticker.

'And according to this story that company is owned by ...' said Tallis, following a link.

'Lord Spencer-Brown.' Claire finished the sentence, placing the sticker (and a wine bottle) above the restaurant names and using two knives to form connecting lines to both *Scarborough Fair* and *Belucci's*.

'Who's Lord Spencer-Brown?' asked Gail.

'He's my ex-father-in-law,' said Owen.

Gail raised her eyebrows at his admission.

'And Barty mentioned the other day something about Lord Spencer-Brown being the investor behind *Belucci's*. I don't think he meant to say it though because he tried to cover it up in a "nothing to see here" sort of way. I bet the money trail went straight from *Scarborough Fair* to *Belucci's*.'

'Which was perfect until Bruno wanted to get rid of me. How would he do that without upsetting my father-in-law and risking losing his investor? Not,' he added wryly, 'that the old Lord particularly liked me – but he loved his daughter enough to tolerate her choice at least.'

'That's interesting,' said Tallis, pausing to take a sip of wine. '*Y Not* has the same address as *Bella Donna*. That can't be a coincidence. I wonder how long it was in between the review being posted, the restaurant closing, and *Bella Donna* taking the space,' she mused.

'Now why hadn't I noticed that?' said Claire. 'Although it had been completely refurbished.' She tapped the end of the marker pen on the table. 'Do we know whether Bruno was in partnership with anyone for *Bella Donna*?'

Owen shook his head. 'I wouldn't have a clue. But I take it you're thinking if the business were going down, he'd need to find a way of exiting it without damaging his own reputation or upsetting business partners that he still wanted to keep sweet?'

'Exactly. Have The Spoonman write a damaging review and then claim it's ruined the business and there's no choice but to close.' Claire put a large question mark on a sticker and sat it above *Bella Donna*.

Gail added an empty wine bottle to complete the picture and grinned and shrugged when Tallis raised an eyebrow in question.

'If that's the case,' said Owen, pulling at his chin, 'perhaps he always intended to set you up for the fall – humiliate you in the way you'd humiliated him.'

Claire shrugged. 'Perhaps.' She stepped back from the kitchen table, which was now a mind map of stickers, utensils and wine bottles. '*Bella Donna* is the only loose link,' she said. 'We need to know who his partner in that one is.'

Tallis was frowning and rummaged through her bag. 'I saw Bruno and Barty on Friday night,' said Tallis, swiping her finger across the phone screen. 'They were with this leggy blonde woman … I took a photo to show you … Here it is.'

'I have no idea who that is,' said Claire, 'but I feel like I've seen her somewhere before. Do you know her Gallagher?'

Owen's brow furrowed the moment he saw the photo. 'I certainly do, that's Julia.'

'As in Spencer-Brown Julia?'

'As in my ex-wife Julia, yes.'

Claire's phone rang as they were contemplating this. 'It's Giles,' she said, walking away from the table to take the call.

'You were quick,' she said, after greeting him.

'To be honest, I'd begun looking into it a few days ago – I was talking to Duncan about something else, and well … That account you asked me about, I can trace it back to Barty. The structure is flimsy – next time give me a challenge, darling.'

Claire laughed. 'Thanks for that Giles, I really appreciate it.'

'Anytime – and anything to help clear this up. In case you're interested, the company was created about five years ago, so Barty's been doing this for a while.' Then in a gentler tone, 'I'm sorry, Claire, this has to hurt.'

'Thanks, Giles, it does.' A lump rose to her throat, and the words squeaked past it.

'Another thing you might find interesting, and this

one came up in my investigations, but you'll never guess who Belucci was in partnership with at *Bella Donna*.'

'I have no idea, but it's something we were literally just talking about.'

'Julia Spencer-Brown.'

'Seriously?' Claire glanced at Owen, who raised his eyebrows. 'You're sure?'

'Very sure. The name came up in, well, I can't say too much more than that, but I'm sure you can guess. My sources told me she was a not-so-silent partner in *Bella Donna* and that The Spoonman review was the last straw for that business – it was haemorrhaging money. I also heard that Julia is telling anyone who'll listen that she's considering legal action against you for the collapse of the business.'

Claire sniggered. 'That is interesting given we think Bruno was behind the whole thing – him and Barty. I wonder what she'd say if she knew that.'

Giles whistled down the line. 'I'd say it's something he hasn't confided in her about – she'd look a right idiot if that came out. My source told me she put up the money and also dictated almost everything from the menu to the staff to the decor.'

'With the exception of the bathroom, I imagine. That was pure Bruno.'

Giles laughed. 'Perhaps. Seriously though Claire, if I were you, I'd close this down sooner rather than later – I heard she'd been seeking legal advice and I have other reasons – other than caring about you – why I'd prefer that didn't happen.'

The final piece of the puzzle slid into place in Claire's brain. 'That's why Barty asked me a few times if I knew what you're working on,' she said. 'Bruno's involved in it, isn't he?'

'Up to his eyeballs, and my concern is they'll try and shut me down through you.'

'So, I need to get in first.'

'You do,' he paused for a second. 'You said "we".'

'Sorry?'

'Before, you said "we" were talking about the ownership of Bella Donna.'

Claire glanced over to where the others weren't even pretending not to listen to her side of the conversation. 'Yes, I'm here with Owen Gallagher and two of the women from the Fenwyck shoot.'

'Your old boyfriend?'

There was silence for a few seconds. Claire squeezed her eyes shut as she waited for him to comment.

'I'm happy for you, Claire. How are you doing?'

'Really well. I'm about to start work on something new, and I'm staying in Brookford, so maybe next time you're in London you might want to come over?'

'I'd like that,' he sighed. 'Anyway, darling, I'd better go, these words aren't going to write themselves.'

'Thanks for everything, Giles.'

'You're welcome. I'll send you through what I

found out but call me if you need anything else.'

When she hung up, the others looked up expectantly. Claire nodded. 'Giles can trace the company back to Barty, and Julia is Belucci's partner in *Bella Donna*. He's sending me through what he found out.'

Owen muttered something under his breath about Julia. 'That's it, Della. We've got the proof we need.'

'So Barty really is Spooner. We don't have the proof though to link Belucci to those reviews.'

'No, we can't prove that he leant on Barty, but we have enough to clear you.' He grabbed Claire and swung her around before kissing her soundly on the lips. 'And we have enough to stop Bruno from hurting you anymore.'

When she came up for air, she said, 'Okay, it's time to finish this once and for all. Fancy a drive into London tomorrow, Gallagher?'

He nodded. 'Absolutely. Let's finish this.'

Gail and Tallis looked at each other, and Tallis began packing up her notes. 'We'd better be getting back so we can feed the kids,' said Gail.

'Who have probably worked up an appetite by now,' said Owen.

'Not helpful,' said Tallis.

'I told you I didn't want to know,' said Gail.

'From all that studying, of course.' Owen's face was comically expressionless.

As they left, Claire gave each of them a hug.

'Thank you both,' she said. 'We wouldn't have got there without you.'

When Gail and Tallis left, Owen took Nigel out for a toilet break, and Claire busied herself cleaning up their plates and cups, leaving the mind-map on the table in place for now. She didn't need to feel the sudden cool air that blew in from outside to know when Owen was back. While Gail and Tallis were here, the cottage was full, but Owen's presence made it feel crowded – he filled the space.

'I can make you something for dinner if you like,' she said, making more of a production of looking through the contents of the fridge than the activity required.

'No,' he said, pulling her gently away from the fridge and into his arms. 'Let's go to the pub. If I stay for dinner tonight, I'll be staying the night.'

Claire mulled that thought over and decided it sounded like an excellent idea.

As if he could read the direction her mind had taken, he said, 'And that wouldn't be a great idea. Not yet. No matter how much those gorgeous flashing eyes of yours are telling me otherwise.' He kissed her lips quick and hard. 'I don't want our evening to end yet though, so the pub it is.'

Claire smiled. 'Me neither,' she said. 'If you can deal with the fire, I'll be ready in five.'

CHAPTER THIRTY-FOUR

Although Owen offered to come with her, she had to face Barty on her own. Rather than going to his office, Claire arranged to meet him in Soho for coffee.

'I'll wait in the deli across the road,' Owen said. 'Call if you need me.'

Claire nodded and then swallowed hard and took half a dozen deep breaths before walking into the cafe.

Barty's Adam's apple was bobbing away in his throat, and his face was pale and had guilt written all over it. He held up two fingers to Lorenzo for coffee.

'Why did you do it?' she asked the second her bottom hit the chair.

He didn't pretend to misunderstand her. 'How did you find out?'

'Does it matter?' The anger that had given her the courage to face Barty with what she knew had dissipated, and now she was just empty inside.

He shook his head. 'I don't suppose so. Do you have proof?'

Claire nodded. 'I have enough. I have enough to

prove to anyone who wants to listen that I absolutely could not have written those reviews.'

'How did you know?'

'I had my suspicions but hadn't been able to prove it, but it was the *strozzapreti* at Ziggy's that gave you away.' When he shook his head with a blank expression, she elaborated. 'The day I ate there it was served with courgettes and tomatoes, but the date that Alex Spooner ate there it was done with cheese and black pepper.' She shrugged. 'I told you I'd had *strozzapreti*, and you assumed the menu wouldn't have changed.'

'That might prove you didn't write the reviews, but you have none that prove that I did.'

'Only the company search for Spoonman Pty Limited.' She shrugged. 'Giles helped me with that.'

He closed his eyes briefly, his shoulders slumping. 'What are you going to do?' His middle finger tapped against the laminate top of the table.

'I haven't decided,' she said. 'That will depend on your answer to my first question.'

'Why I did it?'

She nodded again and showed her thanks to Lorenzo, who had placed espresso cups in front of them.

He sighed. 'At first, it was for a bit of fun, a laugh and the extra money. I'd wondered how you could afford some of the places you took me to, and a couple of times I saw the half-finished reviews on your laptop. When

I saw those same reviews under the Spooner by-line, I put the two together. When you got your column and told me it meant you didn't have to write the horoscopes anymore, I knew it also meant you were giving up the reviews, so I set up an email in the name of Alex Spooner and sent Duncan some sample copy. At first, it was fun – I got to eat at restaurants I otherwise wouldn't be able to afford to eat at, and it put me in the path of potential new clients who thought I must be doing well if I could afford to eat there. It was a win-win for me.'

'And then Bruno Belucci found out?'

He nodded. 'Yes. Bruno found out. He thought it was a great laugh and promised he'd keep my secret. I believed him – or rather, I wanted to believe him, but then he approached me with an offer that I probably should've refused. He offered me money to change my review on *Scarborough Fair*. I didn't ask why, nor did I care – I was picking up the fee from the paper and another from Belucci. Plus, because I was doing him a favour, he knew that he owed me. He paid me to write another one on *Y Not*, and some positive ones on places he had an interest in. In return, he began sending clients my way. It meant that by the time you signed with *Time for Tea*, I had enough business to go out on my own.'

'What about the review on *Belucci's* itself?'

'That was different. Bruno had told me he wanted to get rid of Owen Gallagher but couldn't take the risk of putting Lord Spencer-Brown offside – he was his business partner in that venture, and Owen was married to Julia Spencer-Brown. Any move without cause against Owen would put the financial side of the partnership at risk. I said something about how it was a pity he couldn't get someone to leave a review about how *Belucci's* was in danger of losing one of its Michelin stars as a result of inconsistency in the kitchen under Gallagher. No one would blame Bruno for getting rid of him under those circumstances.'

'Why did he want to get rid of Owen?'

Barty's mouth twisted, his lips thin. 'Jealousy. Gallagher was getting the accolades and the attention. The way he figured it was that Julia and her father might be able to get Gallagher another job, but his reputation would be tarnished enough that the networks wouldn't want anything more to do with him.'

'Giles and I took you there for your birthday and all along you knew Owen was in the kitchen and you didn't tell me.' The bitterness of bile rose in the back of her throat, and she took a mouthful of coffee to chase it away.

He shrugged. 'I remembered that night when you told me how Gallagher had broken your heart. It was easy for me to write the review, knowing it was my revenge for how he'd hurt you.'

Claire shook her head slowly. 'Don't you dare try and twist this to say you did it for me.'

He lifted a shoulder. 'I was just able to justify it by telling myself he deserved it for what he'd done to you.'

Claire ran her hand down the side of her face to cover her mouth. She turned away as she thought through what he'd said. 'What about the risk to Bruno's business?'

'Bruno rationalised that the risk was minimal — the restaurant was established and had been widely and positively reviewed in the past. This piece was purely to give Bruno a reason for sacking Gallagher so he could, as he said in the papers afterwards, regain the trust of his valued diners. And people believed him.'

'And that's why Bruno asked you to do the same with *Bella Donna*?'

'Yes. He'd gone into that business with Julia. She was supposed to be a silent partner, but she'd made most of the design decisions and also had a say in the menu. It was sinking fast, and Julia was blaming him for it. He wanted out, but his ego wouldn't allow him to be seen to fail and again, he needed to keep the Spencer-Browns onside.'

'And me? Why blame me for it all?'

He looked away from her briefly and scrubbed at his eyes. 'I'd told him all those years ago that my housemate used to be The Spoonman before I took over. I have no excuse other than I was trying to impress him. I hadn't used your name, and no one knew who you were back then. When I took over his management about a year ago—'

Claire lifted her eyebrows at that, and Barty seemed to shrink in his chair.

'I let it slip you and I used to share a house. He said nothing at the time, and I thought nothing else of it until he decided he wanted to get back at you for rejecting him and for blocking him from the co-host gig, by leaking the information that you were The Spoonman. He hates you.' Barty lowered his head. 'I'm so sorry, Claire. Belucci told me that if I didn't leak it, he'd expose me – and that would be the end of my career.'

'Instead, it was almost the end of mine,' Claire retorted.

'I know. But I could look after you.' He raised his head and caught her eyes, pleading for understanding. 'I'd make sure you were okay. You've got to have known how I feel about you?' When the silence lingered, he added, 'Claire, I've been in love with you since the day we all moved in together.'

Even though Owen had surmised as much, Barty's frank admission knocked the wind out of her. She searched his face for some sign he was joking, that he would smile and make some flippant remark as he always did. Instead, his face was full of sadness and something that could've been yearning. 'But you've never said.'

He shrugged. 'I hoped you'd see beyond our friendship one day. When you said you'd broken up with Giles, I thought there might've been a chance for us. Then I saw the footage of you and Gallagher in Fenwyck. There was no denying the chemistry between you.' He looked away from her, his voice small. 'I knew Gallagher would turn against you when he found out it was you who had ruined his career and his marriage; and once he knew that, whatever was still between you would be dead. So, I rang Bruno and said I'd do it.'

'But he didn't believe it,' Claire said, shaking her head.

'No, why was that?' he asked with a surprised tone.

'Partly because he knew I'd had no idea that he'd become a chef, but mostly because he knew *me*.'

Barty nodded slowly, resignedly.

'You tried to ruin me, Barty.'

'I know. But I could look after you; please understand,' he pleaded, catching her eyes. 'I'd hoped you'd turn to me, but instead, you ran away to Brookford. And that led you straight back to him.'

'Is that why you offered Duncan a Spooner review on *The Lamb*?'

'I thought Owen would have no choice but to believe it was you if another review came out. The network would back away from you, and you'd have to come back to me. When I came to Brookford, I saw there was nothing between you and him, and that you'd moved onto someone else. I realised then that it had been for nothing.'

A tear slid down Claire's cheek, and then another

one. She rubbed absently at her eyes, but still, the tears flowed. 'What a mess, Barty.'

They sat in silence for a few minutes. Empty cups were whisked away and replaced with fresh coffees.

'Did you know that Julia is talking about suing me for damages to her business – to make me, as The Spoonman, pay for *Bella Donna's* collapse? Was that also part of the plan?' asked Claire.

Barty looked genuinely confused. 'No,' he said, 'I haven't heard that.'

'Okay, have you heard any rumours about Giles and what he might be working on? And think carefully before you answer because I know you've asked me that question a few times.'

'Okay, yes, I had heard whispers of where he might be sniffing about, but how would I know what Julia was planning?'

'Really, Barty? You're still lying to me? A friend of mine saw you – last Friday night having cosy drinks with Bruno and Julia.'

'That doesn't mean I know what she's planning,' he said.

'But if you had to guess?'

'I'd say that any lawsuit against you might go away if there was nothing mentioned about SB Catering Pty Limited in a book that Giles might or might not be writing about underpayment of apprentices in their stables.'

'I think now might be the time to let Bruno know we have proof that he was paying you to write the reviews you did.'

'Do you? Have proof?'

'Uh-huh.' Claire crossed her fingers under the table. 'Giles is an excellent investigator, and there's a money trail from Bruno to you.'

'I see.'

He lowered his head. When he raised it again, his eyes were glistening. 'What are you going to do about it?'

'I'm sorry, Barty,' Claire said eventually. 'I'm sorry I never noticed how you felt about me, and I'm sorry I've hurt you because of that. Mostly though, I'm sorry because I can't ever forget what you've done and because of it I've lost a dear friend.' She was silent for a second or two. 'Make it go away, Barty, and Julia and her father won't find out from me what Bruno has done. If they take it any further, if I hear even a whisper of Bruno or Julia referring to The Spoonman and me in the same sentence, I won't hesitate to use what I have.

'I've spoken to Adrian Ritchie, and he intends to tell anyone in the business who'll listen that it wasn't me who wrote the reviews, that the tabloids got it wrong. Owen is doing the same, as will Ziggy and Jimmy. The media have gone quiet for now, but if I do an interview about it, they will ask questions about the integrity of the journalist who leaked it, and that will then come straight back to you. If it ever comes out that it was you who was not only The Spoonman but also who leaked the story, your clients would all desert you, and you'd be out of business.

'Despite everything you've done to me, I couldn't do the same to you. So, we'll say nothing for now. Ed says we should be able to sail through it as long as it doesn't spark up again.' She hesitated and fixed her eyes intently on him. 'I mean it, Barty, there had better never be another Spoonman review posted on any medium or I won't hesitate to use what I know.'

'That's more than I deserve,' he conceded.

'Yes, it is. You lied to me, and worse, you betrayed me. I'm sorry I didn't know how you felt about me, but that's no reason for you to do what you did. You almost ruined my career; you almost ruined me.'

'Can I ever make up for that?' he asked, staring down at his hands.

She shook her head. 'No, I don't think so. I'll be needing a new manager, though.'

'I understand.'

Claire nodded and stood to leave.

'I'm really sorry, Claire,' he said. 'I'm almost glad that you know, though. It was a relief to tell you.'

'I'm not glad at all. Even when the truth was staring me in the face, I didn't want to believe it. I still don't, but I have to.' She pulled her wallet out of her bag and threw some notes on the table. 'I have no choice. And now I don't care if I never see you again.'

And then she left, without looking back.

Across the road, Owen was waiting for her. The second she stepped onto the footpath, he pulled her into his arms and held her tighter than she thought was possible. While she wanted so badly to cry, she couldn't, not here in the street.

'How was it?'

'Not great,' she said. 'It was as we thought, and it was because of what we thought.'

He said nothing in response to that; there was nothing he could say. He leaned forward and kissed her lips, softly, quickly. 'Let's go home.'

Claire and Owen were back at Curlew Cottage by mid-afternoon. The day had turned chilly, and the forecast was for some snow overnight. Claire shivered as she fumbled in her bag for her key, dropping it on the path before she could slide it into the lock.

'Let me.' Owen retrieved the key and unlocked the door. Once inside, they toed off shoes and hung coats on hooks.

'When do you need to collect Nigel from Gracie?' asked Owen.

'Whenever,' said Claire, rubbing her arms.

Owen nodded, and Claire spoke at the same time as he did. 'Do you want tea?' 'How about I light the fire?'

They both laughed at their sudden awkwardness.

'Why is this weird?' asked Claire.

'Because we want each other so much,' he said, walking towards her.

Owen's eyes darkened with every step until Claire thought she could fall into them and never find her way out.

'We do,' she said, her gaze moving to his lips.

His mouth curled into a small smile, but he made no move to close the few centimetres between them.

'This has to come from you,' he whispered.

She rested her hands against the side of his face and captured his bottom lip between hers. Pulling back slightly, she searched his eyes, before using both hands to pull his head towards hers. Groaning into her mouth, Owen took charge of the kiss, holding her hard as she swayed into him.

'Oh Christ, Della,' he murmured into her throat. 'These last weeks have been torture.'

'I know.' She pulled his shirt from his jeans, her hands desperate to feel his skin. Her head tilted to one side, and she closed her eyes on a long sigh as he kissed his way down her throat and along the line of her collarbone, sending sparks of sensations through her entire body.

'Take me to bed,' she hummed, rubbing against him. She gloried at the shudder that ran through his body as he fought for control. His hands had found their way under her top and cupped her breast; her moan echoed around them.

He lifted her into his arms and covered the few steps into her bedroom. Claire laughed as he struggled to balance her and open the door at the same time; a rush of cold air greeting them.

He dropped her on the bed, and the laughing stopped as he stood and gazed at her sprawled across the quilt, still fully clothed. 'It's been a long time, Della.'

'I've missed you,' Claire said. 'I thought I'd stopped missing you, but I hadn't.'

He swallowed hard and smiled down at her. 'I never stopped missing you either.'

Claire pulled him onto the bed, a heady buzz simmering though her body.

He lifted her legs so they lay across his. 'No, my darling, we're not rushing into this.' He walked his fingers inside the leg of her jeans and pulled her socks down and tossed them away. He held one bare foot in his hand, warming it, rubbing it.

Claire forgot to be cold.

Rolling away she stood and pulled her jumper off; their eyes locked as she slid her jeans over her hips and stepped out of them until she was standing in front of him in just her bra and knickers. She went to unclip her bra and hesitated when he shook his head. 'No,' he said, 'I want to do that.'

In slow motion he unbuttoned his shirt and let it slip from his arms into a pile on the floor. It wasn't long before his jeans joined the shirt. When his final piece of clothing was shed, her mouth went dry. 'Oh my,' she said.

'Yes, yours,' he promised as he closed the distance between them and lingered behind her.

Claire held her breath as he ran one finger slowly over each bump of her spine and released it with a moan when he finally unclipped her bra and caught her breasts in his hands.

'All yours,' he whispered into her ear.

While one hand teased her nipple, the other slid down her body, across her tummy and the curve of her hip, and back again. His hands lingered on her breasts, before skimming across her mound. Hands so familiar, but at the same time, so completely new.

He nipped at her earlobe, kissing and nuzzling his way down her neck, across her shoulder.

'I want to touch you too,' she said, her moan turning into a gasp when his hand finally found its way inside her knickers. She slid them off and held his hands in place – one over her breast, the other between her legs, her hips pushing and rolling back into his nakedness, feeling him growing harder against her, feeling the groan thunder through his body.

'Oh god, Della, much more of that and you won't need to touch me,' he said into her neck.

As his breath grew faster, little mews of pleasure escaped her lips; his fingers played her until she came apart in his arms. She would have fallen to the floor, but he held her tight until she'd finished, turning her gently in his arms to kiss her, and walking her backwards until they both collapsed on the bed. He fumbled in the pocket of his discarded jeans, eventually pulling out his wallet and then a condom, mock-growling when she laughed at him for dropping it in his haste.

Despite the years in between, Claire marvelled at how their bodies came together as they always had done. Owen's skin felt the same, he smelt the same, but he was much more than he had been. More intense, more substance, more experience, more man.

Afterwards, he held her tightly, curled into his body. 'I've dreamed of you over the years, Dells, of this. But this was way better than my dreams. I love you, my darling Della.'

'I love you too.' She kissed his chest and then prodded his hard stomach. 'Please don't leave me again, okay?'

He tilted her chin so she could look up at him. 'Never.' And then he was kissing her again.

A persistent knock at the door eventually drove them out of bed.

Claire groaned. 'Gracie,' she said. 'She must've seen your car out front – she usually just walks in.'

'Lucky she didn't this time.' Owen grinned as Claire rushed around the room looking for clothes.

'Hang on,' she yelled for Gracie's benefit. 'Oh my god, it's cold,' she exclaimed.

She shut the bedroom door as she left, grinning at Owen's muffled chuckle.

Milo and Nigel bounded through the door as soon as Claire opened it, Gracie following behind.

'I thought I saw Owen's car out the front,' she said.

'You did,' said Claire, placing the backs of her fingers on her cheeks to cool them.

'But—' Gracie made a show of looking around the small kitchen and sitting room, mock innocence on her face.

When Owen rather sheepishly stepped into the room, Gracie's smile was wide.

'Fancy seeing you here,' she said, crossing the floor to greet him. 'It's freezing in here, why isn't the fire lit? Or,' she looked between them, 'wasn't there time?'

'Who are you?' asked Milo, looking up at Owen.

'I'm Owen.'

'Are you Aunty Bear's friend?' the child asked solemnly.

'I am.'

'Do you do sleepovers?'

Claire looked across at Gracie, who was trying not to laugh – and failing miserably. Owen appeared not to have any idea what to say.

'I like having sleepovers,' said Milo.

'So do I,' said Owen. 'Do you want to help me

bring in some wood?'

Milo nodded emphatically and followed Owen out the door on men's business.

'Well?' asked Gracie.

'Barty admitted it all,' said Claire, deliberately misunderstanding her.

'That's good and a relief and all that, but *this*,' she lowered her voice dramatically.

'It's new,' said Claire.

'But good?'

Claire nodded. 'Very.'

Impetuously Gracie hugged her older sister. 'I'm thrilled.'

CHAPTER THIRTY-FIVE

Tallis was at a loose end. The mental activity associated with proving Claire's innocence had provided the perfect excuse to put her own issues on the back burner in the weeks since she'd overheard *that* conversation. While she'd been busy investigating The Spoonman, she hadn't had to think about Derek, their marriage or the identity of the woman who Derek had been involved with. Now, though, everything was as it always was: Derek was in Bristol, Adam was at school, Gail was at work and Tallis had absolutely nothing to do.

Claire's text on Sunday morning had come as a welcome relief from the strain of having to pretend to Derek that nothing had changed, that she still had no idea of the affair he'd been having. Although she'd felt a rush of accomplishment when she'd spoken to Jimmy and Ziggy on Claire's behalf, that night at the gala dinner she'd gone back to playing the demure and doting wife on Derek's arm. She'd dressed up and made her face and straightened her hair until it was sleek. Derek had asked her what she'd done that day, and she'd smiled and said, 'oh, you know, some shops and a nice lunch.'

He'd made a noise in reply, but Tallis didn't think he'd listened to her and was glad as she didn't want to be on the end of his mockery.

While she'd been organising the Fenwyck bid for *Time for Tea*, she'd felt energised and useful. She'd experienced the same fulfilment in the weeks since Claire had turned up here in her garden on that morning only a few weeks ago. It had given her a glimpse into a world where she had an identity – one that didn't begin and end with being Derek's wife or Adam's mother. For the first time in a long time, she'd had something to do to fill in those long hours between Adam going to school and when he came home. In a few months, Adam would finish school and would probably go away to university and then what? What would she do then?

Now, though? Now it was back to normal, not that it could ever be normal again. Not knowing what she did about Derek. But what to do about it? The easy answer was nothing – Rosemary had said that it was over, she could sit back and pretend that all was okay or … no, she didn't want to contemplate the alternative. Not yet.

As she considered that which she didn't want to consider, the doorbell pealed. Tallis automatically flattened her hair and smoothed her jeans as she went to open it.

'Claire. What a lovely surprise! I wasn't expecting

to see you until the weekend.'

There was something different about Claire today. She looked lighter and brighter, and something else. When Claire coloured lightly under her gaze, Tallis smiled widely.

'You and Owen?' she asked.

Claire nodded.

'I'm glad,' she said. 'And Barty?'

The smile on Claire's face slipped. 'It was as we thought.' She shrugged. 'So there you go. Anyway, how are you?'

Tallis inclined her head towards the kitchen. 'Come in,' she said. 'I'll make tea.'

'Please. What's wrong, Tallis?'

Tallis flicked the switch on the kettle, got two cups out of the cupboard, and spooned tea into the pot. Then she exhaled and said, 'Derek has been having an affair.'

Claire covered her mouth and gasped. 'I'm so sorry.'

Tallis shrugged and heaved a sigh of resignation.

'Are you sure? Of course you are, you wouldn't have said anything if you weren't.'

'I overheard him talking to her the other week. There's no doubt.'

'Do you know who it is?'

'No. I asked Rosemary, his assistant, if she knew and she said she suspected it was the wife of a client.'

Tallis poured hot water into the teapot and set it and the cups on the table. 'She also said it was over now.'

'Do you want to know who it was?' Tallis shied under Claire's gaze. 'I don't know,' she said. 'It's bad enough knowing for sure he was unfaithful.'

'You suspected something?'

Tallis nodded. 'Yes, and I know the others did too, but as long as I didn't say anything—'

'It wouldn't be real.' Claire answered for her.

'I know it's not the first time,' said Tallis, 'but there's something that felt different about this time.' She poured their tea, and when Claire frowned, asked, 'You're wondering why I haven't left?'

Claire lifted one shoulder. 'People stay in marriages for different reasons, and I'm sure you have yours.'

'I'm content with how things are. I have my life, and Derek has his. I suppose I've always thought if I could maintain the status quo until Adam leaves school … The thing is though, I don't have my own money or any skills to make any. I can't afford to leave him – even if I wanted to.'

'I see,' said Claire. 'Well, I think I can help with that.' She sipped at her tea as if she was looking for the words she wanted to say.

'Go ahead,' Tallis prompted.

'Now that I don't have Barty in my life, I need some sort of assistant—'

'Oh, I couldn't,' began Tallis.

'Hear me out, please.' Claire smiled reassuringly. 'I need someone who can keep track of things for me – to make sure I know where I need to be and when. You know how I mentioned Owen and I were working on something new?'

Tallis nodded. 'But you couldn't say what.'

'Yes, the press release will go out later today. We're doing a new show, and we'll be publishing a companion cookbook to go along with that. I'm going to need someone who can not only help me with my diary but someone who can also keep track of the dishes and help all of that come together. It's an assistant job, but it's also more than that. You'd need to write up Owen's recipes – he tends to create on the fly – and while I'll put the words around them I'll need you to test all the recipes we cook on the show.'

A flutter of excitement began deep in Tallis' belly, so before it could get too far out of control, she attempted to quash it. 'I've got no experience with television or writing recipes,' she said.

'No, but you can organise the hell out of anything, you're practical, methodical, you understand food and, most importantly, I like and trust you. And I really need someone by my side who I can trust. I meant it the other day when I said we couldn't have solved The Spoonman problem if it wasn't for you. Please, promise me you'll think about it.'

Over the next couple of hours, Tallis thought of

little else. Working on the show with Claire and Owen was like a dream coming true she didn't even know she'd dreamt until that moment.

She talked it through with Adam over dinner that night.

'What do you think?'

'That's amazing, Mum,' he said. 'You have to do it.'

'I don't think your father will like it though,' said Tallis.

'Who cares,' said Adam. 'He has his own life, and it's time for you to have one too. It will give you a bit of financial independence and besides, when I go to university you won't have anything to do. I wouldn't even tell Dad if I were you. You know he'll just rain on your parade and try and bring you down like he always does. Remember what he was like when you guys were going on *Time for Tea*? He'll be like that.'

'I have to tell him,' said Tallis.

Adam shook his head. 'No, he'll talk you out of it. If it ever comes up, we'll just say that you've been helping out. It won't affect him at all.'

'I don't know,' said Tallis.

'He has his secrets, Mum.' Adam's face was serious. 'And you never know when you might need a nest egg.'

Tallis' breath caught in her throat. He knew. 'How did you——?'

'How did I know?' He shrugged. 'It doesn't matter, but I do.'

Tallis added up all the times Adam made himself scarce on the weekends that Derek was home.

'It's your business, Mum, but you need something to do, and you need to be useful, and this is pretty perfect as far as I can tell.' He got up from the table and handed her the phone. 'Call her now and tell her yes.'

At the March meeting of The Cotswolds Culinary and Cookbook Society – off to France with Rick Stein – Claire, Tallis and Gail filled Caro and Fee in on the intrigues. They were suitably horrified by Barty and Bruno's behaviour and impressed by the legwork that Tallis had done.

'I always thought Bruno Belucci was quite handsome,' said Fee.

'In that hot Italian way of his,' added Caro.

'But there was always something about his face that I couldn't trust.'

'I thought so too, Fee.'

Even though the press release had gone out, Claire told everyone about Posh or Not, and blushed beautifully whenever one of them mentioned Owen's name.

'You two are as bad as Adam and Anna,' said Gail.

'I think they're worse.' Tallis laughed.

Tallis had been unsure about announcing her new job over lunch, but Claire told her she was being ridiculous.

'Everyone will be so happy for you,' she'd said.

Tallis wasn't entirely convinced, but Claire had been right; Caro and Fee were over the moon, and Gail rushed across and hugged her. 'I'm so happy for you,' she said. 'This could be exactly what you need.'

Fee said, 'Every woman needs to have some financial independence,' and then added, 'I only wish someone had told me about that earlier.'

While she'd suspected as much, all the women in the group had thought there was more behind Derek's absences from home, although it was also clear no one would've said as much. Their thoughtfulness brought tears to Tallis' eyes that she brushed away under cover of opening a new bottle of wine.

'So how will it all work?' asked Caro. 'The show, that is.'

'We'll be filming at The Lamb on Mondays – when the restaurant is closed – but Curlew Cottage is going to be our test kitchen and centre of operations. Owen has promoted Angie to head chef and is taking a step back to concentrate on the show.'

Tallis smiled at the tenderness that softened Claire's face when she spoke about Owen.

'We're into the first few days of activity, and already he can't help but interfere with service. I'm waiting for the day Angie turns around and tells him to leave the day-to-day operations to her.'

'So, everything has worked out exactly as it should

have done,' said Caro.

'Yes, Caro,' said Claire, 'I think it has.'

Tallis smiled but her thoughts drifted to Derek again, the worry circling and weighing heavily on her heart.

'Don't you think Tallis?' Fee's question pulled her back into the conversation.

'He'd be on any "to-do" list of mine,' continued Fee. 'The man is proper fit. I'd be riding that.'

Claire laughed, Caro seemed bemused, and Gail looked quietly impressed, but Tallis choked on her wine. 'Proper fit? To-do lists? Ride? Where did you get those expressions from?'

'I'm on social media,' Fee said, proud of the reaction she'd got. 'And I've been watching James Martin on the telly. He speaks Yorkshire-like and says "proper" a lot.'

'I haven't heard him talk about "rides" though,' muttered Tallis.

'He's yummy,' said Caro.

'It's those blue eyes,' said Fee.

'And his hair,' said Caro. 'I could run my fingers through James Martin's hair.'

'I'd like to run my fingers—'

'Enough.' Tallis laughed, knowing exactly which part of James Martin's anatomy Fee was heading to next.

'What do you think, Claire?' said Gail.

'About James Martin?' Claire asked with a grin. 'I've never even met him, but I think our dogs would get along and we both do like butter.'

As Fee was about to say something else – which Tallis assumed was about James Martin and butter – she stopped her. 'So in April, we're cooking with James?'

'Yes,' said Claire. 'From his Great British Adventure.'

'How good would it be if we could invite some of these chefs to our cookbook club,' said Caro.

'And then James could come to lunch,' added Fee.

'Heaven help the man,' said Gail.

CHAPTER THIRTY-SIX

The remainder of March disappeared in a flurry of pre-production activity. Each morning Tallis and Owen would arrive at Curlew Cottage where they would toss around ideas for each of the weekly themes, tweak recipes, practice dishes and photograph them for the cookbook that would be released following the completion of filming. Claire had interviews to organise and manage, and as she'd reopened her social media accounts, these also needed to be updated in line with what the marketing department wanted.

There was plenty to do, and Claire didn't know how she would've managed if it wasn't for Tallis. She'd taken over Claire's diary, had plenty of great ideas to contribute, and somehow seemed to capture everything that came out of the daily planning meetings. Tallis also had a talent for styling food that had been a surprise to them all. Even when she wasn't at Curlew Cottage, Tallis was spending a lot of time in the background learning about photography, light and the techniques the food bloggers were using.

One Monday afternoon in the middle of April, just a couple of weeks before filming was due to commence, Owen and Claire completed their first rehearsal in the kitchen at *The Lamb*. Tallis had left to go home, and Claire and Owen had just finished their clean down of the kitchen.

Owen lifted her effortlessly onto one of the stainless-steel counters.

'You'll need to wipe this down again,' Claire chided softly as he stepped between her legs to kiss her.

'It will be worth it,' he said, kissing his way down her throat, sending the now familiar sparks rushing across her skin. Then he added, 'It's been hours since I last touched you.'

'It feels like days,' moaned Claire, reaching her hands under his t-shirt, needing to feel his skin against hers, marvelling again at how they'd found their way back to each other.

'Let's take this upstairs,' he said, 'before it gets any further out of control.'

Claire nodded, and he lifted her down from the bench, pinning her against it for another kiss. The ping of an incoming text from Claire's phone stopped them from going any further.

'I'd better check that,' she said, reaching for her phone and trying to ignore Owen nibbling at her earlobe.

'Oh my god,' she exclaimed.

'What's wrong?'

'Nothing's wrong; the message is from Giles – Barty has just sent him through a heap of incriminating emails. It turns out not only did Bruno pay Barty for the reviews, but he also wrote three of them himself!'

'Let me guess: *Belucci's*, *Bella Donna*, and *Lily James*?'

Claire nodded. 'Tallis always thought there was something different in the language of those – she was right. Giles has emailed some of the emails through – it proves beyond a doubt that he was behind the whole thing.'

Owen released her and moved to where he could read the email on her phone. 'Julia won't want any of these seeing the light of day – look at this one: "I only took the bitch on as a partner to keep her daddy happy, but now I need to get her off my back before this disaster of a restaurant she's created ruins my reputation."'

'Giles said he's even sent him evidence that Julia and Bruno knew they were underpaying staff.'

Owen lifted his eyes from the screen to meet hers. 'Barty's done this for you,' he said. 'It could ruin him, but he's made sure not only has Giles got the information he needs, but he also has enough to close down any threat they might still be tempted to use over you.'

'I know,' she breathed, her eyes glistening. 'I miss Barty, you know,' she said after a brief silence. 'He was my best friend.'

'I know you do,' he said, pulling her back into his arms.

On a rainy Tuesday night in the middle of September the first episode of *Posh or Not* aired, and a party was thrown at *The Lamb* to celebrate.

The crew had outdone themselves by festooning the space with enough fairy lights to make Nigella proud and candles on every possible surface. As well as the production crew and the employees of *The Lamb*, everyone who mattered to Claire and Owen joined them.

Jenna and Chris came with their families, Gracie and Bill – minus Milo who was spending the night with Bill's mother who was visiting – were there, as were the Fenwyck ladies with their families. It was the first time Claire met Derek, and Caro's husband, Malcolm. Both were as she'd expected. Caro's Malcolm was a large homely man who seemed a little uncomfortable with the proceedings, while Tallis' Derek would be, she suspected, obnoxious if given half the chance, but tonight was pretending not to be as uncomfortable as he must have felt. He watched his normally quiet and obedient wife as she mingled with the television people and bantered easily with Ed and Owen, surprise – and more than a little displeasure – written all over his face. Tallis hadn't said anything to Derek about the affair he'd had earlier in the year, although with Adam about to go away to university, it could be the trigger for change.

Not long after the show had aired, to applause all round, Ed signalled to Claire and Owen. 'A breaking news alert,' he said, holding up his phone. 'Have a look.'

As Claire and Owen read the article over Ed's shoulder, Owen started to laugh. 'This is priceless.'

On the screen was an article written by Giles exposing Bruno Belucci and his business partner Lord Spencer-Brown for systemic bullying and underpaying of apprentices at his flagship restaurant *Belucci's* and the now closed sister venue *Bella Donna*. The photo that accompanied the story was one of Bruno with Julia in a darkened London club, heads together as if they were making plans. The full story, the article said, could be found in Giles' upcoming book.

'Karma is indeed a bitch,' said Owen, smiling across at Claire.

'She certainly is,' said Claire.

Claire moved from group to group, chatting and smiling, the drink in her hand always miraculously full. Each time she thought she'd catch up with Owen, someone would come between them, and she'd be caught in another conversation. When their eyes met across the crowded room, the air sizzled between them. Claire lowered hers first and gulped what was left in her wineglass.

A moment later, Owen was moving with purpose

towards her, stopping briefly to grab two fresh glasses of champagne. He put his hand under her elbow and steered her towards the kitchen.

Once in the kitchen, he placed the glasses on one of the stainless-steel benches and caught hold of one of her hands, using it to pull her towards him.

'We did good work,' he said, the look in his eyes wreaking the usual havoc within her.

'We did,' she said, clasping her hands behind his head to pull his lips towards hers.

'I love you, Dells,' he murmured.

'I love you too, Gallagher.'

'Marry me?' he said.

She pulled back. 'What did you say?'

'That wasn't meant to come out like that,' he said. 'I had it all planned, a great romantic proposal.'

'So that was a proposal?'

'It certainly was.' He grinned. 'I'll even get down on one knee, but this floor is really hard.'

'If it's worth doing, it's worth doing properly,' Ed called from the doorway, with all of their friends looking on.

'Go on Gallagher,' said Chris, as he and Jenna pushed their way through. 'On your knee.'

'Well,' said Owen, 'seeing as how we have an audience.' He dropped to one knee, still holding Claire's hands in his. 'Della, sweetheart, I've never stopped loving you. Please say you'll marry me.'

'Get off the floor, you idiot,' she said, a tear running down her cheek.

'You haven't said yes yet,' he said in a loud whisper.

'Yes,' she said. 'Yes. Of course I'll marry you.'

As they kissed, Ed's voice floated around them, 'now why couldn't they have waited until we were filming again? This would have been gold.'

RECIPES

You'll find these and other great teatime recipes from the book at www.brookfordkitchendiaries.com.

Beginner Scones

Even if you've never made scones before, this recipe will give you fabulous scones in less than thirty minutes. Go to whoa, including the washing up.

It's these scones that got Gail started on her baking journey. And why not? Just three ingredients – five, if you count the pinch of salt and the little bit of milk you need to brush the tops with – and a very good scone result for very little effort. The trick is, as with all scones, not to overwork the dough.

Ingredients:
3 cups self-raising flour
1 cup lemonade
1 cup fresh cream
Pinch of salt
A few tablespoons of milk

Method:

Preheat the oven to 220°C and grease or flour the base of the scone tray while you're at it.

Put the flour and salt into a bowl and combine.

Make a well in the centre of the flour and pour in the cream and lemonade and mix – an ordinary dinner knife works best for this.

Turn it out onto a floured bench and – I use my hands rather than a rolling pin for this – press it out into a slab 4-5cm high. No, you don't need a ruler.

Using a round cookie cutter – or a small glass if you don't have a round cookie cutter – cut discs in the dough.

Bring what's left of the dough back together and pat it out again so you can cut more scones. Repeat until all the dough is used.

Place the scones closely together on your prepared tray and brush the top with a little milk.

Pop in the preheated oven for 10-12 minutes. The tops should be golden.

Serve with jam and cream – or cream and jam – or just plenty of really good butter.

Pumpkin Scones

These would've been made with leftover pumpkin – either mashed or from the Sunday roast. I roast my pumpkin first, but if you're using mash, ensure it's completely dry and just pumpkin – none of that pumpkin mashed with potato that I (and Claire) can't stand. Also, regardless of whether you're using roasted or mashed pumpkin, it should be fridge cold. Other than that, the usual rules apply for scones – don't overwork them.

As for what pumpkin to use? Butternut is sweeter and much easier to work with but use whatever is to hand. These are lovely with butter, even better with cream cheese, and absolutely fabulous with cream cheese and tomato chutney.

Ingredients:
2 cups self-raising flour
60g butter – straight from the fridge and chopped into small pieces
1 tablespoon caster sugar
A pinch of salt
½ cup (125ml) buttermilk (plus extra to brush the tops)
⅔ cup mashed pumpkin
½ teaspoon ground nutmeg
A good shake of ground ginger, ground cinnamon and ground cloves (optional) if you want your scones to be a little Christmassy.

Method:

Preheat the oven to 220°C (200°C if fan-forced) and line a baking tray with baking paper.

Sift the flour into a large bowl, mix in the sugar and salt (it's just as easy to use your hands for this) and rub the butter into the floury mix using the tips of your fingers until the mixture looks like breadcrumbs. At this point, I pop it into the fridge for ten minutes to chill the butter down.

Mix the nutmeg and other spices (if using) into the mashed pumpkin.

Make a well in the buttery flour and add the buttermilk and pumpkin. Stir with an ordinary dinner knife – this will help avoid overworking – until a sticky dough forms.

Tip it onto a lightly floured surface and gently knead until it's just smooth. This is quite a soft dough.

Using a lightly floured rolling pin (or your hands), roll out to about 2-3cm high and, using a fluted edge cutter, cut out the scones and place them on the prepared tray. They'll rise better and more even if they're just touching. Bring any leftover dough together and repeat.

Brush with buttermilk and bake for 12-15 minutes or until golden brown on top. They should also sound hollow underneath.

Vegemite Spaghetti

This is a bit like Vegemite and cheese on toast, but as with Vegemite toast, it's not really about the Vegemite but all about the butter. It might sound strange but it really is worth trying. I saw it first in Nigella's *Kitchen* recipe book but have also seen it in Ella Risbridger's fabulous *Midnight Chicken and Other Recipes Worth Living For*. There's also a version in Anna Del Conte's *Risotto with Nettles,* which is, apparently, where Nigella first saw it. I love how recipes like this come full circle – not that it's really a recipe, but rather a collection of ingredients.

This quantity will do two people nicely for lunch or one famished person.

Ingredients:
Spaghetti – I have no idea how much, a handful, I guess
Vegemite (or Marmite) depending on where you live – about a teaspoon
50g butter
Grated parmesan (or similar) cheese – I usually grate about a handful

Method:

Cook the spaghetti in the usual way.

Melt the butter and Vegemite together.

Drain the spaghetti, but before you do, save about half a cup of the cooking water.

Mix the buttery Vegemite into the pasta, using some reserved pasta water if you need to.

Serve with plenty of parmesan cheese.

BEFORE YOU GO

If you enjoyed *Escape to Curlew Cottage* I'd love it if you left a review in the usual places. If you'd like to stay up to date with my next happy ending, you can sign up for my newsletter at my website: https://joannetracey.com

You can also drop by and see me – virtually speaking, of course – at any of these places:

Facebook: https://facebook.com/joannetraceywriter
Instagram: https://instagram.com/jotracey

ACKNOWLEDGEMENTS

December 2020

During the first lockdown earlier this year six women, all bloggers – two from Canada and the rest of us from different parts of Australia – formed a group. We called ourselves the Six Stunners and once a week we all hop on a Zoom call and chat about our highs and our lows, books, blogging, and everything else in between. We're all very different people, yet we all just fit.

Like Claire I've never been part of a group before – I've never even been in a book club. This group, though, has become the highlight of the week for all of us. It's a bright spot, a safe and supportive place in the chaos that 2020 brought with it – just like the Cotswolds Cookbook and Culinary Society is for its members. For that reason, I dedicate this novel to The Stunners – you know who you are.

As always, my thanks to my editor, Nicola O'Shea. Writing this story challenged me in several ways, but I'm so very proud of it – and grateful to you for your wise guidance. You push me (ever so gently) to improve my craft and to step out of my comfort zone a little more with each novel. Here's to many more. Thanks also to Keith Stevenson for his skills in turning my manuscript into a formatted book.

This novel has seen two changes to the small team that helps me bring my book babies into the world. To my copy editor Joanne Speirs, thank you. My lack of attention to detail when it comes to grammar continues to astound me, and it's your skills that have helped these words shine.

I have a new cover designer on this outing too and just love what Louisa West has created – and from a brief that could best be described as vague and fluctuating.

My family have had to eat a lot of scones during the writing of this book. Despite that inconvenience, you guys are still my biggest supporters. I hope you're prepared for plenty of Kiwi bakes as I write the next novel.

The biggest thanks go to you, my readers. With all the choices available to you, you've chosen this book, and for that, I'm beyond grateful.

ABOUT THE AUTHOR

Joanne Tracey lives on the Sunshine Coast in Queensland Australia with her husband, daughter and a cocker spaniel who takes her role as resident flop-dog and guardian of Jo's office very seriously. She has, however, been known to sleep a tad too much on the job – the dog, that is, not Jo.

An unapologetic daydreamer, eternal optimist, and confirmed morning person, Jo writes contemporary romance, romantic comedy, women's fiction and what she likes to call foodie-lit – which is the perfect excuse to indulge her baking habit in the name of research. Her characters cook whatever it is she wants to be cooking – or learning to cook. Then there are their occupations; through her characters Jo can try out occupations she'd never conceivably do or the business ideas that her husband says, "maybe that needs a little more thought darling." It's the daydreaming thing again.

Even though she lives in paradise, it's Jo's travels that inspire her stories. From Melbourne to Queenstown, Bali, Hong Kong and The Cotswolds, you never quite know where you'll end up, but it will be somewhere that takes you away from your every day.

When she isn't writing or day jobbing, Jo loves baking, reading, long walks along the beach, posting way too many photos of sunrises on Instagram and dreaming of the next destination and the next story.

Jo's life goals (apart from being a world-famous author) are to be an extra on *Midsomer Murders* (perhaps a dog walker in Badger's Drift), to appear on *Desert Island Discs*, and to cook her way through Nigella's books – yes, all of them.